British Praise for
Waiting for Lindsay

"With her helplessness in the face of events and her struggles for purpose, Annie is a figure for our time, a character who will resonate and live on in reader's minds."

—*Scottish Book Collector*

"An enthralling first novel written with polish and assured style."

—*Pocklington Post*

"[Forsyth's] work is both thoughtful and entertaining, with a style and class which shows great promise. She exposes emotions and brings her characters to life with maturity and skill."

—*Yorkshire Post*

"Partly thriller, partly psychological family saga, and a sensitive study of relationships."

—*South Home Newspapers*

"The writer is excellent on the undercurrents that ebb and flow between people."

—*Highland News*

"Moira Forsyth establishes herself as a name to watch out for in future. It is an impressive debut that . . . provides a vivid impression of the past as a shared experience."

—*Historical Novels Review*

"A warm, sensitive novel which explores the long-lasting effects of a family tragedy."

—*Coventry Evening Telegraph*

"Forsyth forces her characters to come to terms not just with the past, but with a very uncertain future."

—*Belfast Telegraph*

Waiting for Lindsay

MOIRA FORSYTH

THOMAS DUNNE BOOKS
St. Martin's Press
New York

THOMAS DUNNE BOOKS.
An imprint of St. Martin's Press.

www.stmartins.com

ISBN 0-312-27873-X

First published in Great Britain by Hodder and Stoughton

First U.S. Edition: August 2001

10 9 8 7 6 5 4 3 2 1

For my Mother and Father

The author gratefully acknowledges the support of the Scottish Arts Council for the purpose of writing this book.

Contents

The Past

Thirty-four years back – Lindsay

All afternoon the voices called, the two syllables of her name singing through the woods, down the steep garden, and across the sands to the sea. All afternoon, and then through the long bright evening, they searched, and did not find her.

At ten, Christine made the children go to bed. They lay awake, whispering across the landing to each other, listening to anxious talk, the banging of doors, cars on the drive labouring in first gear, more voices outside. Jamie fell asleep, but the others got up and stood at the top of the stairs. All the lights were on; the house was bright as Christmas. Outside the pale midsummer sky was dimmed and the moon rode high, as if searching too, casting her light across the width of the Black Isle, looking for Lindsay.

Jamie woke, and called for his mother. He had a pain in his stomach. His Aunt Christine came upstairs; she was the one left in the house to watch the other children.

'Have you found her yet?' they asked, as she tried to shoo them back to bed.

'Not yet,' she said, going in to Jamie, who was wailing, *Mummy, Mummy!*

'Your mummy's looking for Lindsay,' they heard her say. 'She'll be back soon.' She held Jamie in her arms, rocking him. He tucked his thumb in his mouth and was quiet.

They all stood in the doorway, watching.

'He was asking for his mummy,' Annie said. 'He's wanting Auntie Liz.'

'Go to bed,' her mother scolded wearily. 'You should all be in bed.'

'Will you wake us when you find her?' they demanded.

'Yes, of course we will.' She nodded at Annie. 'I'll come and tuck you in when Jamie goes off to sleep.'

Annie's bed was cold now, and her cousin Lindsay's, next to it, was empty, her felt rabbit flopped where she had left him this morning, next to her pyjamas. Annie got out of bed again to fetch the rabbit and take him in with her. He lay next to her bear, and Louie, the rag doll.

Perhaps she fell asleep before her mother came in. But till the moment she took the rabbit into bed with her, it all remained clear in her memory. On midsummer nights she could recall it vividly, and did, thinking again of the day Lindsay left.

'Left' was the word Annie used, though everyone else referred to her 'disappearance'. But a child, a girl of thirteen, cannot vanish like a bubble, a puff of smoke. Even at six, Annie knew that. Her cousin Jamie, for months afterwards, had a story about his big sister Lindsay being 'magicked' away, as if by a wizard, a spell. Perhaps some misguided adult had suggested this to him; Annie did not know. He grew out of it, anyway.

She had always known Lindsay inhabited the real world, not some fairy tale. Lindsay was solid, substantial, and even Annie's memories of her had a vitality no story ever acquired. She remembered her cousin's ringing voice, her long brown arms and legs, dusted with blonde down, and her hair reaching almost to her waist, thick and fair. When she closed her eyes, she could see Lindsay banging her sneakers against the lintel of the back door to empty the sand out, and picture her racing down the steep garden path, faster than anyone else, yelling *Last one on the beach is a hairy kipper!* It was always Jamie who was last, and he always cried. Then Lindsay would scoop him up and swing him round till he laughed again.

It was not possible that someone so vigorous and beautiful could be spirited away by mere magic. That was why, Annie knew, they went on looking for her so long. She must be somewhere, they must be able to find her.

And yet, however loud and long they called, however far and deeply they searched, they did not find her. Lindsay did not see, or hear, or answer them. When the children woke in the morning, remembering some strange thing had occurred in their world, and then what it was, they went downstairs together, all four, Tom and Alistair first, the little ones behind. In the kitchen their parents, Mrs Macintyre from the post office, and Hamish who worked in the shop with Stuart, Lindsay and Tom and Jamie's dad, were all sitting round the table. They were white and tired, and the air was clouded with cigarette smoke.

'Have you found her yet?' they asked. 'Is she back?'

Outside the sun moved up the blue sky, and far out in the firth porpoises dived and played. A few early holiday-makers strolled past the tennis courts and down on to the beach. In the kitchen of the High House, Liz Mathieson rose from her chair, unhooked her cardigan from the back, and leaving the others in the kitchen, walked out of the back door. She stood at the top of the steep path that zigzagged through the garden to the gate among the blackcurrant bushes at the bottom, that opened on to the track to the beach. She often stood there, watching the sunshine climb the garden slowly, the children scrambling up it fast. Beyond the bushes lining the path, the shining sea rolled to and fro, swaying gently up on to the sand and retreating again.

In a few minutes she must go back indoors so that they could begin looking again, in daylight this time, for her daughter. Absently, she stretched out a hand and rubbed a few leaves from the lemon balm bush by the living-room window. She raised her fingers to her face, and breathed in the sharp citrus scent. Just this moment, she thought, that's all I have, perhaps, for ever and ever, that will not be filled with pain. She was light-headed with lack of sleep, with something so terrifying it could no longer be called mere worry, or fear. The scent of lemon, the shining sea, the leaves of the silver birches quivering, catching the light: all these she held, not wanting the moment to change.

Someone called; she turned and went back indoors. Sunshine lay across the big table where her boys were seated, oddly silent. Her sister Christine sat keeping her own children close, Alistair leaning on her shoulder, Annie on her lap. Stuart was talking on the telephone; the police would be here again in half an hour. They fed the children, who, like the adults, did not want to eat. All the time, unable to help themselves, they told each other there was some mistake, some misunderstanding. Anyway, they would find her today, or she would come back.

'It's just not like her,' Stuart kept saying, 'to wander off without telling anyone.'

'Not all night,' Christine said. 'Not all night.'

The children were going down to look along the beach.

'Stay together,' their mothers said. 'Look after the little ones.' They felt helpless: should they keep the children with them or not? But they had spent all the summers of their lives on this safe familiar shore.

'We'll call you,' they said. 'Don't go past the rocks. Come back when we call.'

And they all trooped back as soon as they were called. All except Lindsay. They went on calling for her down the days and weeks and years to come, till there was no point in calling any longer. But she did not hear them; she did not come back.

Winter

1

'I'm glad you're here,' Annie said. 'After Christmas is over, everything seems so bleak.' She opened the cupboard in the alcove next to the fireplace. 'What about a drink? You haven't had your New Year.'

'Aye, sure.' Tom came over to look at what was left from Hogmanay. One thing about coming to stay with Annie and Graham – they always had a grand selection of drink. He chose his malt, and Annie had the same.

'Canny there. I've still got to drive over to Jamie's later.'

'Oh, is that too much? Usually Graham does the drinks. Pour some back if you like.'

'No, I won't go that far, thanks.' He took his glass, and sat down again. Annie moved around the room switching on lamps, and the suburban street, fading in winter dusk, vanished behind their reflections in the bay window. Then she sat down again, curling her legs beneath her in the big chair. Tom was sprawled on the sofa, growing sleepy with the heat of the room and the early whisky. He roused himself, realising Annie had asked him a question.

'What?'

'You're in Aberdeen to talk to Jamie about the shop?'

'Yes – that's it. To see you as well, of course.'

'Oh, of course.' She smiled. 'Uncle Stuart's agreed then – he's OK about selling it now?'

'I don't know about agreed ... but yes, he's going along with it.'

'He'll miss the place, though, won't he? He's still there quite a lot, when you're teaching.'

'He doesn't do any dealing now – I've been handling the

antiquarian side, mail order and so on, for years,' Tom said. 'I think that's why it's difficult to get him to see there's no future in it. He imagines we can just tootle along indefinitely. But we can't.'

'But that's what you've *been* doing,' Annie pointed out. 'Why does it have to end now? Are *you* fed up with it?' Tom didn't answer this. 'You could do with a change, maybe,' she prompted.

'Aye, I could do with that, certainly.'

'But you won't leave the High House – you'll go on living there?' Of course he would – impossible to imagine Tom anywhere else. But for a moment, Tom didn't answer.

'Oh, I hadn't thought about that,' he said at last. 'But the shop's actually losing money now. That's the point.'

'Oh, I see.'

'And Jamie's joint owner, since Dad handed over to us, so I need to discuss it with him.'

'I know.'

'Don't worry,' he said, smiling. 'One change at a time is enough for me.'

'It's a wonder we don't hate the place,' Annie said, 'after all that happened. Especially you and Jamie. But you don't, do you? I still feel sort of tied to it myself.'

She was thinking of Lindsay, and of his mother's death, a few years later. But Tom did not talk about these things, even for Annie.

'When's Graham home?' he asked, hoping to deflect her.

'First day of term,' Annie said, 'so he might be late.'

'So we can get another drink in?'

'D'you want one? I thought you were driving?'

'I am. Only kidding. Tempted by this wonderful malt.' He leaned back and closed his eyes. 'It's warm in here. This is a very relaxing room.'

'Is it?' Annie looked round, trying to see it afresh. It was too familiar: all she saw was that the life in it came from Tom being there, the pile of books slipping sideways at his feet, the crumpled newspaper he'd been reading, his navy sweater slung over the back of the sofa.

Tom opened his eyes. 'Where did you say Alistair was – not at home for Christmas?'

'Munich. Business, then he stayed with people he knows there. But he's away somewhere else now, I think. What an exotic life he leads,' she wondered, 'so unlike the rest of us.'

'Alistair was *never* like the rest of us,' Tom said.

'I know. Anyone would think you and Jamie were my brothers, not him.'

They contemplated this in silence for a moment, and Tom finished his whisky. He grew drowsy, the room floated, and Annie's voice droned softly on. *Mm*, he said, and *You're right*, or *Did he?* Christmas, her parents, Graham's bad temper over something that happened at Hogmanay, all the family trivia she gathered and stored, and relayed to him each time he came.

Somewhere, a bell rang.

'That's the door!' Annie exclaimed. 'Who on earth—' Tom stirred to wakefulness as she got up. 'Probably someone selling something,' she said. 'Back in a minute.'

She was gone for several minutes, but no one seemed to come in. He got up and poured himself another large dram, having forgotten about driving to Jamie's. Jehovah's Witnesses, he thought, sitting down again. Annie always made the mistake of feeling sorry for them. She'd be there for ages. Maybe he should call out, rescue her. Then suddenly she was back in the room. Her face was flushed, and she carried with her a rush of fresh air, something new.

'What is it?'

'Tom – it's Rob. He's here – by himself.'

'Who?'

'Oh, Tom, for God's sake – Rob – Alistair's boy.'

'*What?*'

He could see she was excited: she loved the unexpected.

'What – is Alistair here?'

'No, that's what I'm saying. He's on his own. He came by himself – I've put him in the kitchen.'

'The kitchen? Are his shoes dirty or something?'

'Don't be daft. I asked if he wanted something to eat and he said yes. He says he's had nothing since yesterday – imagine that, Tom.'

'Annie—'

'He's been hitching lifts.'

'I don't follow this – where's his mother – he lives with his mother, doesn't he?'

'Well, yes, Sussex – no, Surrey, not Sussex. I'd have to look up the address on my Christmas list. But anyway, I keep telling you, he's come on his own. I don't think – I have the feeling no one knows he's here.'

'But he's just a wee boy, isn't he?'

'About fifteen, sixteen – it's hard to tell. With that hair and everything.'

Tom was startled. 'Is he that old? I thought he was only eleven or something.'

'Oh no. Older than that.' Each contemplated, silently, the oddness of not knowing Rob's age. Then Annie turned away, going out of the room. 'I have to admit I didn't recognise him myself – at first.' She paused by the door. 'Come through – I have to feed him. Whatever else.'

Tom followed her into the kitchen.

On a revolving stool, spinning slowly, was a boy in a denim jacket covered in badges, and jeans torn at the knee. His hair was cut brutally short and adolescence had enlarged and coarsened features that might once have made him an attractive child. Tom did not recognise him at all. But then, he couldn't remember seeing him since Alistair and Shona were still living together, and that must be more than ten years ago.

Annie was slicing bread.

'Will a sandwich do just now?' she asked. 'I've a casserole for later, but it's not in the oven yet.'

'Yuh. OK.' This was little more than a grunt, ungracious. Even so, it was clearly a South of England grunt. Good grief, thought Tom, surprised, he's English.

'Hello, there. Don't suppose you remember me.'

'Yuh.' The boy nodded. 'She said. You're Tom.'

'Right.'

'Tuna or cheese?' Annie asked briskly, opening the fridge door. Rob shrugged. 'Don' mind.'

'Mayonnaise?'

'Yeah. Ta.'

Tom sat down at the table. A vase of pink carnations was in the centre, shedding flakes of petal on the pine surface.

'Any chance of a cup of tea, Annie? Or coffee. Something.' Even for him, it was a bit early in the day for so much alcohol. Annie put a plate of sandwiches down in front of the boy and went to fill the kettle.

'Well then,' Tom said, looking at Rob. He had begun to eat, very fast.

'Tea or coffee?' Annie offered.

'Got any Coke?' Rob asked, his mouth full.

'Oh – I don't know.' She opened a cupboard and stared doubtfully at the contents. 'I think there's some lemonade here, left over from Hogmanay.'

It was flat.

'Milk?' she suggested.

'I'll have tea. Tea's OK. Two sugars.'

'Oh. Right. Sugar.' She began to hunt again and eventually found some caked hard in a little china bowl that was familiar to Tom. Perhaps it had been his grandmother's. Annie had a lot of her things.

The hot tea, and some of Annie's Christmas cake, steadied Tom.

The boy did not touch the cake, but he ate two chocolate biscuits. It was difficult to ask him anything while he was eating so much and so fast, but Annie tried.

'Maybe you'd like to ring your mother?' Annie suggested. 'Let her know you're OK. Or your dad?'

'They're in Tenerife.'

'What – Alistair?' This didn't seem credible.

'No, not Dad. Mum and Ken.'

'Ken,' she said. 'Is that—'

'Me step-dad.'

'What – they left you on your own?'

'Na. Had the dog, din' I?'

'Did you?' Annie echoed. Tom could tell what was going to worry Annie, so he leaned towards Rob and said, 'What have you done with the dog?'

'Giv 'im to me mate, din' I?'

'Did you?' This was ridiculous. Annie would have to phone Alistair. Or he would. Just as soon as his head cleared. You needed a clear head to speak to Alistair.

The boy got to his feet.

'I use the toilet?'

'Yes, sure, there's one just on the right.' She got up and opened the kitchen door to show him. Tom got up too and shut the door behind Rob.

'Annie,' he said, 'you'll have to get in touch with Alistair. Now.'

'I've just remembered – he's in New York. He said when he phoned last week. His office'll have a number, I suppose. But he couldn't *do* anything – just worry.' She saw Tom's eyebrows rise. 'Oh, he would Tom. Anyway – better wait till he gets back.'

She began to clear the table and Tom could tell from the vigour with which she wiped up crumbs that she was annoyed.

'Annie—'

'What on earth was Shona thinking about – leaving a boy that age on his own?'

'He had the dog.'

'It's not funny.' She shook her cloth into the sink and ran it under the hot tap.

'Well, look at it this way,' Tom suggested. 'He's here, he's safe, and you can easily put him up for a few days till Alistair gets back. Then he's *his* responsibility.'

'Oh, I know that.' Annie sat down opposite Tom at the table.

'It's just—'

'What?'

Annie had wiped up flower petals along with the crumbs, but more were falling. She pushed them together in a little heap with one finger.

'Why?' she asked. 'Why has he come here?'

'Why not? You're family. All his family's up here, apart from his bloody useless parents.'

Annie let this pass, in the interests of pursuing her own train of thought.

'None of us has seen him for years – since that awful Christmas after the divorce, when Alistair was in such a state, demanding his rightful access, making sure Shona didn't have Robbie for a minute more than she was entitled to. He was such a bonny wee boy, too.'

'Now, presumably because he's big and spotty instead of blond and angelic, neither of them wants him.'

'Ssh!' Annie glanced towards the kitchen door. 'He's a long time, isn't he? D'you think?'

'Shooting up,' Tom suggested. 'Isn't that what it's called?'

'What – *drugs*?'

'Och, don't be daft. I'm only joking. Constipation, more likely, if he hasn't been eating properly.'

They heard the cloakroom lavatory flush and the door opening and closing. Rob came back into the kitchen.

'Right then,' Tom said, getting to his feet. He was taller than Rob, but only just, and the boy was probably still growing. 'I'd better go. Jamie and Ruth are expecting me about half five, and I'll need to walk after all that whisky.'

'Oh.' Annie looked disappointed. 'I'd forgotten you were going there to eat. But you're coming back, aren't you, to sleep here?'

'Well – I'd intended to, but – I mean, I'd eat here too, but Ruth asked me—'

'No, it's OK. Wouldn't be enough food anyway now.' She got up too. Tom nodded at Rob.

'OK – see you again. Have a chat with Annie.'

Out in the street, walking past his own car and Annie's little white hatchback, Tom felt as if he'd abandoned them both, aunt and nephew. But it would be good for Annie to deal with Rob on her own. She hadn't enough to do – that was the trouble. Pity, he thought, as he so often did, she hasn't got her own kids. He tucked his hands into the pockets of his long black coat, hunting for the leather gloves he kept there. It was cold, the sky starry, the air tingling with frost. He tried to think about the shop, about what he was going to do. That was what he'd come to discuss with Jamie. They had to sort something out. He did not want to think about children at all, longed for and unconceived like Annie's, or present and unwanted, like Rob.

2

Once, Annie and Graham had loved each other completely. Annie knew that was true.

'I love you,' she had told him on their wedding night, 'more than anything or anyone else in the world. I love you so much.' And he had lain with his arms round her, his mouth on one breast, tugging the nipple.

'You're a grand girl, Annie,' he had said, his mouth full of young milkless breast.

Maybe, she thought, years later, when she had too much time to think, that was the best moment of all. A moment of letting go. Annie wondered a lot about her marriage, as she did about everything else in the years after she had stopped teaching. But all this wondering wasn't quite enough to fill the days. She seemed to wade through a lot of empty time. Rob's sudden arrival had shocked and worried her, but it pleased her too. She bustled round him.

When Graham came home he could hear the television from the hall, where usually there was quiet, except for the sounds from the kitchen of Annie cooking, and the mild drone of Radio 4. Often, he was so late even these sounds had ceased, and the smell of his dinner drifted through a silent house. Annie would be in her chair in the bay window, the cat on her lap, or the dog at her feet, dreaming. The sight of her like this always roused in him a faint irritation. Had he been the one with all day to himself, he'd at least have listened to music in this empty waiting time, or have found a job for himself. He didn't know how she could just sit there, doing nothing.

He stood for a moment listening, puzzled, to canned laughter, American voices. Then he pushed open the living-room door.

A boy, stocky, with cropped hair, was stretched on the sofa, his feet in grubby trainers propped on one arm, his head supported against the other by three cushions. The television absorbed him, the noise cutting him off from Graham's entrance.

'What the – who the hell are you?'

The boy jerked round, his feet landed on the floor and he stood up.

'Rob,' he said. 'I'm Rob.'

Annie was in the doorway. 'Graham, it's Alistair's boy.'

Graham readjusted several thoughts at once.

'Is Alistair here then?'

'No.'

'He's in New York,' the boy offered.

'And his mother's abroad too,' Annie added. 'He's come on his own.' She turned to Rob.

'Food's nearly ready. I'll give you a shout.' She made for the kitchen, the bustle of her walk indicating that Graham should follow.

In the kitchen the American voices faded. The table was set for three.

'What's going on?'

'He just turned up, when Tom was here in the afternoon. They left him on his own, Graham. Shona and her fancy man. Well I think he's her husband now. Something's upset him – he hitch-hiked all this way.'

'I don't even *recognise* him,' Graham said, bewildered, belliger-ent. 'He could be anybody, for me. How old is he?'

'Fifteen, sixteen.' Annie waved a hand vaguely. 'Something like that.'

'You'd better ring Alistair.'

'He's in New York.'

'Well, ring him in bloody New York then.'

'Oh, for goodness sake – what could Alistair do? We'll just have to keep him here till one of his parents is home. That's all.'

'Well, he can get those godawful trainers off for a start,' Graham said, heading out of the kitchen. 'I suppose that's the way he behaves at home – Shona always was a slut.'

'Graham!'

Annie sighed and went to prod the potatoes. She was just too late: they were turning to mush in the pan. Quickly she drained them and began to mash, the fork sinking into soft white, the knob of butter melting greasily golden, then disappearing. She turned them into a serving dish, marked the surface with a fork, and put them in the bottom of the oven. As she shut the oven door and stood up she grew giddy and had to steady herself, clutching the back of a chair till the moment passed and her vision cleared. Shouldn't have had a drink in the afternoon, she thought, aching now, and weary.

Graham reappeared. He seemed more cheerful.

'Right,' he said, 'that's sorted him out.'

'You weren't unkind to him, were you?'

'Unkind?' Graham echoed, trying out the word as if he'd never heard it before. 'Annie, he's an adolescent. They all have hides like leather. Believe me.'

'Oh well,' she said, putting the warmed plates on the table, straightening cutlery, 'you would know.' She put on oven gloves and waved her linked mittened hands at Graham. 'Tell him to come through then. It's ready.'

Graham stood at the kitchen door and bawled, *'Grub's up!'*

Annie flinched.

'I could have done that myself,' she said. 'I meant you to go and fetch him. He's got the television on.'

'It's OK, I made him turn it down. They're all deaf as well, kids. Too many discos.'

But Rob appeared almost at once.

'You'd better wash your hands,' Annie said. 'Here, use this towel.'

''S OK.' Rob looked at the table and sat down on the chair nearest him. Graham, annoyed, almost said, *That's where I sit,* then decided this was petty and moved round to the side, to the unaccustomed third place, where his bulk was in Annie's way as she dished up the meal.

Rob ate fast, shovelling food, finished long before either of the others. In the pauses between increasingly stilted scraps of conversation, Annie was conscious of the noises of chewing and swallowing. Desperately, she cast around for things to talk about. But Rob was monosyllabic, his responses a series of grunts. She gave up and gathered empty plates.

'I'm not finished,' Graham said, helping himself to the last of the casserole. He was a slow eater; it had often irritated her to watch him laboriously clear his plate while she, setting a good example to the children she'd never had, waited for him.

Rob kept glancing at his watch.

'OK if I watch the telly?'

'What? Oh yes. I was going to make coffee. And there's cheese and biscuits or fruit.'

'No thanks. Had all them sandwiches.'

'So you did.' Helplessly, she watched him scrape his chair back, wipe his hands down the side of his jeans, leave the room.

'Well.' Graham leaned back in his chair.

'Well *what*?' With a clatter, Annie heaped plates and stacked the dishwasher.

'We're stuck with him, I take it.'

'Look, he came to us. That must mean something.' Graham was picking shreds of meat from between his teeth with a probing fingernail. Abruptly, Annie turned away and ran water into the sink to soak the empty casserole dish. She longed for Tom to come back.

But when he did, bringing the smell of cold January air, a whiff of some larger, fresher world, Graham was still scornful, Annie still cross. They sat round the kitchen table, while from the living room came the roar of excited laughter and the blare of cymbals and trumpets celebrating each round in a game show.

'I think,' Annie said, 'they watch TV a lot at that age.'

'Certainly,' Graham agreed. 'But they don't all walk into strangers' houses to do it.'

'We're not strangers,' Annie protested. 'We're his family.'

'Then he should treat us with more respect.'

'Oh shut up,' Annie sighed. 'You must be *so* popular with your pupils.'

'What the hell's my job got to do with it?'

'Just a minute—' Tom broke in. They were working up to a row here. They both turned to him at once. Unnerved, he raised his hands, as if to fend them off. 'He's only a kid. I mean, Annie's right, of course, he's family. But we don't know him. He doesn't know us.'

'Well, now's our opportunity.'

'Annie, what d'you think Alistair's going to do when he gets back? He'll be up here like a shot, dragging the lad home, scoring points off Shona as he goes.'

'Right, it's their problem,' Graham said, 'not ours.'

'I don't think Alistair wants him either,' Annie said. 'Cramp his international style, having a child in tow. Weekends, the odd holiday – that's about it.' She folded her arms, leaned back. 'If he cared, wouldn't he have brought him here sometimes, to meet his family?'

But before either man could answer, the kitchen door opened and Rob came in.

'Sorry,' he said, backing away again as they turned in unison to look at him. 'Sorry,' he said again. 'I just . . .'

'Come in,' Annie said. 'Can I get you anything? Is the programme finished?'

'Yeah. I just wondered – could I get a bath or something?'

Annie got up at once. 'Yes, of course. Come on, I'll show you where everything is.'

The men sat on without speaking, listening to the water draining from the tank, Annie opening and shutting cupboard doors upstairs.

'You want a drink, Tom?'

'No, I'll get back to Jamie's. Ruth said they'd put me up.'

'I thought you were staying here?'

'Well that was the original plan, but Annie's going to need a room for Rob.'

'She can make up another bed, for God's sake.' Graham reddened. 'Sorry. Please yourself, Tom.'

'It's OK.' Tom hesitated. 'Yes, right. I'll have a drink. We all need a drink.'

When Annie came downstairs they were in the living room, and the bottle of malt was on the coffee table.

'He's having a bath,' she said. 'I've made up the bed in the little spare.'

'Tom said Ruth was giving him a bed.'

'Oh Tom—'

'It's all right. I'll stay if you want me to.'

'I do.' She heaved a sigh and pushed her hands through her

hair so that the curls sprang back loose and untidy. 'It's upset me,' she said. 'Rob turning up like this. I don't know why.'

'It's upset all of us,' Tom assured her. 'When I told Jamie—'

'Why on earth should it bother him?' Graham asked.

'The same reason it bothers me,' Annie said. 'Because nobody seems to care about Rob. And yet he's part of our family. It's all wrong.'

'Have you asked him?' Graham broke in. 'Asked him why he's turned up here? Has he run away, or does he think he'll have a wee holiday – what? I mean, he must be due back at school. Even if they broke up later than we did, he must be—'

'Yes, yes.' Annie waved a hand at him. 'I know all that. But I haven't asked. I thought he'd tell us, when he'd settled in a bit. I thought tomorrow, when you'd both gone, I'd have a chat with him.'

She pictured herself sitting opposite Rob at the breakfast table, Graham off to work, Tom driving north again. Thinking of this made her feel different, more responsible. Was this what having your own children was like? Did they push you on a generation, make you adult, by their very existence? But she was adult, sensible, reliable. She was all those grown-up things.

She had imagined herself with babies. In the early years of marriage, while she was still teaching full time but seeing it as a temporary thing, a way of saving money for a better house, a family house, she imagined babies. When she held a friend's baby on her lap, solid and warm, felt plump arms whose skin was tight with newness, she had thought, I'll have babies soon. She had a list of names, she made decisions about prams and cots and where the baby would sleep. The first one would be a boy. They would have two sons, then a daughter. It was all there, planned, in her mind. Later, during years of repeated hopes and disappointments, these imaginary babies grew and changed. It was children she missed having now. Her friends had children: they met them from playgroup or school, took them to Brownies and Cubs, taught them to swim, bought bikes, complained about the cost of bringing them up.

They bought a family house, and eventually Annie gave up teaching. This idea came from counselling sessions Annie had been having, but Graham encouraged her to do it, saying she should relax more.

'Teaching wears you out,' he said. Underneath was the still-living hope: then you'll get pregnant, then it will work. But it had not.

Now there was this cuckoo, a gauche unattractive boy who was not theirs and never could be. He had simply landed, and might just as simply and suddenly take off again. No wonder Graham was annoyed, no wonder Annie was upset.

Rob did not reappear.

'He's got one of those things,' Annie explained. 'You know – a Walkman. He was listening to it in the bath. Do you think that's safe enough?'

No one answered her. Graham put on Vivaldi's *Four Seasons*, which Annie hated. After a few moments, she got up and turned down the sound. She could feel Graham's resentment, but ignored it.

Tom said, 'I'll ring Ruth,' and went into the kitchen to use the phone there. He seemed to be gone a long time.

'Sorry,' he said, when he came back. 'Jamie wanted to talk about the shop again. He was expecting me back tonight. He wanted to come over, but—'

'But what? It's a bit late, I suppose.'

'I said Rob had gone to bed.'

'What – he wanted to see Rob?'

'Well, of course he did. His nephew too,' Graham pointed out.

'Second cousin,' Annie amended. 'Something like that.'

'Family,' Graham said. '*Family*, Annie.' But she did not rise to this.

Winter crashed to an end on the CD player. Tom went to bed before Graham could start on Wagner. Annie followed him out into the hall.

'I'm going to make a cup of tea. Do you want one?'

'No thanks.' He paused on the half-landing, looking down over the banisters to where she stood leaning on the newel post at the bottom, smoothing her hands over the pitch pine acorn.

'It's strange, isn't it,' she murmured, 'the way Rob turned up just when I wanted to talk about Lindsay. As if . . . as if it wasn't the right time for that. I don't know.'

'But you often want to talk about Lindsay.' Tom smiled down at her. 'You weird woman. But in the end, we never do.'

'Don't we?'

'Goodnight, Annie. See you in the morning.'

Tom lay on his back in Annie's spare bed, between ironed white sheets. The central heating had gone off, but the room was still warm. It was a pretty room, the wallpaper blue and white Regency stripes, the curtains a deeper blue, the rosewood dressing table brought from their grandmother's house a long time ago. He lay with the bedside lamp still on, soothed by this tasteful, unused room. All Annie's rooms were pretty, he thought, the colours blending, the pottery bits and pieces matching, the carpets soft. She had plenty of time and money to choose the right things. He reflected on this, and on the unfairness of life. There were sounds from the kitchen, then footsteps in the hall, the front door opening, the clink of milk bottles. Then the front door was locked, the chain rattled up. Annie came upstairs slowly, sighing as she reached the top.

Tom drifted into a doze, thinking about the shop again, and his discussions with Jamie. They were going to have to sell, no question. The sound of traffic on the main road kept him from absolute sleep. He was used to a stillness torn only by the owl's cry, the 'cushie doo' in the trees around the High House. And the wind in the trees, brushing fir branches against each other. In Annie's street the trees were too spindly to give voice to the wind: it shook the leaves with a derisory rustle, and moved on.

In the narrow third bedroom Rob slept hunched beneath the downie, his clothes scattered on the floor, his rucksack spilling out cassette tapes on the pale green carpet. Now and again, the sound muffled by duck down, he whimpered a little, and once cried out. His legs twitched, throwing off the cover, and at two in the morning the cold woke him. He was in a strange house, an unfamiliar bed. He sat up, bewildered. Then he remembered, and lay back, listening. Silence. He hadn't wakened anybody, hadn't been shouting. It was just the dream in his head, the lorry thundering up the M1, the smell of cigarette smoke and diesel, the shaky feeling when he got out at the service station and the driver said, *OK, son?*

Sometimes at home, he woke with a jolt to find his mother in the room, saying, *You having a bad dream? I told you not to watch that horror film, give anybody the heebie-jeebies.* Then she would straighten the covers, and leave the landing light on, as if he were still a kid.

It wasn't a film that did it, he wasn't such a nerd. But he'd no idea what did, that was the scary thing. As long as it didn't happen here. But why should it? He was OK.

After all, he'd got here. He'd made it.

3

With nothing but the certainty of youth to back him up, Graham had started out believing he and Annie would have sons, big and fair like himself, and then a daughter, dark and lively as Annie was. Ironic, he often thought, when she looked so fertile, plump and rosy, that no children came. After a drink or two, he would find himself recalling how he'd felt about her then, when they were still full of hope. They were young and healthy, and it was only (everyone said) a matter of time. She must be brimful of babies, so couthy was she in his arms, her breasts, her bum, such lovely warm handfuls.

He did not feel the same now. The years, the repeated disappointments, had dimmed all that. Each act of love, once so joyfully plunged into, became tense with expectation. It always meant something else. And yet, in the end, none of it had meant anything.

Lately, she seemed to him like a rose overblown, petals faded. Past her best. He looked now with impartial lust on the pale thin girls in his sixth year, in drooping skirts and black jerseys with sleeves so long they came over their knuckles. When they sat writing, only pale fingers were visible, the nails bitten hard, or long talons painted pink or black or red according to fashion. Something about these paw-like hands, scraping across the page, excited him. And their ankles in black tights, and their small breasts enveloped in black wool . . . This was all in his mind, working beneath the surface. No one else knew of it, least of all the girls themselves, who walked home each day hand in hand with lads who turned up at the school gates in denim, or whisked them away on the backs of roaring motorbikes, their black skirts lifting, hair flying, modern witches.

When he caught sight of a group of his own pupils in the city centre at the weekend, dressed differently, the girls with tiny cotton tops low at the neck and high at the waist, revealing white gaps of perfect skin, saw the boys whose arms rested on their bare shoulders or circled the warm curve of a waist, he envied them their easy, untried familiarity. How casual they were, about something so dangerous.

On his fortieth birthday, he had realised these girls could be his daughters. And he tried to put all the unsuitable thoughts he had of them, that so disturbed and appalled him, out of his mind, cramming them into the stuffed cupboard of his subconscious along with all the other thoughts in which he no longer allowed himself to indulge. But he went on feeling the sudden spasms of lust that both brightened and spoiled his days.

On the day that Rob arrived, he'd just gone back to school after the New Year. It was a bad first day: the heating system in his part of the building had broken down. He and two heads of department spent most of the morning rearranging classes, moving pupils, so that the effect of this was minimised. It meant no one settled, no one had any sense of being back at work.

Graham had been deputy head for four years, but he still had a teaching load. Staff cutbacks would have made this necessary even if he hadn't wanted to do it. He took his small fourth-form group into his office this cold Tuesday morning, where there was an electric heater they could use. They sat in a crowded semicircle, pads on their laps, the floor littered with bags and jackets, the carpet darkened in patches by melted snow. It grew stuffy in the room with mingled odours of sharp scent, sweat, fried food. Around one of the boys there always clung a stale, fatty smell: his father owned a fish and chip shop and Ray helped out in the evenings.

The lesson wore on, the girls taking notes assiduously. Then one of the boys broke wind so that they all edged their chairs away from him with loud expressions of disgust. It was Graham's policy to ignore this kind of thing. He carried on talking. The double period seemed endless – and it was only the first day. The girls who had, in the busy active weeks up to Christmas, seemed so lively and flirtatious, were dull and immovable. Too much food and drink, Graham thought: Christmas did no one any good. When the group finally shuffled out, one girl hanging back to smile at him, *Bye sir, see you on Thursday*, he sank into his chair again.

'Shut the door, Caroline.'

'Right sir. Bye then.'

When she'd gone, he put his face in his hands for a few minutes and rubbed his eyes. This made him feel worse, if anything. Someone knocked on his door and he stood up briskly, gathering papers on his desk and tapping them to make them fall into line.

'Come!'

It was a third-year boy whose chemistry teacher was unable to deal with him in class. Graham had not been able to persuade her that the year head was the appropriate person to send him to.

'He doesn't pay any attention to Jan either,' Grace had complained. 'I know it seems a sexist thing to say, but he only listens to men.'

But the Christmas holidays had clearly diminished the good effect of a man speaking to him, if it had ever existed.

'Not you again, Darren?'

The boy grinned, shrugged. 'Mrs Robertson said to come.'

Graham sighed. 'I suppose she wants a daily report form.'

'Aye.' He caught Graham's look. 'Yes, sir.'

Graham rummaged in a drawer and brought out a form. He entered the boy's name and class.

'Right – here you are.'

The boy hesitated. 'Am I nae gettin' detention, sir?'

Graham looked at the boy coldly. The trouble with discipline was that you had to keep it up. This morning he felt he could hardly summon the energy to get himself through the day.

'I can't believe,' he said, 'you've so little brain you're actually reminding me – do you *want* detention?'

'Disna bother me.' He paused. 'Sir.'

Graham sighed.

'Well, let's say I've still got a bit of Christmas spirit left. We'll let you off this time.'

'Right sir. I go then?'

'Yes, back to whatever class you're supposed to be disrupting now.'

When the boy had gone, he went to the year files and looked him up: *Suspected abuse by stepfather*. He closed the file on this and on Darren's catalogue of misbehaviour, and put it back in the drawer. Then he scribbled a note on a yellow Post-it, reminding himself to speak to Jan Patterson, the year head, and stuck it amongst several others on his desk. That at least would be a pleasure: Jan had been at the school less than a year, but at least (and he sighed over Grace Robertson), she knew how to manage the kids. He let his mind linger over Jan Patterson, her endless legs, the swing of fair hair when she turned her head.

Usually, Graham slept before Annie, leaving her to lie awake and worry for both of them. But on the night Rob arrived, he lay and listened to her breathing become slow and light, growing more and more wakeful himself. When he stopped thinking about school, he turned to Rob instead, feeling irritated without knowing why. Then he realised the irritation was with Alistair, not the boy. Alistair always got his back up, could even do it without being here. He shook this off, went back to thinking about work. But this time, it wasn't the central heating breakdown, or the new chemistry teacher's discipline problems, or the pile of paperwork on his desk, or even Jan Patterson. It was Darren Wilson who came to mind. He saw the boy again, shuffling out of his office. And the irritability he felt when he thought of Rob tweaked at him again. No one took responsibility, that was the trouble. For Rob, for Darren . . . Bad parents, they were at the root of it. Bad parents.

Annie moved round, moaning a little as she curled away from him. He turned towards her, fitted himself round the warm curve of her back, tucking his knees behind hers. The scents of her body, her dark hair, consoled with their familiarity. We have to comfort each other, he thought, giving way to the self-pity that grows in the unsympathetic dark.

He must have dozed off. The cry that woke them was so sudden and sharp they were half-way out of bed, shaking, before they knew what had happened.

'God almighty, what is it?'

'I don't know.' Annie was pulling on her dressing gown.

She opened the bedroom door, stretching out her hand for the landing light, but Tom was there already putting it on.

'What is it?'

'Rob – will I go?'

'No—' Annie was on her way. 'A nightmare,' she said, over her shoulder. 'Probably.' The two men stood looking at each other in the sudden light.

Graham shrugged. 'As long as that's – it was the boy, wasn't it? We were asleep.'

'So was I.'

Annie pushed open Rob's door. Her heart was still thumping with the fright of being jerked out of sleep. The room was dark, the boy a hunched shape on the bed. She went over to him, and reached down for the bedside lamp.

'Are you all right?' He was weeping, a strange, uncomfortable sound: not a child's sobbing, but not a man's either. He raised his head.

'Don't put on the light.'

'All right.' Annie took her hand away from the light switch and sat down on the edge of the bed. The boy shuddered, pushed the covers off his shoulders, lay back. 'What happened – were you dreaming? Jamie, my cousin, he used to get night terrors, screamed and ran about – maybe you get them too.'

'Yeah, yeah, it was a dream. I'm OK.' But his voice had a tremor in it.

'Can I get you anything? A drink – some hot milk?'

'No, I don't want nothin'.'

'Are you cold? Would you like a hot-water bottle?' He was shaking; the whole bed vibrated.

Graham came to the door, blocking the light from the landing.

'Everything all right?'

'Just a bad dream. You know – night terror – like Jamie used to get.'

'Oh.'

'Go back to bed, Graham. I'll be through in a minute.'

Graham hesitated, then disappeared. She heard him speaking to Tom. Someone went into the bathroom, then another door closed – Tom's bedroom.

'You c'n go back to bed,' Rob said. 'I'm OK. Sorry I – sorry you got woke up.'

'It doesn't matter.' Annie smoothed the downie, straightening it. 'No hurry to get up in the morning. I'm not going out. Sleep in if you like.'

'Right.'

'Goodnight then.'

''Night.' And as she reached the door, 'Sorry.'

'It doesn't matter. Really.'

She pulled his door to behind her and stood for a few seconds, listening to the silence. Then she went back to bed.

Graham had put the lamp on and was reading.

'Never get back to sleep,' he said. 'Bloody kid – what's ado anyway?'

'I don't know.' Annie got into bed, sighing as she raised her pillows so that she too was sitting up. 'He said it was a dream, so I suppose he's like Jamie – remember Jamie used to get night terrors? Except we always thought that was because of my aunt Liz dying. But Rob – Graham, he was *crying* when I went in.'

'Crying? He's *sixteen*.'

'Fifteen. Just fifteen, Graham.'

'Fifteen, sixteen . . . a bit old to be blubbing in the middle of the night because he had a bad dream, eh?'

'Oh, shut up,' Annie said wearily. 'Can't we just put the light out and go to sleep?'

She tugged her pillows down and lay on her side, away from him. Graham made a token show of turning a few pages, then he switched the light off.

'I'd better try to find out,' Annie said. 'Talk to him in the morning.'

'Well,' Graham said, 'it'll give you something to do, I suppose, sorting out his life for him.'

Annie did not answer. They lay back to back, not touching, in the cold dark. Outside, snow fell in silence, drifting across the city.

4

Tom drove north the next day. He had breakfast early with Graham while Annie, in her dressing gown, drifted in and out of the kitchen, making coffee and feeding the animals. Then he went to Jamie's flat, to make decisions about selling the bookshop.

'I'd better head up the road,' he said eventually, when they'd talked for a long time, mainly about their father. 'I just hope the A96 is passable.'

'Blocked at Huntly already,' Jamie said with a grin. This was what their parents had always fretted about, on those childhood journeys north and south for Christmas.

'I haven't been to see Christine and Matt,' Tom said. 'There wasn't really time. Are they OK?'

'Well, I don't see them much either – but we were all at Annie's at Christmas. They're OK. Getting old.'

'Aren't we all?' Tom got to his feet. 'Right, I'm off.'

'It's all settled then?' Jamie asked. They stood in the hallway, while Tom put on his coat. The flat smelt of Jamie's Gauloises, strong coffee, and faintly of the scent Ruth had sprayed on before leaving for work. This concentration of smells made Tom long for home, though he didn't know why.

'I'll speak to Dad,' he said, pulling gloves out of his pockets. 'He's not going to be *happy* about it, is he?'

'It's up to you, Tom, really. He has to realise that. You're the one who puts the effort in now.'

'Aye well, with less and less return these days.' He sighed. 'Ach, we've been over all that.'

'I wouldn't mind a bit of cash, I have to admit,' Jamie said, opening the front door for Tom. 'But I can manage. It'll probably take a while to sell. Anyway, Ruth doesn't seem to mind me living off her.'

'Just as well, eh?'

Jamie stood by the window and looked down at the street as Tom got into his car and drove away. It was still snowing; by the time he turned the corner the car had become indistinct, blurred by a cloud of white specks. Jamie wished for a moment he'd said 'Ring me when you get back,' as their parents always had. Then he turned away from the window, and began preparing for work.

They had chosen this flat because of its view over the city, and its high-ceilinged rooms. The big north-facing bedroom was Jamie's studio. It had no furniture apart from cupboards for his equipment, a few chairs and his drawing table and stool. He sat at this table now, and unscrewed his pen. He was illustrating a book on Scottish wildlife and had been asked to produce pen-and-ink drawings as margin and chapter head decorations.

Yesterday he'd been pleased with what he'd done: today, as he looked through them, the drawings seemed twee, cosy. He got up and paced about for a while, smoked a cigarette, drank some cooling coffee, and washed up his mug and Tom's. Then he thought of Annie, and his curiosity about Rob was fired again. He'd go and see them, and Annie would insist on giving him lunch. That would take care of most of the day. He could leave before Graham got home.

He was on his way out when the phone rang. He reached it as the answerphone message began.

Ruth Maclennan and Jamie Mathieson are not able to come to the—

'Hi – hello?'

'Oh, Jamie, it's Annie. Has Tom left?'

'About, um, twenty minutes ago.'

'The forecast's awful. I hoped I'd catch him, persuade him to leave it a day. When they've cleared the road—'

'Too late. He'll be OK. Tom's pretty cautious.'

'Well, yes, but—'

'How about Rob then? He still around?'

'Actually, he's in bed. Graham says all teenage boys stay in bed till dinner-time.'

'Blast him with some of Graham's Wagner. That'll get him up. I was just on my way over, Annie, is that OK?'

'Yes, of course it is. Come and have lunch.'

Jamie licked his finger and chalked an imaginary tick on the wall.

'I'll walk,' he said, 'so I'll be about half an hour.'

Outside, he turned up the collar of his army greatcoat and dug his hands deep in the pockets. Ruth took the car to work, so Jamie walked everywhere. He distrusted buses and had never mastered the complexity of their routes, or having the right money for the fare. Besides, he liked weather, didn't mind how bad it was. Snow settled on his woolly hat, his moustache, the front of his coat.

Eventually the blizzard thinned and the snow stopped. This was what he liked: how, after such a storm, a spreading patch of blue cleared the sky, and the whole city sparkled, sun refracting off granite. His steps quickened and he breathed in icy air. With one gloved hand he brushed snow from his head, his face, the front of his coat, where it flattened to a smear of white on the heavy cloth.

He went round to the back of Annie's house, and into the porch. Through the glass door to the kitchen he could see Annie at the table, her hands held high above a mixing bowl, a shower of floury crumbs falling from her fingers. He stamped the snow off his boots, opened his coat and flapped the lapels to dust them off. The kitchen was warm, and smelled of baking.

'Hi!' Annie smiled at him as he came in, and brushed a curl of hair off her face with the inside of one raised elbow. 'Did you get soaked? Snow seems to be off now, at least. Hang your coat over the door.' She smacked her hands together over the bowl, and tipped some water in from a glass jug. 'I'll make coffee in a minute. Just doing a pie. Put the kettle on.'

Jamie did as she asked, and sat down at the table to watch her pat and roll the pastry.

'You're so domestic,' he said. 'It's cosy here. I love your kitchen.'

'Ruth and you have a pretty good kitchen yourselves,' Annie pointed out.

'Clinical,' he said, dismissing several thousand pounds worth of German cupboards with a wave. 'Like something out of a hospital. Appropriate, I suppose, for a doctor. But not cosy.' He looked round, making a show of surprise. 'Where is he then, where's the waif and stray?'

'Rob? Still in bed. I told you.'

'Lucky sod. Doesn't he have to go to school or anything? I mean, hasn't anyone missed him?'

'Maybe they have – at school. But Shona's in Tenerife, Lanzarote . . . one of those places. Package holiday. And Alistair's in New York.'

'Not on a package,' Jamie grinned. 'I bet. Work work work. Making money.'

'Well, we just have to wait for one of them to come back.'

'You're loving it, aren't you? What's the pastry for – apple pie? Someone to cook for apart from Graham.'

Annie lifted the circle of pastry on to a pie dish and laid it gently down, pressing round the edge.

'Kettle's boiling,' she said. 'Make the coffee, eh, Jamie?'

'Aye, sure.' He knew where everything was in Annie's kitchen.

He's like a woman, she thought, watching how easily he found what he wanted, fixed up the cafetiere, whistling softly. He just gets on with it. She thought of Graham, who still, when he helped clear up, said things like 'Where do you keep this jug?'

She had finished with the pie: it was filled, covered, the edges knife-marked in scallops. She put it in the fridge and washed her hands.

'I'll go and see if he's awake,' she said, 'since you're so anxious to meet him.'

'Well, I'm not leaving till I have. He's my cousin, isn't he?'

'Several times removed,' Annie smiled.

'Well, the removal was entirely Alistair's fault. He's the one who sold out and went to England.'

'Och, Jamie.' She paused by the door. 'That's the nationalist in you, talking like that.'

'But of course. Still true, though.'

While she was away he pushed down the plunger on the cafetiere and got out mugs, three of them. Did teenage boys drink coffee? Or just Coke? How old was Rob anyway? He tried to work this out, and failed.

Annie came back.

'He's awake,' she said, 'but not . . . what you might call lively.'

'What's he like?' Jamie asked, pushing Annie's mug of coffee across the table towards her. 'He was an awful bonny wee boy. Blond, big blue eyes. Mind, your mother thought he was the bees knees?'

'He was, he was lovely,' Annie sighed. 'When Alistair and Shona split up she was so upset, my mother. She thought she might never see him again.'

'Do bees have knees?' Jamie mused. 'And what's so special about them anyway?'

'What?'

'Nothing. Sorry.' He patted her hand. 'No, she was right, Auntie Chris, wasn't she? They spirited him away to that heathen land across the border . . . her only grandchild.'

'Yes, it was mean of Alistair. He could easily have come home more often. Shona too. *Her* mother used to visit them, but Mum was never asked. Or not in any way that made her feel she'd be welcome. And – what was Shona's mother called – Norma, I think – she hasn't gone for quite a few years now. She's too arthritic. Waiting for hip replacements.'

'You make it sound very *Becket*,' Jamie grinned. 'Waiting for Hip Replacements.'

'Aye, and they take about as long to come,' Annie said. 'Look at Dad.'

'How is he?'

'Same as usual. Och, OK, I suppose. Doesn't get as much golf as he'd like.'

They sat in silence for a while, sipping coffee. Jamie longed for a cigarette, but knew Annie wouldn't risk Graham's wrath. The kitchen had darkened; outside the sky was slate grey, and it was snowing again. He could stand at the back door, he supposed, risk the blizzard turning his Gauloise soggy. He imagined the smell, the taste, but this only made the craving worse. He was just about to get up and head for the back door when Rob came into the kitchen.

A changeling, Jamie thought, his faded image of the blond
child (he recalled a red jersey, navy dungarees) suddenly incongruous.

'Hi,' he said. 'I'm Jamie.'

'Hi.'

'Coffee?' Jamie held up the pot. 'Made it myself – fully guaran-
teed to wake you up. If, of course, that's what you want.'

Rob looked bewildered. 'Sorry I slept in,' he said, turning to
Annie.

'I told you – it doesn't matter.' She pulled out a chair for him.
'Would you like some breakfast?'

'Yeah, yeah, OK.'

'Coffee, then,' Jamie said, pouring some into the third mug.

'I don't—' Rob hesitated, shrugged. 'OK then.'

'Milk?'

'Yeah, ta.'

Annie had washed out and filled a sugar bowl now, and she
set this down on the table. Rob added two spoonfuls to his mug,
all the time glancing covertly at Jamie.

He thinks I'm a jessie, Jamie thought, amused. A poof, gay,
whatever the terminology is down where he lives. I bet he thinks
all men my age who can make their own coffee and wear Doc
Martens and earrings are bent as safety pins. He looked at the
boy again, at the spotty chin, the brutal haircut, the crumpled
clothes. Poor sod, he thought, I wonder how he gets on with
Alistair.

'Scrambled eggs?' Annie asked.

'No, it's OK. Just toast or somethin'.'

She's overdoing it, Jamie thought, with a pang of pity for both
of them. 'So what are the plans today?' he asked Rob.

'Well, with this weather,' Annie sighed, 'I don't see us getting out.'

'It'll clear up in the afternoon,' Jamie said. 'You wait. I'll take
you somewhere if you like – is there anything decent on at the
pictures?'

Rob looked uncomfortable.

'It's OK,' he muttered. 'You don't hafta—'

'What?'

'Do nothin' wiv me. Take me out an' that.'

'No, that's right,' Jamie agreed, 'but it's a good excuse for me. I'd quite like to see a film. Better than working.'

'You supposed to be at work, like?'

'I'm an artist. Artists choose their own hours.'

'That would be fine,' Annie said, 'if you ever actually got round to working. You're lazy, Jamie, that's your trouble.'

'Absolutely. Nae question.' He turned back to Rob. 'How about it then? Got the *P & J*, Annie?'

'Saturday's. Somewhere. It'll be in that.'

'You come too,' Jamie offered, when she had fetched him the paper. He spread it out on the table. Rob munched toast, watching him.

'Well, what's on?' Annie leaned over the table next to Rob.

The boy was conscious of her spicy scent, and the warm baking smell that clung to her clothes and hair. He drew back, embarrassed, putting both hands on his lap to conceal the erection hardening there. She was middle-aged, she was his *aunt* – God, he must be *sick*.

Rob had seen all the films that were on, but he didn't seem to mind watching any of them again. So Jamie chose.

'Oh, I don't know,' Annie said. 'I don't fancy that.'

''S good,' Rob assured her. He'd finished the toast and his prick had subsided again. He leaned back, tipping his chair up. 'A thriller, like. Fantastic car chase right at the end – this guy, he—'

'Don't tell us!' Jamie protested, and Rob grinned.

Later, Annie thought rather sadly that it was Jamie who'd done that – made the boy look as if he were at ease for the first time. She had taken him in, fed him, come to him in the night when he wept, tucked him in with her kindness, her longing to make it all right. But it was Jamie he'd taken to, she could see that.

Like explorers, feeling festive and daring, they set out through deep snow, sunshine crisping the air to brightness. They marched down the centre of the empty street, making for the main road leading into town. Eventually a bus came, gliding through churned snow, and Annie persuaded Jamie they'd miss the beginning of the film if they didn't take it. Jamie dealt with it all still in explorer mode, as if the bus were native transport in some foreign place. Annie could see Rob was alternately embarrassed and delighted.

Later, when Jamie went to buy them all popcorn, he said to Annie, 'He's like a big kid, in't he? 'S he always like this?'

Annie sighed. 'Well, he is really. He was the youngest – spoiled rotten. So I suppose we shouldn't be surprised if he still hasn't grown up.'

'What – you mean his mum and dad – they wanted him to be the baby, like?'

'Liz and Stuart, yes. I suppose it was because Tom always seemed quite grown-up, and they didn't have anyone else after – I mean, any more children and they—' She stopped, feeling her face flood with colour. All the old horror came rushing in.

'What?' Rob was looking at her. Between them the air seemed to prickle with his curiosity, her confusion.

'Nothing. I don't know.' She looked round. 'Oh, here's Jamie now,' she said. 'Come on – the lights are going down.'

Jamie handed out cardboard cartons, the popcorn smelling honey-sweet in the darkness. Annie breathed it in, felt faint, sick. Rob fell silent; on the screen half a dozen beautiful people had their lives made even more wonderful by a bottle of Martini.

Annie sat between her cousin and her nephew. Two large inexplicable tears rolled down her cheeks. She ate a bloated puff of popcorn and waited for the film to begin.

5

On the Thursday, a thaw set in, and by Friday the streets were clear, the pavements piled with grey slush. Annie rang her mother on Thursday evening and said she'd be up to visit on the following day as usual.

'What about the roads – maybe you should leave it for a day or two?'

'Graham says they're clear,' Annie reassured her. 'It's all right – I'll see you about eleven.'

'Well, if you're sure. Take your time driving.'

'I always do. Oh, Mum – one thing.' She should have told her mother this already. Why hadn't she?

'Yes?'

'I've got a visitor.'

'Tom? Bring him with you, if you think he'll come. He's not at Jamie's then?'

'No, no, it's not Tom. He went back on Wednesday – he was only here a day.'

'He never drove back in all that snow – Wednesday was the blizzard, wasn't it?'

What was she fussing about, Annie thought, that was two days ago. Over.

'He got home fine. Anyway, it's not him. We've got Rob here. Alistair's boy.'

'I know who Rob is,' Christine retorted. 'Robert,' she added. 'Goodness, what's brought him up? Did Alistair leave him with you or something?'

'No . . . he came up on his own.' She wouldn't tell her mother about the hitchhiking. That was over too, but Christine would still be horrified.

'On his own?'

'He's nearly sixteen.'

'Is he really? Well, well. I was thinking he was still a wee boy.' She sighed. 'So what made him pay you a visit? Are the English schools still on holiday?'

'I suppose they must be.' *Who am I protecting here – Rob or my mother?* 'Anyway, he seemed to want to come. Shona's abroad. Spain.'

'Mm. Funny time of year to go abroad. And is he coming with you, then, tomorrow?'

'I'll ask him. You know what teenagers are like – lie in bed half the morning. But he seems quite happy here. Maybe you and Dad could come over on Sunday. See him then.'

'I'm surprised he remembers any of us,' Christine said. 'It's so long since Alistair brought him.'

'He gets on well with Jamie.'

'He's very easy-going, is Jamie.'

'Well, I'll see you tomorrow then. With or without Rob.'

Later, as she stood in the kitchen preparing supper while Rob watched children's television, Annie wondered why she felt uneasy about this conversation. Rob came into the kitchen and slouched against the work surface, cracking his knuckles. Annie switched off the radio. She had heard the news three times today; it was stale by now.

'You can lay the table if you like,' she said. She got out cutlery and put it in a bunch on the table. While he set it out, she began clearing the dishes lying by the sink.

'Me Dad's home tomorrow,' Rob said behind her.

Annie turned. 'Is he? You can ring him then.'

'He'll be jet-lagged.'

'Well, we'll ring him at the weekend.'

'What you goin' to say to him?'

Annie looked down at the table. She moved the side plates and turned over two of the knives.

'Haven't you ever done this before?' she asked, distracted.

'We don' have our dinner like this. At a table.'

'What d'you do then?'

'Sit in front the telly wiv it.'

Annie felt the leap in her throat that meant *my children would have* . . . She thought she'd stopped doing that. All through the childhood of her friends' offspring she'd said to herself how different her children would be, how carefully she and Graham would bring them up. What may have started as arrogance became, as the barren years went by, a kind of helpless pleading with the God who had ignored her.

'Well, anyway,' she said now, 'the side plates go here, and you put the knives like this, and if you have a lot of courses – here, I'll show you.'

She got out more cutlery, and gave him a lesson in place-setting. He seemed bemused, but followed her instructions.

'You never said,' he pointed out when they'd both had enough of this. 'You never said what you're going to tell me Dad.'

'I wasn't going to tell him anything,' Annie said. 'I thought you should be the one to talk to him.'

Rob sat at what was now his place at the table and started fiddling with a knife. Then he put it down and span it fast, faster, on the lip where blade joined handle.

Annie sat opposite him and put out her hand. The knife rang on the table, and was still.

'Rob, why did you leave home?'

The boy looked down and began cracking his knuckles again, one hand crushed inside the other.

'Don't,' Annie protested. 'Don't do that.' He stopped, but did not look up, muttering something she couldn't catch. She often found herself having to ask him to repeat things.

'They all mumble,' Graham had told her. 'Grunt and mumble. Can't make out a bloody word half the time.'

'What?' she said. 'I didn't hear?' Rob scraped his chair back and got to his feet.

'Goin' to the toilet, right?'

Annie listened to his footsteps thumping upstairs. She put out her hand again and span the knife gently. It wobbled and stopped. Then the front door opened. Graham was home.

In the morning, she went out early, just after Graham left for school, and drove to the supermarket. 'I'll be back about ten,' she'd told Rob the night before. 'If you want to come to your

granny's with me, you could get up then, OK?'
'Do I have to?' He seemed younger in the sitting-room lamplight, softer, like a child.
'No, of course not. It's just – she'd love to see you.'
'You said she was comin' on Sunday, though.'
'I think so. All right, it doesn't matter.'
'Watch my bishop,' Graham said. He was teaching Rob chess. They sat hunched on either side of the low table the board fitted on. Graham had ignored Rob's lack of interest, bullied him into playing much as he bullied his pupils into doing homework, revising for exams, turning up for rugby practice. It was simpler to give in and do what he wanted, less hassle. Or so Annie supposed, since it was much the way she felt herself.

But Graham was a good teacher. Despite himself, Rob had begun to be interested, and when Graham praised him curtly for a smart move, he flushed with pleasure.

Annie thought about this as she drifted through the super-market, filling her trolley till it was almost too heavy to wrench round corners. At the checkout, unloading on to the conveyor belt, she was taken aback by how many odd things she had chosen: crisps, cans of Coke, frozen chocolate bars . . . What am I doing, she thought, he needs decent food – look at his skin – why am I buying this rubbish? Too late – the girl had waved these undesirable items in front of the scanner, a bleep for each one.

At home, she unpacked and stacked away. The house was silent; Rob must still be in bed. She went up to look in on him before she left for her mother's, but his bedroom door was closed. She stood for a few seconds, listening, and heard him turn over in bed. Then she went downstairs and put her jacket and boots on again, for the drive to Bieldside.

Annie's parents had sold the house where she'd grown up, just too late for Graham and her: they'd already bought their family house.

'Typical of your mother,' Graham had said, making a joke of it when Matt and Christine finally decided on a new bungalow. But Annie wasn't sure she'd have wanted to buy the house any-way. How could she have changed anything without worrying whether her mother would mind? Her parents' house would have been too big, and the lack of children there, where she and Alistair had fought and played and grown up, would have shown up too much.

Altering their own house was better. She'd enjoyed that, scraping wallpaper, cleaning, washing down walls, going through bottles of Nitromors as she stripped the banisters. And yet, she'd done it all during those bleak months when she'd begun to realise they might never have children.

She found herself thinking about this again, as she drove through suburban streets to her parents' tidy bungalow. Firmly, she pushed it all aside as she drew up and parked the car. Her mother liked her to be cheerful, and she had learned not to dwell on these things any more, now that there was no point.

In the front garden the roses had been trimmed, but were waiting for March to be properly pruned. Flanking the door with its polished brass letter box, were tubs of winter-flowering pansies, bravely gold and blue above melting snow. Annie rang the bell to let her mother know she was there, and opened the door. She was wiping her boots on the mat when Christine came through from the kitchen. Annie stooped to lever off her boots and felt hot. The hall was very warm: the whole house was dense with artificial heat. Alistair and Annie had grown up in a cold house, since even after her parents had indulged in central heating, it was switched on for only two short periods night and morning, and never turned up very far. Then after the move, they'd had a change of policy, or a change of heart. Perhaps, growing older, they felt the cold, or simply realised at last they were well enough off to spend money being comfortable.

'You're just yourself then?' Christine looked round Annie as if she might be concealing Rob behind her.

'Yes, he's still in bed.'

'At this hour?'

'Och, he sat up late last night. Watching a film – him and Graham.'

'Well, well. As you say, teenagers. Come away through. I've the coffee perking.'

The big chrome percolator had been abandoned with the old house – given away to a church sale. Alistair had bought them a modern coffee maker, which Christine complained took up too much space on the work surface. However, she half-filled it on Friday mornings, in Annie's honour. But Annie knew her mother's idea of coffee was still really Nescafe with boiled milk. The gas fire was on in the living room, and her mother had set out china from the second best tea set on the coffee table.

'Now,' Christine said, coming through with the glass jug, 'are you still taking it black?'

'Yes, black's fine.'

'It doesn't seem much, with no milk or sugar.'

'I like it like that,' Annie smiled.

'You'll have a biscuit though. I baked yesterday.' Annie took one; she knew when to give in.

She couldn't remember when the coffee morning had become habitual, something she couldn't miss except in an emergency. It had begun as an occasional Saturday visit, when Graham was playing for a first fifteen team, and her father could take on eighteen holes of golf. Then, her parents were still in the old house. Since she'd stopped teaching, and Graham had given up his captaincy, it had changed to a Friday, and grown into both of their lives, becoming something Annie felt she couldn't neglect. In the summer they sat in the garden room at the back, in cane armchairs with flowery cushions, risking the weather by having the doors open, and talking about family things, what was in the news, and gardening. This garden was much smaller than the old one, but there was a tidy herbaceous border, and clumps of chives and parsley by the back door.

They passed the hour and a half in this easy fashion, only ever skirting the edges of whatever pain either might be suffering. There had once been a breach between them, not healed, but passed over, ignored, and since then Annie knew exactly how much to say, and the kind of thing it must be. Her mother was old, of course, and the old should be protected. But she'd noticed that, growing older, Christine, though still as keen to talk, was less willing – or able – to listen. The weight of the conversation had shifted: now it was Annie who nodded and agreed, hearing her mother's news, that was both trivial and vital, as everyday lives are.

This time, however, Christine was keen for Annie to tell her about Rob. They did travel over the same ground at first: Alistair and Shona, their shortcomings as parents, and yet what a pity it was they ever broke up (Christine did not like Shona much, but liked divorce less), and Alistair's success, praised with the proviso that money isn't everything. But eventually Annie had to tell her mother that in fact, his parents did not know Rob was in Aberdeen.

'Well, that'll be a shock for Shona when she gets home. Have you tried getting in touch with a neighbour?'

'I didn't think of that. But what would be the point? He's all right. It's up to Rob really.'

'Somebody has to be responsible for him.'

Sure, Annie wanted to say, *but should it be me?*

'Are you coming over on Sunday?' she asked instead.

'It's Communion – we'll be late home from church. And your father likes to walk down and back.'

'How is he?' They had wandered off the subject. Maybe everyone gets like this with age, Annie thought, your own world shrinking, the day-to-day life all that matters.

'Graham will come and pick you up about one. You'll be back by then. Save Dad driving at all.'

'I don't know,' Christine said as Annie was leaving. 'It's a great pity you can't get hold of Alistair. The boy might listen to his father. What does Graham say?'

'Not much.' Annie eased her feet back into her boots, and tugged on her coat. 'Don't you worry – Alistair's due back today or tomorrow – we left a message at his office, and on the answerphone at home.' She leaned across and kissed her mother's dry cheek, but only just. Christine always drew away slightly.

'Well, well. Take care now, driving on these terrible roads.'

'Don't stand in the cold.'

But Christine did stand there, and Annie paused at the corner, twisted round, waved again. Resentment folded into compunction, a first taste of the fear to come. *Because she will not always be there.* And yet, it was still a powerful woman who stood there, however frail she looked in her Pringle jersey and soft tweed skirt.

You could tell with men, Annie thought, driving away. Look

at Graham – how large he is, and solid, the hair on his body like a pelt, yes like an animal, compact with power. And Tom and Jamie, long and dark and thin, vulnerable-looking, like their father. She looked in the rear-view mirror, turned her head, moved out for a right turn. And me. She looked younger than forty, was bonny, vigorous, lively. It's an illusion, she thought, with women. My mother was always smaller, more fragile in appearance, and always stronger. She still is. Her words are like blows.

Annie's eyes filled with tears, but she dashed them away. Stupid, stupid, it was all so long ago. And her mother had not said anything so terrible, had she? But it had been enough – Annie had learned that whoever she went to for sympathy, it should not be Christine.

She stopped for traffic lights, watched two long-legged boys cross in front of her, giving each other good-humoured shoves, laughing, their young voices so loud she heard one shout, as the lights changed, *Fit ee fuck's at got tae dee wi it?* She found herself smiling as she drove on, thinking of getting the pressure cooker out, making lentil soup for Rob.

But when she got back to the house, he was not there.

6

'Yeah,' Jamie said, 'he's here. Is that all right? I phoned, and Rob answered. I'd forgotten you saw Christine on Fridays. So I said did he want to come over, see what I was working on, have a sandwich.'

A few hours ago she'd have been annoyed, disappointed – some dreary emotion like that. But there wasn't room for all that now.

'Jamie – it wouldn't matter – I mean, it doesn't. I hadn't made anything for lunch anyway. But—'

'What?'

'Alistair's here.'

A very short pause. 'Tell him to come over then. You bring him.'

'Can't you just bring Rob back here? He's—' she lowered her voice. 'He's a bit *tense*. He flew.'

'In a plane.'

'Yes, in a plane, of course in a plane. But he's got a hire car, it's not that.' She could see from her bedroom window the bright green hatchback, parked in the street. And she could hear Alistair pacing about downstairs.

'I haven't, though,' Jamie reminded her. 'Got a car.'

'Oh, for goodness sake.'

'We'll walk, then, if you want him over there.'

'Oh that'll take ages, and I don't think Rob – boys – like walking much.'

'Too bad.'

'Jamie, you're just being awkward.' You and Alistair both, she thought. And then when Graham gets home . . . Men. She felt outnumbered, as indeed she was. She took a deep breath. 'I'll tell Alistair Ruth's got the car, and we'll come over and fetch him. Oh dear.'

'Poor Annie,' Jamie said, 'devils and deep blue seas, eh?'

She met her brother in the hall. From above, he'd looked vulnerable, the hair on the crown of his head very thin. His colour was high, and he'd put on weight.

'He's at Jamie's. We'll have to go there, if you want to see him now.'

Alistair had come in hard and angry, taking command. Only there had been nothing to take charge of, just Annie chopping onions, the kitchen littered with cooking apparatus, the boy not there, Graham at work. They were all unreachable, unarguable with.

'I'll make you something to eat,' Annie said now. 'There's no hurry, is there? Now you know where he is?'

Alistair took off the jacket of his expensive grey suit and hung it over the back of a kitchen chair. He seemed less imposing without it, a tall man thickening at the waist, a man going grey, his status all in his clothes, his fine leather shoes.

Annie abandoned her soup-making and filled the kettle. The light was on in the kitchen, for the day had never brightened, and she caught her reflection in the window. *I'm always in this kitchen, getting food for people. I'm not a woman, a person, I'm a provider.*

'Will a sandwich do? I was going to make soup,' she added reluctantly, 'do you want to wait for that?'

'What?' He leaned his face on his hands, rubbed his eyes fiercely, saw red and black and red again. 'Anything. A sandwich. God, Annie, I can't make decisions. Jet-lagged.'

Annie made sandwiches, and they ate some, though neither was hungry. Alistair talked about the flight, the getting from New York to London, London to Aberdeen. He seemed obsessed with travelling.

'But you're here now,' Annie reassured.

'And for what?'

'But Shona—'

'Bloody woman. I could murder her, Annie, she's useless. I'd have done better having my son brought up by a chimp.'

'Or a wolf, maybe,' Annie said, taking this to be a joke. 'You know, like Romulus and Remus.'

Alistair stared at her. 'What the hell are you blethering about?' He got up, brushing crumbs from his trousers. 'Come on then – let's get the sod over here. Make him explain himself.'

'Alistair!'

'What's up now?'

'He's your son – look he's just a *boy*. *Something* made him run away.'

Annie had been worrying about the nightmares. These had gone on – every night there was some disturbance. Graham slept through it now. But she got up, though she didn't usually go into the boy's room, as long as he went quiet and slept again. But every night she stood chilled on the landing, listening.

'Well, I've no idea,' Alistair said. 'Why don't you ask his mother?'

'Ally, he's been having nightmares, really bad ones.'

Alistair frowned. 'Has he? God, that takes me back. When Shona and I first split up, he stayed with me quite a lot – before my job got too – you know – and he had them then.'

'Nightmares.'

'Yes. Screaming blue murder in the middle of the night. I'd leap up like somebody had shot me, and tear through to his room. He would be crying, shouting – and he used to push me away, you couldn't comfort him.' He saw Annie's expression. 'No, he didn't know who I was, never woke up. Then just like a light going out, he'd fall quiet, lie down. He was sort of half-awake for a while after that, but OK, he knew it was me then.'

'What were they about, the nightmares? Did you ever find out?'

Alistair shook his head. 'No, no. He never remembered anything in the morning. Shona swore it didn't happen with her, but she was lying.'

'Well, it's happening now, here,' Annie insisted. 'So I think something must have disturbed him. But you and Shona, neither of you seems to *care*.' She paused, but Alistair only shrugged. 'You remember,' she went on, 'Jamie having nightmares? Well, you must, he had them at the High House, when we all stayed there.'

'That was because he'd lost his sister and his mother in the

space of three years. Very traumatic. But he was only a kid –
and Rob hasn't had anything like that in his life.'

'But—' Annie wasn't going to let him off with this. Then, suddenly, she couldn't be bothered. He was hopeless, he wouldn't
even understand if she pointed it out. All she said was, 'It must
be a family thing. I thought – did Tom not say once that Uncle
Stuart got up in the night sometimes, and when he was young
it was really scary . . . his dad didn't even seem to know where
he was – just the kind of thing you're saying about Rob?'

Alistair shook his head. 'Don't remember that.'

'I'm sure – anyway, whatever the reason, I mean if it's
inherited or not, something must have set him off this time.
And you and Shona don't even seem to *care* about your son.'

'Don't be so bloody sanctimonious.'

'I'm not. Come on, you must have some idea. Shona's husband, what's he like?'

'A creep. Hasn't the gumption to get a spider out of the bath,
so you can forget your wild imaginings on that front.'

'Well, at least show you're *worried*, Alistair. All you've been
so far is angry. And he's only a boy, he's *young*.'

'Aye. I know. Maybe you're right.' Suddenly the Scots in his
voice again, the London twang fading, the Englishness taken off
with his jacket. He sighed. 'Come on then. Let's get on with it.'

The sky was so grey and low it seemed to scowl over the city,
lean on the rooftops, the snow turning to icy slush, piled between
pavement and road. They drove in silence, lights on at half-past
two, everyone hurrying indoors.

'No snow in London,' Alistair said as they turned into Jamie's
street. 'New York though. Freezing hard.'

'Was it?' They were in the hire car, that smelled of upholstery
and air-freshener. Alistair parked with all the stateliness of a man
used to a much larger car.

They stood for a moment outside the corner house where Ruth
and Jamie had the first floor.

'Weird,' Alistair said, 'being back here so quickly. New York
. . . Aberdeen. Usually it's London, and the office. And one office
is like another really. Whichever country.'

'I don't know how you can do it,' Annie said.

Alistair shrugged, then went briskly up to the side door.

'It's work,' he tossed back at Annie. 'That's all. And everybody goes to work.'

Well, I don't, thought Annie, and when I did it was a classroom, warm and safe, and all my bairns on their wee chairs, and the drawings and posters on the walls . . . Oh I miss it – why did I ever stop? And it's too late to go back, I'm out of it, out of date.

This was old ground, much trodden. She knew that, and still tortured herself.

Alistair had rung the bell and gone straight upstairs. The pungency of garlic and tomatoes, basil and strong coffee, came down to meet them.

'He's been cooking,' Annie sighed, hurrying up behind Alistair. 'Which is just another way of not working. Any old excuse.'

Jamie and Rob were finishing their meal; the sink was stacked with dishes and there were used saucepans on top of the hob, one with a ribbon of pasta trailing over the side.

'Hi,' Jamie waved a chunk of bread at them, then wiped it round his plate, soaking up sauce. Rob did not look at his father, but stopped eating, and stared at his plate.

'Coffee, you two?'

'No,' Alistair said, and at the same time, 'Yes, all right,' from Annie. So Jamie got up and poured some for both of them, setting the mugs on the table.

Alistair sat down, but did not touch the coffee.

'What's going on?' he asked.

'You two want to talk, eh?' Jamie said. 'Come on Annie, show you my etchings.'

She picked up her mug and followed him.

'I don't think,' she murmured as he shut the studio door behind them, 'they do want to talk, really.'

'I'm absolutely sure they don't, but it's time they did, eh?'

'Oh yes.' She sipped coffee, leaning on a cupboard. Jamie sat at his drawing board, doodling idly on a notepad. There was silence.

'Quiet discussion, d'you think?' Jamie enquired. 'Rational debate?'

'Maybe nothing. Maybe silence.'

'Maybe.'

Annie crossed to the drawing board.

'What are you doing just now?'

'Sweet FA.' He drew a sheet of blank paper over his work. 'Really, Annie. Nothing. I'm empty. I doodle – stuff I do is crap.'

'Maybe if you made an effort – didn't get distracted.'

'Distractions are all that keep me going.'

They heard footsteps, and Alistair came in.

'I'm leaving, Annie. You want a lift back?'

'What about Rob?'

'Well, I guess you're stuck with him, Jamie. He's taken a fancy to you.'

'What?' He's taken fright, Annie thought, looking at Jamie. He didn't mean this to happen. But she was jealous.

'He's not going home with you?'

'Apparently not.'

She saw suddenly the whiteness round her brother's mouth, the tight grip on the door handle. 'Oh, Alistair.'

'He can't live *here*,' Jamie said. 'God, how would I get *that* past Ruth? No way.'

'Your problem,' Alistair said. 'He's a bit big to be dragged out. Coming, Annie?'

'Well, yes, but—' Jamie caught her arm as she turned to follow Alistair.

'What's going on?'

'I don't know. I'll – I'll ring. I mean – he can stay with us. Graham's sort of used to it – that's all right. But—'

'Aye, sure. Ring me then. Eh? He can stay here till Alistair goes back to being a financial powerbroker.'

'Will Ruth—'

'She's away till tomorrow. Haematology conference in Glasgow. It's all right.'

'If you're sure – I'd better go.' She went through to the kitchen, where Rob was still sitting by his empty plate.

'Rob—'

'I'm not goin' wiv him. Right?'

'You don't have to. Look . . .' She hesitated. Alistair had left the doors open and cold air swept round her ankles. Faintly, she heard him start the car. 'Did you sort *anything* out? About your mother, I mean.'

'Na. She's not bothered what I do.'

'Of course she is—'

He was like one of her six-year-olds, sullen, hunched over a difficult word he couldn't manage to read. Instinctively, she put a hand on his shoulder. He shrugged it off.

'I'm OK. Right?' He scraped the chair back, got to his feet. 'He says I can stay here if I want.'

'Jamie? Surely, for a day or two. We can sort something else out later, maybe.' Alistair sounded the horn. Annie went backwards out of the kitchen into the narrow hall, brushing against the rubber plant's cold hands. 'Oh dear, I'm sorry,' she said, but whether to the shiny green leaves, or to Rob, or to Alistair, she did not know.

'What kept you?'

'Alistair, stop it. This is ridiculous. What did you say to him? Couldn't you talk?'

'*Talk* – I told you – he's a cretin.'

'Stop it, stop it – no one uses language like that now. It's obscene.'

'Why *have* children?' Alistair gritted his teeth, swung out on to the main road, ignored the screech of brakes in his wake. Annie clung to the door handle.

'What's the point? They keep you up at night, scream till they're blue, and you never know what the fuck's wrong. Then there's about three years when they're perfect – angels – then the mother screws you up and goes off with them so that's it. End of being a proper father.'

'No, no!' Annie protested. 'You're still his father, you've done—' Alistair ignored this, and went through an amber light turning to red.

'Then they hit puberty, look like something you'd be scared to meet in a dark alley, turn into football hooligans, vandals, Goths, Huns. Christ, what's the *point*?'

Love, Annie wanted to say, love is the point. Don't you love him? But there was nothing she could say to Alistair that would even temper his anger, let alone bring his view anywhere near hers, anywhere near what *she* felt, had always felt, about being a parent, having what he (for all his fury) had so ungratefully experienced. So she said nothing, but let him have his rant out, till they were in her street again, and he had to slow, or skid across slush into a lamppost. He switched off the engine, and took a deep breath.

'Sorry, Annie, sorry. It's not your fault. The mess. All this. You took him in – you'll end up with him, I can see that. The novelty will wear off for Jamie, if it hasn't already, and when Ruth walks back in the door – *she* won't have him. Might dirty her kitchen.'

'Oh Alistair. She's not like that. It's just she's never had kids – she's a career woman.'

'Well, neither have you had kids, and you—' He reddened, gripped the wheel. 'Sorry. Ignore me.'

'I can't.'

'Don't cry. God, Annie, don't cry. I feel enough of a bastard as it is.'

'I'm not, I'm not.' She took his proffered handkerchief and blew her nose, dried her eyes. 'It's just Rob being here has sort of stirred things up again. I suppose. Oh, I don't know what's wrong with me.'

'Tea,' Alistair said. 'We'll have a pot of tea.'

'Yes, all right.'

By the time Graham got home, Alistair had gone again, on the next flight out. When she tried to explain what had happened, she felt almost as if she were making it up. There was no evidence at all that her brother had been there. But Graham thought it was funny.

'He'll be back here soon enough,' he said. 'Rob. What d'you bet, eh? Jamie'll get fed up – or Ruth will put her foot down.'

'That's what Alistair said.'

'And he's right. Anyway – what about his mother? Surely to God *she* wants him?'

'I know – I've been thinking I should ring Shona. After all, she's the one he lives with.'

'You notice, though, she's made no attempt to contact us. If she's back from swanning around her Mediterranean beach.' Graham said this quite cheerfully: he'd had a good day – or as good as they got now. The boiler was fixed, his classrooms in order again. And he'd had quite a chat with Jan about the changes they were going to make in the third year. She was good, capable, he decided, an excellent head of year, for all she'd only had the job a couple of terms. And there was no cuckoo in the nest, no stubble-haired boy in his place at the table. He came up behind Annie as she tested a grain of rice, and put his hands on her breasts.

'Graham!'

'House to ourselves – want to go to bed?'

'The rice is ready. Don't be daft.' But she was flustered by his weight pressing against her, responding despite herself. For she had no interest now. The urgency of being young, the much more desperate times when they had followed a calendar, a thermometer – all those years of losing hope had deadened in her the wish for sex. That was something she did now to keep Graham happy. A kindness. Still, she was flattered for a moment.

But he'd backed off.

'OK. Dinner. You want a drink?'

'There's wine if you want to open that. I'm just dishing up.'

She woke in the night, but there was no cry, no one to get up and listen for. It was the thaw that had disturbed her – pillows of melting snow gliding off the roof, the steady rain, heavy dripping from gutters. She did not mind lying awake. She could lean on Graham's warmth, and the rhythm of his breathing reassured in the bleak night. Her pulse seemed to quicken and she grew wider and wider awake, but not with anxiety. It was excitement she felt, a kind of nervous anticipation. Rob will come back here. Alistair said so, Jamie knows it, Graham expects it. There isn't anyone else. She stirred in the bed, restless, getting colder. She'd go to the bathroom, then she might be able to get back to sleep.

There, the show of blood took her by surprise. *I didn't even notice the date.* What had happened to the heavy days of waiting, knowing this was on the way, hating and longing for it at once? Failure and resolution.

She ran warm water, washed, got what she needed from the pine cabinet in the corner of the bathroom. In a few minutes she was back in bed, cold against Graham's heat, as he stirred and grumbled in his sleep. Oh well, that explains the tears with Alistair, she realised, but still, I didn't even think of that. Maybe, she considered (not for the first time, not that) if I hadn't thought about it so much, it would have been all right. It would just have happened when I wasn't looking for it. But how could you *not* think about it, not look out, or count the days? Annie was aware that she was thinking of all this as if it were in the past. Careful, she told herself, careful, he's a teenager, he's not yours, and good grief, he's not even lovable. It's a temporary thing – like looking after Jamie when he was ill. But hope persisted, as it always had.

7

'You might have warned me,' Jamie said.

'What about?'

They were in Annie's kitchen. Jamie had brought Rob back, and the boy was upstairs, playing his tapes on the ghetto blaster that had accompanied him from the flat. 'He may as well have it,' Jamie had said. 'I only listen to the radio when I'm working, and I can use the kitchen one.'

Annie turned from the sink to face him. Jamie took off his greatcoat and flung it over the basket chair in the corner. He ran his hands through his hair and sat down at the table. His hair was left on end, and what he had once informed Annie was designer stubble, looked simply rough.

'About his nightmares. If that's what they are.'

'I thought I'd told you.' Annie was surprised. 'You had them – remember? Night terrors. But you grew out of them. Then they started up again when you were ill, but only for a wee while. Only till Ruth—'

'Yeah, yeah – I know. What's his angle though?'

'Angle?'

'Why does he get them?'

'I've been asking Alistair that,' Annie sighed, 'but he wasn't very helpful. I reminded him about you.'

'Bloody obvious in my case what caused them. Lindsay – then Mum – all that stuff. But we never talk about all that, do we?'

'Not fair on our parents,' Annie said. 'But we did when you were ill.'

'Did we?' Jamie couldn't remember.

'And now we don't talk about *that*,' Annie pointed out. 'Anyway, as far as Rob's concerned, Alistair says he had night terrors when he was wee, but that was when he and Shona had just split up. I don't know. Rob never says what he's been dreaming *about*. Maybe he can't remember.'

Jamie rarely thought about his nightmares now. The recurrence when he was ill, ten years ago, had been brief, a few nights. But he had recognised Rob's nightmare howls, had broken out in a sweat hearing them. *I bet Rob remembers what he's been dreaming about. I remember. Even now.* But it was the panic he recalled, and something that came and went in his mind in states of almost sleep, even now. A faint image imprinted on his memory with all the illusory distinctness of the Turin Shroud: still powerful, however false, the image of a thin figure in a flowered cotton dress, curled up in a corner, one brown sandal missing, her white sock dirty, the dress stained rusty brown in a long streak over the chest, head tucked down at an odd angle, hair falling over the face, hair once honey-coloured, now damp, streaked with the same rusty staining, stiffened by dried blood into clumps. A limp creature, curled round like a rag doll, legs folded beneath her, pushed into a corner. In the dream he had been backing away, stumbling, trying to get out. But that was finished, and the dream (he remembered now, it was Annie who'd told him this) was anyway not the truth. It had not really been like that.

He wanted to say to Rob, whatever the demons are like, they'll fade and cease to frighten, even to move you. Because although they look like the truth, they are not. But in the night, all he had done was rouse the boy from dream to waking, put on the light, and give him a dram which he took but shuddered over, before lying down again, dazed.

'I'll leave the hall light,' Jamie said. 'You OK?'

'Yeah. Sorry.'

'It's OK. Forget it.'

Jamie went back to bed, and missing Ruth, did not fall asleep again for a long time. But he moved in the shadows of sleep, so that the old nightmare image, which he was able to keep out now, to control, resurfaced as something else, and he was filled with a sense of his mother, who had come to him in the night when he had cried, smelling of warm hay and talcum powder. And then, in hospital, going to see her with his father, she had smelt different, of something bad, sour. He had held back, not wanting to be near her, yet longing for his mother. He had no picture of this, just the smell, no memory he was sure (his memory was second-hand, Tom's, passed on later). No image of his own of how she was so thin she barely raised the green hospital blanket, her skin brownish, with purple bruises under her eyes. Now he saw her. The smell, and the sight of her, and her voice just a hoarse whisper.

Jamie put on the lamp, and sat up.

'*Christ*,' he said aloud, 'no wonder I had fucking nightmares.'

He read, and fell asleep at six, the lamp still on. He slept late and heavily, but Rob was even later. He got up groggily at eleven, saying nothing about what had happened. Maybe he doesn't remember, Jamie thought, or maybe he's just embarrassed. But he didn't know whether, or how, to broach the subject with the sullen boy munching toast, gulping down a pint of milk. Jamie leaned on a kitchen unit, smoking, reading the front page of the *Scotsman* spread out on the marble worktop. He tried not to look at Rob at all.

'I'll take you back to Annie's,' he said, folding up the newspaper, and putting out the cigarette with a hiss in a pool of water in the sink.

'You don't hafta.' Rob wiped crumbs from his mouth with the back of his hand. 'I don' mind stayin' here.'

'Ruth's coming back today,' Jamie said, sounding colder than he meant to. 'Sorry.'

The boy shrugged and got up. A few minutes later, Jamie heard laughter and applause from the television.

'Fuck's sake,' he muttered. 'I'll know I've lost it when I start watching that at eleven o'clock in the morning.' He could imagine only too well Ruth's raised eyebrows, her cool surprise. No. No good.

So here they were at Annie's again. She didn't seem to mind constant television or the trainers and jacket littering the hall floor. She was cheerful and matter-of-fact.

'I'm going to ring Shona,' she said. 'Rob gave me her work number.'

'She's back then.'

'Yes – Alistair got in touch as soon as he picked up his messages. Said he was dealing with it.'

'So didn't she want to come as well, wasn't she in a state over her missing son?'

'Well, I don't know. Don't think Alistair gave her the option. You know what he's like. Probably barked at her down his mobile phone, then leapt on the plane.'

'Are you sorry for her, or what?'

Annie considered this. 'N-no. Perhaps. I'll tell you when I've spoken to her.'

She went up to her bedroom and used the phone there. This was so that Rob couldn't overhear, but Jamie stared at the kitchen extension in some frustration. Annie was away a long time, then eventually he heard the lavatory flush upstairs, so he couldn't tell how long she'd actually been talking to Shona. If at all? He had read all of the *Scotsman* now except the Business Section, which he never felt offered him anything. Perhaps he was wrong. He drew it towards him, but none of the headlines made sense.

Annie came back.

'Well?' But she shook her head. 'She wasn't there? You were ages.'

'Oh, she was there. God, Jamie, you wouldn't believe – I mean, most people you talk to after a few years it's like yesterday, isn't it? Old friends. But Shona – I can't believe I ever knew her.'

'Annie dear, she was never exactly your bosom buddy. Anyway, is she coming up to claim her son?'

'Uh uh.' Annie attempted an imitation of Shona's voice, London dissolving into her native Doric, speaking fast, so that there was nowhere to break in, or disagree.

You can't argue wiv 'em, can you? I thought he was at Kevin's, but it was the dog, Annie. We come back an' I says to Ken, where's the dog? Robbie, he's out a' the time, but if it's the evenin', he leaves the dog, ken? Nae that he's much cop as a guard dog, but it's a deterrent, like. You wouldna believe the burglaries we've had round here – they cut round doors and athing. Alistair, he's on at me for leavin' him, Robbie, I mean, but he wouldna come with us. I thought he'd be fine, he's a quiet laddie, Annie, ken. Nae trouble, as a rule.

'She wasn't worried,' Jamie said now, 'I mean, panicking about how he'd got here, any of that stuff?'

'Well, she didn't really get time to, I suppose. She thought he was at his friend's, then Alistair called. I think he's been having such a go at her, she's reacting to that.'

'So, does she want him back, or what?'

'Well, as she says herself, how do you make him? I said we were happy to have him here for a while, and she said that was OK with her. Apparently he was threatening to leave school anyway. She's going to talk to him on the phone later.'

'What about the dog?' Jamie asked.

'Och, you're as bad as she is,' Annie sighed. 'You'll never believe this, but I suspect—'

'Don't tell me,' Jamie grinned. 'She'd like you to have the dog as well.'

'Well, she didn't actually say that. But I gather Rob's very fond of it.'

'You wonder, don't you,' Jamie said, 'what Alistair and Shona saw in each other in the first place.'

'She was very pretty.'

'Sex,' Jamie answered his own question. 'Good old sex. Then he got ambitious, and sex wasn't quite enough.'

'But Rob was born,' Annie said. 'And Rob's the one who suffered for it. I can't understand . . .' She fell silent, and gazed out of the window. Jamie put a hand over hers, twisting together on the table.

'You're the best person he could be with just now, really,' he said. 'It's a myth that parents are the only ones who can bring up their kids. His are bloody useless. You'll give him a bit of stability.'

'Yes,' Annie agreed, stifling hope, something like joy. 'But I'm not having the dog. I mean, I'm sorry for Rob, if he misses it, but—'

'What kind is it?'

'What on earth does that matter?'

'I wondered how it would get on with Mac – or worse, Tibby.'

Annie smiled. 'Catch Graham agreeing to it anyway. But it's funny, I don't think he minds Rob staying with us.'

'Suppose he's used to grunting adolescents.'

'That's what I mean.'

Jamie got to his feet.

'I must go,' he said. 'Ruth's home this afternoon. Better tidy up a bit.' He paused by the door. 'Keep in touch – if I can do anything—'

'Aye, sure.'

When he had gone, Annie went to find Rob. He was watching television.

'I spoke to your mother,' she said. Rob clicked the remote control, switching channels. Annie tried not to look at the screen.

'Right,' he said.

'She's quite – she doesn't mind if you want to stay here. But the school – anyway, she said she'd contact the school.'

'It's me birthday next week.'

Annie halted, then took this in. 'You'll be sixteen.'

'Yeah, don' hafta go to school.'

A throb of irritation rose in Annie. 'You have to do something.'

'Yeah. Get a job.'

'But you've got no qualifications.'

Rob shrugged.

Annie, about to launch into a series of reasoned arguments, abruptly changed her mind. Leave it to Graham. For it was pity she felt, for all his surliness, the stupidity of the things he said. The bitten nails, blotchy skin, feet awkwardly large, hands still childishly small – these made him both ugly and vulnerable, someone to be pitied and cherished. She felt angry with Alistair and Shona, for so easily abandoning him.

'Anyway,' he said, 'that's good. Staying here.'

'Is it?' She was startled, flattered. 'Won't you miss your friends?'

'Yeah. A bit.'

She was going to say, and the dog, what about the dog, but she was afraid he'd say yes, can he come here. She knew her limits, knew Graham's, felt sure the dog was large, a Rottweiler or German shepherd. Then the telephone rang.

'Annie? It's Cath – I'm back. How's things?'

Cath was Annie's closest friend. They had taught together, till Cath had her twins, who were sixteen now, and off her hands, or almost. She had been away on a course, part of a programme training people to become crisis counsellors. Annie couldn't imagine Cath doing this very well: she wasn't particularly calm. Cath herself seemed to have some misgivings, for all her enthusiasm. *You would be better at it,* she often said to Annie. *Why don't you join? I mean, you've got experience, haven't you, however sort of buried or long ago?* Only Cath could say these things.

Now, with all that had happened getting in the way, Annie struggled to recall where Cath had been.

'Hi – how was the course?'

'Fantastic. At least – I had a great time. Some reservations about the actual *content.* Don't know if I'm as equipped to deal with post-traumatic stress disorder as they seem to expect . . .'

'Oh, I'm sure you are.'

'Anyway – what about coffee? So we can catch up. What's doing?'

Annie realised that to this question she always said on a breath of laughter, *Oh, nothing much.*

'I don't know where to begin,' she said now. 'Do you want to come over – or will we meet – tomorrow?'

'What day is it?' Cath never knew the day, or date. Neither did Annie, though once they both had, for the children had copied it from the board into their books every morning. *Friday, 15th January.* Green was the colour for Friday. But Annie felt more like red now, a confused Saturday red.

'What's today – Saturday? We could meet next week.'

'Wednesday? Art Gallery?'

'Yes, all right.'

'Coffee shop at eleven, then. So a lot's been happening?'

'I'll save it for when I see you,' Annie said, hearing the scrape and whine of the garage door as Graham opened it. The dog went to the front porch, tail sweeping to and fro.

'Hi,' she said, as Graham came in. 'Rob's back.'

8

'No, no,' Cath declared, wiping up the crumbs on her plate with a damp finger and popping it in her mouth. 'Mm – you can't counsel your friends.'

But she continues to do it anyway, Annie thought, practising on me. Cath listened with her head on one side, smiling a little, saying 'um' now and again, giving encouraging little nods.

'You forget,' Annie said, dividing the last of the coffee from the cafetiere between their cups, 'I *had* counselling. For ages. So long I got to recognise all the things she did – the nodding, and saying back to me in a slightly different way the thing I'd just said to her. So you think, *Goodness, I did say that didn't I?* And you have the quite mistaken impression you've learned something about yourself.'

'Wow – you're cynical today.'

'No. I've thought this for years. I used to believe all my family should have had the kind of counselling you're being taught. Sometimes I still think so. Then I remember how utterly useless it was to me, how all it did was perpetuate false hope.'

'Ah me.' Cath sighed, but looked cheerful. The week away had done her good: she was still high, full of it.

They had talked about Rob, and Alistair, whom Cath remembered better than Annie realised, as a good-looking sixth-former. She hadn't often seen him since. Then Cath had described her counselling course. Now they were back to Rob.

'I must go,' Annie said eventually. 'Rob's been with Graham at the school, but he'll be back for lunch. He didn't want to go, but Graham said he didn't have a choice – it was that or back home on the train. I don't know – maybe Rob believed him. He went anyway.'

'They're not playing rugby in this weather?'

'Oh no, pitch is still covered in snow and slush. But the sports pavilion needs clearing out. Graham had some of the second year timetabled to do it. Rob's supposed to help sort them out.' She paused. 'It would be better for Rob if he went back to school – but he won't.'

'Graham can't make him do that too?'

'Even Graham's power has its limits.'

'Get him into college, then,' Cath said briskly. 'Goodness, I know what sixteen-year-old boys are like. You have to keep them occupied or they *slump*.'

'If they were still little,' Annie said, 'I could bring him over and he'd play with your two. But you can't just produce friends for them when they're teenagers.'

Then she realised, as they gathered up coats and bags, that if he'd been little, Rob wouldn't be here at all. It cheered her, anyway, to have a boy to complain about, as Cath did about hers.

She went on seeing her mother on Fridays, and sometimes Cath on Saturdays. She gave them different accounts of the same events. But with both of them, she made light of serious things. She did not want her mother to worry; she did not want to appear foolish to Cath, who was used to having children, and had worked so hard at bringing them up on her own. Her former husband had remarried immediately after the divorce. Cath saw through Annie's apparent casualness, just as Annie had seen through Cath's apparent indifference when Pete remarried. But there was no need to discuss this. They covered up for each other, emotionally.

'Rob's on a college course,' Annie announced in triumph, one Saturday morning, setting her bags down beside the table where Cath was already seated.

'Good for him. Or is it good for you?'

'Well, I got the details for him. But he's quite keen. Will I get the coffee?'

'No – get your breath back. I'll get it. Sit down.'

'Sorry – I've been dashing – running late this morning.'

'Again.'

'I know. It used to be me waiting – and you rushing in at the last minute. What's happened?'

She sat down abruptly, struggling out of her coat, turning it over the back of the chair.

When Cath came back, she said, 'You know fine what's happened.'

'Sorry?'

'Why you're late these days.'

Annie laughed. 'Och, it's ridiculous. But he seems to need as much looking after as a bairn. And you've got two – how do you do it?'

'By giving them a lot less attention – novelty wore off a long time ago.' She smiled. 'Don't worry – you're doing a great job.'

'Am I?'

'He's doing what you want, isn't he? Graham's got him helping with football coaching at the school, you've got him studying again, he's signed on, got his name down for umpteen things—'

'I suppose so. But we've pushed him into all that. He's only doing it so he can stay.'

'Well – he obviously wants to. That's something, isn't it?'

'But he needs *friends*, that's the thing. He's coaching twelve-year-olds, living with two middle-aged people and a dog and a cat. What can I do about getting him some real friends?'

'Nothing. It's up to him.'

'A youth club or something?' Cath raised her eyebrows. 'No, right, OK. I'm out of date. I just worry that he's so solitary.'

'Most mothers worry about the *friends*,' Cath said. 'Bad company, where they're going, what they're up to.'

'Well, that's normal. Teenagers are supposed to be a worry to their folks, aren't they?'

Later, Annie thought, I am like a mother, just one who's come to it a bit late, so I'm out of touch. She watched a group of boys about Rob's age move down the pavement towards her: once she'd have felt threatened by such a phalanx of male youth. One had a woolly hat and two were in football shirts, despite the cold; several had tattoos, earrings. Now, she let them part and flow past her, still jeering at each other in loud, confident voices, and she felt not threatened but reassured. They are all the same, she told herself, he is normal. But she wanted him to be part of one of these rough groups, shoving, calling insults, laughing loudly.

Graham was no help.

'Annie, you've got to let him do *something* for himself. It's his problem. If it is a problem. He's not in any hurry, is he, to launch himself into the social scene?'

'I wonder why not.' Annie was fretting. 'Maybe he doesn't know how to set about it in a new place. I thought Cath might invite him over to meet her boys. But she didn't and I couldn't ask somehow. He's quite presentable, isn't he, now his hair's grown a bit? And I think his skin's clearing up.'

'You're like a bloody mother hen.' Graham said, ruffling her hair as he went past. Annie smoothed it down, irritated.

When the phone started ringing she ignored it, thinking he was nearer. But it went on ringing, and she realised he'd gone upstairs.

'Hi, this is Jan Patterson. Is Graham about?'

'Yes – somewhere – just a minute.' He was at the top of the stairs, leaning over the banister that ran along the landing.

'Jan somebody.'

'School,' he said briefly. 'I'll get it in the bedroom.'

She waited till he'd picked it up, heard his warm *hello* and replaced the receiver.

Later, she thought she'd phone Jamie, and left the ironing board in the kitchen to make the call. Jamie liked discussing other people: he'd sort out Rob's social life. But when she picked up the receiver, Graham was still talking. Then the woman interrupted, and they laughed. Graham began to speak again, hesitated, aware of a difference, a slight hollowness in the space between his voice and hers.

'Oops, sorry,' Annie said, sounding breezy, though she was taken aback. 'Thought you'd finished.' Hastily, she put the phone down and went back to ironing shirts.

Rob was in the kitchen, hunting through biscuit tins.

'I get somethin' to eat?'

'Help yourself.' She hung Graham's blue shirt on the back of a chair, and picked out a pillowcase. As she smoothed it on the board, she watched Rob cut awkward lumps from a pound of cheddar. It was peaceful to go on ironing, the kitchen warm and smelling sweetly of clean laundry, while Rob cut cheese, piled crackers on the plate beside it, poured half a pint of milk in a mug.

He balanced mug and plate, and began to edge past Annie.

'Eat it here,' she said. 'I don't want crumbs everywhere.'

'I'll be careful—'

'No, you won't.'

'Promise?'

'Eat it here, Rob.'

'Watchin' *Brookside*, though.'

'Too bad.' She smiled and he grinned back.

'OK, OK.' He ate fast and untidily; she folded the pillow case and began on one of his T-shirts. The telephone rang once and stopped. A moment later Graham came into the kitchen.

'Jamie,' he said.

'Oh, I was just going to phone.' She switched off the iron, knowing she'd probably be gone half an hour. 'Sorry,' she said as she passed him, 'didn't mean to interrupt you. You're not usually so long on the phone.'

'Work,' he said. Rob looked up, catching something unfamiliar in Graham's tone. But Annie had reached the hall and was settling herself in the basket chair.

'Hi, Jamie, how's things? I was just going to ring you.' Rob went past her, back into the living room, with another plate of crackers. Graham was putting on his jacket.

'Taking the dog,' he said, patting Annie on the head as he went past her. Annie shook her hair out.

'Don't *do* that – sorry – Jamie, was there something – or did you just ring for a chat?'

'There's something,' he said. 'What about you?'

'What – hang on, Graham's just going out.' The front door banged; she got up and shut the living-room door too. 'I wanted to talk over what we should do about Rob.'

'I thought he was staying – turned into a fixture?'

'Well, he has, I suppose. Shona sent him a horrible football top for his birthday. He did like it, though. And she phones quite a lot, to speak to him, and to me. I think she was kind of strange at first because she was so embarrassed. Poor Shona. She tells him all about how the dog is. And his pals. He's always a bit quiet after the phone call. Quieter than usual. Oh, and Alistair sent a cheque for his birthday, so he bought CDs to put in the ghetto blaster you gave him, and Levis.'

'What about Alistair, then, does he phone and give news about the goldfish or something?'

'Don't be sarcastic. He phones about once a week, but it's me he speaks to. Rob just grunts a bit and passes the call over. I can't imagine what they *ever* spoke about. Anyway, it can wait – we can sort out his social life some other time. Or lack of it. What about you – something good or bad?'

'Good – fantastic. Sort of.'

'Sort of?'

'No, really. Fantastic. Amazing. Can you come over, Annie? It's not a phone call situation, if you see what I mean.'

'Are you all *right*?'

'Oh yes, fine. No crisis. Just – you are coming?'

'Yes, yes, I will. Soon as Graham gets back with the dog.'

'Leave him a note – I can't wait that long. Rob will tell him, anyway.'

'I suppose so. OK – right, coming.'

The temperature was rising; the long winter was easing at last. Annie drove across to Jamie and Ruth's flat through persistent rain. Jamie's mood had infected her: without knowing what there was to be excited about, she was filled with anticipation. And yet, when she got out of the car and looked up at the lit windows, a spurt of fear pierced this.

'Where's Ruth?' she asked, following Jamie into the hall, kicking off her shoes, leaving her coat on a peg.

'Work,' he said. 'Some meeting. But she's OK.'

'What, has she been ill?'

'No, no.'

He could barely keep still. Annie sat on the sofa, watching him. She thought he'd been drinking; he was flushed. He fussed round, getting himself gin and tonic, disappearing to the kitchen for ice and apple juice for Annie. She sat on the leather sofa, her stockinged feet sliding into the sheepskin rug, clean and soft as when Ruth had bought it two years ago. It wasn't a cosy room, Annie thought, but it was beautiful.

She admired the art deco lamps, and the prints by artists only just becoming well known, all over again. And scanned the shelves of the ash bookcase they'd commissioned from a local cabinet-maker, even though it was full of thrillers. It's like a room in a West End play, Annie thought, and Jamie was like someone in a play too, keyed up, restless, full of momentous news.

'Goodness, sit down – you're like a demented hen,' Annie scolded. Jamie laughed, and sat down beside her.

'Sorry.'

In sudden silence, they looked at each other. Then Annie knew what he was going to say, and she knew her flash of fear had been real.

'It's the weirdest thing – I never thought I'd feel like this about it – but Ruth's pregnant. We're going to have a baby.'

Annie heard that *we* and noted it, somewhere in the rational part of her. But she had no idea what to say.

'That's – that's – how's Ruth?' She saw Ruth, her lean elegance, the dark cap of hair, the long cool fingers. But she could not see a baby.

'Oh, she'll get used to it.'

'What – she's not – not sure? She didn't, *you* didn't mean it?'

'Well, we never did anything to stop it, if that's what you're asking.' A broad smile took over his face. 'But after all this time . . . and she always thought it wasn't possible.'

'Why not?' Annie was readjusting her view of Jamie and Ruth. 'I thought it was just that Ruth wasn't interested – she's always been so set on getting a consultancy.'

'Well, that's true as well. But she thought she couldn't anyway. Have children.' He hesitated. 'Look, don't say anything, Annie, well, I know you wouldn't, but she had an abortion, years before me. She was ill after, something went wrong. So we thought – but it wasn't true. She's really pregnant.'

Annie took a deep breath.

'Oh, Jamie, I am glad.'

'It's amazing, isn't it? I'm actually going to be someone's *father*.'

Annie couldn't imagine this. Then she could. Why did she

have this sort of imagination? It wouldn't let her alone, it had no pity. She saw Jamie with a baby in his arms, then holding a child by the hand, then pushing her on a swing. They would have a daughter, dark and composed as Ruth herself. Annie's eyes filled with tears, and they spilled over, blurring the whole room. She sat still, unable to stop them, unable to raise her hand and brush them away. Jamie put one arm round her, and with the other, used the cuff of his jersey to dab at her face.

'See,' he said, 'I thought you'd be so pleased – because if it can happen to Ruth, who had a total mess made of her insides – well, it could still happen to you.'

'You're such a fool, Jamie,' Annie wept. 'But I am happy for you, I really am.' He held her close and she pressed her hot tearful face in his neck that smelt of Gauloises and aftershave.

'Don't tell Graham yet,' he said, when they had both blown their noses on Ruth's peach tissues.

'Why not, if Ruth's all right?' Not that she *wanted* to tell anyone.

'There's a job – she wants to go for it before anyone knows.'

'Yes, but what's the point?'

'She's been working towards this for years, but women in medicine still have a much tougher time than men. She thinks they wouldn't give her it if they knew about the baby.'

'But Jamie—'

'I know about the sex discrimination stuff. They'd say it was for some other reason. Anyway, it's only a few weeks.'

'No, but Jamie, what about after – you mean she's going back to work?'

'Women always do, nowadays.' Jamie looked cheerful about this. 'And let's face it, her earning power's a million times what mine's ever going to be. So it made it no contest really. Especially as I'm the one who *wants* to do the looking after, and I can work at home. While he's sleeping. Or she. He or she.' Jamie had a foolish, dreamy look on his face. Annie wanted to slap him. And Ruth. *I hate Ruth.* She stood up. *Got to get out of this, I'm not responsible. I'm not being fair.*

'I have to go,' she said. 'But tell Ruth – well, it's lovely. And I hope she gets the job.'

'Oh she will,' Jamie said. He grinned, hugging Annie fiercely.

It did not seem possible he was the man who had once lain so close to death too deep a breath might carry him across the fine whispering line between here and there, now and nevermore. Annie laid her head on his chest for a moment, and closed her eyes.

She drove home wondering how she could keep from blurting all this out to Graham. But it was Rob who looked up when she came into the living room. The television was off; he and Graham were in the middle of a chess game.

'Hi, Annie.' He grinned, then turned back to the board, concentrating.

'This bugger's starting to give me a hard time,' Graham said. 'Look at my bloody king.' He hesitated over the board, then moved a pawn.

'I'm going to bed,' Annie told them. Graham nodded, still without looking up.

In the kitchen, she heated herself milk to take up to bed. That and two paracetamol, she told herself, then I might get to sleep. Rob came in.

'You're on the scrounge, are you? Hot cross buns in the bread bin.'

'Yeah, I know. I've had one.' He opened the fridge and got the milk out. There was about half a pint left in the carton, so he drank it off, not bothering with a glass. As he wiped a smear of milk from his upper lip, he said, 'You OK?'

'What? I'm fine.' I wonder what I look like, Annie thought. The crying must show. Mothers were not supposed to cry. Her own mother had cried so rarely that when it happened, the world itself seemed to cave in. Adult tears were serious, frightening.

'Somethin' wrong?' he persisted. But he did not really want to know; he wanted reassurance.

'No, no, I'm fine. Just tired.'

'Right then,' he said. 'Got him beat, Annie.' He meant the chess game.

'Have you really?'

'You should see him – he's gutted.'

Annie smiled. 'He must be. You're not supposed to win, just give him an opportunity to show off.'

Rob grinned. 'Tough.' He went out with his hot cross bun, taking advantage of her vulnerable mood to eat it in the forbidden living room. Annie saw this, but didn't care. Let him. What did it matter?

'What does anything matter?' she asked aloud of the milk pan, as she dumped it in the sink and ran water in. 'Nothing's fair. Nothing.'

She went up to bed, skin forming on the milk, knowing she didn't want to drink it. Now she despised herself. I was mean to Jamie, I hope he didn't see it.

She lay back on the pillows with a book open in front of her, but could not read. She wanted to tell Tom, since that would be a comfort. And Graham. They weren't close in the way they used to be, but there were no secrets, nothing important divided them. She longed for him to come to bed.

When he did, he seemed distracted, distant.

'Well,' she said, 'did he win, then?'

'Did who win?'

'Rob, of course. The chess game.'

'Oh, that. Yes, he got one and I got one. He wanted a decider, but it's too late. School tomorrow.' He got into bed. 'You reading?'

'Yes, I suppose so. Trying to.'

''Night then.' He turned over. She looked at his back, the incongruous bulk of his shoulder above the broderie anglaise edge of the downie cover, the springy burnished hairs, the familiar moles. And she gazed at the patch on the back of his head where the hair was thinning. Then she looked down at her own hands holding the book. There were little brown spots on the backs she had taken for freckles. But this was winter, so perhaps they were not.

'Graham,' she said.

'What?' He sounded gruff, sleepy.

'I'm not supposed to tell you this, but—'

'Don't then.'

Silence.

'Graham, this *matters*. Only, you mustn't say anything. It's just that I can't not tell you.'

'For God's sake.' He turned over on his back. His face was

shadowy in lamplight, the chin dark. She remembered suddenly how when they were first married, he'd shaved again at night, so that the bristles on his chin wouldn't fire up her skin, which was so sensitive then, and easily marked. And a tenderness for this memory softened her towards him. She slid down beside him in bed.

'Jamie—'

'Oh, him. Rob said you'd gone charging round there. What's he want now?'

'Ruth's pregnant.'

He did not let the tiny pause turn to a silence that might mean something.

'Christ – bet she's pleased about that. Superdoctor.'

'Jamie's so happy – ecstatic. I didn't see Ruth. It's got to be a secret because she's after some job, doesn't want anyone to know yet. So you mustn't—'

'Oh, don't worry. Who would I tell? It's only your family would care anyhow. Sorry. Right, so Jamie's pleased, is he?'

'He's going to stay at home with the baby. Ruth'll carry on working. I suppose that makes sense.'

'It'll suit *him* – he can stop even pretending to work.'

'Graham!'

They both sat up, wide awake. How were they ever going to sleep tonight? Graham thought of the next day, his bottom set fourth years, the disks missing from the computer room, seeing Jan when the staff meeting finished.

'I'll be late tomorrow,' he said. 'Staff meeting after school.'

'Oh. Right.'

He laid a hand over hers, twisting the downie cover so hard it might tear.

'Annie, wait till that baby comes – Jamie'll be round here with it every bloody day. He'll need all the help he can get.'

'Is that supposed to cheer me up? Ach, I don't *grudge* him – he's so happy. It's just – I thought I was over all this, but it's brought it back. I thought – well, that I'd stopped hoping.'

'Don't.' Graham got up and reached for his dressing gown.

'Where are you going?'

'Downstairs, for a drink. You go to sleep.'

She started to get up.

'No, Annie, I'm not starting one of those all-night sessions. We're not going back to that.'

Annie subsided on the pillows, and let him go, so that she could weep in peace.

Downstairs, Graham poured himself whisky in the cooling living room, and stood turning the glass in his hands, after one fiery gulp. It was all going to start up again, he could see that. Bloody Jamie and his ice queen wife. The unfairness of it tightened his chest. And after all he'd done.

He'd supported Annie, hadn't he, through all those tests, the operation? He remembered all too clearly those nights in the house on his own, when she was in hospital. At first, he'd let himself believe it would work. Like Annie, he'd imagined the kids they'd have. Seen himself playing football in the park with a couple of robust blond boys, almost been able to conjure the touch of his daughter, flirting with him as he tucked her up in bed. Good pictures. He clung to them.

Then one day, when he was still Head of Department and had a register class, he'd been entering the birth dates of his new first years. And he realised he and Annie had been trying to have a baby for all of these children's lives.

They're what I should have, he thought, looking up at the rows of expectant faces, fresh out of primary school, still too nervous to misbehave.

So he went home and told his wife they had to give up. He hardened himself to her tears and pleading, certain he was right. At school, he kept his distance now. It was easier, in his present job, not to get fond of the kids. And when his colleagues complained about their children, or boasted of their achievements, he tried not to feel left out. But he was, he was – a whole life denied him, the love and energy he could have given to his own boys, his own lass, fallen into ashes, dust.

He swallowed whisky, rubbed his eyes. Pathetic to mind about it now. And then, through all this self-pity, the thought of Jan. A different kind of discomfort. But why should he feel guilty about that? It wasn't as if Annie wanted him now. All she'd ever wanted was his sperm. As long as she thought it was some good to her. Whereas Jan – she just wanted *him*. And she'd had her kids, took them for granted. That was a relief, he realised. Two sons, a divorce, a decent career – and still those long legs, that wicked smile . . .

'*Christ*,' he said aloud. 'What am I going to do about it?' And answered himself, 'Nothing, nothing. That's what.'

Upstairs, Annie had put the light out, and all she said when he came to bed was, 'I'm going up to Tom's. Next weekend.'

'Fine,' he said. 'Do you good.'

He fell asleep quickly, while Annie lay awake for a long time. But although she had cried, although there was pain in every breathing thought, she had learned something in all these years of failing. It was not so bad now: there were ways of numbing yourself to the worst of it, so that the pain was a little way off, standing perhaps in the corner of the room like a shadow. The sense of numbness grew, like the aftermath of a sting, and gradually, it sent her to sleep.

The Past

Five years back – Annie

Annie's parents never talked about it. They must have talked when it happened, no way round that, but not any more. If Annie referred to it, her mother simply changed the subject, not answering. If she tried again, Christine said, *What's the point in raking that up? It's in the past. Best forgotten.* But it had not been forgotten. Annie knew that.

This morning, her period still had not come. Three days now. She got her diary out again, thumbed through the last dog-eared month, counted and recounted. Well, two days really. But still.

'I'm sure you'll have no problems,' Christine said, when Annie first told her mother she and Graham wanted to have a baby. 'You're so regular.'

'Dead on,' Annie nodded, pleased to be getting something right. 'Don't tell anyone, though, not yet.'

'Och, it's nobody else's business,' Christine said. 'We won't count chickens.'

So they had tried to talk of other things, but both women kept coming back to this, and making plans.

'Let's hope you don't have long to wait,' Christine said as Annie left. 'But don't get anxious – it can take a wee while.' They walked up the path together, and stood at the gate. It was a hot June afternoon, and the scent from the flush of pink roses that filled the garden was sweet and heady.

'Have a buttonhole for Graham,' Christine said, snapping off a bud with her strong gardener's fingers. Annie took it, and bent to pluck a blue pansy.

'Pink for the girls, blue for the boys,' she said, smiling.

'Oh my, how many are you going to have?' They both laughed.

'A lot,' Annie said, closing the gate between her mother and herself. 'Four, six, who knows?' She waved the flowers at her mother as she set off down the road, feeling light, as if she might float away.

That had been ten years ago, when she was twenty-five. Now she was thirty-five, and there were no children. For nine years, she'd kept charts, taken her temperature, marked the days, known every shade and sign of her body's cycle. She had exploratory operations, her Fallopian tubes were checked, she took fertility drugs that made her sick and headachy, or bloated and miserable. But for the last year, she'd done none of this. Oh, she counted the days, that was like breathing now. How could she ever stop? But nothing else. She'd been seeing a counsellor, who was helping her realise she was too tense, and had allowed an obsession with her infertility (hers and Graham's, but that's a whole story in itself) to take over her life.

She had heard, of course, about those couples who gave up trying, adopted a child, and then, miraculously, conceived their own. Annie couldn't imagine adopting someone else's child. What if she didn't love it? There were no babies to be had anyway, only older children, abused or handicapped. But Annie didn't want to be a social worker, to put right someone else's wrong. It was weak of her: she ought to love any child who might need her. But she couldn't. She did enough for other people already, with Barnardos, the Church, Oxfam . . . all these good things that over the years had filled her useful days. No, when it came to children, she wanted her own, completely: to carry and bear and bring up.

But she still thought of those miracle babies who came unbidden at last. So she tried to give up trying. That was partly why she went on with the counsellor. In that hour, in the featureless room with its oatmeal tweed chairs, low table and box of tissues, she was able to feel hope, not so much for a child, as for the possibility that one day her life would be better; she would feel all right.

It was July. Her counsellor was on holiday, and they wouldn't meet for at least a month. Cath, Annie's best friend, was also away. But Cath was in the middle of a protracted divorce, and had far more need to be supported than she had means to support. So there was no one to talk this through with just now. Not Graham, certainly. It was because of him that Annie had gone to the counsellor in the first place.

It was another night when they were both still awake at three in the morning, another bout of hopeless crying, another wasted month. Annie eventually put on the bedside light, as if it might make it less terrible, not to be in the dark. Graham put his head in his hands, pushed his fingers through his hair, and looked up at her bleary-eyed.

'We're going round in circles, Annie. Christ, what's the point? I'm sorry, I'm as sorry as you are, but I don't want to talk about it any more. I don't even want to think about it.'

'All right,' Annie said, growing cold, the night itself hardening round her. 'We won't talk about it any more.'

When she spoke to Cath, Cath said, 'You should go to Marriage Guidance.'

'But there's nothing wrong with my marriage. Well, nothing that having children wouldn't put right.'

'Yes, but you can go anyway – it is a sort of relationship problem, isn't it?'

'I'll think about it. I have to do something.'

And so, because she had to go on talking about it, she talked to the counsellor. It would not have been true to say she never talked to Graham, or even that they didn't sit up most of the night any more. But it happened much less often, and things had improved. Or so she told herself.

She was on her way to her mother's house. She went there most Saturday mornings, while Graham played rugby and her father had his round of golf. They had coffee, and discussed unimportant things. She stopped at the newsagent on the corner to buy the gardening magazine she got for Christine every month. It had a free packet of plant food, attached to the front cover with sticky tape. The glossy paper of the cover was slightly torn, where the packet had started to pull at it. Annie stood at the counter waiting to be served, holding the magazine carefully so that the paper didn't tear any further. On the wide counter, all of the day's newspapers were spread out. The headings on most of them said *Police search for missing eight-year-old*.

She and Graham had gone out the previous night, and she'd

been up working in the garden from early morning. She had not seen or heard the news. So it stung her, this headline. She'd come face to face with it many times, but it never ceased to sting. Sometimes it was a girl who was lost, sometimes a boy, and the age varied. Sometimes the child was found alive, and sometimes not. Occasionally, the child was not found at all, but the headline slipped from the front page to an inside one, and eventually vanished altogether.

'One pound fifty,' the newsagent said, so she came to herself again, and handed over the money. But she did not buy a newspaper. And though there was one at home, folded and unread, she wouldn't look at it. She knew better.

In her mother's garden, the roses were blooming, and in the sitting-room window, facing the street, she could see a bowl of red ones, fully open, so that a few crimson petals had fallen on the polished surface of the table. She rang the doorbell and walked in. Everything in this dim hall with its long mirror, red and brown patterned carpet and oak hallstand, was utterly familiar. On the hallstand hung her mother's navy coat, her father's check cap and waterproof jacket. On top of the drawer was the last of the Indian Tree cereal bowls, full of oddments: spare buttons, keys, some loose change. Annie had grown up in this house, and it had not changed since she and Alistair had left home, Alistair to go to university, she to be married. Usually, this sameness was a comfort. Annie liked tradition, old and shabby things, a safe world. But today it seemed claustrophobic. She was full of words she could not utter.

Christine was in the sunny kitchen at the back of the house. The door was open to the porch, whose windowsills were filled with geraniums, red and pink, and there was a smell of baking.

'Now then,' Christine said, 'I've just boiled the kettle. Coffee won't be a minute.'

'No hurry,' Annie said, sitting down at the table and resting her elbows on it. She had the magazine in front of her. 'Free gift this month.'

'Oh aye – what is it?' Christine looked round. 'Oh, I've a whole bag of that stuff in the shed.'

'Oh well, now you'll have some more.'

'Could you not use it?'

'All right. Thanks.' Annie tried to detach the packet without tearing the paper further, and failed. Silently, Christine handed her a pair of scissors.

They had coffee in the porch, but even with the back door open, it was still too hot. Annie felt stifled, then sleepy.

'Late night,' she yawned. 'I'm tired.'

'Oh – where were you?'

'We took Cath's boys to see the film of *Peter Pan*. But then after we'd run them home we went for a drink, and met Gill, a woman Graham teaches with, and her husband. So we ended up back at their house for coffee.'

'I thought Cath was away?'

'She is. The boys are staying with Pete.'

'Ah.' A crease of disapproval appeared on Christine's brow. 'Those poor bairns.'

'They seem all right.'

'Maybe. But you can't tell with children. Pete and Cath should think about them for a change, put their bairns first.'

'Well, I think they tried, Mum, for long enough. Pete's with someone else now, anyway.'

'And what kind of example is that to set?'

'She's quite nice. Even Cath thinks she's all right, and it's made Pete more co-operative.'

'I don't know.' Christine shook her head. 'It's a different world.'

'Mum – I can't be sure yet – but I'm late. I'm definitely late.'

She had blurted this out, and it was a mistake. But Christine took it calmly, in the way of someone who had gone through hope and disappointment so many times, hope was illusion now. Annie should have been the same, of course, but she was not.

'Aye, well. Wait and see.'

Annie was suddenly enraged. 'Oh, I always do that. I'm so sick of waiting.'

'Well, Anne, there's nothing else to be done. A lot of life is just waiting.'

Christine had seen the news, and read the paper. Her mind had been full of the missing child all morning, and she had been thinking (for all she told herself she never would again) of the past. She could not help but imagine the terrible waiting of the child's family – though it wasn't just imagination that summoned this horror, it was memory.

Annie rushed on, thinking of the two days' grace, the glimmer of what might yet be. Only, she knew full well it was another false alarm. A familiar cramp told her that, but she was ignoring it.

'Sometimes,' she said, and her eyes were filling with the ready tears that so often irritated Graham, and caused the emptying of several of the counsellor's tissue boxes. 'Och, sometimes I feel life's not worth living. What's the point? Nothing ever comes of it. And all I want, all I've ever wanted, is to be like everyone else, just ordinary, with my own children.'

Christine looked at her daughter: the flushed bonny face, the pretty clothes and sparkling rings. Then she saw instead, for a few distracting seconds, the gaunt pallor of her own sister, hands twisting on her lap, the scrawny hollows of cheekbone and collarbone, and the tight line of her mouth, the dry eyes.

'You know,' she said, 'it seems to me all you're doing now is wallowing in self-pity. Maybe you havena got bairns, but you've a good man, a fine job, and a very nice home. We can't have everything we want in this life so maybe it's time you realised that, and just accepted your lot.'

Appalled, Annie burst out – 'You don't understand – you don't know what it feels like!'

'Whatever it feels like,' Christine said, 'it's nothing compared to what Liz went through. Never forget that.'

That her mother should instruct her now to remember what all her life she had been taught not to think of, stunned Annie into a silence so absolute Christine had no choice but to continue. But her spurt of anger against Annie was spent. Wearily, she forced out the words.

'If you'd known that kind of suffering – well, then you might talk about life not being worth living. Not that Liz ever did such a thing. She was so brave, all the way through. After the first – after – I don't believe anyone ever saw her cry.'

No, Annie thought, she just died of cancer three years later. Instead. But she could not say this, could not answer her mother.

There was the sound of a car on the drive, and the engine purring while her father got out to open the garage door.

'I'll just go and speak to your dad,' Christine said. 'I'm sure you don't want him coming through while you're in a state.'

She went out, and for a moment Annie sat immobile, unable to move, or think, or do anything at all about the tears coursing down her face. She heard the murmur of her parents talking in the hall, then the kitchen door closed and their voices were shut off. Like a sleepwalker, a drugged person, Annie picked up her bag and went out of the back door and round the side of the house to the front garden. She had to get home.

She walked slowly, carrying her misery like an unwieldy parcel. She was blind to the world around her, and found her way home by instinct. When she got there, she went straight upstairs and lay on the bed, wearing her sandals, the strap of her bag still on her shoulder, holding on to something that must never be opened again, never spilled out. They would not come after her or look for her. They would think she was best left to herself. On her own, she would reflect, and realise in time the truth and value of what Christine had said.

In their kitchen, Christine had not put the potatoes on, and the table was not laid. Instead, she sat turning the forgotten packet of plant food in her hands.

'I shouldn't have said that to her,' she told her husband. He sat on the chair nearest her, awkwardly patting her arm. But he said nothing, because he didn't know what he could say. Christine, anyway, went on. 'I don't say I'm not right to think it, because self-pity doesn't help anyone, but I wasn't right to speak of it. She's a good lass and she was only a bairn when it happened. It's nae her tragedy. God knows, we've tried hard enough nae to let if affect their lives.'

Her husband's hand closed over hers, and she sighed.

Annie, lying silent and tearless on her bed, feels the blood seep from her body and soak through her underwear and skirt. She feels it spread in a sticky pool beneath her, uselessly, and for the first time since all this began, with anticipation and love, she despairs.

And yet, she goes on waiting. She's conscious of waiting for something, and that she must not move till it happens. But nothing happens except that the room grows lighter and lighter, she seeming to float within it, as if the bed itself has risen from the floor, or the mattress taken slowly to the air, all weight evaporating. And the burden she's been holding so tightly begins to move away from her too. She lets it go, unresisting. It is no more than a dark shape dissolving in the light that is minute by minute whiter and more brilliant. Unable to bear it, Annie shuts her eyes, but this makes hardly any difference. The light penetrates. She feels warm, that perfect transitory warmth of the minutes before the alarm clock rings, every inch and particle of her warm, and filled with light.

She is weightless; there will be no more worrying.

The front door banging woke her so abruptly it was as if the bed had flung itself back on to the floor with a jolt. Aching, she slid her legs off the bed and sat up. She was giddy, but it passed. The dream faded and she remembered what had happened with her mother. Then, surprised, she realised she was dry, clean. There was no blood. That must have been part of the dream too.

Graham shouted from the hall, and she answered him.

'Just coming.'

She smoothed her crumpled skirt, and in front of the mirror, combed her hair. She was flushed, sleepy-looking. Some of the brilliance of the dream still clung, protecting her. Now she understood the tight frailty of her mother, the way she had guarded herself all these years. How could Annie, how could anyone else ever have a sorrow to match theirs, when she and her sister were the age Annie is now, and the world grew so dark. She understood this, and pitied her mother.

And yet, going downstairs, she wondered if all she was feeling, her heart light, was the absurd persistence of hope.

Spring

1

Tom had had a good line in his head all day, a strong ten-syllable line. When it had come to him, as he mashed up dog food for Bracken, whose jaws were weaker and teeth fewer these days, his heart had leapt at its perfection, and he had risen giddy, seeing red, hearing the line, rhythmic and sure. Where are you going, he had asked it, listening for the next line, for a clue about what the poem would say. But it was afternoon now, and he was at the table in the front shop, piles of books on either side, checking invoices. The line was still alone, had nothing to go with it but a phrase, a fragment. There was no poem. The line itself seemed less strong now, less a powerful beginning than an idea stranded in an open space.

The bookshop was empty. There would be children in after school, and one or two teachers, but at two-thirty on a March day when the rain had not stopped since ten o'clock, and the wind blew in gusts down the street, seeking out cracks to whistle draughts through, there was no one. Tom was alone, his father having stayed at home after lunch, as he usually did. He snapped shut the metal fastener in the ring binder, closed it, and put it on a shelf in the back shop. He switched on the electric kettle to make himself tea. It was warmer in the back room, and smelt of dog, since Bracken had lain in front of the two-bar electric fire all morning before going home with Stuart at lunch-time. Tom got his pad out, and sat at the table here, knowing the bell would ring if anyone came into the shop.

Every time he wrote, he marked the date at the top of the page in tiny Roman numerals, an affectation left over from school. He put his glasses on to peer at the last page where half a dozen lines reproached him, shapeless and unfinished. The light in here was not so good. He switched on the study lamp, which didn't help much: the date sprang out clearly, too clearly. He'd written nothing since before Christmas. Resigned, he turned the page, looked at blank paper, wrote his good line, and a little further down the page, his fragment. The clock ticked, the electric fire heated the backs of his legs and rain spattered on the window that looked on to the yard, with its dustbins and stone wall. Then he caught sight of the *Scotsman*, lying on a chair where his father had left it in the morning, folded back at an article on Seasonal Affective Disorder, explaining how this would come to an end for many people depressed by lack of sunlight, when the hour changed at the weekend.

The hour will change, and daylight will come again, he thought, then said aloud, with one syllable less, 'the hour will change and daylight come again.'

Twenty minutes later, the bell rang on the shop door, and he looked up like a man roused from sleep. He shook himself back to here and now, and the sound of footsteps. But as he got up, someone came through.

'Meg,' he said. She wore a long raincoat with the collar turned up, and her half-closed umbrella dripped water on the piece of thin carpet between table and door.

'Hi.'

He took the umbrella from her and stuck it in the wastepaper basket, then unbuttoned her coat so that he could slip his arms round her, feeling her thin straight back under his hands, beneath lambswool jersey and cotton shirt. She stood still, submitting to this, and leaned her head on his chest. Then she drew back.

'Tom, the house is sold.' His arms slipped away, let her go.

'When?'

'This morning – the offer was accepted this morning. They want to move in in four weeks.' She was looking at him anxiously, but he turned to the shelf with the kettle and mugs.

'I'll make tea,' he said. 'I put the kettle on earlier, but I forgot to make any.'

'I would have told you,' she said, 'only we've had so many false starts with this selling business. You know.'

'So,' he said, with his back to her, swilling hot water in the brown pot he and his father had used, almost entirely unwashed, for years. It was thick with tannin. *You hardly need a tea bag in that,* Annie had said once, visiting the shop. 'So . . . you'll be away in four weeks.'

'Well, the boys are home at Easter, so I hope by then we'll have a rented place. Till we find a house.'

'No more travelling for Keith, then.'

'That's right.'

He turned and handed her a mug of tea. She held it carefully, but did not drink from it. Eventually, as he talked, she set it down on the table, next to his poem, which she did not notice.

'I suppose it had to happen sometime,' he said.

'Yes.' She looked tired, the tiny lines at the corners of her eyes more noticeable than usual, the skin white round her mouth, which was pulled tight.

'It's a good thing,' he went on. 'Time it was sorted out.'

'Oh yes.' Her voice was faint. 'I have to try, anyway. It might be better when we're together all the time again.'

'I'm sure it will.'

'Tom—'

'It's all right. *I'm* all right. You want a biscuit?'

'Tom—' She was flushed with the heat from the fire, almost girlish in the lamplight as she moved towards him. But he brushed her aside.

'Off you go –' he said, '– home. You must have plenty to do, if you're moving in four weeks.'

'I will see you, though.'

'Is there any point?' He smiled at her, softening this.

'Surely—'

'Off you go,' he said again, brisk, giving her no opening.

The shop bell clanged. She whirled round, and went out quickly, forgetting her umbrella. As she turned, the end of her coat belt flew out and caught the edge of a heap of letters and publishers' leaflets. They slipped sideways, knocking over the mug of tea. But he had followed her into the shop and it was only later, when his customer (Mrs Macleay from the post office, for a Catherine Cookson and a birthday card), had gone, that he went back and discovered a pool of brown tea had obliterated his poem.

*   *   *

Tom closed the shop early, turning out a couple of teenage girls who had come to talk about boys somewhere out of the rain before they went home. It was no longer dark at half-past four, but the steady rain made it seem so, and along the street people had switched on lights indoors. He could see framed all the way out of the village, different living rooms, different lives. And yet, despite the variations in curtains, pictures and furniture, it seemed to be the same scene he glimpsed, in every one. Television, slouching children, women crossing the room purposefully, the bright interval of the hour before tea.

The rain had lightened. It was like a fine mist in his face now, and the air was fresh and welcome. He strode out, heading for his father's cottage to collect the dog on his way home. He did not go along the seafront in winter, but back through the village and by the top road. There were open fields on either side, and little shelter from trees, so on windy nights it was grim, but it braced him. That was what he needed. However, if he'd known it was going to rain so hard, he'd have taken the car in the morning. He told himself this, filling his head with tiresome details, so that he would not think about Meg.

But he did. Her face, her voice, and if he was not careful, her thin body, so often and so beautifully naked in his arms, under his hands, drawing his body into the neat fit of hers. The wind was stronger here, and blew in from the sea, sweeping open his Barbour jacket, cracked with age, windproof but not warm. He turned the collar up, thrust his hands back in the pockets. The lines of his lost poem revolved, faded.

Two years of intimacy, forbidden, guilt-charged, would come to an end in four weeks. She would follow her husband south at last, and his midweek nights would be his own again, free for writing, doing other things, getting on with his life. This was what he told himself, but his self was not fooled.

He had reached his father's place. He banged the knocker and opened the door. The dog barked once, and came to greet him.

'Is that the time?' His father roused himself from an armchair. 'No – the news isn't on yet.' He was watching children's television and eating toast. 'You must be early.'

'I am.'

'Now then,' his father looked round vaguely. 'Anne phoned. I wrote it down – I told her I'd write it down, so I wouldn't forget to tell you.'

'Tell me what?'

'Ach,' Stuart snorted, 'I forget.' They both laughed. Stuart put his glasses on, went hunting on the open bureau desk that was littered with papers.

'Here – is this it?' He held up a scrap torn from a notepad. 'Aye, here, Friday, she's coming on Friday, with wee Robbie. Not so wee now, she tells me.' He took his glasses off again and sat down by the fire. 'Now then, what was the story you told me? When you came back at New Year. About him running off and neither Alistair nor thon hally-racket Shona bothering to come looking?'

'Dad, you know fine.' Tom cut him short. His father more and more affected to be forgetful, even slightly senile. Tom disliked this, knowing it to be an act, but fearing that one day it would not be. Perhaps that's why he does it, to get us used to the idea, he wondered. I wouldn't put it past him.

'So Annie's coming on Friday,' he said aloud. 'I'll ring her when I get home.'

'She tried you there first, thinking Wednesday was early closing. Then she rang me, just for the crack, I suppose. She's a great blether, Anne.' Stuart, seeing Tom had stopped listening, and was being inexorably drawn to the television screen, shrill voices in the corner, aimed the remote control and switched it off. 'Do you want your tea?'

Tom shook his head, irritable. 'No, no, I'm off home.' He whistled the dog, and they set off for the High House.

After his wife's death, Stuart would not live in the High House. When Lindsay disappeared, he had stayed on only for her, who could not leave, but clung to the shadows in the garden of three children playing, her lost daughter still given voice by the wind in the trees, made visible by sunlight moving across the lawn. So when Tom and Jamie had both left to go to university he shut it up and rented a cottage on the seafront at Rosemarkie. He was still there. Now Tom lived alone in the High House. Before he met Ruth, Jamie had stayed there between jobs or girlfriends. People often told Tom it was a big house for a man on his own, as if this might be news to him. Behind their comment was unspoken what they all said to each other, but not to him, all the people in the village who remembered that far back: *And so much tragedy.* They thought he should get out, sell it and start afresh somewhere else. At least, they had thought so while he was a young man, a clever young man, who seemed full of promise, bound to go far.

But I have not gone anywhere at all, Tom thought, as he climbed the steep path, the dog plodding behind. I am still here, where I was born, like a farmer who cannot leave the land. I cannot leave this house.

He stood by the back door, looking down the long garden, obscured by shadows spread so thick they made a darkness in themselves. Below were one or two lights on the path along the seafront. Here the wind and the sea were blent to one soft roar that seemed always to be hushed, retreating, and yet never did retreat. He listened, his hand on the cold iron knob, till Bracken pushed her nose against his thigh, and he opened the door to let them both in.

The kitchen was always warm: since he'd had the Aga converted to oil, there was no risk of its going out during the day, no need to come home at lunch-time to stoke it. He did not always light a fire in the sitting room, even in winter. There was a Windsor chair in the corner of the kitchen, where he settled with book and whisky on the nights when he did not see Meg, and had no other company. The crimson cover of the chair was faded and worn, with loose threads he picked at absently as he read, and the seat cushion had no resistance left in it. But he was used to the chair; it fitted him, as the house did. He knew the house looked neglected, and there were rooms he hardly ever went into. He must, though. Since Annie was coming, he'd make an effort. Clean the kitchen perhaps. Meg was the only woman in his life who had never made any attempt to do this for him. Women usually saw him, and the house, as a challenge, at least for a while. They set to, tried to make a difference. But Meg had not. She came, and they made love, talked, slept. Then she went home again. The most she had ever done was make tea, or help him wash up.

Once she had said, *It's very restful here. I never have to think about doing anything in this house.* When she had a bath, she used his towel, or took a clean one from the linen cupboard and left it crumpled on the floor. The warm imprint on the other side of the bed, a damp towel on the floor, a toothbrush she used: these were her only marks here. It would be easy, then, surely, to let her slip away.

When the telephone rang as he was finishing his meal, it was Annie.

'Did Stuart tell you? Is it OK – if Rob and I come up at the weekend?'

'Certainly. On Friday, Dad said. How long are you staying?'

'A couple of days.'

'Any particular reason?'

A pause. 'Oh, you know. Just fed up. It's been a long winter. And Rob could do with something to . . . cheer him up. A change.'

'Hasn't he got a job yet?'

'No.' She lowered her voice. 'And it's causing a bit of friction with Graham. As you can imagine.' She raised her voice suddenly, talking to someone else. 'It's in the top drawer – I told you. Tom. I said – just for the weekend. Yes.' A pause. 'Sorry – he's gone out now.'

'Well, then.' Tom's phone was in the chilly hall with no chair nearby. He pictured Annie in her warm bedroom, settling back on the pillows for a nice long chat. 'I'll see you sometime on Friday then. Dad'll take the shop for me in the afternoon, so just come to the house.'

'Right. We might have lunch at that place in Fochabers – what's it called?'

'Annie,' he lied, 'I have to go. Got something in the oven. See you Friday.'

'Is something wrong?'

Well, yes, he thought, but now's not the time. He touched the storage heater in the hall: cool, as it always was by this time of day. Why did he bother? Why did he even live here?

'I'll talk to you at the weekend.'

'All right, Tom.' Her voice caressed him. 'Take care – see you soon.'

Later, he called Meg, and she came over.

2

Meg left him early to go home and feed her cats before she went to work. Like Tom, she did supply teaching in the local secondary, but her subject was more often in demand than his. She had three regular days a week at the moment. He lay in the cooling bed for half an hour after she had gone, watching daylight spread across the sky in a wash of pale blue, the horizon fading pink and lilac. He must get up and see to the dog, and put these sheets in the washing machine. Last night Meg had said, *This bed smells – of old sex, probably.* He'd laughed, but now the rumpled covers did smell stale. She was right; he was getting careless.

Still he lay there. On Thursdays, Stuart played golf, so there was only Tom to open up the shop, go through the post, and send off any orders that had come in for antiquarian books. This was the only part of the business that still paid, and lately, he'd been neglecting that too. It was difficult to care now they'd decided to sell up. The first ads had gone in a week ago. But it had taken Meg and Keith over a year to sell a very pleasant house in Fortrose. How much longer was it likely to take for a small bookshop, specialising in antiquarian stock, and with very low profit margins, to take someone's fancy in Edinburgh or York? Advertise nationwide, the agent had advised. It's just the kind of thing someone retiring early might fancy. But Tom didn't hold out much hope. He would be sitting there, most days of his life, for some time to come.

At this thought, which in the past had been a comfort, such a wave of despair swept over him that it left a weight pressing on his chest. He could hardly breathe, hardly dared to open his eyes again. *What can I do?* he asked himself. But he had been passive all his life, and now there was nothing else he could be. It was not just the shop. He had chosen passivity in everything. What could be more passive than waiting for poetry? And as for women – he had loved only women with whom it was impossible to be happy – lovely women with the plain names of queens – Elizabeth, Anne, Mary . . . and now Margaret, Meg. But not his sister, with her aristocratic boy's name. He had not loved his sister.

How strong she had been, Lindsay, and sure of herself. When she was there, everything was organised, controlled by her. Annie followed her like a wee dog, comical and clumsy, copying everything she did. Tom, dreaming with a book, would rather have stayed alone, letting them all go off without him. But he'd had, even then, a vague sense of having to look out for Annie, since her own brother wouldn't. Then, Alistair and Lindsay quarrelled, both wanting to lead, but Lindsay always winning because she was the stronger.

What he remembered about her disappearance was the large empty space her going created. How quiet it was, and restful. But without her, he was even more conscious of having to take care of his brother, of Annie.

The small hot bedroom in his friend Alex's house. Both of them, reading the forbidden newspaper reports, Tom sick with guilt and fear.

Later, at night, whispering across the bedroom to Alistair what he knew, and Alistair saying, *We should go and look, we could do it.* Then – *had they* – had they gone to look?

Always, here, he couldn't remember the order things happened, or even if they had happened at all. But he could see himself in the woods, standing in a clearing next to Alistair, his heart beating fast and hard.

That must have been some other time. *If it happened.* It must. They would never have been allowed to search on their own like that.

The bed was cold, and he was rigid, tense. What the hell had brought all that up? More than thirty years, and it still couldn't just disappear, leave him alone.

Tom flung back the covers, got up, and went to run his bath. Peaty water spat from the tap, cleared, then ran scalding hot, steam rising like a cloud in cold air. He turned on the radio, wiped the mirror with the back of his hand and lathered his face for shaving.

After breakfast he took the dog down to the beach. There was a softness in the air, as if spring might really be coming. In the garden, soil and grass were pierced with green spikes, and there were scents everywhere of the wind changing, the earth waking. The breeze that swept them along the shore was kinder this morning; even when Bracken had had enough and they turned to face into it coming back, he did not feel cold. How easy, he thought, to see in all this renewal a sign of hope. You could not help it: the heart lifted, however unreasonably, every year at these first signs.

'Aren't you tired of being on your own?' Annie had asked him once, when he had told her about Meg. She had known about Mary too, and with both affairs had been more sympathetic to the women she had scarcely known, than to him.

'Oh yes,' he said, 'often. Tired of myself, I suppose.'

'Then – why don't you do something about it?'

He thought of this now. Should he ask Meg to stay? But it was one thing to sleep with another man's wife, quite different to break up a marriage, even when the children were grown and had gone away to be students. Or so he told himself. There was also, just as terrifying as the prospect of her agreement, the possibility that she might say no.

'I've brought it on myself,' he said aloud to Bracken, who was looking up at him, puzzled that he'd stopped. 'Eh? What d'you think?' She nuzzled his hand, searching for a biscuit. He would have to wait for Annie to tell him what to do, what he should be thinking.

But when she arrived with Rob early on Friday afternoon, she seemed subdued, going at once to warm her hands, holding them above the closed hotplate of the Aga. The weather had turned cold again. Rob stood awkwardly, gazing round the kitchen.

'I had a clean-up, in your honour,' Tom said, 'but Annie won't think it's good enough, and you won't know how bad it was before.' Tom grinned at Rob, who almost broke into an answering smile, before bending to pet the dog.

'He's great with dogs,' Annie said. 'Mac's been walked to death this last month.'

'Bracken's a bit old for long walks.'

'A bit fat,' the boy said, leaning back to look at her critically. 'Ain't ya?' Bracken wagged her tail.

'We'll take her out now,' Tom suggested, 'if the pair of you want to stretch your legs.'

'Yes, we could. Might get me warmed up again. I don't know why I feel so shivery – the car has a good heater.' Annie pulled her gloves on again.

'You coming Rob – along the beach?'

'Aye, OK.'

They went down the steep path in single file. Annie hung back, murmuring to Tom, 'Hear him? He's beginning to lose that awful accent.'

'Aye,' Tom mimicked, smiling at her. 'Turning him back into a Scot, are you? That'll please Jamie.'

'Och, Jamie.' She looked annoyed. 'I hardly see him.'

'He's coming up at Easter, with Ruth.'

'Oh—' Annie frowned. 'When did you last speak to him, then?'

'Oh, a week or two back. To tell him about the ads going in.'

Tom turned to shut the gate behind them as they left the garden and followed the coast path down to the sea. Rob was ahead with the dog, hands tucked in the pockets of his denim jacket, so that it was pulled tight round his waist. He looked different – it wasn't just his voice.

'His hair's grown too – see that?' Annie pointed out. Her face had cleared, and she looked pleased. But something was wrong. He wondered what, knowing she'd tell him soon enough.

'So how's things?' he asked.

'Oh, you know. Much the same.'

'But Graham's fed up with the cuckoo in the nest, is he?'

'Well, I don't think he'd mind if he felt Rob was pulling his weight. But all that lying about in front of the TV . . .'

'Doesn't it get on your nerves – you're at home with him all the time?'

Annie seemed puzzled how to answer this.

'I like having someone in the house, I like having him around.

It's not that . . . and he's good, he helps if I ask him. Sometimes off his own bat, now.'

'Helps?'

'You're laughing at me.'

'No . . . no. It's just the way women talk about men. *Oh, he's very good, he helps with the shopping, he cuts the grass, washes up one or two dishes every few months . . .*'

'Who're you making fun of – men or women?'

'Both . . . both. When you live on your own you do it all, however inadequately. It's got nothing to do with being male or female.'

'Ach, Tom, you're on a hobby horse – that's not what we were speaking about.'

'No, sorry. Go on – tell me about Rob.'

'That's it. He helps. I did get fed up about three weeks ago. Lost the rag. I need time on my own in the house, I told him. That's what I'm used to.'

'So does he go out and walk the streets, or what?'

'I made him go to the job centre. And the college. He's enrolled on a computing course – there were places left, so he got one. One day a week.'

'That's progress, I suppose. So who's paying – you?'

'No, it's free – a course for unemployed people.' She sighed. 'It's not Rob . . . I actually get on all right with him. It's Graham, mostly. I think he's jealous. Or maybe not. He's out a lot.'

Tom said nothing, but in his mind picked among the possibilities, worrying about Annie. He let the silence last too long, for she had been following a different track, and said, 'What about you?'

'Oh—' Tom shrugged. 'Tell you later. We'd better go back. I'm making a curry – time I got it started.'

'Bliss,' Annie said, smiling up at him, her face rosy from the keen wind, the woollen hat pulled down so that only a few curls escaped. Childlike, bonny, she laid a hand on his arm. 'It's lovely coming here, lovely to be cooked for. Luxury.'

'Well,' Tom said, 'let's wait and see how the curry turns out.' He waved to Rob and whistled the dog. They all turned, facing into the wind now, to begin the walk back.

*   *   *

'Where's the telly then?' Rob gazed round the living room. He had been kept busy since they got back, unpacking, chopping vegetables, bringing in wood for the fire. Now they had eaten, and the fire was warming the big room almost to the edges. However, the corner window, Annie knew from experience, would still be chilly. It was set in the round end of the room that looked from the outside like a turret. Immediately above this, upstairs, was a tiny separate room, where Jamie had once slept. Now Rob was to have it; it was so small it was easily heated.

'Oh dear,' Annie said, 'I forgot.'

'Forgot?'

'You probably wouldn't have come if I'd told you.'

'What – there's no telly?'

'I'm afraid not.' Tom stood swaying gently, back to the fire, hands deep in his trouser pockets. Rob looked not so much dismayed as perplexed.

'What d'you do then?' he asked.

'Do?'

'When you come home from work, like. In the evenins.'

'He's a snob,' Annie said. 'Pretends to be too highbrow for television.'

'Ach,' Tom said, settling himself in one of the big chairs that sat either side of the fire. 'She knows fine – I'm an addict. If there's a TV, I watch it. All the time. This is the only way to break the habit. Total withdrawal.'

'Yeah, but – what d'you *do*?' He sat down in the other chair, easing off his trainers, stroking the dog with one foot as she lay stretched out, belly to the fire. She twitched, dreaming, and gave a faint whuffle.

'Chasing rabbits, eh?' Tom prodded her gently, then looked up at Rob. 'I listen to music, cook . . . read.'

'What – every night?'

'Have friends round,' Tom went on, as if Rob hadn't spoken.

'He writes,' Annie said suddenly. 'He's a writer.'

'How's that – books?' He looked at Tom. 'That right? What kind?'

Tom laughed, caught between embarrassment and pride, as he always was at this. A hard kind of pride, you needed to be a poet, but far more, to admit to it.

'The failed kind,' he said. 'No need to get excited – no best sellers, or anything like that. A couple of wee volumes of poetry – the last one published ten years ago.'

'Not so long as that—' Annie protested.

'Well, I was finishing the work on it when Jamie was ill. Getting better.'

The little frown between Annie's brows cleared. 'Oh,' she said, 'yes, so you were.' She sighed. 'That was quite a year.'

Rob looked from one to the other. He wasn't interested in poetry, but something else had caught his imagination. What was here that he did not know?

Annie had pulled the rocking chair forward so that she was near the fire too. There was a long, battered sofa, covered in olive green velvety stuff that had worn bare on the arms, but it was too heavy to drag across the room. In summer, though Rob could not know this, it collected the morning sun as it came up glittering from the sea and washed the room with light. If you lay there, as Jamie once had, every day, it was the warmest, most golden place to be in the Western world. Now it was at the cold edge of the room, cast out of the light, shaded and dull. The three of them sat in the glow of the standard lamp behind Tom's chair, and gazed at the yellow flames as they darted up from a fresh log of wood, sparking blue, spitting resin.

'We used to read, Tom, d'you remember?' Annie asked him, tipping her chair to and fro, so that it made the floorboards beneath the old carpet creak. 'Read to Jamie.'

'That was summer,' Tom said. 'Long summer evenings when the light didn't fade till midnight.'

'And came back at three,' Annie recalled, 'so that when you woke with it, you knew there were hours to go before morning.'

'He was always awake,' Tom said. 'If you went in to him, he was awake.'

'He dozed so much during the day.' Annie stopped rocking and was still.

Rob said nothing; he was waiting for them to go on. He felt he was close to the mystery they'd all kept from him. He knew there was a mystery about what they just called 'Lindsay disappearing', this terrible thing that had happened years ago when they were all children, his aunt and uncles, and his father. His father had answered questions curtly: *Nothing for you to worry about. It was a long time ago,* and his mother, who had been the one to rouse his curiosity in the first place, said vaguely, *It all happened before I knew your dad.*

As a child, he'd grown used to being kept out of things, and the reaction of adults when he tried to find out, taught him eventually not to ask at all. It was like sex, drugs, alcohol – you had to find out the best way you could. They knew but they weren't going to tell you. Under the scanty information he'd managed to glean was always a line that went *and don't you think you can try it, my lad*. Embarrassed silence, an uneasy shrug: *Ask your dad,* Shona used to say. *That's his job.* And if he did – though that was never easy – all he got was *Hasn't your mother explained that?*

He learned from his friends, from books and magazines. But they couldn't tell him about his parents splitting up, they couldn't tell him about Lindsay. He felt different about these things: his parents' marriage, or lack of it, was a private embarrassment, less important as he grew older, and many of his friends became like him, with mother and father in two places, or more often, no father at all.

But about Lindsay, his curiosity grew.

'What you wanna do,' his friend Kevin said, 'is get the old newspapers – look them up. They got them in the library. See, I did this project at school on the bridges in our town – there was about a thousand bridges, I'm not kiddin' – when I lived in Yorkshire, like. Primary school. Anyway, Miss Mitchell, she was the teacher, she took us to the library and they had this what d'ya ma call it. Like a film reel – you could put it up on this screen and there was the papers. Eighteen hundred and somethin'.'

'You mean look through all the old newspapers – it would take months.'

'Don't ya know the date?'

He and Kevin sat on the wall outside Kevin's house, smoking rollies and picking loose cement and bits of moss out of the bricks along the top. Kevin's mum wasn't home till six, so it was OK to smoke.

Kevin was the only one he'd told. After all, he didn't know

what might come out once he started looking. Better not to tell other people. He was torn between a terror of embarrassment and a longing to talk to someone else.

'I could find out the date.' He stubbed out his cigarette end so that it frayed on the brick, disintegrating. 'I know the year – my dad was twelve, and he's forty-six now, so that makes – what year?'

Kevin struggled with subtraction. 'You're the maths genius – not me.'

'No, I'm not.'

'Comin' in then?' Kevin asked, losing interest. 'See if Juventus is still top of the league?'

They played football league games on Kevin's computer. Usually that was what they discussed every afternoon, as they shrugged off school. They slid off the wall, and picking up sports bags heavy with school books and trainers for PE, went indoors.

Later, Rob thought over what Kevin had suggested. He'd have to go to Aberdeen, though. It would have been in the local paper, something like that. Later, he discovered he could have done the same thing at home: what happened to Lindsay made headlines in the national press. Even when common sense should have told him this, he persisted in thinking of it as something local, private. But then, he didn't know what he was dealing with.

Although this was not what had finally brought him to Annie's door on a cold January night, it was still in his mind. He did not consider asking Annie directly. He meant to find out the truth, unfudged, and it was best to do that yourself. So he went to the library. Annie was pleased he'd asked where it was. It distressed her that he seemed to read nothing but football magazines and the sports pages of the newspapers.

'Look at it this way,' Graham said. 'Now he's reading football reports in quality papers. I imagine all he saw at Shona's were the *Daily Express* and the *News of the World*.'

'Oh hardly,' Annie protested. But she thought he was probably not far wrong. Still, books were the thing.

'It's a wonderful library,' she enthused. 'Take something with you for identification – then you can join.'

'What for?' Rob asked.

'Well – to take books out.'

'Oh,' he said, going red, 'I don' wanna borrow any books.'

Annie was nonplussed. 'I thought – what do you want the library for then? To study?' She brightened again, thinking he might have homework for his computing class. She didn't know much about computers.

'Na – just to look somethin' up.'

'Oh – what? Is it something we could help with?'

'Na. Just somethin'.' He knew Annie better now. 'Something about football.'

'Right,' she said, losing interest, as he'd known she would.

The library was forbidding: wide steps up to a huge granite frontage, and a bewildering choice of places to go once you were inside. He toiled up more stairs to what turned out to be the wrong department.

'The microfiche is downstairs,' the woman said, so he went back down. This time, three people were queueing to speak to one man behind a desk. He waited for a moment or two, then gave up and went to the shops instead. He told himself he'd come back when it was quieter, but he forgot, his mind on the tapes he'd bought, and took the bus up to Annie's.

That night, she told him she was going to Tom's at the weekend.

'Come with me,' she said. 'You'll love the High House and you don't have your computing class till Wednesday, so you won't miss anything.'

Tom lived on the Black Isle, lived in the house where they'd all been when it happened.

'All right,' he said. Annie was unpacking groceries. 'You want a hand?'

'Yes,' she said. 'You do this – I'll get the tea started.'

He knew where everything was kept. He was at home in Annie's house. He knew better than Graham where she stored things, how she organised the housekeeping. As he put tins and packets away, and washed the fruit, he told himself it didn't matter about the library. He could go to the one in Inverness instead, and anyway, so close to the heart of the mystery, he was bound to learn what it was.

Later, he asked himself why it had taken him so long even to get to the library. After all, he'd been in Aberdeen for nearly three months. Too many other things, he thought, doing my head in. Couldn't hack it. But the other things were fading, leaving some space, a sense of clearness, room to move. His head felt lighter these days.

Now, in Tom's shadowy living room, with the sound of the sea lost in the fire's crackle, conversation between the adults, he thought again about Lindsay, who had been born here, lived here. He knew, of course, that she had disappeared and never come back. His mother had said that. *She was the oldest one, your dad's cousin, your Uncle Tom's big sister. They were all playing on the beach, all the kids, and she just upped and went. Wandered off – your Uncle Tom says he saw her away up the beach, and he shouted but she never heard him. Never saw her again. And none of them's got over it, your grans and grandads – and if you ask me that's what gave your Auntie Liz cancer.*

What had happened? His mother had shaken her head, then his dad had come in to get him, and the look he gave her – that was after they stopped living together, stopped speaking really. She must be dead, Rob had decided, long ago. If she wasn't, she'd be ancient now, older than his dad. Maybe she was going about somewhere in another country, not knowing where she came from. When he was a kid he'd had this fantasy about meeting her, and she was mega-rich, and when she found out about him, her memory sort of flooded back, and she goes – *You must be my nephew* – and she doesn't have kids, so he inherits all her worldly goods.

He didn't have those fantasies any more. Life doesn't work out like that. You don't win the lottery, rich women don't leave you all their money. But when things get so bad you can't stand the thoughts banging away in your head any more – you can leave. So he had left.

He closed his eyes, listening to the murmur of Tom's and Annie's voices, the dog's head a warm hard weight on his foot.

'You remember,' Annie was saying, 'how we got through all of *Tom Sawyer*, chapter about, and *Coral Island*, and *The Scarlet Pimpernel*, then when he was a bit better—'

'Managed to wean him off our old kids' stuff,' Tom interrupted. 'Only he got hooked on the Russians.'

'*Crime and Punishment*,' Annie sighed. 'God – that was hard going.'

'I made him switch to James Thurber after that.'

'And *Wuthering Heights* . . . and *Gatsby*.'

'Your choice.'

'It was about time I had a choice,' Annie laughed. 'What was yours – the Thurber?'

'McCaig, MacDiarmid – and John Donne.'

'Oh, poetry,' Annie sighed. 'Not Jamie's thing really.'

'Well, what does he read now?'

'Thrillers. Junk. Airport blockbusters.'

'See – we chose all of them really.'

'I suppose we did.'

Rob opened his eyes as Tom leaned forward to put another log on the fire. He hadn't heard of any of these names. They meant nothing. But it seemed to be a lot of reading.

'It was an extraordinary time,' Tom said.

'What was wrong with him? He musta been ill years to get through all them books.' Rob leaned forward, wide awake again. But Tom and Annie had been looking backwards, inward.

They had to refocus. Tom answered him.

'Not years, thank God. But months, yes. It took him months to recover.'

'Yeah, but what from? I mean, he have a car accident, or what?'

Silence.

Tom and Annie looked at each other. Tom shrugged.

'Didn't Alistair ever say?' Annie asked.

'Christ, nobody in my fuckin' family ever answers a straight fuckin' question.'

Rob got up suddenly, dislodging Bracken, who heaved herself to her feet, thinking it must be time for her last walk of the day. But Rob was going without her.

'I'm goin' to bed, OK?'

'Yes, sure, you must be tired. Travelling's so tiring,' Annie murmured, knowing, yet remembering too late, that sixteen-year-old boys are not worn out by a two and a half hour drive and a walk on the beach. 'And the change of air,' she added, more and more inanely. 'The change of air – it always tires me out.'

Rob stared at her in disbelief – as well he might, Tom thought. 'We'll answer questions,' he said. 'There's no secret. It just doesn't seem fair to Jamie now it's all so far in the past. To discuss him, I mean. So we don't.'

'You was discussing him now,' the boy pointed out.

'Well, no,' Tom said, 'we were talking about books.'

'We don't want—' Annie hesitated. 'I mean, you're family, after all. We don't want you to feel left out of anything. But as Tom says, it was so long ago . . .'

He looked at their kind, reasonable faces. Then he shrugged and went out, leaving the door open, and went upstairs to bed.

Tom and Annie sat in the draught from the open door, then Tom got up to shut it. Bracken, further confused, followed him.

'Better take her out,' he said. 'You coming?'

'No – I'll make a cup of tea. You want one?'

'Whisky?'

'Yes, that's better.'

'When I come back then. Or you start now, if you like. Bottle in the cupboard. Enough left for tonight, I think.'

'Right.'

'Think we need it.'

When he had gone out, Annie banked up the fire and fetched the whisky and two of the big crystal tumblers. Should she go up and see Rob? But for once she didn't want to, wanted only to sit by the fire with Tom, and talk. And listen. He looked quite grey: something was wrong. She was half ashamed that she looked forward so much to finding out what.

3

'Well,' Tom said, 'what was wrong with Rob, d'you think? Marching out in the huff.'

'He thinks we're keeping a secret from him. I suspect he wants to know about Lindsay, and maybe your mother. He was hinting, in the car coming up.'

'I'd be surprised if that has any interest for him. It was years before he was born. I assumed he was getting het up because he thought there was something about Jamie we were keeping from him. He took a shine to Jamie, you said.'

'Well, we are. Keeping something from him.'

'You think we should have told him – *explained* exactly what ulcerative colitis is, described an ileostomy, so he'd understand why Jamie made up his mind life wasn't worth living. How even when we got him home, apparently no longer a suicide risk – ha – he made sure *our* lives weren't worth much either – watching him twenty-four hours a day.'

'Oh Tom, it wasn't – I never felt—'

'You think it's OK to tell a sixteen-year-old boy all that stuff about his uncle?'

Annie looked uncertainly at him. 'I don't know,' she said. 'I mean, I think he's old enough to take that – understand, a bit. It's Jamie we're protecting, isn't it, not Rob? But I never knew you were so *angry* about it.'

'I'm not, I'm not. Not now, not even then. Scared. I was scared we'd go in and he'd have had some secret store of tablets all along, we'd go in and he'd be – sorry.'

'No, no. I understand, I was scared too, but it wasn't so bad for me, I wasn't there when he first came home. But I saw him in hospital, all those drips and things.'

Tom did not answer. He lay back in his chair and closed his eyes.

Annie remembered again how Jamie had been when she first went up to visit, soon after the operation. Stuart had met her at Inverness station, and taken her up to Raigmore.

'How is he?' Her uncle looking tired, and wearing his golfing trousers and red V-necked jersey, straight from Strathpeffer golf course to pick her up.

'Ach, he's not making anything of it, Anne.'

'But I thought—'

'The operation was fine, very successful. The doctor said he should be fitter than he's been for months, once he's up and about. But—' he cruised the huge hospital car-park, looking for a space. 'Here we are – it's busy in the afternoon.'

'So what's wrong then?'

They stood outside the car, looking across the top of it at each other. Stuart frowned.

'You'll see for yourself, Anne. See for yourself.'

Along the wide corridors, a drift of visitors with flowers, chocolates, carrier bags holding clean nightdresses, library books. And Jamie at last, in a small room off the ward, lying on his side, turned away from the window overlooking the car-park with its acres of empty cars, and his curtains drawn anyway, cutting out the glint of sunlight, so that the room was shadowy. He was asleep, the dark lashes long and soft on his face, and though he had not shaved, looking young, young, a boy again.

'Oh,' Annie said, and sank on the chair beside the bed, her warm hand brown on his white bony arm. His eyes opened, gradually focused.

'You're not to die,' she said, 'you're not to die.' And tears rolled hot over her face.

Weeks later, Jamie said, 'You told me not to die, so I thought I'd better not. You'd have given me an awful row.' And that, Tom said to Annie, was his first joke. Not up to much, but better than dying.

It had taken more than that, of course. Over and over, even when he was sitting up, eating again, off the drip, he would say to Annie or Tom, *Who's going to look at me now, eh?*

Annie looked across at Tom, and he opened his eyes again.

'He was so young,' she said at last. 'Too young for something as awful as that. I used to think, too, that he wasn't fit to cope, how could he be, what with Lindsay and then your mother.'

'Let's leave it,' Tom said. 'It's over, in the past. And Jamie hates to be reminded. He felt . . . mutilated. That was what bothered him most, not the past or any of that stuff. Just that no woman was ever going to look at him again.'

'I know. It was only Ruth . . . I mean, whatever I might feel about Ruth myself – apart from just pure sort of admiration, envy . . . whatever . . . she was the right person, the only one who could have made him feel OK about himself.'

'We helped,' Tom said. 'You and I.'

'But we couldn't fall in love with him.'

Tom let himself laugh. 'No, we did need Ruth for that.'

'Anyway,' Annie sighed, 'you're right. It's a long way in the past. Though not as long as Lindsay. But with that – with all of it – these things must surely diminish, lose their power, for each succeeding generation.'

'They do.'

'The emotion goes out of it, at any rate.'

'Our parents stamped the emotion out of it pretty quickly themselves, don't you think?' Tom asked, getting up to pace about the room with his glass of whisky. He came to a stop in the shadows by the round window, where the curtains remained open, so that he seemed to be looking out over the garden. But all Annie could see were their reflections, and the flicker of faint firelight, as if in another, dimmer room beyond, a different Tom and Annie talked of other things.

'That's why we don't talk about the past,' Annie said. 'To spare their feelings.'

'But –' Tom turned round, '– we go on talking to each other about it.'

'Well, I suppose I do. Why do you want to now, Tom? Has something happened? It has, what is it?'

'Och, I'm in a philosophical frame of mind. That's all. Meg is leaving.'

'Oh Tom. Another.'

'As you say,' he murmured, his voice dry. 'Another.'

'But she was married,' Annie sighed. 'Why have you never fallen for anyone suitable?'

'Free, you mean? Unfettered.'

'Who could marry you, have children . . .'

'Maybe I didn't want that.'

'Didn't you? Oh Tom, you must.'

Tom came and sat by the fire again. In the lamplight his thin face was softer and younger.

'A catalogue of loss, that's my life, Annie,' he said. 'Eh? Lindsay, and my mother. And then Mary, and nearly Jamie too. A pattern of loving and losing. So I don't exactly feel surprised that Meg's going too.'

'Och, that's rubbish,' Annie exclaimed. 'Mary would have married you if you'd given her the least encouragement. And Jamie *didn't die.*'

Tom laughed.

'You sound like your mother! Fat lot of sympathy I'm getting.'

Annie shook her head. 'Don't say that. I mean, my mother's right, anyway, when she says there's no point feeling sorry for yourself. I do, though, just as much as you.'

'How are things, anyway? You've seemed so cheerful since Rob appeared. Well, on the phone you do.'

'I'm fine. Graham's being a bit peculiar. Distant. Probably work. It's usually work. And I think he's not always as keen on Rob being there as I am. You get sort of set in your ways when you've no children to keep things changing, moving.' Her hands twisted in her lap for a moment. She seemed to be on the verge of tears, or of some revelation. But she gave herself a little shake. 'Never mind that – tell me about Meg.'

'They've sold the house at last. That's all.'

'She could stay, though? I mean, her kids are both away from home now.'

'I haven't asked her to.'

'Oh Tom.'

'It's no good. I'm fond of her, but a lifetime – not now, Annie. As you say, we get set in our ways. I'm too old and too crabbed.'

'You may think that – but you've got to fight against it! That's what's wrong with Graham – ach, I can't bear all this negative stuff. It's so *dreary*!'

'Well, maybe I'm dreary. A failed poet, I don't even write any more . . . let alone publish. No wife, no kids, a bookshop that makes no money, and I'm still living in the place where I was born.'

'You're back at the beginning,' Annie pointed out. 'You should be knowing the place for the first time.'

'You and your pal, T.S. Eliot,' Tom mocked. 'Got it taped, eh?'

'Oh, have some more whisky,' Annie said, picking up the bottle.

'Are we both drunk?' Tom asked. 'Or is it just me?'

'Both,' Annie said. 'Oh bugger, I've spilled some.'

'Here – watch. That's it. However drunk you are, my dear, mustn't waste a drop of this.'

'Mm. It is lovely, isn't it?'

'So are you.'

'What?'

'Bonny. A bonny woman. I often say as much to your husband.'

'Do you? More than he says, at any rate.'

'Aha. So that's it.'

'What's it?' Annie gulped whisky, frowned at him.

'He's got a floozie, has he? A bit on the side?'

'Ach, away with you, Tom. You don't know anything.'

Tom stretched out one foot in a worn argyle sock and touched hers. Their toes met, pushed gently against each other. Tom smiled.

'You are, you know. You're a bonny woman. In fact, that's the real reason I've never married. You're my ideal, perfection. No other woman could hope to measure up.' Annie laughed, shaking her head. 'No, I mean it – Graham's a real shite if he's having it off with somebody else. Tell him I said so.'

'Well, he's not, so blethers to you.' She smiled back at him, flushed and bonny, just as he said, in the glow of firelight.

In bed, Annie woke after an hour or two of heavy sleep, cold and sober. A jumble of dream pictures zigzagged in her head for a few seconds, then dissolved. She pulled the bedclothes up, tugged them round, turned over in a cocoon. But it was a chilly cocoon, and she was wide awake, worrying. It must be about three o'clock, she thought, all this negative thinking is worst at three o'clock. She tried to stop thinking altogether, but the demons crowded in, and her head throbbed. In one of those lost dreams, whose faint taste lingered meaningless and threatening, Graham had been smiling, but not at her. Then she remembered about Jamie, and the baby. How strange that the worst thing could lie in wait, minutes after consciousness. Why had she not told Tom?

She sat up and switched on the bedside lamp. But the bulb had died in the night. She rose and went unsteadily in the cold dark to the doorway and put on the main switch. Dazzled, she felt her way back to bed and picked up her watch. Four o'clock. Just as bad. And her bed as she got back in was chilly, with a hot-water bottle gone flabby and cold.

She wanted, very urgently, to phone Graham. What had come into her mind was the long visit she had made here when Jamie was convalescing, and the weekends she'd gone home. Oh, the lovemaking, she thought, it was the best ever. For an astonishing few seconds lust swelled, and she ached for him, or *no, for sex.* She lay with her eyes wide open, waiting for this to pass. I'll go downstairs, she thought, fill the bottle again. Then I might get back to sleep.

Thrusting her feet into slippers and pulling on her dressing gown, she went quietly downstairs, not putting on the lights, but feeling her way. The house was so cold she was shivering by the time she reached the kitchen. Tom must have left the light on: a line of yellow showed beneath the door. She opened it, blinked in brightness, entered warmth.

Rob was sitting at the table with a mug of tea.

'Oh – what a fright you gave me!'

'Sorry.'

'No, no, I couldn't sleep – got too cold. I thought Tom must have left the light on.' She lifted the kettle. 'Enough left for me? Yes, it'll do.' She raised the Aga lid and felt the heat flow out, warming her face and breast. Rob had only just made his tea, so the kettle boiled in a moment.

'What about you?' she asked, adding milk to her mug, and sitting opposite him. 'Did the cold wake you as well?'

'Yeah. I suppose.'

'Not . . . not a nightmare?'

'No.'

'You've been – well, it's a while since you had one. Isn't it?'

'I'm OK.'

'I know.' Annie sipped tea. Rob looked round the kitchen.

'He live here on his own, then?'

'His father – your great uncle Stuart – used to, but he moved out when Tom came back. Well, before that. The house was empty for a while.'

'Weird house, eh?'

'Did you never come here? When you were wee – I thought your mum and dad brought you.'

'Did I?'

'I'm sure—'

'I wasn't in that room, though, with the monkey? I'd have remembered that.'

'What?'

'There's a monkey – a toy, like – on the mantelpiece.'

'Oh, in the turret room. It was Jamie's – the monkey. It's a puppet, but he was too wee to work it when he got it, so Lindsay cut the bars and strings off to make it a toy he could play with.' She stopped, shrugged. 'Oh well. Anyway, that was Jamie's room when he was growing up.'

'Right.'

'You know about Lindsay?'

'Yeah, Mum said.'

'Not your dad – did Alistair not speak about her?'

'Not really.'

'So—'

'There was somebody in it, though,' Rob interrupted. 'I remember now – in the room I'm in. When I came here with Mum and Dad. Somebody was stayin' in it then, because Dad wouldn't let me go in.'

'Jamie,' Annie said. 'It must have been Jamie. Now, how old were you – d'you remember that? I'm trying to think when Jamie moved out—'

'So it was always his room, then?'

'No – later, after he got better – he was very ill, for weeks, and after that he didn't have a job. So he stayed on, but he moved to the room Tom used to have, at the back. It's much bigger. Stuart had left by then, and Tom took the big front bedroom.'

'So they was all, like, comin' and goin' – stayin' in the house, then goin' away, then back again?'

'You could say that. Yes, it's been a bit like that.'

'So the times they left, where'd they go?'

Annie, thinking of her conversation with Tom, wondered if perhaps Rob wasn't interested in Lindsay nearly so much as in the uncles he was getting to know for the first time. The living.

'University,' she said, answering Rob's question. 'Tom to Edinburgh, Jamie to Aberdeen. Then Tom travelled a bit, and Jamie had a series of jobs that seemed to go nowhere. He lived on Skye for a few years – well, one year, maybe. I forget. That was after Tom had come back. Tom taught in the Commercial College in Aberdeen for a while, hated it, came up to see his dad. Stuart suggested he work with him in the bookshop till he'd decided what to do next.'

'So when was that then?'

'Oh dear,' Annie sighed. 'Twenty years ago? Something like that.'

'So none of you's doin' a proper job then?' He grinned. 'Apart from Graham.'

Annie laughed. 'Well, Tom does supply teaching, and he runs the bookshop with Stuart. Not much money though. Jamie is an illustrator, who doesn't work all that hard at it, and lives off Ruth, and is very comfortable indeed. And I – well, I have Graham. I used to teach primary – years ago.'

'So why you so keen for me to get a job?'

'Oh hey, that's different.'

'How is it different?'

Annie wanted to say, look at us, you don't want to end up like us. But that would be disloyal to Tom and Jamie – and it seemed to admit too much. So instead she said what adults are supposed to say.

'The world's different now. And you're young, you should plan for the future.' She leaned towards him, tapping the table lightly with one hand. 'I want you to have an exciting life, Rob. A really full life.'

'So . . . you and Tom and Jamie – you all wish you'd got different lives?'

'Oh, I don't know.' Annie got up and went to the sink to pour away the rest of her tea. She had underestimated him. He's been watching us, she thought, sizing us up. If it hadn't been the middle of the night, if reality had not slipped away from her in this familiar kitchen, this loved house, more than once before – she might have shooed him off to bed with another platitude or two. But she sat down again, and pushing her hair away from her face with both hands, leaned on her elbows, her face framed by pretty well-kept fingers, and said, 'It's not easy. I mean, we've had easy lives, in many ways. But there's always the past. You don't get away from that – it kind of hangs over us.'

Rob seemed restless; he fidgeted with a spoon lying on the table.

'How d'you mean?'

'What happened to Lindsay—'

'That was years ago, though. Years and years.'

'I was eight,' Annie said.

'I can't hardly remember bein' eight,' he shrugged.

'Already?' Annie sighed. 'Me neither. It's not what we remember so much – it's what we don't remember, but our parents do.' She thought about this. 'Sorry, I'm not explaining it very well.'

'Doesn't matter.' He shifted on the kitchen chair, looked round.

'It was just that,' Annie persisted, 'it made it so important that *we* were all right. Behaved well, did the right things. Made up to our parents for what happened. Not that they ever said – only, you can't. Nobody, nothing, could make up for that.'

Suddenly, she wearied of this. Why bother? He was right, it was years and years ago.

'Anyway,' she said, 'what about you? If you're down here in the middle of the night at your age, there must be something bothering you.'

He scraped his chair back. 'I'm OK.'

'Oh, come on, Rob. You've been staying with me since New Year, and all I get out of you is that you were fed up and wanted a change. I just don't believe it. I never did, but I thought I'd give you time, a bit of space to sort yourself out.'

'Yeah, I'm fine. I'm OK now.'

He would not look at her. He was lying. But this was what always happened: the more she pushed, the further he retreated.

'But Rob,' she insisted, not caring now, for hadn't he been with her three months, got himself on a course (or she had, all right, she'd done that), and look at his hair, his skin. He could play chess better than Graham, he was even thinking about going along to the rugby club next season to train with the under 18s. No, she wouldn't back off this time, just because she was afraid he'd run away from her too.

'Something's happened. Were you in trouble of some sort?'

A fleeting grin lit his face for a second. 'You could say that.'

'Well?'

'What?'

'What sort of trouble?'

Then the telephone began to ring, making them jump. They both stared at it in disbelief.

'It's five o'clock,' Annie said, 'who on earth—' She got up. 'I hope there's nothing—' She was thinking of her mother. 'Hello?' Faint breathing, just a soft sigh, and the line went dead. 'That's odd. They hung up.'

'Wrong number,' Rob said. He'd got to his feet. 'I'm goin' back to bed, OK?'

'Right. Do you want a hot-water bottle?' She hoped not, wanting her own, and not being sure if any of the old ones left in the bathroom cupboard were fit for use. But he shook his head.

'No, it's OK.' He paused by the door. ''Night then.'

'Good night.'

When she reached the landing, Tom called from his room.

'Annie, is that you?'

'Yes. Couldn't sleep, went down for a bottle.'

'I thought I heard the phone.'

She went to his door and pushed it open. She couldn't see Tom in the darkness, but she made out the shape of the bed.

'You did. But whoever it was hung up when I answered. It was a woman, though.'

'How d'you know?'

'Just – oh well, I think it was.' She hesitated. 'Could it have been Meg? She must be feeling pretty low.'

'What time is it?'

'About five – quarter past. Something like that.'

'Christ.'

'What?'

'I hope it wasn't. It's not like her. She's very rational. Calm.'

'Oh Tom, you're absolutely hopeless. If she loves you—'

'She doesn't. Not like that.'

Annie lost patience. 'Tom,' she said, 'you're a fool. You don't have the first idea. No wonder Rob thinks we're all pathetic.' She went out, closing his door, and padded along the landing to her own room.

Tom was wide awake now. What did she mean – pathetic? No, he knew. And Rob was right. He lay in the dark, missing Meg. Not her, on the phone, at five in the morning. Someone suicidal or drunk, dialling the wrong number – no one they knew. Not Meg. She didn't care in that way, anyway, wasn't involved to that extent. Was she? He turned on his side, his arm reaching out to the empty place where she had lain, a still and quiet sleeper after lovemaking, her breathing so faint he would lie listening for it, touch her sometimes to make her stir, prove she still lived, was not a phantom, part of a dream. The bed was cold, and he missed her. This was the worst part, and it had happened with Mary too. Not just the itch for sex, though that was bad enough, a thing not solved or laid to rest whatever fantasy you indulged alone in the unsatisfactory dark. It was the warmth of the woman, her neat round bum tucked into your crotch, the fullness of her breast cupped in the hand you curved round her sleeping body, the scent and tickle of her hair under your chin.

Sometimes he did not know why he had sent Mary away. If she had simply hung on, they'd have ended up together. Probably. But she had given him an ultimatum to which there was only one answer. Marriage or nothing, she said. All right, he told her, you're not going to bully me into something we'll both regret.

Nothing. He had chosen nothing. So she had taken him at his word and gone. In a year, her sister was only too pleased to tell him, she had a good job in Edinburgh and was engaged to an accountant. In another year, she was pregnant. Would it have been better, or worse, he mused, if she and her husband hadn't gone to Canada, but appeared every summer with an increasing number of bairns, so that all he might have had was paraded in front of him, not just relayed by her sister? As it was, he still saw Mary childishly slender and young, full of dreams, wanting none of him if she couldn't have it all.

Was there any chance now of getting back to sleep? I'll count to five hundred, name the counties of Scotland, the Munros I have climbed, he told himself, reviving childish solutions, and if I'm not asleep, I'll put on the light and read. Or just get up. Sometimes, in these early hours, images formed and re-formed, and a poem was written by breakfast. He had written so much after Mary went. Mary gone, Jamie close to death, and yet he had written ceaselessly, faultlessly. His best work. My only work, he thought now, consumed with the self-pity that embraces the hour before daylight, annihilating.

Annie curled herself round her hot-water bottle, wishing Graham were there too. I wonder, she thought, if he would care enough to lie awake and phone me at five in the morning, if he thought we were breaking up. She couldn't imagine it. But anyway, it was too remote and terrible a possibility. Not that she didn't entertain it from time to time, especially when she had been with Cath. But people like us, she always decided, stay together, work things out. And yet, as she thought of the way they had parted, and of how he had absolutely refused to discuss Jamie and Ruth, she had a sense of something not quite strong enough to be called misgiving. No, it was no more than an uneasy movement in her chest. She sighed and shifted on to her other side, turning her back on doubt.

4

Annie didn't often go away from home on her own. Graham couldn't remember the last time, though it must have happened since the summer Jamie was ill. That was long ago: he looked back on Annie and himself at that time as if they were different people, young and full of hope. Odd that – they'd had a terrible couple of years, with Alistair and Shona splitting up, Jamie nearly dying, and all through it, her periods dead on every month, no sign of pregnancy, despite the many tests they'd had, the operation to clear her tubes, all that stuff. This time, of course, she wouldn't be gone so long.

And yet, on that Friday morning as she packed for Rob and herself, and prepared to leave, he felt as if he was about to be set free. He had to go to work, of course, but that was fine, work attracted him. Like an adolescent drawn to school by a sudden crush on a teacher, some unattainable, infinitely desirable other – that was how daft he was. But he knew he'd been difficult at home.

'I've a lot on my mind,' he had told Annie the night before, by way of apology when she complained he was grumpier than ever.

'What?' she asked. 'What have you got on your mind?'

'Work,' he said, 'what d'you think?'

'Oh, work.' She shrugged and turned away, dismissing this.

'Aye, work. You don't mind the cheque at the end of the month, I notice. Just the fact that earning it gives me some grief now and again.'

'You were the one who said I should stop work,' she snapped.

'What's that got to do with it?' He was genuinely bewildered, but that irritated her even more.

'Well, saying I don't do my share – just live off you. I run after you like a *slave—*'

'No one's ever asked you to.' He was tired of this – what a nag she was turning into. He hated the way his own restlessness provoked her, making something of nothing, so that he was all the more conscious how awry their lives were, getting worse. And yet it justified him too, justified all the other feelings that away from home, overwhelmed him.

Then he picked up his half drunk coffee, leaving the kitchen, leaving it to her.

'God, Annie, it's years since you left work. You've had plenty of opportunity to find yourself something else to do.'

'I never stop,' she protested, 'I'm on the go the whole time, doing things, for *other people*.'

'Good works,' he sneered, going out unfairly on this exit line, leaving her furious, helpless, and then in tears.

But after a few minutes, she dried her eyes, and got up to clear the dishes and tidy the kitchen. The *Archers*' music surprised her: she realised she'd not heard a word of the programme. All those pretend lives – how could she have been so interested in them? But she had been, for years. Those unreal people were more present for her than the starving, the wrongly imprisoned, the flood and earthquake victims who crowded the news.

She made herself a mug of tea, and took it through, a little uncertainly, to the living room where Rob was lying along the sofa watching television, while Graham marked papers. She was surprised to see him there, and not in the study. Usually, he insisted he couldn't work if there was any noise – the buzz of her sewing machine in the next room annoyed him.

'Shove over,' she said to Rob, who moved his legs, but put them back across her knees as soon as she'd sat down. She rested her arms on them, the mug of tea in both hands. 'Mind my tea.'

She couldn't follow the programme he was watching. Something about aliens, who were recognisable only by the third eye in their foreheads. For the rest, they were very like the human crew of the spaceship. Both sets of creatures were solemn, and all (she decided) terrible actors. She said so to Rob.

He grinned. 'Yeah, but it's good.'

'What's happening?' she asked. 'Are they stuck on the ship, is that it, held to ransom?'

'Not really.'

She waited, but he went on watching. 'Well, what then?'

'Oh, for God's sake, Annie, let him watch it in peace.'

Tears sprang to her eyes again. He was impossible – it wasn't just that he was tired. Why should she put up with this? And in front of Rob.

''S OK,' Rob said. ''S finished, any road.'

'Oh, right.'

They watched commercials instead, and the cat came up and tried to curl round between Rob's legs and Annie's lap. She kneaded them both, purring, digging claws in.

'She's mad, your cat,' Rob said. 'We never had a cat – just Rebel.'

Annie wanted to say, *Do you miss him a lot?* but she was afraid he'd say, *Yes, can I have him here?* Partly, that was what she wanted too. If Rebel came, he'd be more grounded with them, fixed, permanent. But she couldn't face raising this with Graham. So instead she murmured, 'Oh we've always had cats.' Graham looked up and closed his file.

'I'm for dogs,' he said. 'A dog is faithful. Basically a yes man, but faithful.'

'Cats can be faithful too,' Annie protested. 'And they're more interesting.'

Graham snorted. 'How can you say that? Remember Tiger?'

'Oh, Tiger. But he was the only cat I've ever known do *that*.'

'What did he do, then?' Rob wasn't much interested in cats, but Graham and Annie suddenly seemed so animated, as if they'd discovered the one thing they had in common, and were bursting to talk about it.

'Oh, we had this cat, Tiger, we didn't call him that of course, he came with the name. He belonged to an old lady up the road – when we were not long married, in our first house. Not here. Anyway, he came round a lot.'

'She encouraged him,' Graham interrupted. 'Kept giving him food. Big mistake.'

'Well, the old lady was a bit forgetful. In the end, they carted her off to a home, and the cat was left. Her niece was clearing out the house, and I said, was she taking the cat.'

'No, you didn't – you begged her to leave him for you.'

'She didn't seem very kind.' Annie defended this. 'I didn't like the look of her.'

'So you got the cat?'

'*He* got *us*.' Graham shook his head. 'He knew which side his bread was buttered. Or his tin opened.'

'He stayed,' Annie said, 'for about a year.'

'Then the ungrateful beast buggered off. Moved in with an elderly gent in the next street. Higher quality of cat food, I assume. Plentiful supply of mice and sparrows.'

'You do get cats like that—'

'Opportunists. Eye to the main chance.'

'Some of them just stay with one set of people for a while, till you think they're settled. Then they suddenly move on – for no apparent reason. Maybe he was always looking for an old person to replace his old lady. Someone who'd be at home all the time. I was working full time then.'

Annie and Graham were conscious that this brought them uncomfortably back to the argument in the kitchen. But before she could dwell on it, Rob heaved his legs to the floor.

'I get a bag of crisps?'

'Yes, help yourself.'

'Get me a beer,' Graham said. A pause. 'You want one, Rob?'

Rob hesitated. 'No, it's OK.' He turned at the door. 'Thanks.' He began to go out, then stopped again. 'You want anythin', Annie?'

'No, no, I'm fine.'

Alone with Graham, she said, 'He's really at home now, don't you think?'

'I'm not having the dog,' he told her, getting up to put a file back in his briefcase.

'I didn't—'

'No, but you're thinking it.'

'Ach.' She got up, impatient with him now. 'I wish—'

But she didn't know what she wished. For a few minutes they had been almost companionable, the three of them. Like a family. But it was an illusion, it wouldn't last. She was glad to be going away with Rob, and she looked forward to talking to Tom, who would comfort her.

So when, at the weekend, she had gone, they were both aware

of not parting well. Graham knew Ruth's pregnancy stirred the old longings, but he couldn't do anything about them. That was the trouble all along – he never had. He turned from all this with relief. Beneath his irritability at home, he was carrying around all the time, like a kind of inner torch, a sense of excitement, impending disaster. On the Friday, he found he was unable to go on doing nothing about it.

It was the end of the afternoon. He and Jan had been discussing a pupil, who was more often out of school than in it. In the end, they decided to tackle the parents again.

'It won't work,' Jan said, 'but I suppose we'd better try.' She got up to leave.

'You doing anything tonight?' he asked, not wanting her to go now. 'Busy weekend?'

'No, not really. TV, I suppose. Sad, isn't it, when the highlight of the week is a bottle of wine and the gardening programme?' She smiled at him, making for the door.

'I just wondered – fancy a drink instead?'

'Tonight?'

'Yes – I'm not a gardening fan. More of a pub fan, I suppose.'

'Me too,' she said, 'when I get the chance.'

'Well,' he offered, taking courage, making the leap, 'you get the chance tonight.'

'But—'

'Annie's away for the weekend. Could slump in front of the TV, I suppose . . . but I'd rather have some company.'

'All right,' she said slowly. 'I'd like to.'

'I'll pick you up about eight?'

'Yes, fine.'

He knew where she lived: her house was only a ten-minute walk from the school, but three weeks ago her car had been in the garage for several days and he'd given her lifts home. She had a pile of marking, and her leather briefcase, well-worn, sagged with the weight. They had sat outside her house for increasing periods of time, talking. On the last night before she was due to pick up her car, they'd left school late, after a parents' evening. She'd invited him in for coffee, but he'd said no, thinking her son would be there. He knew the older one was away at university, but the younger was still at home. Thinking of this, as he drove home, half sorry he'd turned down her invitation, he wondered how old she was. Must have started young, to have adult sons. But this was almost all he knew about her life. They'd not talked about themselves, just school: pupils, exams, meetings, guidance – all the things they shared at work. And in the thick of all this, something had ignited between them. That was how it seemed to him.

The house was silent except for the dog's bark when he heard Graham's key in the lock. The cat, waking from sleep in the basket chair, stretched out her front paws, claws extended and yawned fishily at him, her teeth tiny white fangs in a clean pink mouth. Both animals made for their empty dishes. He fed them, changed out of his suit, then fetched the lead and called the dog who came at a trot, having been let out only briefly at lunch-time by the neighbour who helped when Annie wasn't there. The cat sat on the front steps as they drove off, washing her chest with long smooth strokes.

He meant to walk in Hazlehead woods for an hour. It was light till after eight now the clocks had changed. It had been a blustery day, the sun appearing in fits and starts between scudding clouds. There were crocuses on the verges, and signs of green in buds on the bare trees. Graham was surprised to find himself noticing all this. He was full of energy. On Friday nights he usually slumped on the sofa with a can of beer, telling Annie he was knackered, letting her run round him. Only – since Rob's arrival it hadn't been quite like that. The boy had taken up most of her attention.

'She spoils him,' he said aloud to the retriever waiting at a fork in the track. They took the left branch, and he strode on, thinking about Jan again, and the weekend ahead.

What he felt, he realised, was the kind of tingling excitement that vanishes after marriage. Well, before that. What did he think was going to happen? But the answer to that was obvious. However often he told himself there was no chance (what the hell was he playing at anyway, even *thinking* about it), he could not make the thought lie down, any more than he could make his cock lie quiet. It rose up, as his hopes did, anticipating. He hadn't felt like this since – no – he had never felt like this. On the edge of his excitement was the black shadow of guilt. That was what he kept pushing away. They were back at the car-park, and he had walked the last half of their circuit without noticing he'd done it. He unlocked the car, and called the dog. Then he drove home telling himself he'd be a fool to take the risk.

But when Jan opened the door and asked him in, all his common sense dissolved.

'I'm not ready,' she said. 'Sorry. I'd to take Colin to his friend's house. They're going to see a film and he's spending the night at Steven's.' She stood back. 'Sorry – come in.'

She had just washed her hair; it was still damp, and lay like dark shiny wings on either side of her thin face. She wore a tartan man's dressing gown too big and bulky for her. Her neck rose fragile from the wide collar, and in the hollows of her collarbone, the skin was still moist from her bath.

'Would you like a beer?' she asked. 'I won't be long.'

He drank a can of Export and flicked through her evening paper while he waited. Her house was a nineteen-fifties Dutch bungalow, granite built, set above the street, with a neglected rockery in front and a square drying green bordered by shrubs at the back. The living room where he sat was plain, the chairs good but old, and there was a heavy oak table in the window. The wooden shelf above the gas fire was bare except for some opened mail and a brass clock. There were no pictures and no flowers, but a long low bookcase took up almost the whole of the wall behind the sofa. He went to examine it. Science fiction, a few modern novels, travel and biography. The science fiction probably belonged to her sons. The books, the room, did not tell him much. None of it answered the excitement he'd been feeling since he'd left her at school that afternoon. He had made a mistake, this was all a blunder.

'Right – shall we go?'

He gulped the last of his cold beer and stood up. 'Sure.'

He had lost the knack. What did you say, how did you get the two of you out of the house and into an appropriate drinking place without embarrassment? In a flash of self-pity, he longed for the familiarity of Annie, her anxious but routine *Do I look all right?* his habitual *Fine, come on, we're late.* Then he pursed his lips, gave a low whistle.

'You look great.'

She coloured, smiled. 'Thanks.'

At school she wore grey or black suits, he seemed to recall, with a white blouse. Neutral, functional. She seemed softer now, no longer teacherish and smart. He opened the car door for her and drove away with a surge of confidence.

They went out on the South Deeside road, to a country hotel.

'This do?' he asked, turning into the car-park.

'Wonderful – I haven't been here before.'

'They've done it up – it's a lot better now.'

They passed the restaurant, where people were dining at pink clad tables by candlelight.

'The food's supposed to be good here, isn't it?' Jan asked, as they went into the lounge.

'So they say.' Maybe they should have come for a meal, he thought. No, that would have been overdoing it. Wouldn't it?

They found an empty corner.

'What would you like?' He glanced round. 'They have a great selection of malts here – what about one of those?'

'All right,' she said, 'but I don't know anything about them. You choose.'

He bought something he was sure she wouldn't know, showing off, not quite realising he was doing so. But he wanted to be a different man from the one in the office, on the school stage at assembly, in the classroom. What was it about teachers, he wondered, makes them want to prove that really, underneath, that's not what they are. She was doing the same, as she ranged over her past life, the other jobs she'd done before having children. Teaching had suited her when the boys were young.

'I suppose you could say I've made a career of it now,' she said. 'And it came just in time – when John and I split up.'

He expected the divorce story, but it didn't come, and he held back from asking, not wanting to talk about his own marriage. Then his hand brushed hers, lifting her empty glass to take it back to the bar. As he rose, she looked up at him, and the tilt of her head on its long neck made him feel guilty and reckless.

When he came back with another drink for her, Coke for

himself, since he was driving, they did not talk any longer about school. A little fuelled by alcohol, flushed, she relaxed. Eventually, the bar became very crowded and noisy, and Graham suggested they go on somewhere else.

'Well, actually, I don't mind going home,' Jan smiled. 'I'm really tired. Friday night syndrome.'

'Fine, let's go then.'

In the car she leaned back with her eyes closed.

'Oh dear,' she murmured. 'Shouldn't have had the last drink.'

When he stopped for a red traffic light, her throat, her hands folded in her lap, were bleached pale by the street lamps. His hands tightened on the wheel.

As they turned into her street, she opened her eyes and said, pulling herself up in the seat, 'Hey, I'm falling asleep here. Sorry. You want to come in for a cup of tea – toast?'

'You're too tired,' he hesitated. 'Otherwise . . .'

'No – I'm OK now. I could do with something to eat, anyway. Too much drink, not enough food. I didn't eat much tonight.'

'Well – there's the dog,' he said. 'I'm later than usual. I have to let him out.'

'Oh. Right.'

He drew up at the door, and they sat there for a moment in silence, the engine purring.

'Thank you, then,' she said at last. 'It's been lovely. Really nice.'

'I could – it's not far, and he's had quite a walk today. I could take him round the block, and then come back here for the toast.'

'Yes – all right. If you want to. OK.' She opened the car door, slid her long legs out, picked up her bag from the floor of the car. As she did so, her smooth hair swung forward, fanning out. He wanted to touch it, stopped himself in time.

'Twenty minutes,' he said, 'at most. If you're sure . . . ?'

'Yes,' she said. 'I'm sure. I'll put the kettle on.'

Walking the dog briskly to the end of the street, he did not change his mind. It was as good as done. He drove back to her house very fast through the quiet suburbs, slowed as he reached her street, cruised quietly to her door.

'I'll just make the tea,' she said as she let him in. 'You weren't long.' She waved him towards the living room. 'Have a seat.' The gas fire was on; it felt warm.

They were both awkward now. She seemed more distant, and he began to wish he hadn't come.

'Any chance of a drink?' he asked. 'For someone who's spent the night in a pub, I feel unnaturally sober.'

'Sure,' she said. She opened a cupboard in the hall. 'No malt, I'm afraid.' He waited as she retrieved first one bottle, then another. 'Sherry – no. Been here since Christmas, half-finished. Cans of Export . . . here's some whisky, will that do?'

'Great,' he said. 'But I hope you're still making the toast?'

She laughed. 'I am. I'm starving – don't know why.'

He felt better with the whisky burning in his throat, and leaned on the lintel of the kitchen door, glass in hand, while she made toast. The smell of it filled the kitchen. But she was still out of reach, busy in her own place. Could he have misread the signs after all? Then she brushed past him with the plate of toast, butter melting in pools on thick slices, and beneath the aroma of that, he scented something else, and his body beat a strong pulse in answer.

He did not think her beautiful. Annie was still his ideal of beauty for women – plump and dark and rosy. Jan was long and lean, but there was something in the turn of her head, the way she crossed one long leg over the other, the rasp of her tights, that made him unsteady with lust, utterly single-minded. Yet here they were talking about work again, schools they had taught in before this one, and he was repeating things he'd said over and over in the past, mouthing memories that had no interest for him now.

They reached for the last slice of toast at the same time, and their hands collided.

'You have it,' she smiled. But the smile vanished as his fingers grasped hers, and she shook her head. 'Oh dear.'

'Sorry,' he said, drawing back.

'No, it's all right. Really.' And she moved over smoothly, sank down beside him, let him draw her into his arms.

'Bed,' she said a moment later, taking her mouth from his with a gasp. Graham was reaching beneath clothes to skin, skin to a deeper place, and did not pause. 'Bed,' she murmured, 'easier there . . .'

Afterwards, he was astonished at his own urgency; at the time, what he was conscious of was hers.

In bed, he felt in control, since she was pliant, willing, open to him almost at once. Then she seized him as he entered her, and her nails were sharp on his back, her legs gripped him. She's hungry, he thought. I wonder how long? And he pitied her, her solitary life, till pity dissolved in lust again and he drew out only just in time.

'Sorry,' he said. 'Should've . . .'

'Me too,' she sighed, grabbing a handful of tissues, cleaning them both up. 'Sorry, I do have condoms – I just—' she exhaled, lay back. 'It's been a while. Well, a long while. Probably past the sell-by date.' She grimaced, as if it were herself she referred to.

They lay side by side; he reached out and took her long-fingered hand in his. She grasped it, rolled her head on to the curve of his neck and shoulder.

I should feel guilty, he thought. What a bastard. But in truth he felt only relief. A long time for him too, since this sort of savage satisfaction.

Later, she hunted out the packet of Durex.

'It probably doesn't matter now,' she said. 'I haven't had a period for over six months.' For a moment, he didn't realise what she meant. How old was she? Older than Annie, older than he was. And yet she didn't look it. Even naked, all that showed of the children she'd had were a slight slackness in her belly, and faint white papery scars she said were stretchmarks. He traced them now, gently, with one finger, as they lay down again. She was still holding the little packet, and she held it up, explained she'd had it since her last affair, a short-lived one, that had happened not long after her husband left.

'I had something to prove,' she said. 'But I don't know whether I proved it or not . . .'

'You're terrific,' he said. 'No need to prove anything.'

Slowly, steadily, they began again, and he stayed till morning.

In the High House, on Saturday morning, Annie and Tom

took the dog along the shore, and she told him Ruth was
pregnant.

'I don't know why I didn't say last night,' she said. 'It was on
my mind, oh, all the time, but Jamie didn't want me to, and
Graham was so difficult about it.'

'It's hard . . . hard,' Tom said, 'to take it in. The last thing I
– God, I know it's ridiculous, he's nearly thirty-nine, but he
doesn't seem old enough, somehow. Jamie. And Ruth – what
does she think?'

'How would I know?' Annie threw a stick for Bracken, who
lumbered after it, picked it up, dropped it again, and stood
looking at them both. But they had stopped, and were looking
not at her but at each other.

'Ach, Annie, I'm sorry. Are you all right?'

'No, of course I'm not, but it's utterly mean of me to be
anything but pleased for Jamie.'

'And Ruth.'

'Oh, I don't know. I don't think *she's* thrilled, not like Jamie.
And the worst thing is, that gives me some sort of perverted
satisfaction. I don't know why. I must be a horrible person.'

'You're not. Of course you're not. Oh Annie.'

'I'm sorry, Tom, it's only you I could say this to – only you.
No one else could understand.'

Not Graham, he thought, but did not say. He took Annie's
hand and tucked it under his arm, so that they walked on linked
together. More calmly, she related what Jamie had told her about
Ruth's job.

'It hardly seems fair, does it?' Tom said. 'That she should care
so much about her job, so little about having kids, and yet she's
the one . . .'

'Oh, it's not as simple as that,' Annie broke in. 'Of course it's
not fair, but I've thought that for years – when men are arrested
for abusing their children, when mothers neglect them, leave
them to get burned by unguarded fires, when a child disappears
because no one was looking after her properly – I used to get so
angry and upset. But not now – what's the point? *All* of life is
unfair. And I'm very lucky. I have an awful lot.'

'I used to think,' Tom said, 'you got upset about all that because
of Lindsay as much as anything else.'

'No, not really.' She paused, looked up at him. 'Perhaps it was all mixed up in my head for a long time. Your mother's grief, and then when she died, my mother's. All that loss and pain.'

'We can't compete, can we?' Tom gave a bark of laughter. 'Not a chance. What on earth could we suffer, as terrible as that?'

'That's what *I* kept thinking! And I felt so guilty complaining about *anything*. In fact, I never do now – to my mother.'

'So,' Tom said, 'we'd better just be pleased for Jamie and Ruth, and they'd better just be pleased for themselves.'

Annie tucked her hand into the crook of Tom's arm again, and they walked on. But the tide was coming in, and they had to move apart to negotiate the rocks and jump over pools. As they reached a stretch of flat beach again, the sun broke through and the air seemed warmer. Annie unzipped the front of her fleece as they stopped to wait for the dog to catch up.

'We'd better go back,' Tom decided. 'She's wearying.' They turned, facing into the wind now. But still it seemed warm, with the sun on their backs.

Annie was thinking about Ruth, but Tom said abruptly, 'I'm going to miss Meg.'

'Oh Tom, can't you ask her to stay?'

'She's married. I won't do that.'

'It's a funny kind of morality you have,' Annie commented.

'I don't know what that means.'

'I think you do. You seem to be saying it's all right to sleep with her when her husband's away, but not to want to have her altogether.'

'That's it,' Tom said. 'Anyway, it's not my decision. It's hers.'

'But how can she stay, if you don't ask?'

Tom shrugged. 'Well, I won't, that's all.'

'You're a fool.'

'Probably.'

'Let's not quarrel—'

'I'm not.'

'It's just – poor Meg – yet with me you're so kind and understanding—'

'That's different.'

Annie did not ask why; she could see from the tightness in his face that he was unhappy. Damn Jamie and Ruth, she thought, upsetting us all. And yet now there would be a child in this childless family. It must be a good thing. *If I can't be a mother, I'll be an aunt.* That might be really lovely, and if Ruth's working – she stopped it there, afraid of what her imagination might conjure, afraid to let it run on.

Tom was wondering how Stuart would take to being a grandfather.

'Do you think he'll like it?' Annie asked.

'Och, you never know with him,' Tom said. 'He pretends he's out of it, too old to care what happens. That's his line. *I'm old, son, don't you bother about me.* Then when Jamie and I do take matters into our own hands, get the shop on the market – he's done nothing but girn that nobody considers him at all.'

'But don't you think,' Annie suggested, 'that when people get older, all their most prominent characteristics get stronger, exaggerated. He was always a bit awkward.' She laughed. 'He'll adore the baby, though – just to wrong-foot us.'

'Aye, maybe.' Tom smiled. 'You'll be looking forward to old age with Graham then.'

'What?'

'All his familiar traits getting exaggerated.'

'Oh Tom, don't. Graham's all right. He's been very good with Rob.'

'Thought he was fed up with him?'

'No,' Annie said, being honest, 'I think it's probably me he's fed up with.' And she sighed, filled with a longing for home, and making it all right again with Graham.

In Jan's bed, Graham woke groggy, hungover. This was unfair: he hadn't had much to drink, had he? He shifted, and became aware, with a shock of astonished memory, that the woman whose body curved into his was not Annie.

Good God, what have I done?

He opened his eyes. It was daylight, and the thin curtains made the room only shadowy. Jan stirred. He moved his hand down her flank and over the slope of her hip, round her belly, and down between her thighs. She turned in his arms smelling of sex and sleep and smoke from the bar they'd sat in the previous night. How often he'd wakened with an erection like this, bursting with it, and felt it to be useless, wasted. Her legs parted and he moved over her, and though her hand came down to guide him in, there was no need, he was finding his own way. She moaned as he pushed deep inside, her legs came up and round him as they had the night before. He was held, desired, enveloped. The blood pounded in his temples, and the room darkened round them.

They lay together for a long time afterwards, sealed by sweat, cooling, not speaking. Graham began to wonder how he was going to extricate himself, from the bed, the house, what he had done. Because he had to, there was no question. This couldn't happen again. It wasn't the start of anything. It wasn't an affair. But he felt grateful to her, and he thought she was grateful too.

'I have to go now,' he said at last.

'Want some breakfast first?'

'What about your kids – when do they get back?'

'There's only Colin, and he won't turn up till lunch-time at least.'

'All right. Breakfast. Then I'll get back.'

'OK. Right.'

He lay and listened to the shower running, music from the radio. Then she came through, still naked, her hair wet, and gave him a clean towel.

'Have a shower if you like,' she said. 'I'll put coffee on. You want bacon?'

'Great.'

In the morning, her kitchen was sunny and warm. He had a bacon sandwich and strong coffee, and felt better. They divided the newly delivered paper between them, and read it companionably, in silence.

'Look,' he said at last, finishing his coffee, 'I'd better go. See to the dog . . . and so on.' She looked up, smiling at him. Her hair was lightening as it dried in sunlight, and gleamed as she moved her head. She wore jeans and a loose T-shirt, and looked younger than she ever did at school. And yet there were fine lines round her eyes; she was pale and slightly wan, not young. A spasm of lust twitched at him again.

'Thanks,' he said. 'It was – well – thanks. I loved it.'

She grinned. 'So did I.'

She went with him to the front door.

Graham hesitated. 'I – what about tonight? You fancy a meal out, or something?'

She looked at him with her eyes narrowed, appraising the situation, or him.

'How long have you got?'

'What – on my own?' Something kept him from saying Annie's name. Guilt. Shame. Some emotion he didn't want to feel yet. 'Monday or Tuesday. So—'

'All right,' she said.

'No strings,' he said, ashamed of this, at any rate, but knowing he had to say it. 'I can't—'

'I know,' she said. 'I do know.'

He drove home in a wave of triumph, relief, singing along with the tape he was playing, loudly.

The house smelt stale, as if Annie had been gone a long time. He let the dog go into the garden, put out food for him and the cat. The cat sniffed her dish and stalked away, ignoring him. She was Annie's cat, and acknowledged him only as a favour which he did not often seem to deserve. *Bloody animal, you'd think it knew.*

There were three messages on the answerphone, in ascending order of guilt.

Annie? It's Alistair. Look, I'm going to come up for Easter weekend, see Rob, sort something out a bit more – I've spoken to Shona. I'll ring again. Right.'

Oh – oh, it's that machine. Anne? It's Mum. I must have missed you, I thought you weren't going till today. Will you phone me when you get home? Ah – yes. Goodbye then.

This is Debbie from Debenham's, with a message for Mrs Gibson. The curtains you ordered are ready for collection. Thank you.

I am knitted into this house, he thought, this marriage, her family. But Jan had wanted him, taken him. She didn't want kids, or a home, or a listening ear for all her disappointments, losses, the clinging past. And her family – whoever they were – had nothing to do with him.

He went upstairs to change, then he whistled the dog and drove up to the woods to take him for a long walk.

*   *   *

In their German kitchen, over a table laid with Denby breakfast china, the air perfumed with good Colombian coffee and wholemeal toast, Ruth and Jamie faced each other, she in defiance, he in helpless protest.

'You can't,' he said. 'You just can't, Ruth. We'll manage, it'll be all right. It's meant to happen – you *can't*.'

But he could not reach or touch or move her. They gazed at each other without understanding, and for the first time since she had come to find him, without love.

5

When Graham had gone, Jan went into her living room. She sat on the sofa where last night he had leaned over, putting his arms round her, and she had lain back, waiting for his kiss, his next move.

Some years ago, she had been in a car accident. It was a bad one, but she'd come out completely unhurt. The day after it had happened, she had felt like this: unreal, shocked out of herself. And combined with this white shock in her mind, a blank space of otherworldliness, she had had all through her body, over and over, waves of langorous sleepiness.

She lay back on the sofa cushions, heavy, washed by fatigue. This room did not get the sun till afternoon, so it was cool and dim. But she felt it would be hours before she cooled too, she had become so absolutely warm, all the way through. For what seemed a long time, she lay there, allowing the crowded images of last night, this morning, to pass through semi-consciousness. She recreated every word and touch and cry and kiss.

Eventually, this faded, and she opened her eyes.

'What am I doing?' she asked aloud. 'What's going on?' Then she got up and went back into the kitchen.

Graham was not the sort of man she liked, usually. When she'd first come to the school, she'd thought him abrupt, difficult. Everyone said he was notoriously short-tempered. He terrified first years, and probationer teachers. He won't intimidate me, she thought, determined to stand her ground, make a good thing of this new job. But she saw quite soon that the manner and the man diverged. He was a patient teacher, kind when pupils were struggling, though sharp with bright but lazy ones. Once, as she passed a classroom where he was teaching, the whole class erupted into loud laughter, and looking in, she saw his pleased beam: they liked his joke. She warmed to him, paid him more attention.

But she'd thought of nothing but work, hadn't intended this. Of all the stupid things to do, having an affair with someone at school was the stupidest. She'd despised other foolish teachers for it in the past. But of course, it wasn't really an affair. She checked herself, stopped in the middle of drying glasses, gazed out of the window at her small square of back garden. It was only sex. One off, not to be repeated. A mistake. But oh, oh, the *sex* – she tingled again, lust thickening at the core of her, spreading outwards to thighs, breasts, throat. Weakened, she leaned on the work surface, closed her eyes. It had been such a *long time*.

This, the warm ache of desire, it confused everything. Because she wasn't *in love*. And yet, when he asked her out, it was as if a door had opened that she had been gazing at for ages. But it was no good, he was married. No children though. She'd asked him once, some time ago, when she'd been talking about her own, and he seemed interested. 'No,' he'd said curtly, 'none.' So she had changed the subject, aware of touching the edge of some pain she didn't really want to know about. Now she wished she did know. Then changed her mind. Better not.

But how would they – could they – meet in school now, pretending nothing had happened?

'You fool,' she exclaimed. 'You bloody *stupid woman*.' And wept briefly, hating herself, and him. Then the phone rang, and it was her son, wanting to know where she was, she was supposed to be picking them up for football training.

'I forgot,' she said. 'I forgot it was my week. I'm sorry – I'm on my way.'

Graham was having second thoughts.

He shouldn't have said he'd see her tonight. As if it were the start of something. It wasn't. They had to go on teaching in the same school, for one thing. At the thought of this, he shuddered. Rooks gathered in the tops of the trees, raucous, mocking. The wind shook the branches, blew clouds off the sun. It was a fine Spring day, the sort of day he was usually glad of on a Saturday, when he could get out of the house, and walk the dog for miles.

Certainly he had walked a long way. He took stock: where were they? The dog looked round, waiting for him. 'All right,' he said, 'on you go,' and the animal did, nosing the ground, seeking new trails. Graham followed, more slowly. *As long as no one found out.* He kept his personal life separate from school. He did not talk about Annie or family matters when he was at work. If pupils dared to ask him personal questions, he lied outrageously. No one older than twelve believed a word he said. But now? The utter stupidity of what he – they – had done, rose up and confronted him. *Oh God.* And yet, he wasn't sorry. He threw a stick for the dog with enormous force, so that the retriever had to bound after it, his golden coat catching the sunlight as he slithered to a halt, seized it in his jaws. *I'm not sorry.*

He whistled the dog, and they set off down a track that would eventually lead them back to the car-park. Just this weekend, he promised himself, and I'll make it clear, so she'll understand. She's a bright woman, she knows already. And there was no . . . persuasion. She knew what she was doing, she wanted it for Christ's sake. We're adults, we both know the score. This sounded weak, even to him. But he kept telling himself it was how it had to be.

Jan called for him soon after seven. She had offered to drive, so that he could have a drink this time. He came out at once, and followed her down the path to her car. She was wearing something long and silky, that clung to her thighs as she walked. Lust seized him again, crippling.

'Am I late?' she asked as they fastened seat belts. 'It was a bit of a rush – Simon came home today.'

'Your son.'

'The older one, back from Glasgow for Easter. I wasn't expecting him so soon, but he's fixed up a job for a couple of weeks with my ex-husband's firm. So he's back to spend a few days with me first.'

'Your . . . ex lives in Glasgow, right?'

'Yes.'

They drove on in silence. I don't want to know, Graham was thinking, about her life, her family, her kids. I just want the sex, and so does she. That's all.

'What's he studying, your son?' he asked.

'Electrical engineering.'

'He like it?'

'Yes, it's OK. Likes the social life, anyway.' She laughed. 'Don't they all?'

'I was at Glasgow,' he said. 'It was great.'

He had booked a table at an Italian restaurant in the city centre. It was busy and the waiters wore red aprons and shouted at each other in what sounded like Italian, though they spoke to the customers in broad Aberdeen. Graham and Jan followed one of them to a table near the back. There was a checked tablecloth, a candle stuck in a wine bottle, and two giant menus.

'This do?'

'Lovely. I've never been here – everyone says the food's good, though.'

'Not bad,' he said, as if he had some personal responsibility for it. They sat down and discussed what to eat.

'I can't ask you back – like last night,' Jan said, when they had reached the tiramisu and coffee.

'No – sure – your kids are there.'

'Yes, with the boys at home . . . I mean, you're welcome to come and meet them, have more coffee—'

'No.' He was quite definite about this. 'That's OK.' But he was all at once dismayed. Where then, if not her place?

His house. His and Annie's. Out of the question. He looked across the table at Jan, digging her spoon into layers of dessert, the fall of her pale hair framing her thin face with its high-bridged nose. She had strong hands, bony wrists.

Conscious of his eyes on her, she looked up, smiled.

'You look great,' he said. 'You're gorgeous – why is there no man?' He'd had most of a carafe of red wine, didn't care what he said.

She flushed. 'Too busy,' she said. 'Kids, job . . . no time.'

'Can't believe that.' He was out of the way of paying compliments, and yet he wanted to. 'I'll get the bill,' he decided. 'OK?'

'Yes, but let me pay my share.' He was out of the way of this, too.

'Certainly not.'

'Really.' She dipped into her bag, took out two ten-pound notes and handed them over. He took one, gave the other back.

'OK, thanks.'

She leaned back, feeling somehow patronised, as he raised his hand for the waiter. He was a handsome man, even if he wasn't her type. Her husband had been thin, a graceful man, ascetic. When they were young, people had said they looked alike. Graham's breadth, his burly strength, both repelled and drew her.

She drove him home carefully, taking her time. They did not speak for she was thinking of her marriage, and the way it had ended, and he was struggling with something he did not want to call conscience.

Annie had rung him at six, as he was getting changed.

'I'm going out,' he told her, when she asked what he was doing. 'Crowd from work – the Italian place in Torrance Street.'

'That's nice. I'm glad you won't be lonely.' She asked after the dog, the cat, her house plants, and talked about Tom, telling him about some woman Tom had had, but who was now leaving.

'Didn't that happen before?' he asked. 'A woman he was going to marry, or something. She left too.'

'This is another one,' Annie sighed. 'I don't know.' There was a pause, then she said, 'Have you seen Jamie?'

'No. Alistair phoned. I was out – message on the answerphone. He says he's coming up at Easter, to sort something out about Rob.'

'Oh.' He could hear her inward breath, her anxiety. 'Right, that's OK. Have you rung him back?'

'No, no. You can do that when you get home.'

'But it's next weekend—'

'When are you coming home?' How could she know that this time, he wanted her to stay away? A bit longer, a few days. He needed longer.

But all she said was, vaguely, 'Monday or Tuesday. I don't know yet.' She began talking about Rob, but he broke in on this.

'I must go. I'm being picked up at seven.'

'Any post – other phone calls?'

'Electricity bill – and your mother rang – and oh, some curtains you ordered are ready.'

Now, as Jan brought him home and drew up outside his house, he thought how easily he'd lied. But Annie was all right: she had Tom, Rob, Alistair coming up next week, Jamie and his pregnant wife. Already, he had heard enough about that. It would go on though . . . on and on. Yes, Annie was OK, she had her family.

'I'm going to take the dog along the road,' he said. 'Want to come?'

'Yes, sure.'

She made a fuss of the dog, but minimally, as if she thought she should. She had no animals herself.

'The boys used to want a dog,' she said, 'but my husband didn't agree. And we were both working, anyway.'

They walked round the block, and stood for a moment by the front gate.

'Tea?' he asked. 'Toast?' She laughed.

'I couldn't eat another thing.'

'Tea then.' He didn't care now.

'Yes, all right.'

But in the house he was embarrassed. It was so familiar, and the situation so alien. Nothing fitted. He fussed about, trying to find a teapot, then gave up and put tea bags in mugs. He was doing this when Jan came up behind him and slipped her hands round his waist. He turned in the circle of her arms.

'We don't want tea, do we?' he said.

'No.'

He took her hand, and led her back to the living room. No question of going upstairs – not that – but he drew the curtains and they sat on the Chesterfield. The cat, curled in an armchair, raised her head and looked at them, clear-eyed.

'Listen,' Graham said, 'Jan, I feel I should say something – make it clear—'

'You don't have to.'

'No, but—'

'I know,' she said, and her hands took his face and held it gently. 'I know you're married, this is just one weekend, it can't go on, it's crazy as it is. I know all that. I just don't care right now.'

'Neither do I,' he said, 'neither do I.'

But they had not got far, were still struggling, half-laughing, to take each other's clothes off, when the doorbell began to shrill, on and on, with a finger on the button, refusing to give up.

'Christ – what the fuck—' He was on his feet, zipping his trousers, buttoning his shirt. He went out, shutting the living-room door behind him.

Jan fastened her bra, smoothed her hair, put the cushions straight on the sofa. It was like being a teenager, she thought, caught by your parents coming home early. Her heart beat fast. But his wife was on the Black Isle, and she wouldn't ring the doorbell. It was all right.

It was Jamie. For a few seconds, Graham thought someone must have died, some major tragedy had occurred. Then he realised Jamie was very drunk. He lurched in, grabbing at Graham's arm.

'Annie,' he said. 'I gotta speak to Annie.'

'She's not here. For God's sake – what's wrong?'

'Annie's gotta tell her – she can't – she can't, it's my baby too, I got rights – tell her, Graham.'

'What?' He gripped Jamie, almost shook him. 'God's sake, man, you're pissed.'

'Drove here, though,' Jamie told him. 'Shouldna done it, eh? See, if the bobbies had got me – over the limit, eh?'

'Too right. Come on – come into the kitchen. I'll make coffee, get you sobered up. You stupid bugger.'

He would have to phone Ruth. Jamie slumped on a kitchen chair and began to cry. Then Jan appeared in the doorway.

'What is it?' she asked. 'Is he – all right?'

'Pissed,' Graham said. 'It's my wife's cousin – I'll sort him out. I'd better ring his wife. Don't even know if she's any idea he's here.'

'I'll go home, then,' she said. He stopped, faced her.

'Yes,' he said, 'I think you'd better.'

She left, closing the front door very firmly behind her.

Graham turned back to Jamie. 'For Christ's sake,' he snapped, 'stop that bubbling – what's happened?' But Jamie was incoherent. He beat on the table with both fists, and sobbed. Graham leaned back on the work surface, covering his face with his hands. That's it, he thought, that's it. I never did have a chance. Then he pulled himself together, put the kettle on, and went to phone Ruth.

In the morning, he woke from sleep confused, cold, the downie flung away from him. He pulled it round his shoulders and turned on his side. Then he remembered Jan's calm face, as she looked at him, and left. Jamie, blubbering in the kitchen, then silent in the car, eyes closed as he drove him home; Ruth, opening the door to them as he held Jamie up, her face white and unrevealing. She thanked him, but did not ask him in. He went anyway, to find out what was going on. He had to be able to explain it to Annie. So Ruth told him, and then she asked him to go. *I'll manage him,* she said. Jamie had his head in his hands, he looked green. For the first time Graham pitied him, was sorry to leave him with his competent and beautiful wife.

He turned on his back, wide awake, with a sudden urgent erection. Well, he told it, that's a waste. And yet – what time was it? Ten. Nearly ten. He reached for the telephone and dialled her number, knowing it by heart now. If one of her sons answered, he'd hang up, take it for a sign. But it was Jan who spoke.

'It's me. Sorry about last night.'

'That's all right. What was wrong? I thought something awful must have happened.'

'Not yet,' Graham said, 'not yet.'

'What?'

'Nothing. Tell you later. Fancy a walk? Looks a fine day – thought I'd take the dog along Deeside.'

'Well, maybe later. I'm in the middle of getting Sunday lunch organised.'

'Oh sure. Right.'

'You're welcome to join us.'

'No. No, I won't do that. Pick you up about – when?'

'Half-past two. I'll be clear by then. Might even have managed to finish my marking.'

'Right.'

He lay back, breathed deep. Why had he done that? Annie would come rushing home as soon as she knew about Jamie. Maybe he wouldn't tell her. Nothing had happened, and she would only be upset. He threw off the downie and got up, singing an aria from something – what? Knew the line, the words, couldn't remember which opera. Rossini?

He turned on the shower, stepped in, went on singing.

There was a walk on the banks of the Dee Annie had introduced him to, years ago. They'd gone there with her parents, when they were engaged. But they hadn't gone that way for a long time, and he wasn't entirely sure he could find the path to the river, down past a farmhouse, and a massive horse chestnut tree.

It was not much changed, but there was a fence in the way, and they had to walk further than he remembered to reach the water. There were primroses on the bank, and daffodils, that he'd forgotten about, but which he pointed out now to Jan as if he'd meant to bring her here only for them.

'They're lovely,' she said. 'What a peaceful place.' As they walked, she asked him again, tentatively, about the night before. 'Are you OK? You got your cousin home all right?'

'My wife's cousin,' he said. 'Yes, I think Ruth's coming to fetch their car today.' He brooded, then decided to tell her. It would certainly be easier than telling Annie. 'Ruth – his wife – she's a doctor. Very successful – career woman, I suppose. And she's pregnant, but doesn't want to be. So threatening to abort. He's distraught. End of story. Or beginning of story, I suppose. Depending on whether she gets her way, or he gets his.'

'God, how awful,' Jan said, but that was all. She put her hand in his as they walked, and spoke of other things.

Eventually, they found somewhere among the trees that was secluded enough, and he laid his jacket down for them to lie on. Then they made love again. The dog wandered away, bored, settled some distance off, and went to sleep.

There were only birds, and the sound of the water, and the crackling of twigs and leaves beneath them as they moved. Far away a cow lowed, and another answered. It was warm and sheltered, and in the quiet aftermath, Jan dozed off too, her mouth open a little, her outward breath a faint rasp. Graham lay awake, and thought how strange it was that sex caused such destruction, and yet you would sell your soul to get it. What had driven him? He looked at her, the bluish cooling skin, the tumbled clothes half dragged on again. She was hard, and strong: there was none of Annie's soft roundness, her yielding. She had struggled with him, given back, active as he was. No wonder she slept now. But, he told himself, she was not in cold daylight so very attractive. Her skin was sallow, she was bony, lean. He told himself all this dispassionately, trying to analyse what had happened. He was a fool, to risk so much for sex.

The trouble was, sex never came by itself, was not just an itch, a crazy firing up of lust. Think of Annie, and her terrible longing for children, think of Jamie and Ruth, who had started in such a glow. No question, he had to get out now, before all the other stuff moved in, took over – the love and the loss and the guilt.

He sat up, and began to fasten his clothes, so that Jan stirred and woke.

'Better get back,' he said. 'It's getting cold. You OK?'

She sighed. 'I suppose so.'

When he drove her home, all he said this time was *See you tomorrow, back at the ranch, eh?* She did not look at him.

'Yes. Thanks for . . . the walk. It was a lovely place.'

He did not wait for her to reach her door, but drove off, gunning the engine.

6

On the Sunday, Annie and Tom slept late, so Rob got up and fed
Bracken. Then he unhooked her lead, and took her out himself.
He walked up the back road and across a hillocky field, empty and
scattered with molehills. It was difficult to work out here what
land was all right for him to walk on, and what was private.
Annie had told him there was no law of trespass in Scotland.

'Theoretically,' she had said, 'you can go where you like.' That
word *theoretically* filled him with doubt. He kept looking round,
expecting a red-faced landowner to leap out at him, brandishing
a stick. But it was Sunday morning silent, and he saw no one.
He'd climbed a long way. The sea sparkled in the distance; on
the other side, hills shimmered smoky blue against the brighter
blue of the sky.

'Nice here, innit?' he said aloud to Bracken. She nuzzled him,
devoted. It was easy to get dogs to like you. A yank of regret for
his own mongrel. But his mother said Rebel was all right. She
was walking him every day (the exercise, she said, helped her
keep her figure), and sometimes Kevin came and took him out.
People were supposed to get to look like their dogs; sometimes
he thought that must be right, that he was like Rebel, a bit of
everything, belonging nowhere. But Annie, now, she wasn't like
her own retriever, more a spaniel, friendly and jumping up, soft
as anything, with big feathery paws. He laughed aloud, thinking
of this. And Tom wasn't like Bracken at all, for Bracken was stiff,
and getting stout. Tom was like one of those wolfhounds, huge,
but skinny, hungry-looking. Maybe that was a bit too fierce, and
Tom wasn't fierce, no way. His mother (he sighed) was a white
poodle, wearing a pink ribbon. He had a spasm of longing for
her too.

On the phone (and she phoned every week, sometimes twice a week) it wasn't the same, especially as he'd lost interest in all the people she talked about – except Kevin of course.

'I gave Kevin your address,' she told him. 'He said he was going to write.' But he hadn't had any letters. Well, he'd had one, and thankfully, he'd picked up the post himself that morning from the mat behind the door. Stuffed it in his pocket, heart sinking. His mother had said, when she rang him, 'I sent on a letter, in a lilac envelope. Did you get it?' She laughed. 'A girl, I says to Ken. I bet it's a girl.'

Sometimes, she asked when he was coming home. When she did that, he had a picture of himself in the living room at home, him and his mother and Ken, eating chips in front of the telly, the strong fatty smell of the chips, Rebel sitting with his ears cocked, waiting for one, and a game show blaring out music and applause. Then, briefly, he longed to be back there, where it was easy to live up to what was expected of you, it was so little. But he always told Shona he didn't know when he'd be back.

'Well,' she said, 'it's up to you. Got your own life to live. It's nice, there, is it, with Annie and them?'

'Yeah,' he said. It seemed disloyal to show enthusiasm, or to praise. 'It's OK.'

'She's a nice person, Annie,' his mother said. 'I says to Ken, he'll be all right there. Shame she never had her own kids.'

Once, when he was about twelve, he'd gone to stay with Kevin. It had started with one night sleeping over, then Sunday dinner, and somehow, he was still there on Monday. It was a bank holiday, no school. Then he'd got his school stuff from home, and gone back there on Tuesday for tea. Kevin's mum didn't say anything, just dished up his food along with Kevin's and his dad's and his sister's. But eventually, on Friday, Ken turned up, said he'd got to come home.

'Sorry,' Ken had said, standing in Kevin's hallway, 'hope he hasn't been in your road.'

'No trouble,' Kevin's mum had said. 'Any time.'

Sometimes he wondered, if Ken hadn't come for him, if Shona hadn't been planning to take them out for a curry to celebrate her new job, whether he might still be living with Kevin. No, that was daft.

He climbed the fence, and held the barbed wire wide for Bracken to get underneath. They were on a path that widened as it wound downhill. But it must be someone's land, because there was a cottage with no glass in the windows, a broken-down shed, a Land Rover beside them. A man was taking something out of the back of the Land Rover. Rob hesitated, but Bracken was a long way ahead, and he didn't want to shout for her. The man turned, saw the dog, and they greeted each other like old friends. Then the man looked up and saw Rob.

He was old, like Tom's father who'd come to dinner the night before, and whom Rob remembered only dimly. But this man was much taller, and gaunt, in a tweed jacket and plus twos, with a flat cap. He had a thick white moustache bristling on his upper lip.

'I know this dog,' he said, 'but I don't know you.'

'It's my uncle's dog,' Rob said. 'I'm staying with him.'

'Tom? You're Tom Mathieson's nephew? Well, well, didn't know you existed.'

Well, Rob wanted to say, I didn't know you existed either. So what? But he just stood there, looking at the old man.

'Give me a hand – you seem to be a strapping lad.'

He was taking long planks of wood out of the Land Rover. Rob went up and supported one end, while the man fed the wood out bit by bit. They stood several feet apart, holding three of the planks. They were narrow, but heavy.

'Into the house,' the man said.

'What they for, then?'

'You'll see.'

He did see. The main room of the cottage had no floor, just joists, and a smell of dust and damp.

'You layin' a new floor?'

'Absolutely. Spot on.' They leaned the planks against the wall of the tiny passageway between the two front rooms. The other was smaller, and had a stone floor.

'Kitchen through there,' the man said. A narrow stairway went up the centre of the house. 'Bedrooms upstairs, bathroom along there.'

'This your house?'

'Belongs to me, yes. Don't live in it. Well, obviously. I'm doing it up for a holiday cottage, to make an income from it.' He looked round. 'Eventually.' He turned back to Rob, eyes narrowing. 'I say, you're not free by any chance?'

'Free?'

'School hols – student vacation – how old are you?'

'I've left school. Not got anything else yet.'

'Right, splendid. Poet in the making, no doubt – like your uncle.' Rob began to deny this, but the man went on. 'Like a job? Good with your hands?'

'I can do plumbing, my mate's dad was a plumber,' Rob offered, inspired. 'He got us to put a toilet in and a sink for Kevin's gran. He kind of watched us, like, checked it. But I could do it again all right.'

'Oh I say – champion. That's it then – fifty quid a week and beer and sandwiches in the Plough at lunch-time. How does that sound?'

Not much, thought Rob, but he wanted to do it. He wanted to go back down the hill, and wander into the kitchen and say to Annie and Tom, 'I got a job.' And it would be, though he scarcely realised this yet, a reason to stay.

'Aye,' he said, 'right. You're on.'

Annie and Tom were sitting at the back door on garden chairs dragged from the garage, and growing drowsy in the warm shelter of the house wall. The Sunday papers were spread round their feet, the corners fluttering a little.

'I wonder how long he's been gone,' Tom said. 'He was out before I got up.'

'Bracken will be exhausted.'

'Dog's too fat. Do her good.'

'I'm so sleepy,' Annie sighed.

'Change of air.'

'Nonsense – I'm used to this air. Been coming here all my life. It's stress, I think. Or the absence of it. One or the other. When I go back, I'll start worrying again. At the moment, it's like having a holiday from myself.'

'If you say so.' Tom turned a page of his paper, and read about backpacking in Morocco.

After a moment, Annie said, 'I don't know why, but when

I think of home I get a kind of anxious feeling. As if I'm homesick. Isn't that strange? I never used to feel like this. I want to be here, I love it, it's right, but I've got this tingling anxious feeling. I thought speaking to Graham last night would make it go away.'

'But it hasn't?'

'No, it's worse.'

'Go home then,' Tom said promptly. 'Trust your instinct. Go home.'

Annie sat up sharply. 'You think there's something wrong?'

'How would I know? But usually, our instincts are true.'

'And what's yours,' she asked, 'where Meg's concerned?'

'Oh stop it, Annie. I don't have any instincts left.'

The garden gate opened, and Rob came through, followed more slowly by Bracken.

'Well,' Annie said, 'you were up early.' He stopped in front of them against a background of sunlight and bright sky, so that she had to shade her eyes to see him.

'Bracken's knackered,' he said, grinning.

'You want something to eat?'

'Yeah – I'm starvin'.'

'We're just making sandwiches,' Annie said. 'We thought we might go through to Inverness at night, for pizza or something.' She yawned and stretched. 'Oh dear, must move myself.'

'Got a job,' Rob said. It was as easy as that: just do it, just tell them. But he held his breath, not knowing how they'd take it.

'What?'

'When – this morning?'

'What sort of job?'

'Not a real job, like. Hard enough work, I bet, though. With this old guy.'

'Hang on,' Tom said. 'Start at the beginning.'

'That's it. I met this old guy, up the hill. Helped him take stuff out his truck. And he says he's doin' up this holiday cottage, do I want a job helpin' him. So I says yeah, OK. That's it.'

'Oh God,' Tom said. 'It's Hamish.'

'Tall geezer. English – posh voice.'

'Not English,' Annie scoffed, 'just went to Fettes.'

'Eh? Went where?'

'It's a school,' she told him. 'You learn to sound like a pseudo-Englishman. He's as Scottish as we are.'

'He said he knew Tom.'

'He does,' Tom agreed. 'Lives in a crumbling wreck of a house on the road up to Cromarty. Took it into his head a year or so back to let out rooms to tourists. But that was crazy – place has got mice in the bedrooms, dry rot, God knows what all. So he hit on doing up the but and ben instead. He's got great hands on him, I will say that.'

'He should've been a joiner or something,' Annie agreed. 'Instead of a toff.'

'So,' Tom said, 'you're going to work for him?'

'Yeah, said I would.'

'How much is he paying you?'

Rob wanted to say *None of your business*, but couldn't. He told Tom, who gave a yelp of laughter.

'We'll see,' he said. 'Get him to put it in writing, that's my advice.'

'But Rob,' Annie protested, taking this in, 'you can't just stay here.'

'Why not?' He nodded at Tom. 'He doesn't mind. I mean, there's plenty room.'

Tom grinned. 'Sure. Make yourself at home. You could always move in with Hamish, of course. He has even more space for a growing boy.'

'Oh no.' Annie felt this had gone far enough. 'If he's staying here, Tom, he's staying with you. Hamish is off his trolley, you know he is.'

Then she went indoors, leaving them.

Upstairs, in the quiet white room where she always slept at the High House, she sat on the bed with its faded cotton cover and gazed at herself without satisfaction in the mirror of the oak dressing table. She looked blurred; the mirror was old and spotted. What's wrong with me? she wondered. He's not mine, he can stay if he wants to. Alistair won't be pleased, having to come all this way further to see his son, and he doesn't like Tom, but that's not my problem. But his computer course – what about that?

Underneath all this, a thread of anxiety kept tugging at some other part of her subconscious. What was it? A wave of longing for home, for Graham, ran through her, left her so giddy she lay back on the bed. Tears slid sideways over her cheeks, dripped cold in her ears. I must go home, she thought, I must go home and see Graham.

7

'Don't,' Graham said when Annie phoned him on Sunday evening to say she was coming home next day. 'Jamie's on his way up, first thing.'

'But why?'

'He's in a bit of a state.'

'I knew there was something wrong. I'll phone him now, tell him I'm coming home.'

'I think Tom should see him as well. Anyway, it's not a bad idea for him to get away for a couple of days.'

'But – is it Ruth – is she all right?'

'She's fine. *She* knows what she's doing.' He sighed. 'Ach, Jamie was round here last night, out of his head, plastered, looking for you. I told him you were away, I drove him home, Ruth took over . . . Then tonight, when I stopped off at Oddbins for some beer, Ruth was there. She says he's decided to go up to Tom's, and see you both. Maybe it was her idea, I suspect it was.'

'But Graham, what's wrong – why did he want to see me?'

'About Ruth, and the baby. Or not, as the case may be.'

'She's not threatening to *lose* it?'

'You put it very strangely,' he said, with a laugh she did not recognise, 'but aptly, I have to say.'

'Graham, I don't understand any of this—'

'Yes, well, better let Jamie tell you himself. Have to go – got something in the oven. I haven't eaten yet.'

'What about last night – was the meal nice?'

'What meal? Oh – that – yes, fine. Very good.'

When they had rung off, Annie went into the living room where Tom was coaxing the fire to life. Rob had gone down to

Stuart's house, where there was television, and someone else who liked watching Rugby Special. They had decided against the pizza in Inverness; Annie hadn't wanted to go in the end. She seemed subdued now.

'Jamie's coming here tomorrow, apparently. Taking the train up in the morning.'

'What on earth for?'

'Graham wouldn't say. Or he doesn't really know. I'm not sure. He was in a funny mood.'

'So – are you staying then?'

'Yes, at least till I've seen Jamie. It must be something to do with Ruth. Or the baby. Graham says he got very drunk last night and turned up at our house, looking for me.' She sank on to the sofa. 'I'm so tired. I wish I knew why.'

'I'm tired too.' Tom came and sat beside her. 'But I think I'm just tired of being alive.'

'Oh Tom.' She looked at him. 'You're just joking, though.'

'Sure.'

Annie lay back again, with a sigh.

'Rob's a bit of a wanderer, isn't he?' she said. 'Or is it just that I'm too boring a person for him to stay with?'

'It's the first,' Tom reassured. 'He'll not last long with Hamish, wait and see. And the lack of a television here will weigh fairly heavily, I should think. It'll be back to the comforts of Deeside Walk, and your home cooking.'

'What on earth is Alistair going to say?'

'Oh God,' Tom said, 'I hadn't thought of that. He'll be up here raging at me.'

But Annie was preoccupied, not listening.

'I wish I were going home,' she said. 'I feel torn in two now. I want to see Jamie, I want to talk to you, and be with Rob, but – I don't know what it is. I feel I should really be at home. My instinct, you know – like you said.'

'Well, wait till you've seen him. Have a talk, then shoot off down the road. You could still be home by tomorrow night. What's a few hours?'

'Yes, you're right. That's what I'll do.'

Tom got up to look for a train timetable. 'I'll ring him,' he said. 'Find out which one he's getting.'

But when he tried, there was only the answerphone. He spoke briefly, telling Jamie to let them know which train to meet. Then he went back to pour stiff tumblers of malt for Annie and himself, feeling they needed it.

'Too bad if Alistair turns up at Easter,' he said as they settled themselves by the fire. 'I won't be here. I'm hill-walking. I said I'd go out with the club.'

'You haven't done that for ages. Good. Why don't you take Rob?'

'Good God, I was hoping to get away, not take my problems with me.'

'Rob's not your problem.'

'Not yours either,' he reminded her.

Annie jumped up and went to the window. She meant to draw the curtains, but the quiet garden, with a cat stalking across the lawn in fading light, caught her and she paused.

'It's so peaceful here,' she said. 'Why can't I be peaceful too?'

'It's not peaceful,' Tom told her. 'It's just sad.'

In the morning, Annie hung around, waiting for Jamie to call. She had packed her bags. Tom had gone up to the shop, telling her to ring him as soon as she heard from Jamie, and he or Stuart would go into Inverness for him. Rob had risen at the same time as Tom, eaten two rolls, and walked up the back road to Hamish's cottage. Bracken watched him leave, ears cocked in puzzlement, then she lay down in her basket with a grunt, and slept.

Annie made coffee, scanned the Sunday papers for something she might not have read yet, fretted. She had stripped her bed, put the sheets and towels in the washing machine, and hung them out to dry when the machine (ageing, like everything else here) rumbled to a halt. Now she had run out of things to do. She could not settle to read, and as she was dressed for going home, couldn't garden. She could do some weeding, she thought, if there were still gloves in the shed somewhere. But it was overcast and windy this morning, and much colder.

At one, Tom shut the shop and came home for lunch.

'No sign?' he asked. Annie had made soup, in the absence of anything else to do. They sat down to eat together.

'Nothing,' she said. 'When's the next train due?'

'Half-past three – something like that.'

'Maybe we should ring him at home again – just in case he's not coming after all.'

'OK – I'll finish my lunch, then I'll do that.'

It was still the answerphone.

'Well, Ruth's at work,' Annie reasoned, 'and presumably Jamie's on his way here.'

'Bloody nuisance,' Tom said. 'And I must get back, someone's coming to look the place over at half-past two.'

'A buyer?'

'I hope so. We'll see.'

'Then what will you do?' Annie asked, as if thinking of this for the first time.

'I suppose I'll have to get a job. More supply teaching – I could try the college.' He grinned. 'Maybe Hamish will employ me as well.'

'You could make some use of the house,' Annie suggested. 'Do Bed and Breakfast.'

Tom groaned. 'What a terrible idea!'

'It is, isn't it?' Annie said, laughing.

Tom held up a hand. 'What's that?'

'What?'

'I thought I heard—'

It was Jamie, coming in the back door.

'Hi folks.'

'I thought you were going to ring us – did you drive?' Annie rose to her feet.

'I hitched from Inverness,' Jamie said. 'Got a lift at the Kessock Bridge took me to Fortrose. I walked the rest.'

Annie began reheating soup, and Jamie sat down. Tom thought he looked terrible. As Annie put a bowl of soup down, and cut more bread, he experienced that sense of *déjà vu* that belongs not to a trick of consciousness but to real memory. They were all ten years younger, and he and Annie were looking after Jamie. Then, he had been ill, but now he looked, if anything, worse. And more worn, since a man of thirty-eight, dissatisfied with his life, cannot have the freshness of one of twenty-eight, even one who has walked close to death.

'I have to go up to the shop,' Tom said. 'I'll get back as early as I can. Dad'll come in for me – I'll see you later.'

Annie came to the door with him, and they stood outside together for a moment.

'Maybe you'd better stay with him till I get home. Is that all right?'

'Of course it is.' Annie lowered her voice. 'He looks awful.'

'I know. But Graham said he'd been on the booze?'

'Yes, but it looks—'

'I know. I'll see you soon – right?'

She went back to the kitchen, where Jamie had managed to eat a few spoonfuls of soup.

'It's good,' he said, 'but I'm not hungry. Sorry.'

'It doesn't matter.' She put her hand on his arm. 'Come through and sit in the living room. You need a soft chair.'

'I do.' He eased himself to his feet like an invalid, an old man.

It was cool in the living room, but Tom had laid the fire before leaving in the morning, so she added a couple of logs and some coal and set a match to it. They took the chairs that sat either side of the fire, facing each other.

'Jamie, what's happened?'

'Nothing,' he said. 'Nothing yet. It's Ruth – she doesn't want the baby. She says she'll have an abortion, soon, before it goes any further.'

'*What?*'

'I know, I know, I can't believe it. I thought she was OK, had accepted it, we'd sorted everything out—'

'But *why*?'

'Well, she never wanted kids, she made it clear at the start, but that was all right then. And she thought because of the messed up abortion she had, that she couldn't conceive anyhow.'

Annie didn't know what she thought or felt about Ruth now. Well, yes she did. I hate her, she thought, sitting close to Jamie, letting him talk. *I hate her*. To think we were glad when she fell in love with Jamie, married him, and he got so well and happy. We didn't mind her not being close to us, the way she always knew what she wanted, where she was going. She was such a success.

And she didn't even *want* a baby. God, she got rid of a baby once before. What's to stop her doing it again? Annie felt the force of this for the first time. *She's killed a baby already.* Now she was going to murder another one, and it was theirs, it belonged to their family. A panicky ball of loathing rose up in Annie. Oh, the injustice of it, the bloody miserable *unfairness.*

No, this was no good. She must stop. Stop. She made herself calm down, began to hear what Jamie was saying.

'I mean, I didn't really think about it when we were first married, all the more of her for me, right? But she *really* didn't want kids – and she's scared, I think, not of *having* a baby, but all that comes afterwards – our lives being so different . . .'

'But that's the reason we have children,' Annie said. 'To change our lives.'

'I'm sorry, I'm sorry.' Absorbed in his own story, Jamie nevertheless heard the change in Annie, the tightness in her voice. He touched her hand. 'I know how it must sound to you, and I'm so sorry to burden you—'

'She hasn't done it, though, I mean everything's still . . . all right?' How could they make Ruth keep the baby? That was all that mattered now. Annie had no doubts. Jamie and Ruth must have this child.

'No, no. She's promised to wait a week before she does anything about it. A week! "I'll give it a week," she said this morning, "and then if I feel the same, I'm going ahead."'

'I could talk to her.' But how could she? She couldn't even bear to see her just now.

Jamie shook his head. 'She's quite cool about it, absolutely determined. There's no arguing with her. She always gets her own way, Annie, it's only in bed it's ever any different with us. In bed – at least there it's me, I'm the one—'

Annie interrupted, not wanting to hear this. 'She can't have decided finally, though, or she'd just have gone ahead. She's got to change her mind. You have to go on talking, Jamie, keep talking to her. You shouldn't have left her.'

'She said she needed space, time to think.'

'For goodness sake—'

'It's all right, I don't think – no, she promised. Anyway, I'd have to give my agreement wouldn't I, sign something. God, as if I *could*. So I had to come, I really had to – I needed you and Tom. I'm so scared, Annie, I feel I'm fighting for my life, my baby's life.'

'Oh God,' Annie cried, 'what an awful thing!' She put her hands over her face. Jamie came off his chair and slid to the floor beside her, his head in her lap, her arms round him.

Eventually, he raised his head and looked at her.

'I'm sorry, Annie. This isn't fair to you – I am sorry. It's just – who else could I come to?'

'It's all right – I'm glad you did. Who else could care as much – understand – there's just you and me and Tom.'

Jamie sighed and turned, leaning on her, stretching his legs out to the fire.

'Yes,' he said, 'Saturday night, when we had the row about it, I was desperate to get to you, ask you what to do. I came charging out – in the car – must have been crazy – I'd had about half a bottle of gin by that time. But I had this mad idea you'd put it right, make her see sense. So there I was, on your doorstep at some godawful hour, midnight, something like that, drunk as a skunk – did Graham tell you? Crying like a fucking baby myself, and this woman's there. God knows who she was, she must've thought I was off my head. Graham looked *sick* – but then he's never been all that keen on me.'

'What woman?' Annie asked. Silence fell; the fire crackled. *'What woman?'*

'What? Oh, I don't know. Like I said, I've never seen her in my life. Though, actually, now you come to mention it, I think I have. That's why I remember. I mean, I was out of my skull, but that sticks, God knows why. She's sort of tall, straight fair hair. I saw her with Graham one day, she was in his car, I passed them on Queen's Road. Maybe he was giving her a lift somewhere, maybe she's a teacher. It must have been about half-past four.'

Annie pushed Jamie away from her, and got up.

'I have to go.'

'What?'

'I'll phone Tom, he'll stay with you. I have to go home.'

'What is it?' He got to his feet, struggling out of his own obsession, realising she was no longer even thinking about him. 'Have I said something?'

Annie looked white. 'It was just Graham?' she asked. 'When you went round – just Graham and this woman? Not a crowd of people?'

'God, Annie, the state I was in he could have had a football team in there, and I might not have – no, sorry, I'm being – it was just Graham. Graham and this woman.'

'Midnight, you said?'

'Well, maybe not as late. About eleven, probably. Annie – I—' He ran his hands through his hair. 'Oh shit. Look, I'm sure – not Graham. I never even thought – I wish I hadn't said now—'

'Just as well you did.'

He had not seen Annie like this, she had never seemed so cold and distant from him. He was afraid: he wanted to get her back for himself.

'Don't leave,' he said. 'I need you to stay.'

But Annie had realised the most important thing was not, after all, whether Jamie and Ruth had a child. It mattered, of course, but to them, not to her.

On the telephone to Tom, she was quiet and steady.

'They've just gone,' he said, 'the prospective buyers. Coming back tomorrow when they've seen their solicitor. Thing is – I suspect what they want is a teashop, not a bookshop. I may have to sell the stock separately – well, I've started doing that already, really, bit by bit. I thought—'

'So you can come back *now*, Tom?'

'Yeah, I'm on my way. Dad's here.'

When he came in, she hurled herself into his arms.

'What the – where's Jamie?'

'Oh, he's all right. Started on your whisky, I think, since there's no gin. He's not too happy I'm leaving. But I have to. Now.'

'Yes, right, that's OK.' He held her arms, drew away slightly. 'What's wrong?'

'Graham was with somebody, a woman. Something's been happening while I've been here.'

'Oh Annie, surely not—'

She told him what Jamie had said.

'Ach, he said himself he was out of his head. Wait – don't jump the gun. It's probably nothing.'

'It's not nothing. I do know that.' She would not stay, would not wait for Rob to get back, or even see Jamie again.

He went out with her to her car, put her bag in the back, and opened the gates. He hugged her briefly before she got in to drive away.

'Take care,' he said. 'Drive slowly, Annie – promise?'

'Why do I feel,' she asked him, as she turned the key in the ignition, 'as if everything's falling apart?'

It was only when she was through the gates, disappearing down the drive, that he permitted himself to say, *Because it is.* And I suspect, he told himself as he turned indoors to meet his brother again, this is just the start.

When Annie finally reached her own street, she expected Graham to be at home; it was after six. But the house was empty. She knelt in the hall, the dog's eager head between her hands.

'I'm home,' she said. 'I'm home – have you been fed?'

But Graham had not been back since morning. She let the dog out, fed the animals, then took her bag upstairs to unpack. As she passed the telephone in the hall, she paused, pressed *play*, listened for messages. Her mother again, then an incoherent few words, a long buzzing noise, and suddenly Alistair, clipped and clear.

'Annie – call me as soon as you get back. Office number – my direct line.' Here he rattled off the number, not trusting her to have kept a note of it, but not giving her time to write it down. *Now what?* she thought, not caring. She was at the top of the stairs when she heard Graham's key in the lock. No garage door. She went into their bedroom and looked out. His car was still in the street, as if he meant to go out again. She went back on to the landing.

'Hello,' he said. 'You're home.'

'I said I would be.'

'Sorry, I had a long meeting. And I've got to go out again for another one. Guidance. Sorry about that.'

'I don't believe you,' she said.

He checked, looked up at her. 'What?'

Annie came downstairs slowly.

'You see Jamie?' Graham asked. 'How was he?'

Annie hesitated. What was she basing all her fear on? Jamie's confused, drunken memory. And yet . . .

'I saw him. He's all right – you should have told me what was going on.'

'I thought it was better coming from him.' But he looked away as he spoke, and she knew he hadn't been able to face her reaction, hadn't wanted to discuss Ruth with her at all.

'Do you want something to eat, then?' she asked. 'Before you rush out again.'

'Um, well, yes. Right. I was going to buy chips on the way.'

'I'll get something out of the freezer,' she said. 'Or pasta? Would pasta do?'

'Anything,' he said.

Annie went into the kitchen. It was tidy, and it did not look as if anyone had eaten there, lived there, all weekend. She filled a saucepan with water, and set it on the cooker.

Graham hovered in the doorway.

'I'll just go and sort my stuff out for tonight. Be in the study, right?'

'Yes,' she said. 'I'll give you a shout when it's ready.'

But neither of them could eat. And when she saw Graham, who relished his food, loved it, poking his fork around among the ribbons of tagliatelle, she knew her instinct had been right. But she was too much afraid of what she might learn to question him. She held back, waited.

'Do you have to go to this meeting?' she asked as she took away his plate without commenting on the food left on it, or on hers.

'Yes, why?'

'I want to talk to you.'

'It can wait,' he said, 'if it's about Jamie.'

'No.' She turned to face him. 'It's Rob.'

'Where is he?' Graham glanced round, as if, she thought scornfully, the boy might be concealed somewhere. 'He stay on with Tom?'

'Yes,' she said. 'He's got a job.'

'Well, good for him.'

'I don't know,' she said. 'It's only with Hamish.'

'Oh God, not Hamish.' Graham laughed. For a moment, it was

easier, they were almost like themselves again. Then Graham
plucked his jacket from the basket chair in the hall, and left.

'See you about . . . half ten or so. Don't wait up,' he told her.
'We might go to the pub after.'

What pub? He came home from school meetings as soon as
possible, complaining bitterly about his evenings being hi-jacked.
She almost ran after him, had to steel herself not to. He had only
just gone when the telephone shrilled. She was standing next to
it, and picked it up on the first ring.

'At last!' her brother exclaimed. 'All I get is bloody answer-
phones.'

'Is it about Easter?' she asked, heart sinking. She couldn't cope
with Alistair just now. He'd have to wait – not that he would.
You couldn't stop him.

'I can't make it,' he said. 'It's crazy here, we've got this
takeover bid threatening. You'll have seen it on the news.'

'No,' Annie said. 'Tom doesn't have a television, remember?'

News? She had lost sight of the news, lost interest, since Rob's
arrival. Alistair sounded irritated.

'It's been going on for weeks. God – you really are in the sticks
up there. Surely you read a newspaper – I don't mean the *P &
J*.' He snorted. 'Anyway, we're still fighting it off – our Board
are dead against it, but I'm beginning to think it could happen
anyway. Then everything's up in the air. I thought you were a
shareholder – I told Graham to buy, ages ago. Haven't you been
reading all the bumf we've sent out?'

Alistair always had this effect: Annie felt bullied, belittled,
annoyed.

'What bumf? I never read things that come in big white enve-
lopes – you should know that. Graham reads them. Anyway, I
didn't know you were so important – it can't actually affect you
much, can it?'

'Oh ho – can't it? I can't leave, Annie, just take my word for
it. Can't take the chance – might come back and find I haven't
got a job.' He laughed, a mirthless bark.

'But that's terrible—'

'Well, we'll see. Show's not over yet. Anyway, point is, if Rob's
OK, I'll leave it for a while.'

'Yes, he's fine. He's at Tom's.'

'Oh. I thought he was doing some course or other – he's not going to *stay* with Tom?'

'Well, yes. For a while.'

'Hm, I suppose he can't actually come to any harm. I'd rather he was with you, though.'

'*Actually*,' Annie snapped, 'he's got a job.'

'What job?'

'Labouring. For Hamish.'

'Good God, is he still on the go?'

'You know he is – don't be such a pretentious *sod*, Ally.'

'No, no, really. Tell me.'

'He's doing up a holiday cottage. Rob's helping him.'

'Well, that's fine, Annie, as far as it goes, but we have to get him a few qualifications – training of some kind.'

'I did try!'

'Yes, yes, you've done wonders. Better than his bloody mother, at any rate. Look, I'll have to go. Someone's wanting me – and I'd better check the e-mail. I'm expecting to hear—'

'You're not still at work?'

'Naturally. Here till ten most nights.'

When he had rung off, Annie went back into the kitchen to clear up the supper dishes. Oddly, she felt better. Alistair was appalling, but he had an invigorating effect. Or the anger and indignation he induced did. So she was fine now.

She was fine till about ten. Then she watched television with the sound off, something she had not done since the last bad spell with Graham, when he had finally told her to give up, that they had to think of themselves as childless now. That had been very bad, but different from this. She kept looking at the clock. At half-past, she took the dog out, then had another whisky, her second. At quarter-past eleven she went to bed.

She lay back on the pillows with the lamp on, trying to read. Without meaning to, she dozed off, then jerked awake as the book slid to the floor. It was almost one o'clock, and Graham had not come home. Annie rose and flung on her dressing gown. Where was he? Perhaps he'd had an accident, driving home after a couple of pints. But he never did that.

Where was he?

She went down to the kitchen and put the kettle on. She'd

have a cup of tea, and at two, no later than two, she'd ring the hospital, the police, check there hadn't been an accident. She made tea, and stared at the newspaper, pretending to read.

This had never happened before, in all the years of her marriage.

At two-fifteen, as she got down to reading the sports pages, shaking with terror and indecision, Graham came in. They faced each other in the hall, and she knew he had not been drinking. He hadn't even been in a bar, for there was no smell of cigarette smoke clinging to him. For a moment, they looked at each other, then his eyes slid away. Annie heard again in her mind what she had said to Tom as she left him. Tom, Jamie, Alistair – and now me, she thought. Things are falling apart.

The Past

Ten years back – Jamie

Because they know now that Jamie is not going to die, Tom and Annie have become childish and irresponsible. With Jamie they're still careful: he has light wholesome meals, he has warmth and company and rest. It's as if they've exhausted all their common sense looking after him. On their own they're hilarious, and after he's in bed, drink too much and eat ice-cream at midnight. The air in the kitchen is thick with the smell of Tom's French cigarettes.

'You'd think we were kids,' Annie says. Her stomach is aching because they've laughed so much at something ridiculous, a fantasy built round a woman who comes into the bookshop. She's an odd woman, rude and abrupt, but their ideas are getting more and more ludicrous.

'I don't know how I'm going to keep a straight face next time she comes in for one of her get well cards,' Tom says, pouring himself another dram.

'What d'you mean, *one* of her get well cards?'

'That's what she buys.'

'Nothing else?'

'Not much.'

'She's poisoning her friends, then,' Annie decides. 'One by one.'

'She can't have many left,' Tom points out. This sets them off again.

'Oh, hush, hush,' Annie cries. 'We'll wake Jamie.'

Jamie is in his turret room at the High House, with the curtains open to catch the moon as she rides pale above the sea, seeking the darkness that does not come. He's too far off to hear them, except faintly, and anyway, he's not asleep.

He sleeps only in short dozes, as much through the day as at night, as if he were still in hospital. Sometimes he wakes sweating, from a dream of being back in the ward, and for a few seconds is desolate. Then he opens his eyes and sees the shadowy chest of drawers, its brass handles gleaming in moonlight, and the tiled fireplace in the corner, with his First World War model planes on the mantelpiece, the wooden monkey puppet propped at the end. He hasn't added much since he's come back home, nor has anything been taken away in his absence. The Lloyd loom chair, the faded rag rug, the bookcase with a pile of *Victor* and *Superman* comics on the bottom shelf . . . it's all familiar, and in the night reassuring.

And yet, in daylight, he often thinks of saying to Annie, *Clear this lot out, will you? Put it in the loft.* It goes back too far, to a boy he can't even remember being. Grown up, he moved to one of the large front bedrooms, Tom's when they were young. Now Tom sleeps in the room that was his parents', overlooking the sea. Jamie prefers to see the garden, tangled and overgrown, stretching up the hillside beyond the house. It's the back of the house that looks down to the sea across the vegetable garden. The drive winds off to the left, through woodland down to the road to the village.

Now, he can hear the sea all night, and in the morning, when he manoeuvres himself to his feet to go along the landing for a pee, he sees the sun bleached white on shining water.

He is getting better, no doubt about that. Each day he can sit up for longer, sleep less, do more. In the afternoons, if it's fine, Annie and Tom put the garden chairs out, and he lies on a sun-lounger which they move down the slope with the sun. They stay at the back of the house, as the steep rise of trees at the front means the sun is not there for long, and there is anyway less to see. At the top, by the back door, where once their mother had tubs of herbs, but now Tom has tubs of weeds, you can just see over the hedge to the sea, and hear the children playing, as their cries drift up from the beach.

The terrible things in the past happened when Jamie was barely five, Annie only eight, so there is no pain for Jamie in the sound of children playing. He can lie and read, or listen to the radio, and all he is conscious of is the warm sun on his face, and the mug of tea waiting beside him. Mostly, he dreams, dozes. He has little energy yet even for reading, and amuses himself with old children's annuals. In the evenings Annie and Tom read to him, Annie first, while Tom is writing, then Tom, then the two of them chapter about. The lemon balm by the back door, whose pungent leaves he crunches in his fingers as he goes indoors for supper, is later always to be associated with the Bash Street Kids, Pa Broon, PC Murdoch. In the evening, the big living room, curtains floating in a breeze that bumps against the open window, is filled to its corners with a host of fictional characters who do not seem to vanish altogether when the story is ended, the book closed. Sometimes, his night dreams are haunted by the elusive Pimpernel, Jay Gatsby solitary by his swimming pool, Heathcliff on the moor . . . They are more real to him than any of the people who have inhabited his world till now. The boundaries between the real and unreal dissolve, cease to matter.

But for Annie it is different. At the end of three weeks she snaps out of fiction into reality, and carries herself back to Aberdeen.

'I have to go,' she tells him, leaning down to collect his empty cup, so that a raw breath of scent assaults him and a fall of dark hair sweeps against his face.

'I suppose you miss Graham,' he sighs, feeling sorry for himself. He doesn't want her to go. Tom is at the bookshop most days, and his father comes only in the evenings, and falls asleep in the rocking chair, long before the end of the reading.

'Maybe,' Annie smiles, 'he misses me.' She leans forward again, and kisses him. 'Anyway, it's the date – I have to go. But I'll be back in a few days.'

'Why, what's special about the date?'

'Nothing – it's—' Annie blushes. 'Tom will explain.'

Tom comes home early, so that Jamie won't be alone. But he's fretful, and the pain is bad today. It is the pain of recovery, they both know this. There is no threat in it any more. And yet it troubles them.

'Dad'll be round later when he closes up. He's doing the shop for me. Are you OK if I go and write for an hour? I'll make tea first – any of Annie's scones left, d'you know?'

Jamie shrugs, trails after Tom into the kitchen, and sits at the table. Tom gives him the scones to butter.

'What's she gone to Aberdeen for?' Jamie asks. 'I mean, why can't Graham come up here? Schools are on holiday now, aren't they? He could come here, if they're missing each other.' He licks butter off his thumb. 'Not that I'm actually desperate for Graham to come and read stories to me . . .'

Tom laughs.

'History of rugby union in Scotland . . . Reader's Digest DIY manual?'

'No, seriously though . . .'

'Well, I'm sure he does miss her,' Tom says. 'But he can only take so much of our family. That's what I think it is. Then his friends are in Aberdeen, and there's the house and the animals.'

'Oh well, as long as Annie comes.'

'She's family. And she's soft about you. Since you were a miserable spoiled brat.'

Jamie ignores this. 'So why's she gone off *now*? She hinted it was for something special. It's not their anniversary or anything, is it?'

Tom shakes his head, smiling, as he pours mugs of tea.

'It's the time of the month, I think.'

'*What?*'

'Do I spell it out? You should know by now, Jamie. About three days in the month she thinks she's most likely to be fertile, so that's when they . . . make the hit, you could say.'

Jamie is silent, and pokes at the crumbs left on the plate.

'She might have said,' he mutters at last.

'It embarrasses her. And I suspect she thinks it's bad luck to speak about it.'

'But she tells *you*.'

'I know anyway, by now. How long have they been trying? Four, five years? It was really bad, just before you went into hospital. She was going to a clinic . . . and year before last, was it, she had some operation, remember?'

'Oh yes,' says Jamie, but he doesn't. He was in Skye the year before last, living with a girl who'd just inherited her grandfather's croft. In the end, he decided living off the land wasn't really his thing. And the girl had thrown him out anyway. Now, pushing this uncomfortable memory aside, he feels he's missed out on something important.

'*I* tell *her*,' he says, 'all the stuff that's going on with me. When I started shitting blood, it was Annie I told. So how come she didn't just say she was going home to screw her husband?'

'She doesn't use that sort of language for a start,' Tom says, leaving Jamie in the kitchen, and going upstairs to work.

He's been itching to get back to this all day, but as he climbs the stairs, he feels guilty. Jamie is miserable, and unused to being alone. Their father will be here in a couple of hours, but two hours is long to fill on your own, when there's so little you can do to vary the minutes. But at least he's safe to be left now. He seems resigned at any rate. *I'm not in such a hurry to die as you think*, he said irritably after he'd spent the first week at the High House constantly attended by Tom, or his father, or Annie. They had taken turns, afraid to leave him. Now, as Jamie begins to seem himself again, however weak, they feel they have to trust him. Resolutely, Tom shuts his bedroom door, shuts out Jamie, and the guilt. The call of his desk, at the window overlooking the sea, is too strong.

It's a large, airy room, sparsely furnished. But the bookcase overflows, the desk is covered with papers, and the set of cheap shelving bought in a DIY store in Inverness, is stacked with files and notebooks. Here, in the bentwood chair with its flattened, faded cushion, at this desk, Tom feels most at ease, most himself. He sits looking out of the window or down at the scattered papers for some time, before he picks up his pen.

The desk is a big one, bought from a depot selling second-hand office equipment. Pushed to one side is Tom's Olivetti typewriter. He means to buy a computer when he gets some money for the book. He thinks of his work now as *the book*, not as an amorphous collection of poems, some published, many not, bundled together in three envelope files.

He is supposed to be making a final selection for his editor to read through. In reality, he's still writing. In the two months since Mary left, he has been writing like a man possessed, who must somehow get down on paper an unstoppable surge of ideas, words, lines, and catch them before they vanish, use them before they dry up. And the best thing is that these poems are good. They are good as they tumble off the pen on to the page. There has been almost no reworking. It won't last; he knows this, and so doesn't dare stop.

The excitement of it is only intensified by his sense of loss – the loss of Mary, the near loss of Jamie, the terror of those weeks when death breathed down their necks. The excitement of the work has carried him through. He's listened to Annie, read to Jamie, with only the thin surface of his attention. The rest – all that matters – has been with the poetry, its sweet seductive rhythms.

He bends over the desk now, drawing to him the latest in a series of dolphin poems. He and Annie take Jamie to the point on fine days to watch the dolphins, and from each visit has come a poem. These verses are all to do with Mary, with her going from him in a way that is more significant than any parting yet that he has known.

There is no way of telling, when the dolphins leave, each curved leap from the dark water further and further out to sea, till they are mere specks, indistinct, that they will be back. Another day, another summer, and perhaps different dolphins, who can tell? But they do reappear, and each summer parents tell their children the dolphins are coming back. You just have to have faith in that. With Mary, with love itself, there is less and less room to have faith. He has turned his back on the moving sea, all the possibilities Mary once offered. The poignancy of his loss moves him almost to tears as he works. But it is exhilarating, all the same, this pitch of emotion, when it spills out with the springy grace of a new metaphor, a perfect couplet.

Two hours pass, and he is in this other world. He's roused from it only by his father's shout.

'Tom, will I get the tea?'

He comes downstairs dazed, unable to think what food they are going to eat. But Annie has left them a casserole, and between them Jamie and Stuart have put it in the top oven, and set a pan of potatoes to boil on the hotplate. Jamie has stopped sulking; Annie phoned from Aberdeen and he's been able to tease her about her reasons for going home. She laughed at him, told him not to sit up late, promised to bring back a present.

'Do you mind if we don't read tonight?' Tom asks later. His head is peopled with his own creations and he can't be doing with anyone else's. 'I'll put a record on. Mahler, OK?'

The fifth symphony fills the room. Stuart falls asleep with his mouth open, snoring a little, and Jamie makes a half-hearted attempt at the *Scotsman* quick crossword. They miss Annie.

In Aberdeen, Graham has greeted Annie with lust and relief.

At first he liked being on his own, with no one to tell him not to leave beer cans on the mantelpiece or lights on all over the house, no one to sigh with exasperation when he farts in bed. Briefly, he thinks he should have remained single. But the house, by the end of a fortnight, seems empty, and even he notices the stale air in the living room, the dead flowers in the vase in the hall. He flings open the windows and stands by the open front door, smelling the roses Annie has planted and tended, and wondering if she's got the morning train. She's phoned every other night, so he's not been without contact. But he feels, despite this, neglected.

The phone rings.

'It's me, I'm at the station – train was early. Can you come down?'

'On my way.'

He's had two weeks of useless morning erections, so almost as soon as he gets her home he has her in his arms, hands under her clothes, tongue in her mouth. They go straight to bed.

Afterwards, lying embraced, afternoon sunlight moving across the rumpled bedcovers, Annie smiles to herself, and nudges even closer. His arm tightens round her and he looks down at her flushed face.

'Nice to have you home,' he says.

They lie there for a long time, Graham because he has dozed off, Annie because she is holding carefully his milky injection of semen. She pictures, as she so often has before, a billion spermatozoa swimming upwards, spreading outwards. How can they miss? And yet, they always do.

No. This time it will be all right, it must be now. When Jamie was dying, she used to tell herself, *If he gets better, it will all be all right. It's a sign.* She meant that if he lived, she would have children. She could not say why these two survivals

– his life, her hopes – should be linked. But she believed they were.

When she was eight, she invoked charms in just this way. Running down the steep garden she whispered, *If that blackbird doesn't fly away before I get to the holly bush, Lindsay will come back.* Squeezing half an inch of toothpaste on her brush in the cold bathroom, Alistair banging on the door, (*Hurry up, Mum says!*) *If I finish cleaning my teeth before Mummy comes upstairs, Lindsay will come back.* Raising her skipping rope, preparing to jump on the flat paved area at the back door, *If I get to twenty without tripping, Lindsay will come back . . .*

All her life, she has evoked charms, courted disaster. For they come true, they work. The blackbird flew off, her mother came along the landing (*Aren't you in bed yet, Annie?*), the rope caught between her ankles on the tenth jump. Lindsay did not come back. She does not mean to tempt the gods like this, but she can't help it. She longs for signs, confirmation, the right to hope.

Graham wakes at last, and goes to make sandwiches for both of them. They eat them in bed, and make love again. She hasn't been so open to him, so loving, for a long time.

'It's worth being on my own for a couple of weeks,' he tells her, 'if I get this when you come home.'

Annie giggles, moves closer, touching him.

'No more!' He throws up his hands in mock horror. 'I'm finished, floppy as a wet dishcloth. A broken man.' But she is having some success, and laughs at him as he quickens again and moves inside her for a few minutes more.

'I don't know,' she says, when they subside at last, and lie still, 'I don't know why I feel so hopeful suddenly. After all this time. It's got something to do with Jamie, I think. Now he's getting better, I just feel it's all going to come right.'

Graham grows cold beside her. He's a fool, why didn't he realise? It's not him she wants, her rush of desire wasn't for him. It's the right day, that's all, the right time of the month. He gets up without another word, and goes through to have a shower. The bathroom gets the sun only in the early morning, so it seems darker in here, and cold.

Annie stretches out in the empty bed, confident, happy.

*   *   *

When Annie comes back, sooner than she meant to at first, Jamie has sunk into depression. Even though she is here before he was expecting her, he is surly and resentful. And the weather has changed: rain sweeps in over a pewter sea, and the trees toss themselves about like fretful children. Water runs down the roof and drips from a hole in the guttering on to the paving stones at the back door. Tom, reading the newspaper in the kitchen, is conscious of the Aga's putter, the clock's tick, and the drip of water outside, like an echo. Above these, the wind makes forays through branches, rain spatters on the window. He is alone. Annie has hung her wet jacket over a chair and gone up to see Jamie. She's so cheerful, Tom hasn't managed to tell her about the nightmares. But she'll find out soon enough.

Jamie's bedroom is both stuffy and cold. She doesn't know whether to air it by opening the window or by putting on the electric fire.

'What you need,' she says, 'is a real fire.'

'Hasn't been lit for years.' Jamie is huddled in bed, in pyjamas and a navy Arran sweater with holes in the elbows. He is unshaven, and his skin looks greasy.

'Minute my back's turned!' Annie cries. 'Look at the state of this place.' She straightens bedclothes and sweeps crumpled tissues into the waste bin along with two empty beer cans and a full ashtray. 'No wonder it's foul in here.' She should have stayed with Graham. He'd have got over his moodiness, whatever caused it. Maybe he just didn't like to hear so much about Tom and Jamie. Once or twice, she's wondered if he's jealous. She tugs at the sash and the window shoots up with a jerk, letting in a sweep of cold air, a sharp peppering of rain.

'Annie, for God's sake – d'you want me to get pneumonia now?'

'Go downstairs then – it's warm in the kitchen.'

'I don't want to sit in the fucking kitchen. I want to stay in bed.'

'Oh Jamie, you'll never get strong at this rate.' Something of Graham's impatient vigour has infected her. All that sex – she has more energy than she can use, and can no longer be bothered with illness. Then she stops, looks at Jamie's peevish face. 'Oh dear. You're not well, are you?' She shuts the window with a bang and the room is still again. But her energy must go somewhere. 'I'll try the fire, eh?'

'It'll just smoke.'

'Och, it should be OK if we get it going properly.' She rushes off to find kindling, newspapers, to fill a bucket with coal. Jamie huddles under the downie, and sighs.

'There now.' The fire is laid: sticks crisscrossed on balls of newspaper, a few lumps of coal set on top. Annie, kneeling by the grate, strikes a match and the paper catches. In a moment, a cloud of smoke is pouring out into the room. 'Oh God, sorry – hang on—'

'I was right,' Jamie says. 'You dunderheid.'

'Wait, wait—' Annie sticks her hand up the chimney, knocks back the forgotten baffle plate. Soot falls, but not enough to put the fire out altogether. She stands up, grasps a fresh sheet of paper, shields the smouldering grate. In a moment, the smoke has begun to drift up the chimney instead. Annie stands back, sooty but triumphant. 'There now.'

'Annie – this room reeks – I can hardly breathe.'

'I'll open the window a wee crack – that'll clear the smoke out. Come on – you come down for a cup of tea and by the time you're back the room will be nice and cosy.'

There's nothing else to be done. He yields without grace and lets her help him downstairs.

Later, however, he's forced to admit she is right, and grudgingly forgives. The room is scented with burning wood, for she has brought up logs that were drying off by the Aga, and the fire is burning brightly. Annie runs a bath, and while he is soaking, changes his sheets and tidies the room.

'Right then,' she smiles at him as he settles back into bed, feeling clean and fresh at last, 'you're glad I'm here now, aren't you?'

'Daft besom,' he says, grinning, well enough to tease her now. 'Did you click then – hit the jackpot? Is this an incipiently pregnant Annie I see before me?'

'Shut up, don't speak about it.' But she glows; it must be all right.

Tom has taken advantage of Annie's return to go out, so she and Jamie spend the evening in his room, Jamie in bed, Annie in the armchair from the landing that she's dragged in. It's a greedy little fire, so she has to run up and downstairs for logs several times, and once brings a bottle of whisky back with her too. First they are merry, later melancholy sets in, and reminiscence.

'It was stormy like this after Lindsay went – d'you remember?' Annie says, listening to the hollow pipe of the wind as it swoops round the turret. 'After all that sun, those hot days . . . it was weird. The pathetic fallacy comes true – weather does seem to reflect human emotion.'

'So are you feeling stormy tonight?'

'A bit.'

'I've been thinking about it, you know. Being ill gives you too much time to dwell on stuff. Bad stuff.'

'Lindsay?'

'You remember those nightmares I used to get? Well, they're back. Since you went to Aberdeen.'

'I had to go,' Annie protests.

'Oh, it's not your fault,' he says, as if it is.

'The same nightmare? Or don't you remember?'

'I remember.'

'When you were little,' Annie reminds him, 'they didn't start right after Lindsay disappeared. You were about eight, nine. Not long after Auntie Liz died – so I'm sure that's why you got them. The loss of your mother.'

'Well, maybe. But they were *about* Lindsay. I don't know what started them off, but I associated them with a vague memory of seeing this old guy on the beach one day, sort of mumbling to himself. I think it was after that. Something about him brought it all up again. I never dreamt about Mum – you'd think I would, wouldn't you? Not about something that happened when I was five that no one even properly explained.'

'What guy on the beach – an old man?'

'Yeah, but I never saw him again. Maybe he was on holiday, some family's old grandad, I don't know. He was talking to himself. At least, talking as if there was somebody with him. Somebody he was mad at. But he was on his own. Scared me.'

Annie hesitates. 'Jamie, you say the nightmares were about Lindsay – what happens in them?'

'Same dream I had when I was a kid, would you believe that? Twenty years later, nearly. Eighteen.'

'Are you sure? How can you remember?'

'Aw, come on, Annie, remember your worst dream as a kid?'

'Yes,' she says. 'I was shut out, out of the house. Couldn't get back in. And my mother was there, I saw her through the window, but she didn't see me. Or hear me.' Her face darkens. 'Yes, I see what you mean.'

They listen for a moment to the wind, and the logs cracking on the fire.

'I'll tell you, if you like,' Jamie says.

Annie isn't sure she wants to hear it, but it might be thera-peutic for him, might stop the nightmares, if he tells them out loud. She can't say no. But his dream is terrible, and she was right to be afraid. What if she is tainted with it now? And yet it doesn't waken anything in her own memory.

'That's horrible,' she tells him, leaning forward to poke up the fire a bit. 'No wonder you woke up screaming.'

'Sorry,' Jamie says, realising too late that this might be lying in Annie's memory too. Perhaps she will have nightmares now, and she could be pregnant as well . . . *illness makes you so bloody selfish*. For the first time since it all began, he knows he wants to get well.

'It's all right.' Annie straightens up and looks at him. 'I had horrible pictures in my head too, of course I had. And Tom, and Alistair. All of us. But it's not true. I mean, whatever ours are . . . yours is wrong.'

'Well, it could easily be, of course. I mean, I wasn't there, for God's sake. They burned the bloody place down, didn't they? Some locals.'

'The hut? I thought the Council did that, to stop all the ghoulish tourists coming to look.'

'Anyway, even if the hut's . . . wrong . . . it's true in essence. True about her.' And he sees her again, his sister made different, the life knocked out of her, limp.

But before this can take hold, Annie says firmly, 'No, it's not, not true at all. She wasn't so little, for a start, she was thirteen, tall for her age. A big girl. And she wasn't wearing a dress, it was shorts.'

'What?'

'Oh, I'm sure about that. I longed for shorts like hers – boy's shorts. And it was so hot – the one hot week, Tom said, in a miserable summer. He was eleven, Alistair was twelve, so they remember more. You and I were – what? Five, eight. No memory survives on the surface from that sort of age.'

'That's my point about this picture I keep seeing in the dream – it came from deep down—'

'Deep down in what? You never saw her, you weren't there – how could you be?'

'Unless—' His face is full of new horror, but Annie stamps on this.

'No,' she says, 'you were never on your own. Not one of us – even Alistair – had a minute away from everyone else all the rest of that summer. What d'you think? They were terrified to let us out of their sight.'

Jamie leans back on his pillows.

'Right.' They are both thinking of the emptiness of memory, that can so easily be occupied by falsehood. 'Shorts?'

'Blue shorts, white Aertex shirt,' Annie confirms. 'Tom says they were blue – he remembers reading it in the paper, which he wasn't supposed to do, but he saw it at a friend's house, and he thought it was so strange, to read this description of his sister.'

'What do you mean, description?'

'I don't know – I suppose, about what she was wearing.'

'When she disappeared.'

'Yes.'

'But, Annie, if it's not true, my picture, where did it come from? I couldn't have made up something like that – not at seven or eight years old, could I?'

'No-no.' She hesitates. 'I suppose, maybe somebody else said something.' Some cruel child at school, she thinks, but can not really believe this. 'Och, no, Jamie, you must just have read some book, or seen a film—'

'A film? I was seven when Mum died, we never saw films. Well, *Snow White*. I remember *Snow White*. I mean, we didn't even have TV for years.'

'Well . . .' Annie falls silent, gives up.

'You said,' Jamie begins again, 'you said you had horrible pictures too.'

'Ally did, I think. But he read all those gory comics.' She saw Alistair standing at the door of her bedroom at home in Aberdeen. They were home, so it must have been later. When had they left the High House that summer? She could not remember. But she did remember being home, feeling safe again, then Alistair coming in and saying, 'Lindsay's not coming back.'

'Yes she is.'

'No she's not. She's dead now, she's in the woods and she's dead.'

And Annie had started screaming, so that both her parents came running upstairs and she was held tight, tight, both of them with their arms round her. But Alistair had not got into trouble. She remembers that too, and how she'd been disappointed and relieved at the same time. But as she drifted off to sleep, she heard her father's voice, low and steady, in Alistair's room next door.

Annie doesn't want to think of this any more, and Jamie is white-faced.

'Look, let's stop speaking about it. It's too miserable and awful. There's no comfort to be had from it – except in knowing it's over, and can't happen again.'

'But it does, Annie, to other kids.'

'Not to us, to our family. That's over. And Lindsay's at least . . . still perfect. No more suffering.'

'Perfect!'

'In memory. A golden girl. She was so beautiful. All the time, I wanted to be like her, I wanted to *be* her.'

'*Perfect?*' Jamie sits upright in bed. 'She was a bully – a bossy, snappy, mean-spirited—'

'Oh, come on, you can't remember her death, so how could you remember her life – her personality? You were five!'

'She was my fucking sister. And she left me out of everything – *You're too wee*, she was always telling me, *You can't come*.' A bark of derision. 'And once she said, listen to this, *Why have I always got to trail you with me everywhere?*'

'Oh Jamie, she wasn't like that, she was kind, she was kind to me. She used to comb the tangles out of my hair, all that salt, the sea – it hurt so much, I had such thick hair. She was the only one who did it gently.'

'Everybody,' Jamie says, not listening to any of this, 'had to dance to her tune. And all my fucking life I've had to be sorry she's dead, sorry about what happened and all the time I just don't care. I remember thinking, I really thought this, *Now Mum and Dad'll let me do all the things everybody else does—*'

'You were so spoiled!' Annie cries. 'You got your own way the whole time – no wonder Lindsay was fed up – you girned and girned and you couldn't play the games properly anyway—' She stops, suddenly, in mid-breath, shakes her head. 'Oh God, Jamie, this is ridiculous, you'd think we were still bairns.'

'Well,' Jamie says, his face sullen, as he yanks his bedclothes straight, 'she was my sister. I should know.'

'Jamie!'

A grin spreads slowly, obliterates the sulky mouth, the resentful brows. 'Yeah, OK.'

Annie gets up and crosses to the window, so that she can look down the steep slope of the garden. For all the storm, the dark sky, it is still daylight, and the wind has seen off the rain. The sea looks oily and grey. It is only because the wind is so strong, bends and parts the branches of the hedge, that she catches a glimpse of something moving on the path beyond.

'What can you see, Annie?' Jamie asks. 'Tell me what you see.' They are children again, looking over the wall, through the hedge, between the banisters.

'Just the garden, the trees leaning a long way down in the wind. And a cat under the hedge, I think. Not enough light to see which one.'

'No people?'

'No – at least – I thought – oh.'

'What?'

'There's a girl, a woman, coming in the gate. She can't work the catch – no wonder – now she's got it.'

'One of Tom's? Tom's Mary?'

'No, no, she's gone. He says she's gone for good. But she was fair, anyway, and this one's dark, and much taller. Quite . . . well, elegant.'

'Nobody I know then.'

'A holiday-maker? Got lost?'

'A new woman Tom hasn't told us about?' Jamie is beginning to struggle out of bed.

'Oh, it's Daisy. The cat, I mean. She's gone up to say hello. The girl's stroking her.'

'She's all right then, we approve?'

'She's very . . . well, from here, she looks really *striking*.'

'God, I must see this – who—' Jamie has reached Annie, so she puts out an arm to steady him. He looks down, reddens, whitens, retreats to the bed.

'Are you all right?' Annie is beside him, helping him to lie down again.

'Yeah, yeah. It's my doctor – that's who she is. Doctor Maclennan.'

'What – the one I kept just missing when I came to see you in hospital? How on earth—'

'Well, when I told her where I was going to convalesce, she said that was funny, she had friends in Cromarty, and she was going to stay with them in the summer. So I said come and visit me then, see how well I'm doing. She said – but I never thought she would. I told her about the house. But I didn't think—'

'I'd better go down,' Annie says. 'That bell at the back door doesn't work, and I don't think Tom's home yet.'

As he waits, Jamie pushes his rough thatch of hair back, straightens the bedcovers again, thanks God for Annie's tidying up, his hot bath, the log fire. He hides a *Beano* annual, but leaves lying on his bedside table the poems of John Donne, which Tom had been reading the night before. He is conscious that he's breathing loudly; the thudding of his heart is uncomfortable in his chest.

After he hears the voices downstairs, it seems a long time before footsteps come up. Then Annie puts her head round the door.

'You've got a visitor,' she says.

Then she comes in, followed by Ruth.

Summer

1

During the weekend Tom and Rob spent with them in May, Annie and Graham managed to behave like a couple whose marriage was still in existence. But Tom saw with dismay that both of them thought it was not. He didn't know what was going on, since for the first time in years Annie was no longer ringing him regularly, confiding. She must be talking to someone, but not him.

Within an hour of their arrival, Rob too saw things were not the same. He'd looked forward to coming, to Annie's food, and the little green-carpeted room where he'd shivered, and been afraid, then gradually become reassured by the solidity of the things and the people around him. But in his absence, some change had occurred.

'You've got your old room,' Annie said, as if he'd been in it for years before moving to Tom's. He felt as if he had – it was all so familiar. The room hadn't changed.

Annie opened the window a little further. 'It's warm today,' she said, turning back to face him.

'Summer's coming.' She smiled, but he thought she looked as if her face might pucker into tears, any moment.

'Are you all right?' he asked.

'Yes . . . a bit tired, that's all.'

'Sure?' For a moment, she thought he really wanted to know, so tender he seemed, looking at her. Then she saw that all he really wanted her to do was reassure. And she was touched by that too.

'I'm fine. I'll get the lunch, then you and Graham can go off to Comet or wherever you're buying this computer.'

'It's a Computer Discount Centre. There's Comet in Inverness, but Graham said to come to Aberdeen, this place is better, it's got the best deals. It's good he's coming – Tom doesn't know nothing about them.'

'Well, I think he wants to see Jamie and Ruth while he's here.'

'Yeah, that's how I got him to come, right enough.' He grinned. 'But he's sick of me goin' on about the computer, so he said OK, Graham could help me pick it.'

'This is instead of a television?'

'Kind of. It's so he can do his writin' on it, and I can have all the games and stuff. Championship Manager, World Cup Soccer . . . Gavin and Fraser and them have got them all.'

Annie didn't know who he was talking about. Or what. But it sounded as if he'd got some friends. He must be all right.

'But,' she said, 'if they've got them, why don't you get something different?' But to this, Rob gave her only a look of pity in reply, so she went downstairs to lay the table and put the quiche in the oven.

In the afternoon, when Graham had taken Rob off to study computers, and buy one on Tom's behalf, Tom drove Annie to the hospital.

'Jamie didn't want us to pick him up?'

'He'll be staying on, so he said he'd take his own car.'

It was difficult to park; they had a long way to walk, in a burst of hot sunshine, to the hospital entrance.

'Should I get some flowers?' Tom asked, hesitating by the shop with its buckets full of carnations and gypsophila, its magazines and chocolates and fruit.

'She's got plenty, believe me.'

'How was she – when you saw her last night?'

'A bit groggy. I'm sure she'll be better today.'

'She lost a lot of blood, Jamie said.'

'Yes, she did.'

'But she's OK? I mean, I could get her chocolates or something?'

Annie almost laughed. 'Chocolates?' Then she saw he was nervous, shifting from foot to foot, hands in his pockets to keep them still. 'It's all right, Tom. We don't have to take anything, really.'

'*Private Eye*,' Tom said, plucking it from the magazine rack. 'Then if she doesn't want it, I can read it.'

Annie hesitated between *Woman's Journal* and *Cosmopolitan*. Somehow, even ill, Ruth seemed too grown-up for magazines. But she must have liked them, for Annie had seen them strewn about the flat: glossy and expensive, full of articles on improving your body or keeping your man, and interviews with famous women.

'You don't buy these things, do you?' Tom asked, as Annie paid for both, and tucked them under her arm. They set off towards the lift.

'No. They seem to be about people who live in another world from me. I quite like the old-fashioned ones, with a lot of recipes.'

There was a crowd in front of the lift, so they squeezed in with half a dozen other people and a male nurse with a patient in a wheelchair. They all rose in silence. Annie smiled at Tom, but he did not smile back.

'She was in a room by herself,' Annie said as they came out of the lift and headed for the ward. 'But we'd better ask – she might have been moved.'

'I hate hospitals,' Tom said.

'Because of Jamie.'

'And my mother.'

Annie stopped and turned to face him. 'You don't have to come in.'

'I told Jamie I'd be here. If I can't even manage *that*.'

Annie put a hand on his arm. 'We won't stay. She'll not be fit for a long visit, anyway.'

'How long's she going to be in here?'

'A week, ten days. It depends. A hysterectomy's a big oper-ation, you know. And hers was an emergency.'

'So – she's out of the game for a while, then?'

'Off work for about three months. I don't know how she'll cope with that. And no lifting.'

They had reached the ward. Annie went up to the nurses' station to ask about Ruth. Tom waited, trying not to breathe in the hospital smell.

'She's in a side ward,' Annie said, coming back to him. 'So she must be a bit more like herself.'

'It seems ironic, doesn't it?' Tom remarked, following Annie along the corridor.

'What – that she's lost the baby after all? Worse than that. It's so *sad*.'

'After all that drama in March – was it only March? Then after it's all settled, and she's given in to him—'

'Is that how you saw it?'

'No. I suppose not. Maybe.'

They were at the entrance to a four-bedded ward.

'This is it,' Annie said. 'There – oh – her parents are here, as well as Jamie.'

'I won't stay then,' Tom offered at once. 'I'll say hi, and then I'll go down and wait for you in that lounge place we passed near the shop.'

'Right – I won't be very long either.'

Tom was barely half-way through *Private Eye* when Annie came to fetch him. She sat in the chair opposite his.

'She's not that great. And I thought there were more than enough people. Her mother's a very tiring sort of woman. Never stops talking.'

'I saw what you meant about the flowers.'

'That was Jamie. Came in with armfuls yesterday.'

'He seemed fine.'

'He feels needed. He likes to think Ruth needs him.'

'I thought he'd be distraught – he wasn't bad on the phone, but—'

'Well, he's not distraught. Neither is she. Just ill.'

'I thought she looked pretty washed out.'

'Being beautiful helps,' Annie sighed.

'Well then.' Tom closed the magazine. 'We're going, are we?'

Annie was brisk, going home. It was Tom who felt low and vulnerable. But suddenly, as she made tea for them in the kitchen, she broke down and stood by the sink with the hot teapot in her hand, weeping. Tom came and took the teapot from her, poured the tea, took it through to the living room. He made her sit down, staying by her on the sofa.

'Is it Graham—' he began, thinking she wanted to tell him about this now, but she broke in, her voice loud and anguished.

'Why can't we have children – what's so wrong with us there are no children?'

'I suppose we can't count Rob,' Tom said, putting his arm round her.

'Well,' Annie sobbed, 'it's Alistair – what sort of father is he?'

'I wish I'd had kids myself,' Tom said, 'if it would have made you happy.' For a moment, he meant this. He peopled his mind with the children he might have had with Mary, had he not been – what? – immature, fond of his shallow freedom? Afraid.

He put his arms round Annie and drew her close, sheltering. Her dark hair gave off a puff of fragrance, and underneath, he could smell her acrid weeping. She was warm and solid, leaning her weight on him, sighing as the sobs died away.

'I'm sorry,' she said. 'I don't know why I'm crying, really. I'm just so *tired*. And it's a sort of general sense of hopelessness. Everything.'

'And Graham – what about him?'

She drew away. 'Oh Tom, I don't want to talk about it. Even to you. It's so horrible – we don't talk properly to each other now.'

'Is he – I mean, is it still going on?'

'He says not, but it is, I know it is. So I won't sleep in the same room with him any more. I mean, we have to, while you and Rob are here, but I made him move to the spare – I wasn't going to have him near me while – I couldn't bear it!'

'Oh Annie.'

'It's worse than that.' But she could not tell even Tom how she had pursued Graham to the spare bedroom, desperate for him to make love to her again, and annihilate the other. How could she both hate and desire him? And how could they go on with so little sleep, and so much anger and grief between them? She was exhausted. She leaned on Tom again, and closed her eyes.

She had wept for Ruth too, not knowing who most needed pity. All that anger she'd felt, the real hatred of Ruth, it seemed stupid now, a waste. Poor Ruth. There was nothing to envy now except her career, and you couldn't get worked up about that.

Really, it was herself she thought about, through all this drama, herself and Graham.

'Why don't you come back with Rob and me for a while?' Tom asked. 'Give yourself a break. Rob would love it.'

'Would he?' She smiled at him and dabbed at the tears drying on her face. 'I do miss him. But it's as well he hasn't been here with all this . . . No, I can't, Tom. If I left, he'd see her all the time, it would just get worse, and it might even be here, in my house. And then I couldn't come back and *live* in it.' Her voice rose, panicking.

There was something here whose depths Tom could not touch. Annie had gone somewhere he could not follow. He had not the experience, but more than that, he wasn't capable of this kind of desperation. But perhaps that is my loss, or lack, he thought later, lying awake in the spare bedroom, from which Graham was temporarily given reprieve. His thoughts swung between Annie and Jamie. Jamie had come in on his way home from the hospital in the evening.

'She's doing really well,' he said. 'And all these other doctors keep coming in to chat to her – you can see she's not up to it, but she really wants to talk to them about work. It's awful for her, being a patient.'

'I suppose it is.' Tom didn't know what else to say. 'You can let me know, anyway, how she gets on. We're going back tomorrow.'

'What's the hurry?' Jamie seemed surprised. 'You've only just got here.'

'Rob's working.'

Jamie grinned at this. 'Oh yeah, for Hamish. Send him back on the train, then. You could stay on.'

Tom hesitated. Annie was out of the room, but he wasn't sure how much Jamie knew of what was going on. But why should his loss protect him from everyone else's? And he looked all right; he seemed (Tom tried to find a word for it) less tense.

'It's not all that comfortable here,' he said at last.

Jamie looked round at the large, restful room with its quiet watercolours and ample furniture. It was less tidy than it used to be, much less, but uncomfortable?

Tom sighed. 'For God's sake, Jamie, I think Annie and Graham need to be on their own, to sort things out. They can do without visitors.'

'It's serious then?'

'You've managed to notice something's wrong?'

'Well, yes, but—' Jamie reddened. 'I've had a lot on my mind, for Christ's sake. And Annie never said – she just kept telling me they were having a few problems. I thought it was this business about being childless, and with Ruth and me – I just thought it was best not to say too much. It didn't seem fair.'

'She was protecting you, I imagine. As she always has.'

'Fuck off, Tom, if whatever's going on hasn't anything to do with Ruth and me having a baby – not that we are, not that we *ever* are—'

Between them, an angry and painful silence.

'All I'm saying,' Tom remarked mildly, after a moment or two, 'is that I knew what it was, and I'm living a hundred miles away. I'm not blaming you for anything.'

Jamie took a deep breath. 'It's Graham. You're telling me he's shagging someone else, right?'

Tom winced. 'As you so quaintly put it.'

'Sorry – I wouldn't say that to Annie, you know that. What a bastard.'

'Well, that's one way of looking at it.'

'I thought she looked – I don't know. I thought she was just – oh, shite, she's got thinner, hasn't she? I've never seen Annie look thin.' He got up and went to the glass cabinet. 'Think I'll drink his gin, then, the bastard, maybe I'll even finish it.'

'Lay off – you've got to drive home.'

Jamie added a splash of tonic water. 'Just one, then. A large one.'

He sat down again, facing Tom, on the edge of the chair. He took a gulp of gin, and shoved his free hand through his hair, in the familiar gesture of perplexity, dismay.

'Have you talked to Graham?' he asked.

'Christ no.'

'But Annie – she's sure there's something going on? They're in a bit of a crisis, right?'

'Yes.'

'Should I say something to her? After you've gone home – I

mean, I can't get involved, I've got Ruth . . . and . . . what about marriage guidance, that stuff?'

'I think she suggested it, but Graham wouldn't go.'

'The bastard.'

'So you keep saying. Does he look a happy man to you? But then, you weren't here when he rammed down a minimal amount of food, as if it choked him, and shot out of the house again. He hasn't said more than a dozen words to me since I came. He must have talked to Rob, but that'll all have been incomprehensible jargon. They went out today and spent a vast sum of my money on some computer.'

Jamie finished his drink, and stared down at the empty glass.

'Now I need another one. Maybe I could get a taxi home.' He sighed, setting the glass down on the low table next to him.

'Better not,' Tom said, his voice conciliatory now, 'I think we should keep out of it. They'll get through it themselves, one way or another.'

'Aye, maybe.'

When Annie came in, they both looked up guiltily.

'Sorry, I was talking to Rob. How's Ruth?' Rob followed her in, and sprawled on a chair. The cat, who had ignored invitations from both Tom and Jamie, leaped at once on to his lap.

For a few minutes, they all talked about Ruth, then Jamie went home, refusing coffee.

'I'll ring you,' he promised Annie as he left. 'We should sort out the visiting a bit – she really can't cope with more than one or two at a time.'

'I'll ring you before I go, then.'

'Well,' Jamie grinned, 'it was her family I was thinking about really.' He hesitated. 'Annie, are you OK? I mean, is there anything I can do?'

Annie reddened. 'No, don't be daft. You've got enough to cope with.'

But he put his arms round her and she leaned on his shoulder. Who was comforting whom, she wondered. 'I hope it'll be all right now – you and Ruth.'

He shrugged. 'Yeah, it's queer. I'm wrecked, you know, about the baby. Wrecked. But somehow, because Ruth's so upset as well, we're close. We understand each other, we're together, right? And she needs me now, so I feel I'm some *use*. Does that make sense?'

Maybe that was what he really wanted all along, Annie thought, closing the door after Jamie had left. Ruth to need him, to be useful, necessary. Then she heard Graham's car, and the weariness of her own anxiety came down like a blanket again, obliterating everything else.

Later, alone with Tom in the hall for a few minutes before they went to bed, she said, 'Graham was early tonight, earlier than usual. That's for your benefit – or more likely Rob's.'

'He's often late, is he?'

'Sometimes. Mostly, it's after school – he doesn't get in till eight, nine. Says it's school stuff, but it didn't used to go on so long . . .' Her eyes filled with tears. 'I can't bear it, Tom. I can't bear this. How long will it go on? I've no life, no life any more.'

What could he do but hold her in his arms? But the easy comfort he'd given, for years and years, it seemed, since they were children, was inadequate now, a thin sort of solace. He felt bad about it, but he was glad he and Rob were leaving the next day.

And Annie was glad enough to let them go, though it meant she was on her own with her unhappiness again. But she was disappointed in Tom, understood for the first time how he had let other women down, being afraid of pain, even other people's. He'd been so close and kind, through all those bitter childless years. But when it came to men and women, he chickened out. She saw that. Still, she missed the comfort she was used to finding in him, and felt lonelier than ever. But perhaps you had to go through this kind of thing, to understand it. That was why she could talk to Cath. Indeed, they went over it compulsively, or Annie did, and Cath listened.

'Yes,' she would say, 'that's how I felt,' or 'Pete used to do that.' Cath knew what it meant, to be suddenly without a future, as if all the life to come has been eaten up, and the present frozen.

'We don't seem to get out of the bit,' Annie told her. 'We're stuck, in this awful misery.'

They sat in the art gallery coffee shop, analysing their marriages, trying to explain – more to themselves than to each other – what had gone wrong.

'In the summer,' Cath reassured, 'he'll be away from school, so that'll give you both a break – you could start to sort things out. He won't be seeing her every day.'

'That's what I keep telling myself.' Annie stirred the milk into her second cup of coffee, watching it marble and blend to a uniform dark brown. 'But then I think, maybe he'll get desperate – go and see her anyway. What if – what if – oh God, he might leave me, Cath.'

'I don't think so. I had to throw Pete out, in the end. They like their comforts.' But Annie was still stirring her coffee, biting her lip. 'It's that serious, then, you really think it's that serious?'

Cath had not thought it possible, likely, that Annie's marriage would come to an end, as hers had. Annie and Graham were different – solid, close. *You're my rock,* she had said often to Annie in the past, *You're the white hope for the survival of marriage as an institution.* No, they were going through a bad patch, that was all. Annie dramatised – Graham probably just fancied this woman, had maybe had a wee fling. Now she was not so sure.

'Give him an ultimatum,' she said at last. 'Tell him he's got to sort himself out or go.'

'I can't.'

'Why not?'

'He might do it, that's what I'm telling you. He might go. He could live with her, couldn't he?'

'But Annie, that might not be as bad as this – the way things are now. When Pete went – it was – God, such a relief. I mean, I cried myself to sleep every bloody night for a month, but the rest of the time . . .' She hesitated.

'What?' Annie looked up, and two tears brimmed over and rolled gently down her face.

'It was peaceful. Very very peaceful. Empty.'

'Oh God,' Annie sighed, 'maybe you're right.' She scrubbed away the tears with a crumpled paper napkin and gathered her things together. 'Come on – let's go and look at the *Blue Pool*.'

'Och,' Cath sighed, 'you and your *Blue Pool*.'

But she stood quietly at Annie's side as she gazed at the

small Augustus John canvas. She couldn't see why Annie liked it, really. It wasn't her taste – too plain, she thought, the colours crude.

'See that water?' Annie asked, gazing past the girl lying down with her yellow book, at the blue water. 'I could jump in there, and go down down down, and never come back up.'

'God, don't say things like that.' Cath clutched at Annie's arm.

Annie turned, half-surprised, and looked at the woman beside her, a small fair creature in a hotchpotch of layered skirts and cotton waistcoat and floating scarves, her thin nail-bitten hand with its silver rings (not one a wedding ring) laid on her arm. Cath, who drifted from one unsuitable man to another, haphazard, aimless. I don't want to be like that, Annie thought, I want to be married. That's what I'm used to.

And yet, in the gallery shop, where Cath was buying birthday cards before they left, she caught sight of herself in a mirror and changed her mind completely. I look different now, she thought. Perhaps I could be independent, get a job, be my own woman. Look how thin I am, she considered, what a strange thing.

But it was exhausting, all this emotional swinging to and fro. In the morning, when Graham left for work, she despaired, wept, rang the Samaritans. By evening, having walked all afternoon on the beach or in the woods, the increase in oxygen, or adrenaline, raised her hopes too. She had never thought of herself as a moody person. Now she seemed to be at the mercy of every tick of the minute hand on the clock. But Cath was right: if, when term ended, it was still as bad, she would give him an ultimatum. She would force both of them out of this terrible dark place.

2

The living room of the cottage had a floor, and there was now a newly fitted bathroom. The plumbing hadn't been quite as straightforward as Rob had thought, but Hamish was experienced in things going wrong. In the end, between them, they managed pretty well. At Ross Building Supplies in Dingwall, Rob was now almost as well known as Hamish himself. They seemed to have spent hours pottering there, holding up first one joint or fitting after another, asking each other, or the boys who worked there, *Would this do? What about this one, and then put it with the one you got?*

Some time ago, Rob had started going to Ross County matches with Gavin, who was working in the building supplies depot for a year before going to university. By the end of the season, Rob was as anxious as Gavin to have the team promoted out of the Highland League to the Third Division. He lectured Hamish relentlessly about it on the way back to the cottage, their purchases rattling in a cardboard box in the back of the Land Rover.

Spring dissolved to summer, slowly. Then at the end of May, just after he and Tom got back from Aberdeen, it suddenly became hot. Rob was doing the outside paintwork; Hamish was fitting cupboards in the kitchen. The paint dried too quickly in the heat; the smell of it mixed with the smell of chipboard shavings as Hamish cut the worktops to size. A lark lifted from her hidden hollow in the field behind them and fluttered invisible in shimmering air. A peewit called over and over on her two notes, high low, high low. It was so still that when Hamish stopped sawing and banging, they could hear the sea.

Hamish had rashly advertised that the cottage would be available in July and August, and already had a booking, so he and Rob felt purposeful, keenly racing against time. They were both desperate to finish, and at the same time enjoying themselves so much neither could imagine their lives beyond getting the place ready.

'What about furniture?' Rob asked one day, as they sat on the grass outside, backs to the wall, eating sandwiches. They didn't go to the Dolphin till they finished at night, because there wasn't time. In the Dolphin, Hamish had two pints and Rob had two halves, and then Rob went back to Tom's, or Stuart's, for tea. What Hamish did then, Rob had no idea. He suspected he stayed on in the Dolphin quite late, and that he ate there. *Shepherd's Pie last night*, he sometimes said, or *Microwave's a wonderful thing – Mhairi had that curry ready in two minutes.*

'Furniture?' Hamish paused, sandwich in midair.

'You've got to put furniture in.'

'Oh yes. Tell you what, come up to the house later – we can pick out a few things.'

'But – are you not goin' to buy new stuff – not dear, like. MFI, that's what I thought you'd get.'

Hamish looked blank, as if he'd never heard of MFI. Probably, thought Rob, he hasn't.

'No, no. Plenty of good pieces at the house. I admit, might need – ah – dishes – linen – that sort of thing. I'm still using what my mother got when she married. Wonderful bottom drawer, my mother. They did have, in those days.'

In the afternoon, between coats of paint, Hamish drove them up to his house, Rob silent with doubt. He had been to Hamish's house two or three times, and it seemed to him a great pity to spoil a good holiday cottage by filling it with the kind of things Hamish had as furniture. People wouldn't come back, that was all. But he couldn't think how to say this tactfully.

From the outside, a little distance away, the house was beautiful: early Victorian, apricot-hued stone, and set among silver birches. Tourists, passing through, catching a glimpse of it from the road, would say to each other how lovely it was, and wonder who lived there. Coming closer, you could see the paint on the gables was peeling, the window frames rotten, the garden gone to jungle behind, weedy grass in front.

Inside, cobwebs hung in the high corners of ceilings, dust gathered on the stairs in grey fluffy balls, grime adhered to the pitch pine skirting boards and in the door mouldings. There was a smell of something that was not damp: the house was set on a hill, and had always been airy. Tom said it was dry rot: a mouldy, rank smell, of something gone bad. The whole house was permeated with it, but it was worst downstairs, and in the front rooms.

The kitchen was at the back: it was large, with windows on to the garden, but in a fit of modernisation twenty years before, Hamish had had the old Rayburn taken out and an electric cooker and fitted cupboards with yellow laminated doors put in. So it was often cold: there was a faint warmth in the area of the storage heater, but in winter that merely prevented the water from freezing in the kettle overnight, something which Hamish assured Rob had happened in the scullery when he was a boy. *Coldest house in the Black Isle*, he told Rob, who believed it. The long passageway down the centre of the house, from front door to kitchen, was a conduit for every possible draught. Even on a hot June day, the air struck chill when you went in. It was a mystery to Rob why Hamish, who was so energetic and capable in the matter of the cottage, had done nothing with Brae Mhor. Hamish blamed his mother.

'She didn't care much for the changes in the kitchen – they were her idea in the first place, mind you. The old range was a bit temperamental, time it went. But after that, she wouldn't hear of any more alterations. And I hadn't the heart after she died.'

'She must have been a right masochist then,' Rob muttered, but out of Hamish's hearing.

Now, they went from room to room, Rob with a pad of paper and a pen, so that they could make a list.

'What about this tallboy – never liked it much?'

'Too high.'

'Ah yes. Low ceilings. Right, good. Get our specification first, eh?'

'It's all a bit big,' Rob pointed out.

Hamish looked crestfallen. 'You may be right. Beds, though,' here he cheered up, 'single beds – I've about fourteen of those, scattered about.'

Rob couldn't think of any objection to these, or to the ugly nineteen-sixties dressing tables and chests of drawers standing in the dozen unused bedrooms. But he did wonder if they all had the bad smell right through them. Maybe it would fade in the cottage, with the tang of new paint competing, and the windows open to the sun.

'You'll need removers,' Rob said, as they came along the landing to the linen room.

'Fraser's van,' Hamish said. 'George will see to it for me.'

He opened the door of the linen room. The hot-water tank was in here: it was both the warmest and the pleasantest place in the house. A yellow-eyed cat crept from the lowest of the slatted shelves where it had been asleep on some towels, and slunk off downstairs. Hamish shouted at it, but half-heartedly.

'Bloody cat,' he said.

'Is it yours?'

'No, no, from the farm. Might have been here for days, actually. Can't remember when I was in here last.' But the skylight was ajar, so perhaps the cat had got in that way.

This room smelled of old linen and dust, but nothing worse. However, when they unwound some of the sheets, to look them over, they came to pieces along the folds.

'Well, well,' said Hamish, 'there you are.'

'How long has this stuff *been* here?' Rob wondered, but Hamish was vague. Probably since his mother's marriage, or his grandmother's.

Back in the kitchen, Hamish put the kettle on for tea.

'How long's your family been here?' Rob asked. He was checking Hamish's milk, which was often sour. But this was all right.

'My grandfather came here in eighteen forty-something. You might have a look in there while you're at it. See what needs turning out.'

Rob looked deeper into the fridge. A packet of bacon stank, and there was a piece of orange cheddar with some fungus attached. He removed them both, and put them in the bin.

'So what did you do?' he went on, as Hamish poured the tea

and they sat at the table eating chocolate digestives. Rob knew they were all right: Hamish had bought them on the way home the day before.

'Do?'

'Before you started on the cottage . . . well, when you were younger, I mean.'

'Army,' Hamish announced, and Rob suddenly saw him as a soldier.

'I thought of that,' he said. 'But I came up here instead. My mate Kevin – that's what he wants to do, except his mum and dad say he's got to get A levels first. You get to travel . . . an' all that. Kevin was dead keen – got me persuaded an' all.'

'Well,' Hamish looked doubtful, 'I dare say he's right. It's different now of course. And it doesn't last for ever. When you come out, it's a bit difficult to decide what to tackle next. I helped Tom's father for a while.'

'What – in the shop?'

'A bit of this, a bit of that,' Hamish nodded. 'Mother kept to her room, so I didn't like to leave her again. I couldn't go far, at any rate.' He sighed, and drank his tea, straining it noisily through his moustache. 'After the business with the girl, though, I stopped that too. Couldn't face it. Couldn't face Elizabeth, I suppose. And Mother was nervous after that about being left. Not that there was any risk to *her*. And anyway, they got the bugger.'

Rob suddenly caught on to this. He hadn't been listening properly, but now he wished he had.

'You were in the bookshop,' he said, 'when Lindsay disappeared?'

'Indeed I was. That very day. All afternoon. Perfect alibi, place was mobbed, always was in the season, in those days. People like a book on holiday, and we did postcards then, newspapers, magazines. I said to Stuart, that's the way to go, you know, not these fusty old books nobody's ever heard of.'

'Alibi? Alibi for what?'

'Girl disappears, they question everybody. Everybody.'

Hamish had turned dark red, and his blue eyes glared at Rob.

Suddenly Rob longed to say, *So did they find her?* Something in Hamish's rigmarole (what had he said?) made him realise now that they had. A spasm of fear gripped his arms, his chest. He got up and rinsed his mug.

'We better get back – I want to give the front door its last coat. Then I can get on with the inside tomorrow.'

'Right oh.' The colour faded from Hamish's face; he too got up and rinsed his mug.

They went out to the Land Rover. Hamish looked normal again, his usual self. He kicked at the ginger cat which was sunning itself on the front doorstep. It leaped up and was gone in a streak of orange, across the grass.

I could ask Tom, Rob thought, as they drove back along the road and turned up the rough track to the cottage. He did not want to ask Hamish any more about it, he'd seemed really angry and upset. It was weird, the way something that had happened so long ago (it seemed another age to him, so distantly before his own birth) could go on affecting them all. His curiosity about what had happened to Lindsay had all but vanished. Not even being here, at the High House, had stirred it much. He'd had too many other things to think about. Now he began to wonder again. Yet as he worked through the rest of the afternoon, painting with smooth steady strokes the dark blue of the cottage front door, using a small brush for the mouldings, the edges, he tucked it away again. Sometime, when Tom had had a few drams, and was mellow, he would ask outright. That was the best way with Tom, who, really, was always quite mellow. Sad though, he was a sad kind of guy.

He spent a lot of his time on the phone these days, dealing in books, he told Rob. The shop had been gutted, fiercely altered. There were round tables with yellow check covers, pots of trailing ivy and geraniums and a clean white counter. It smelled of ground coffee and home baking, and it had opened for business in one short month.

Tom was still getting rid of the stock. A lot had gone to a dealer who had come up with a van. The rarer books Tom was selling off in twos and threes, getting the best prices he could. The dining room at the High House, which had a piano, an oak table and eight chairs, and was never used, was now piled with books. When he wasn't packing books, or on the phone, Tom was writing. He did a country diary for a national paper; he reviewed books. It was the exam season, so there was no supply teaching.

'It's not enough,' he told Rob, 'but it'll do for now.'

'You should write a novel,' Rob suggested. 'A best seller.'

'Aye, right,' Tom mocked. 'Just hand me that computer you're always using and I'll get on with it.'

'No, but you could though.' Rob considered this. 'A thriller – eh – car chases and gun-runners and all that.'

'Yes,' Tom murmured, 'I could base it all on my own experiences in the SAS.'

For a few seconds, Rob thought he meant it, that it was true. Tom acquired a glow of glamour. Then it dissolved: he was kidding, he had to be.

Rob finished the door with a careful upsweep. Then he went to clean his brushes. Hamish was screwing handles on to the cupboards.

'You should have cupboards like that in your kitchen. They'd look all right – the pine.'

'Better than mustard yellow, you're thinking?'

'Yeah, well . . .'

Hamish rose creakily to his feet. 'Some day,' he said. 'Some day.' He stood back, admiring his handiwork. 'You know,' he said, 'if this cottage lies empty all winter, I think I'll move in myself. Nice little place – easy to keep.'

'What about your house, though?'

Hamish narrowed his eyes. 'Come off it. Place is crumbling round my ears, eh?'

'Well . . .'

'And who's going to have it when I'm gone? Tell me that?'

'I don't know,' Rob said. 'Don't you have kids?'

'None that I acknowledge,' Hamish said loftily, as he packed up his tools.

It was still hot when they drove away at six. Rob wanted a bath, and something to eat. Then he'd walk along to the Dolphin, taking Bracken with him. She'd lie outside, waiting. There was a darts match tonight; he'd said he would play.

As he came up the path towards the gate into the High House garden, there was at the back of his mind, the question of Lindsay again. He thought he would ask Tom tonight. Once he knew, it could be finished with, tidied away. But it was Hamish, not Lindsay, he was thinking of. Something about the way Hamish had spoken, his sudden fury, made him uneasy. And yet, as he pushed the gate open with his paint-stained hand, came into the now familiar garden, it was another, stronger and less known emotion that wavered gently through him.

I'm happy, he thought. Weird – I'm happy.

As he shut the gate and turned to walk up the garden to the back door, he saw there was a man in the shadow of the doorway, not as tall or thin as Tom, wearing a T-shirt and shorts. With a jolt of something so strong it might equally have been joy or dismay, Rob saw it was his father.

3

Silence, apart from here and there a sigh, the turning of a page, occasionally the faint clatter of a dropped pen. All down the main hall, pupils sat in rows, heads bent. Higher French.

Graham was on the dais at the front; the other invigilator strolled slowly between rows. His left shoe creaked a little. Growing conscious of this, he stopped, turned, creaked back to his desk at the rear of the hall. Graham looked at the clock on the side wall, watched the second hand move noiselessly in tiny jerks, counting down. He cleared his throat.

'Fifteen minutes,' he said aloud, and his voice raised one or two heads. Here and there a pupil gazed sightlessly, then bent to write again. Near the front was the empty desk of a boy who had stopped writing after half an hour, shut his answer book and leaned back, gazing at the ceiling. A few minutes later, he left. Graham did not know him well, but made a note to speak to his teacher. Now one or two others left the hall.

No one liked invigilating: it was a bore, and you couldn't do your own work to pass the time. But today Graham found it soothing. When his replacement had arrived half-way through he'd told her he would carry on, if she brought his coffee in. Relieved, she'd agreed, and gone back to writing reports.

Here, in the quiet hall, there was order. Everyone had a purpose, however well or poorly they pursued it. At least, Graham thought, we all know what we're supposed to be doing. The outside world ceased to exist, and he had nothing to do but gaze up and down the rows, or walk slowly between them.

He was conscious as he did so, of the girls' scent, both floral and chemical, and a guff, once or twice, of sweaty trainers kicked off under a desk.

After the brief week before Easter, when it was warm enough to lie on the ground at Deeside and make love, it had been a bleak spring. Now, in the thick of exams, it was hot. Outside, beyond the ceiling-high hall windows, blue sky and sun blazed. Between exams, pupils lay against the warm stone wall, sunbathing. Graham held himself suspended, in the last few minutes of the exam. When it was over, the papers collected, the pupils gone, erupting into conversation, exclamations, as they moved into the corridor, he'd go back to his office and work with the head of maths on next year's timetable. But the comfortable blank space in his head would vanish, and he'd start thinking again. Involuntarily, he groaned, so that two or three in the front row looked up, and a girl giggled softly. He looked at his watch.

'Pens down,' he said.

With his colleague, Graham packed the exam papers and left them in the main school office where one of the secretaries was dealing with them. Jim Bruce wasn't yet at the computer, pursuing mysterious gaps in the timetable, so Graham sat at his desk, and went through the day's mail, which he'd not had time to look at yet.

But it swam and blurred, made no sense. He put his head in his hands, felt his fingers grip bone, breathed deep. He had made his life impossible. It was only a matter of time before the affair with Jan was common knowledge throughout the staff. Schools do not hold secrets. An occasional comment, eyebrows raised across a meeting, had several times recently made him wonder if – no. The holidays were only weeks away. That would kill any rumours. Everyone would have other things to think about by the time they came back.

In April, during the Easter holidays, he'd told himself it had been no more than a temporary madness. And yet afterwards, back at school, he had known as soon as they met in the corridor, that it was going to start again. It did not make any difference that he kept telling himself he was crazy, making a complete fool of himself, nor that he said over and over *Right, that's the last time*. His feeling for her had grown stronger, his ability to keep away from her vanished. So when she looked round the door, as she was doing now, he was stirred with longing, on fire again, and ceased to care what anyone else knew, or thought.

'When are you finishing?' she asked.

'I don't know. An hour, hour and a half. The timetable.'

'Right.'

'Are you off then?'

'God no – you should see the state of my desk. And only – what – four weeks left?'

'Well, look in before you go.'

'I will.'

A look, a pause, and she had gone. *I'm like a kid.* Over and over, he chided himself – *acting like a kid* – but had no answer, no way out.

In the past, he'd had no sympathy for men who cheated on their wives, thought it a cheap trick, and anyway stupid, to put at risk so much, for so little. Only now, it did not seem so little. It dominated his every waking thought. And the main emotion he felt was not love or hate or anything so absolute. It was guilt, a great lump that had settled somewhere around his solar plexus, but now and again shifted heavily, displacing reason.

Jim Bruce came in, so Graham got up and switched on the computer. For almost two hours, they lost themselves in the complexities of turning the third year into the fourth year, a process which had mysteriously lost them a number of individual pupils. Laboriously they were going through the year, pupil timetable by pupil timetable. Both of them, turning aside from all else in their lives, gave themselves up to logic, calculation.

At six, Graham realised the time, and rang Annie.

'Timetable,' he said. 'Sorry, another hour or so. Can you fix me something I can just heat up?'

'Sure,' she said. 'Don't I always?'

On the phone she was cold, and he became resentful. It was the bloody timetable, for Christ's sake! If Jim hadn't been in the room, he might have said this aloud, complaining she was suspicious about nothing. But as he hesitated, Annie hung up.

How was he to know she was huddled in tears by the phone? And if he had known, all he would have felt (Annie knew) was irritation. In her imagination, furiously overworked, Graham no longer loved her but Jan, was repeatedly unfaithful. She was sure they both despised and mocked her. She knew Jan's name now, and thought she knew her face. She waited in her car near the school gates one day, watching the pupils swarm out fast, the staff follow in staggered relays. Sitting there, she had felt both excited and ashamed, but most of all she had felt frightened.

Her glimpse of Jan, the woman she thought must be Jan, made her heart pound with excitement and fear. *She's not even pretty – if that's her – how can he? He must hate me, to betray me with her.* And yet, bizarrely, some of the pain eased. It would have been worse (though she didn't know why) if Jan had been a prettier, younger version of herself. But she was not, she was middle-aged, lean, sharp, with an air of cool confidence. Annie shifted the focus of her obsession from Graham to Jan. *I could follow her home . . . I could speak to her, tell her . . . what?* She shrank from such a confrontation. Jan looked sure of herself, strode easily towards the school gates. What if she laughed in Annie's face? Annie tortured herself with imaginary scenes. She had chosen this day to watch for Jan because she knew Graham was in Glasgow for a deputy heads' conference. But she didn't do it again, afraid of the humiliation if he saw her.

Later, gazing at her own sad face in the dressing-table mirror, she said aloud, 'I just want to be ordinary.' But what was ordinary? They had never 'just been' anything. They had always wanted to be other than they were. Parents. Still the word hurt. But not the way it had. 'I was all right then,' she scolded her reflection. 'I didn't know when I was well off.' But this sounded too much like her mother. She grimaced, and turned away.

She had not, of course, told her mother there was anything wrong. But Christine had guessed. One day, going up to the bathroom in Annie's house, she had seen signs of occupancy in the spare bedroom, whose open door stood opposite, and since she knew there were no visitors, no Tom come to stay, realised with a lurch of her heart that what was wrong with Annie these days had nothing to do with what Christine called her 'problem'.

A discreet and painful silence continued between them. Christine would not ask what Annie was reluctant to tell: marriage, with all its secrets, was sacrosanct. And though Annie wasn't used to keeping secrets, was a talker, confiding, this secret was somehow easier to keep than to disclose. There was too much shame mixed up in it.

She had Cath, of course. Who did Jan have? Did the whole staff know?

'It would be best,' Graham had suggested to Jan, 'if you didn't tell anyone . . . connected with school.' He knew women had to have friends to talk to.

'I'd go mad,' Annie had sobbed, 'if I didn't have Cath – she's the only one I can tell.' He had wanted to say, *You are mad, we're both mad.*

'Do you think I'm crazy?' Jan had laughed. 'Telling someone from school?' There were friends she had told, but they lived elsewhere: there were long phone calls, on Sunday evenings. Now she came closer to Graham, her hand moved across his chest, slipped between shirt buttons, her fingers caught in his chest hair. 'I have you,' she murmured. 'I have you to talk to.'

'And I have you,' he had answered, turning to her, his mouth finding hers, his tongue entering, her head bent back with the weight of his kiss.

The times they had together were too short for quarrels, for things to go wrong, and yet sometimes they did. Misunderstandings wasted whole hours, and they were both too tense when they met, to shed all of that in each other's arms, every time. And there was no space to make things right, no long evenings together for anger to cool, no comfortable going to bed, where it's hard to turn your back, keep your distance. That was why, Graham thought, sleeping apart from Annie had made it easier to go on with Jan. That had been Annie's idea, but now he didn't want to go back. In the coolness of the spare bed, his hand moved inexorably to his groin, and he thought of being with Jan.

He thought of being with her wherever he was, however inappropriate the place, the context. Only hard concentration on something as complicated as the timetable took his mind from her completely.

As Graham and Jim Bruce worked on, the school grew quiet and empty. Jim leaned back in his chair, took his glasses off, gripped the bridge of his nose between finger and thumb, and eased the place where a red mark had formed.

'Let's call it a day,' Graham said. 'I think we're winning.'

'Aye, I hope so.' They grimaced at each other, then Jim smiled. 'Beat it tomorrow, eh?' He got up, putting his glasses back on, so that his thin face was schoolmasterly again, protected.

Graham shut down the computer.

'How's Sarah?'

'About the same.'

Jim's daughter had ME. At least, they called it that. She'd left school in the middle of taking Highers the previous year, and had not been back. Maybe, Graham thought, as Jim's glasses glinted in the light, and the daze of weariness became invisible for a few seconds, there's something to be said for not having kids.

When Jim had gone, Graham gathered up the papers he needed, and stuffed them in his briefcase. He'd been thinking about work, but he'd not forgotten that Jan was still in school. At the back of his mind, the promise in her eyes. As he fastened his briefcase, she came in.

'Still here, then?'

'Still here.'

'I'm just going now.'

'You want a lift?'

'No – why do you always ask?' But he just shrugged, hands still resting on the briefcase. 'Are you—' she hesitated.

'I'll follow. See you in ten minutes or so. Is it all right?'

'Colin's working till nine.'

'Right then.'

She went, and he stood for a moment breathing in the faint citrus of the scent she'd left behind.

Simon, her older son, had a job in Glasgow again, for the summer. He was coming home to see her on Friday for the weekend. Colin had taken his last exam a week ago, and was working in a supermarket till he too went south, to Strathclyde.

'I'll be on my own,' she had said, 'come September. They'll all be in Glasgow but me.' But she did not say it like a woman soon to be released to be with her lover. She said it with a dry sadness, as if she were being abandoned. Graham did not answer, not knowing what was in her mind.

He stopped to put a few things aside for the secretary in the morning, then went out to get his car. He drove slowly, thinking he might overtake her. Jan lived a ten-minute walk from the school, and did not often take her car. But he rarely drove her home now. Before they were lovers, it hadn't mattered who saw, or what they thought.

She was putting her key in the door as he drove up. She waited, and they went in together.

'You want tea?'

Graham shook his head. 'I've been drinking mugs of tea and coffee all day. Up to here with it.'

'Well, then . . .' They faced each other.

'Let's go to bed,' he said.

Jan laughed. 'What – cut out the dalliance on the sofa, the leisurely courtship?'

'What? Yeah, cut the crap. Bed.'

She came into his arms still laughing, till his mouth shaped hers to his, and they became still, fused.

Neither could have said where lust ended and longing began. *I don't want to get too fond of you,* she had said, back at Easter. *This is going nowhere, we both know that. It'll have to stop soon.* It was as if she was the one with the other life that had to be protected, kept intact. And that was what she seemed to have achieved. Her sons did not know; her work (as far as he could tell) had not suffered. He, for his part, had not told her Annie knew, only that things were bad between them. *I guessed that,* she had said.

Now he followed her upstairs, hot and hard already, his hand on her rump as they reached the bedroom.

'Surprised you've got the energy,' she mocked, 'after such a long day.' His hand slid down between her thighs; she paused to let him do this, let his hand come back up under the gathers of her cotton skirt. She'd stopped wearing tights in the hot weather, and when his fingers reached under her knickers she twisted round, caught his head in her hands, fastened her mouth to his. Stumbling, locked together, they reached the bed.

This was what they did: not every day, but perhaps one or two days in the week, since Easter. They had an hour, sometimes longer. They made for each other in the desperate greedy way of lovers who keep insisting, *This could be the last time, it can't go on, it has to end soon.* Soon, but not now. There is this hour, this bed, skin on skin, a hot and damp devouring of the minutes and each other.

Soon, means the long summer holiday. Seven weeks when they will not see each other. But Graham doesn't know any more how he can do without the sex for that long. It's like a drug; he's hooked. The long body beneath him, the way her legs move apart, the yeasty smell of her sex, the warm wet grooves of her vulva where his fingers seek and stroke, till she rises, moves over him, the blonde fall of hair feathery on his face as she fits herself on to him, pushes down, and he strains his head upwards to take one of her dipping breasts in his mouth, the brown nipple rubbery between his lips. Then she sinks again, her breast on his face, her thighs gripping him and he is a long way inside her, lost.

It is only lust, he has said, she has said, only sex, and yet it is only with each other they have ever gone beyond themselves like this, on and on, out over the edge of consciousness so that the other body is as known as the self, and it is like swimming in clear water that buoys you up, then flows through your lungs, and you are not man and woman but one amphibian creature blent from the two of you, formless, the rise and fall of sensation only.

But they have not said any of this to each other, having no words for it.

'That was great,' he said, pulling her close, so that the sweat cooled between his skin and hers, and the sheets beneath were damp. The window stood wide open; outside a thrush tried his notes, and all their variations, over and over, in an ecstasy of song.

'It was, it was lovely.'

She wanted to say, *It gets better all the time, doesn't it?* but there was no room for words like that, words that might lead dangerously to the questions they did not ask, the doubts they did not want to acknowledge. He would be gone in a few minutes.

Graham peeled himself carefully away from her.

'Christ, look at the time.' He rolled off the bed, and stood looking down at her. 'You're so . . .'

'What?' She smiled, holding him there a few seconds longer.

'Relaxed. Gorgeous. You—' He hesitated. 'OK if I have a shower?'

'Sure – you know where the towels are.'

Then he was dressed, smelling freshly of her soap, her bathroom, and on top of that, the staleness of the shirt he'd worn

all day, and just put back on. He bent to kiss her briefly, then
was gone.

On her own, she lay on the cold sheets, and wept. But not for
long – there was no point. The sun moved on, the room was
shadowy. She drew the downie up, and went into a half-sleep,
drifting. Then roused herself, showered, and dressed in clean
clothes. She went back to straighten the bed, and as she did
so, kicked the edge of the newspaper she'd pushed under there
days ago. She drew it out, and sat on the edge of the bed, looking
again at the two advertisements she had circled six weeks before.
Graham had not told her Annie knew. She had not been truthful
either. Each of them had kept back the most important thing. If
he told the truth, she might end it; if she did, he would assume
it was over.

'It's got out of hand,' she said aloud. And yet, why should she
not have him, if he was so unhappy at home? She deliberately
did not think of Annie, who was a ghost, a cipher.

Graham drove home at first invigorated, alive again, then as he
neared his own street, a daze of weariness ached along his limbs,
immobilised his brain. I'm shattered, he thought, I'm in bits. He
put the car away, and went indoors. Always, as he pushed the
door open, and slipped into the hall, the great ball of guilt rose
up, dividing his ribcage, choking. He fought it down, called for
Annie, stooped to greet the dog.

Annie was in the living room, watching television with the
sound turned off. Graham stood for a moment, gazing at the
animated people on the screen, apparently arguing in mute
anger, then running silently down a busy street.

'You've got the sound off,' he said.

'Yes,' she answered, not looking at him. 'It's better like that.'
She shifted in her chair, tucking her legs underneath her. The
cat rose uncertainly on her lap, turned and settled again. Still
she did not look at him. 'There's cold meat and salad in the
fridge.'

'Nothing hot?'

Now she turned. There he was, meek and quiet at the edge
of the room, but flushed, rumpled.

'Where have you been?'

'School. You know that. Not long till the end of term, thank
God. It's always like this the last few weeks. You *know* that.'

'Do I?'

'Annie, don't start.'

He'd almost convinced himself he really had been at school
all this time. He felt indignant, as if he merited the trust she no
longer had in him.

'I'm not going on, Graham.'

'What? What are you talking about?' He went cold.

'You know fine. I'm just not going on like this. Either end it,
prove you've ended it, or leave. Right?'

'It is – I have . . .'

'Well, I don't believe you. Maybe you should just leave. I'm
sure she'd be delighted to have you.' She rose, tipping the cat
on to the floor. Her skirt was creased, her T-shirt crumpled, and
he saw suddenly that they hung loose on her.

'I'm going to bed.'

'Bed? It's not nine o'clock yet—'

But she did not answer him; she was half-way upstairs.

Graham poured himself a drink, and put on Vivaldi. He sat
listening to the opening bars of *Spring*, watching the manic
silence of television commercials, one after the other. He could
not think, he could not think.

Suddenly, Annie came running downstairs, flung open the
door, and flew across the room where she yanked out the plug of
the CD player from its socket. Vivaldi screamed, then stopped.

Graham got to his feet. 'What the hell—'

'There's one thing,' she hissed at him, two spots of red on her
cheeks, her voice triumphant, 'when you move in with your
floozie, I won't have to listen to bloody Vivaldi *ever* again.'

When she had gone, the door banged behind her, Graham sat
on in the silence vacated by Vivaldi and his wife, the whisky
bottle diminishing by his side.

Leave. He had not thought of leaving.

Move in with Jan.

He'd taught with someone once, who'd done that. Left his wife
and moved in with a girl who worked in the bar they all went to
on Friday nights. But she'd thrown him out after a fortnight, and
his wife, exacting revenge, had changed the locks and wouldn't

have him back. He'd ended up sleeping on the floor in Graham and Annie's living room. This was a long time ago, when they were newly married and in their first flat, tiny with no spare bedroom. They'd been sorry for Neil, but privately thought him ridiculous, pathetic.

Graham shuddered at the thought of this humiliation. He leaned back in the armchair, saw his favourite watercolour on the opposite wall, a tractor in a field, green smudge against autumn woods. Where had they found that one? In Yorkshire, on holiday. The vase on the mantelpiece had been his mother's; the brass fire irons came from Annie's grandmother's house; the William Morris curtains had been bought with money given them by Annie's parents when they moved here. What belonged to him? None of it, it all belonged to this house, to their marriage, to both of them.

Leave. How could he leave? He wasn't thinking about Annie or Jan any more, but about his place, the shelves in the bathroom he'd put up, his workbench in the garage, the shed door he'd fixed, the golden acer he'd helped Annie to plant. Briefly, he transplanted the gold and green vase to Jan's bare sitting room, then closed his eyes at the impossibility of this. Her house was functional, masculine, without the softening of clutter.

'I had no heart,' she'd said once, talking about leaving her husband, 'for starting again with all that stuff about choosing wallpaper, buying bits and pieces. Neither of us had been much interested in the first place. On my own – it seemed pointless. At least the boys could kick a ball around in the house, and nothing would get spoiled. And as long as they were happy – that's what mattered, not a load of useless ornaments, frilly curtains.'

Jan wanted the sex, loved it, but in her mind, he came second to her children. Leaving home, they did not leave her. Already, he suspected, she wanted to move nearer to where they'd be. But with Annie, he'd always come first. No kids of course, but look at the way she'd been with Rob. Maybe he'd come first only because there *was* no one else. Graham gulped whisky. I was jealous, he thought, of that spotty kid. I'm pathetic.

The door opened.

'I can't get to sleep,' Annie said. She stood like a ghost in the doorway in her pale nightdress, dark hair in a cloud around her anxious face.

'Have a drink,' Graham said. 'Here, sit down. I'll get you a glass.' So he did, and they sat opposite each other by the summer-empty grate, which Annie had hidden with a copper bowl full of peonies from their garden.

Annie drank whisky, and shivered as it burned down her throat.

'Oh,' she said, 'oh, it tastes funny when you've cleaned your teeth.'

'Maybe,' Graham offered, looking across at her, 'maybe – I don't know – you want to talk?'

4

The train was hot. It had started cold, but now it was hot. Alistair had chosen the wrong side, for sunlight glared across his face. There was no escaping it, however he turned his head. And if he closed his eyes, it pressed against the eyeballs, orange and insistent. It was years since he'd gone this far by train, and when he did, he travelled first-class. This time, for some reason he could no longer recall (he wasn't on his uppers yet, not by a long chalk) he'd bought a second-class return. Return. Oh yes, this wasn't an escape, a one-way route back home.

There were songs about it – Dr Hook, Van Morrison, Neil Young, Christy Moore . . . who else? Everybody has a song about going home, once the gold-plate of the city has shown itself tinny and false. But he belonged in the city, loved it. That was his home. Still, everyone has a crisis, to go with the song, and this was his. It was curious, he was on a kind of high, had been since the morning he'd cleared his desk. Now, with the rhythm of the train, the long hours of sitting, that strange elation was still there, it was what kept him going. He had even been able to tolerate the family on the other side of the aisle, just the sort you didn't get in first class, young parents and very young children, going on holiday. Since shortly after leaving King's Cross, the younger child, a boy, had been asking how soon they would get to Grandma's. By now, nearing Edinburgh, his parents had long since ceased to pay attention to this, or to any of his other questions.

'Shut it, Justin, sit still, play with your cars, look, that's what we brought them for. Read your picture book. Well, just look at the pictures, then. I read it to you already. Not yet. In a while.'

They had brought with them enough toys and food, Alistair

thought, to cater for a dozen children. The girl, who'd been colouring in assiduously if not skilfully, for the last fifty miles or so, all at once abandoned this, and amused herself by kicking her brother under the seat. The parents dealt with the row by opening another can of Coke, and producing a selection of crisps. Their accents were urban west of Scotland, Alistair noted, the children's a south of England whine.

He'd bought the *Scotsman* from the steward as they neared the border, having exhausted both *The Times* and the *Independent* long ago. But he was sick of reading, and anyway, couldn't help staring, however covertly, at the family opposite. They clamoured for attention; it was impossible not to watch.

'Give 's it, give 's it!' The boy hauled at a packet of crisps.

'I had it first!' His sister clutched the corner.

'But I only *like* salt'n'vinegar – Mam – Kerry's got the salt'n'vinegar an' 's the only kind I *like*.'

'Stop that racket – there's plenty crisps. Here – you have smoky bacon.'

'Don' *wan'* smoky bacon, bacon's a pig's bum, Kerry says—'

'I'm havin' 'em, he had all the chocolate rolls, din'ee?'

Both children gave a final violent tug, the packet gave way and crisps flew into the air, which instantly became rich with the smell of vinegar. The mother smacked the child nearest her, who happened to be the boy, and he set up a howl of indignation.

'That's not fair – I never did nothing – hit her an' all, then.'

The girl grinned, and picked up the remaining, unopened packet of crisps, which she proceeded to eat slowly.

'*Pig's bum, pig's bum,*' the boy muttered, but under his breath.

At a glare from his mother, he subsided against her side, thumb tucked in his mouth, sulking. The father had kept out of all this by pretending to be asleep, his head against the window, a folded jacket between him and the glass. In a moment or so, his mouth fell open a little, and he snored. He really was asleep. One of the disputed crisps had landed on Alistair's arm. He picked it off, and dropped it on the floor.

At Pitlochry, the family packed up toys and food, put their jackets on, and sat expectant, red-faced with heat and weariness, till Aviemore, where they all got off to be greeted by an elderly couple with a fat dog, waiting on the platform. The table and seats they'd occupied were littered with papers, plastic wrappers, Coke cans, crisp crumbs.

'Some folk, eh?' the steward remarked to Alistair, as he swept all of this into a black plastic bag, on one of his forays up the train.

'Beats me,' Alistair said, 'why anyone would take kids on a long train journey.'

'They like it – kids like the train. Not so boring as the car, is it?'

To this, Alistair made no reply. He leaned back, and like the man trying to ignore his children, attempted to sleep. But what stayed in his mind was not the children's squabbles, the slaps, the impatient retorts, but the way the boy leaned against his mother, the girl cuddled up to a sleeping, indifferent father. They were a unit: they had come all this way together, endured the journey for the sake of spending a week in Aviemore, as a family. In his present frame of mind, Alistair could take heart from this. Children loved even the most useless parents. It was possible Rob loved him. Might even be pleased to see him.

Before he left, Alistair had called Shona, not so much to tell her he was going to see Rob, as to make it clear that from now on she needn't expect any money for their son's upkeep.

'Not,' he pointed out, 'that you've had to spend a penny on him since Christmas. I sent a cheque to Annie as well, you know, and I suppose I'd better give Tom something. Though at least Rob's earning his keep now. After a fashion. But the point is – I'm not going to be able to carry on. Don't know what I'll be doing in six months time. Still on the dole, probably.' But a shiver of excitement went through him as he said this, for he didn't believe it. He just didn't want Shona to be let off. 'I hope you've been putting the cash aside for him – for when he eventually goes to college, sets up on his own. This is a very difficult time for me, I hope you—'

Shona interrupted him, a thing she very rarely did. Usually, when he was in full flow, she set the receiver down, and lit a cigarette. When the tiny buzz of his voice halted at last, she picked up the phone again, and agreed with whatever it was he'd been saying. This time, however, she couldn't be bothered.

OK, so he'd been made redundant. Well, so had Ken, more than once, and he'd gone out and got himself another job, hadn't he, and without Alistair's fancy qualifications and his posh friends.

'You'll get something else,' she said. 'With all your business contacts, eh? They won't see you stuck. Anyway, I—'

'For God's sake, Shona, jobs like mine don't grow on trees – have you been listening to a single word—' What was the point? His world and hers had divided years ago; it was like talking to someone who doesn't really speak your language. But he'd no inclination to translate for her, the way he still did for his parents.

Shona, meanwhile, made another attempt to tell him what he really ought to know. 'When you see Rob, I think you'd better—'

But Alistair, while no longer having any deadlines, anything to hurry for, still felt he had no time. 'I'll give him your love,' he said. 'See what his plans are. Maybe I should try to get him to come home.' He offered this, proving that in the middle of his own troubles, he still considered other people. 'You'd like that, eh? Right, speak to you when I get back.'

So Shona did not manage to tell him about a far worse trouble (it seemed to her) than redundancy heading his way. She could have shouted him down, she'd done it once or twice before. But he'd find out for himself soon enough, and then all hell – no, leave it. Let someone else break the news. But she worried about her son, didn't want him to have to face his father on his own. She'd phone Robbie, sound him out about speaking to Tom, warn him his father was on the way. She glanced at the clock. After six, when it was cheaper. She'd try then.

But Ken had met an old mate in the pub on his way home, so in the evening she went out with him to meet this Brian, and his wife. By the time they got home, it was too late to ring Tom. Later, she changed her mind anyway, having lost the confidence to do it.

Coming north, Alistair did not feel a failure, someone returning home beaten, breaking bad news. The euphoria which had inexplicably overtaken him when he left his office for the last time, and strode through home-going crowds to the tube station, had blotted out lesser feelings. He didn't see himself as redundant, finished. He saw himself as a man in crisis, a heroic figure, about to face his greatest challenge: what should he do with the second half of his life? And yet, and yet, as he sat on in the airless train, dozing, waking to a once familiar landscape, closing his eyes on it again, most of this excitement evaporated, and he arrived at Aberdeen Joint station crumpled, weary, and stiff with sitting.

There was no one to meet him. As usual, when he had tried to tell Annie he was on his way, he'd got their bloody answerphone. Where was she all day? She didn't even go out to work, for God's sake. Annoyed, but with a sense that the drama of his announcement would be greater if he delivered it in person, he had not left a message. Now, in the glare of Aberdeen sunlight, made more brilliant in the blue sky by the way it refracted off hard granite, he wished he had. Annie would be here, looking worried, ready to comfort him. Irritably, he went to stand in a queue for taxis.

As the taxi inched its way up Bridge Street through the city centre, it occurred to him that Annie and Graham might be away on holiday. When did the schools break up here? There were no youngsters on the streets in school uniform to reassure him. He could of course go to his mother's, she'd be there and happy to see and feed him. But he hoped Annie was at home. Christine wasn't too keen on surprises and the double shock of his sudden appearance and the news he brought might be a bit much. They were getting on, his parents, he noticed that afresh each time he came. They were old people now, and you had to be careful how you put things to them. He leaned back and closed his eyes. Maybe he was losing his grip already, maybe this was what being unemployed did to you.

'Fit number did ee say?' The taxi driver turned into Annie's street, cruising along the granite-built Edwardian terrace, gardens bright with roses, front doors gleaming with varnish or fresh paint. A comfortable, well-tended street. Alistair leaned forward.

'Near the end, on the left,' he said.

His spirits rose a little, and he wondered (not for the first time) if Graham realised how lucky he was, with his safe job, his house in a good area (bought before the boom, with a mortgage that looked like peanuts now), and a wife happy to be at home for him, waiting with a proper dinner, every night of his life. Pity they'd had no kids, pity Annie'd been disappointed, but then, you couldn't have everything and anyway, look at Rob. Having kids was a mixed blessing.

Alistair pushed open the gate, and the taxi moved off. Yes, he envied Graham in some ways, for all he was stuck in Aberdeen. But Aberdeen was a thriving place, look at the oil business. An idea flickered, but he tucked it away, for later.

Since he and Shona had separated years ago, Alistair had never had anyone waiting for him at home. The women he'd been with had their own flats, their successful careers. That was best, really. Even Laura, who'd been around longest, who was still around in a way, hadn't wanted to give up her independence to be with him all the time. And neither had he, of course. With his lifestyle, what would that have amounted to, anyway? Weekends, the odd evening. Which was what they'd had anyway. I haven't missed a thing, Alistair told himself, not a thing I really wanted.

The door was ajar. Gently, he pushed it open, and stepped into the hall. There were no flowers in the blue vase by the phone, and the air smelled dusty.

'Hi!' His voice sounded thin and unsure in the stillness. A tremor of uncertainty. No, no this was the way to do it, see your family, tell them straight. Annie and Graham, then his parents, then Ruth and Jamie. After that, north to Tom, and his uncle. And his son.

Silence.

'Anybody home?' He dropped his bag on the floor and headed for the kitchen. A fine evening, still warm. They'd be in the garden. The kitchen was empty, though there were signs of a meal over but not cleared away. Pity. Still, Annie always had plenty of food. She'd rustle up something for him. The back doors, to the porch and outside, also stood open, and the porch, mostly glass, was stifling after a whole day's sun. Sweat broke out between his shoulder blades, at his temples.

Annie was on her knees by a flower border, a fork in her hand, but she was doing nothing with it, just sitting there. She looked round, gasped.

'Hey – well – Alistair – where did—'

'Hi, hi, hope this is OK.' He flung himself down on a deck chair left out by the back door. Mercifully, this was in shade now. Annie got to her feet.

'Where did you come from?'

'Up on the train. All bloody day. Never mind, I'm here now. Glad to be. Don't worry, I won't stay long, just see the folks, then head on up to the Black Isle. You'll give me a bed, eh?'

Annie was still in sunlight; he couldn't see her face. He held up a hand to shade his eyes, and she moved towards him, out of the sun. He thought she didn't look too good. A queasiness that wasn't just the effect of travelling in heat, or mere hunger, gripped him.

'All right?' he asked, as if for the first time wanting to know. 'You OK, Annie?'

5

What Rob saw, when he took one swift look at his father, was not a redundant executive, a lost middle-aged man going through a crisis. He had no means of seeing his father like this, no knowledge of what had happened to change the view he'd always had of someone remote, incalculable in his mood, but utterly predictable in all his opinions. He saw neither the failed Alistair, nor the successful one he assumed his father still was.

All he saw was Nemesis.

His mother must have told him. Then his father had come straight here, to confront him, drag him back, make him face whatever music was about to play. So he turned immediately, went out of the gate, and quickly, quickly along the path, back the way he had come.

Where the path opened out, he broke into a jog, but it had been a long day, and he was tired, so he soon slowed again. They weren't coming after him anyway. Maybe they hadn't even seen him. But he knew Alistair had: his father's eyes had met his, locked for a second in bleak recognition. Rob took the fork in the path that led down to the beach, and on to the hard sand near the water. The tide was out. Most of the holiday-makers had gone home to tea, but a few remained, to shake the sand from towels and call the children in.

Lindsay had come this way. Not down the path, but on the shore, over the rocks, along this stretch of beach. Had she got as far as the caves? Did she meet someone, beyond the families sprawled behind windbreaks, near the caves, maybe? How far had she come? But she was only a kid, couldn't have been running away from anything, the way he was. Only a kid, like the girl coming towards him, with the wet collie jumping to lick her arm, her parents following more slowly behind. They passed him, and there was no one now but a couple with another dog, and they were going up on to the path. Soon he'd have overtaken them. Where was he going? He'd sit by the caves, think what to do.

His mother's phone call had been less than a week ago, and for once she hadn't bothered with the preliminaries, telling him how Ken was (as if he cared), but got straight down to it.

'But it's not right, is it, Robbie, what this lassie's saying? She's well on, the dates would fit, my God, did you nae ken any better? I thought you got all that at school these days – anyway, it's on the TV enough.'

She's feeling guilty because she never told me to use condoms, Rob thought. But they don't always work, doesn't she know that? *He* knew, had good cause to know. He *still* couldn't believe this had really happened. He'd been pretending for months it hadn't, since he'd left, really, since her first letter had come in its lilac envelope. What would happen – would he have to pay her to bring up some kid, for ever and ever? His kid. But he hadn't any money, not that sort of money. And they'd been underage, would he get prosecuted, go to a Young Offenders or something? A boy at school had got sent to one of those, Mick Ashford, but he'd gone into a post office with an air gun, terrified the old biddy behind the counter, got out with five hundred quid. You could see why they put *him* away. But sex – how could they put you in prison for sex? It was private, and it didn't hurt anybody. But having a baby hurt. She'd be mad as hell, she couldn't stand even a stone in her shoe. The fuss that time they went up to the woods, when she discovered a drawing pin spike in her trainer, and they had to stop and wiggle it out. It took ages. *I'm not putting that back on till it's out,* she said. *It went right into my foot – like somebody stuck a needle in – look.* He looked, and there was a tiny red dot on her pink heel. Having a baby, though. You couldn't wiggle out of that, once the baby had started.

Why hadn't she had an abortion? That was what people did now, it was easy. Kevin's older sister Amy, she'd had one, not that Kevin was supposed to know. Only when he'd come home from school she was in bed with a hot-water bottle, and she'd been crying. She told him it was because she had a bad period.

Kevin was only ten, he didn't know what she was on about really. Then when he was fourteen and his sister was getting married she warned him Dave didn't know anything about the trouble she'd been in before. Kevin said, *What trouble?* Amy bit her lip. *Nothing, it doesn't matter, you keep your mouth shut, that's all.* So later, he went and asked his mother, and she told him. She was good like that, Kevin's mother, if you asked her a straight question, you got a straight answer. Rob wished that was what happened in his family too.

So why hadn't Lucy done the same? Scared to tell her mum till it was too late – that was what Shona thought. Scared! She wasn't scared of nothing, that one. Especially not her mother. All she was really frightened of was pain, and having a baby must be worse than having an abortion. Not that he wanted to think about either of them. *Either of them.*

He sat down on the sand, the sea in front, the caves behind. Not that they amounted to much, as caves, you couldn't go way inside, as he'd thought at first. If you could, that's where he'd go, deep inside the hill, down and down, into the dripping darkness, then it would open out to a huge hall and the Master of the Caves would be there in his long robes, and the whole place lined with precious stones, the walls dazzling . . . and all around, creatures that were half dog, half monkey, yapping and chattering . . .

He looked up, and there was just the sea, and far out, a boat that didn't seem to move. The fantasy faded. All that *Lord of the Rings*, Terry Pratchett stuff. Magic. If you could magic them away, all the bad things you didn't want, couldn't handle . . .

It's not right, is it, Robbie, what this lassie's saying?

But it was. He was caught. Trouble. All the things he was going to do, play for Ipswich, go to university, work in the States, backpack round Europe, get a hole in one on the Strathpeffer golf course next time he went round with Neil and Gavin, the plan Hamish and him had got, and college . . . None of that would happen now. It was never going to, he was stuck, he'd have to go back, get a job, any job, just one that paid.

He was in trouble. She was in trouble. Worse for her, he supposed, in a way. She didn't deserve it, neither did he. It wasn't fair. God, they'd only *done it* three times, and the first time it wasn't even . . . And then the third time – it really wasn't *fair.*

What was he going to *do*? He couldn't go back, couldn't face his father, or Tom. Or Annie, for all she was soft, like his mother. Not that his mother had sounded so soft, this time.

'Say something, Robbie. The truth mind. If this is right, Robbie, you've to come back here and face up to it. Sort it out. Ken thinks—' But he hadn't wanted to know what Ken thought, so he'd hung up.

She'd phoned again, of course, and in the end, he'd said, 'OK, I'll come down in a couple of weeks, just don't say anything to anybody else, OK? I got to finish this job, then I'll come down.'

'Oh well, at this stage, what's a couple of weeks? It's too late to do anything – you know what I mean. What kind of lassie is she? Her mother seemed a nice woman, well-spoken, not the sort to have a lass in trouble. Anyway, I'll speak to her, Mrs Philips, I'll say you're coming home.'

Why, he had asked his mother, earlier in this terrible conversation, did Lucy's mother come and see *her*? If Lucy wouldn't say who it was.

'Well, the two of you were going out together, weren't you? You were round at her house often enough. Nae that you bothered telling us, I felt a right fool not knowing, but that's boys for you, I says to her. What are you saying, son, that she's the sort that sleeps around?'

His face went scarlet, sweat broke out. How could his mother say these things – was she going to say them to his face, if he went home?

'No, no, I just wondered.' He could imagine Lucy clamming up on her parents, picturing herself as some character in *Neighbours*, refusing to say who the father was, the whole audience knowing, but no one in Ramsay Street being able to guess. Lucy was a great fan of *Neighbours*, of every soap you could think of, just like all girls.

Rob sat with his knees up, arms resting on them, still hot with the embarrassment of remembering this. Now he put his head down on his arms, hot forehead on warm brown arms, and shut his eyes. *What was he going to do?*

There was a faint scrabbling of claws on sand, and a cold nose against his upper arm. He looked up. The dog belonging to the couple on the path had run ahead of them and was standing beside him. It bent and picked up a pebble in its mouth, then dropped it again, and went on looking at him, pink tongue hanging out. The couple were still on the path, the man pointing out Fort George, across the water.

'You want me to chuck something for you, eh?' The dog waited hopefully. Rob found a sea-bleached stick, threw it down the beach. The dog bounded after it.

He hadn't missed his father at all. What was there to miss? He wished he had, wished for a different sort of father, really. But he hadn't missed his mother all that much either. She kept phoning, anyway, so he'd been able to go on speaking to her, about as much as when he lived with her, more, probably. But he'd missed Kevin quite a bit, and he'd missed the dog. He was missing him now, as the black mongrel came back with the stick, and dropped it at Rob's feet. He stood up and threw it again, with more force this time. He could not see where it went, for his eyes were full of tears.

'She'll let you do that all day!' The couple had come down on to the sand, and the woman smiled at him. But he did not answer her, could not trust himself to speak, and turned away instead, walking back along the shore.

That was at six o'clock.

'There's thunder in the air today,' Annie said. 'We don't often get thunder here.'

'So what's happening then?' Tom got a beer from the fridge for himself and put some of the can in a glass for Annie. Then he filled hers with lemonade.

'Thanks. Can you put ice in a shandy?'

'I don't see why not. Except I don't think I've got any ice.'

'Never mind – it's lovely and cold.' Tom watched her drink, then lick the froth from her lips.

'Tell me then – what made you change your mind and come up with Alistair?'

'Och, partly because he was in such a state, I thought he needed someone with him.'

'And?'

'I just felt I'd had enough.'

'Of Graham?'

'Of . . . being so miserable. He is too. He's miserable and guilty, I'm miserable and jealous. Just awful.'

'I can imagine,' Tom said, but knew he could not.

'So when he told me she was going away—'

'The woman's going? What's her name again?'

'I don't even say it. I hate her name.'

'Right.'

'I mean it, the sound of it in my mouth makes me sick. Anyway, she's leaving. Got a job in Glasgow. Her sons are both students there.'

'That's good, isn't it? It means she doesn't want any more than she's had. Just an affair.'

Annie sighed. 'An affair seems quite significant to me. But I suppose that's what it means. She could easily come back, though. Her mother lives out at Bucksburn. And Graham's often in Glasgow, if he has a meeting there he stays with Sheila and Dave. His cousin and her husband. So it could go on. I'll keep thinking it's going on, anyway. How can I trust him now?'

'I don't know. What's *he* saying – Graham?'

'He says he wants us to sort it out. He wants to end it with her.'

'But you don't believe him?'

'Well, I think he wants everything. His house, the chance to apply for headships – no scandal you see, nothing to slur his good name. And all the home comforts. But he wants . . . the sex.' She seemed to choke on this, the word, the idea. 'The kind of sex he has with her, I suppose. He wants that too.'

'You can give him that, Annie.'

Silence. He'd gone too far. Tom swallowed Export, gazed into his glass. When he looked up, he saw she was crying.

'I'm so pathetic,' she wept, 'I know I should throw him out, that's what other women would do, but I just want him back, I just want things to be the way they were.'

'They were hardly perfect.'

'No, but it was all right. And nothing's *perfect*, is it?'

'No.'

'It *was* OK – I mean apart from there being no children.'

'Apart – Annie, you were obsessed with that.'

'What is it – you OK?'

'Yes. It's nothing. Just – I never look at that stretch of the beach without thinking of Lindsay. Even now.'

'Good God, Annie, that was more than thirty years ago.'

'I know.'

Alistair turned too, his gaze following hers. 'You can't see it anyway,' he said, 'the way she went. Not at this time of year.'

'No, but it's there.' She sighed. 'If only – if only one of us had gone after her, if only I'd gone with her.'

'Then the bastard might've got the two of you.'

Annie shuddered. 'Don't, Ally, don't.'

'You were only a wee thing,' he said. 'If anyone should've gone, it was me. And I—' He stopped, and Annie looked at him.

'You remember it then, the day she – that day?'

'I remember.' He came up to where she stood, and took her elbow. 'Come on, for God's sake. Let's find this son of mine. Wherever the hell he's gone.'

So they went on together, not looking back.

'Was I? Not *obsessed*.'

'Obsessed.'

Silence again. Then, in a voice so faint it did not seem to be hers, she said, 'That's what Graham said.'

'Maybe, maybe you've got the chance to put all that stuff behind you.' Tom took a deep breath, risked saying what he'd thought for a long time. 'On the other hand, maybe with someone else you could have kids. Cut your losses, get out now. Who's to say why you never got pregnant? No one ever came up with an answer, did they? And you're a very sexy lady. Lots of men would be delighted—'

Annie blushed, laughed despite herself. 'I'm not – I'm past forty, I don't even have a proper job, just all this voluntary palaver. I'm ordinary.'

'Crap. Look at yourself – all you need to do is put a bit of weight back on. You're a bonny woman, Annie, Graham doesn't know when he's well off.'

'Tom – why did you never say any of this before? It's so strange, hearing it now.' Too late, she almost said. But Tom went red.

'Och, you know. Families. You don't say that kind of thing.'

But what he was thinking was that till now she had been comfortable with her marriage, out of reach of the world, and he could not interfere, could not disturb her safe life.

'Anyway,' he went on, 'all I'm saying is, don't think you couldn't survive outside your marriage, away from Graham. All you need to do is get a life – as Rob keeps telling me.'

Annie smiled. 'Does he?' She glanced at the clock. 'He'll be home soon, won't he?'

'Any minute.'

'Tom, do you think—'

But he wasn't to find out what she wanted to know. Alistair came into the kitchen and sat at the table with them, looking from one to the other, perplexed.

'I know this is crazy,' he said, 'but Rob just came in the gate—'

'He's home?' Annie half rose.

'– and then went out again.'

'What?'

'It was him. God, maybe I'm hallucinating. This bloody heat.'

Annie went out, and down the garden. She opened the back gate, but saw no one on the path. When she turned back, both Tom and Alistair were standing at the back door.

'I don't see him.'

'He just turned and – ran. I swear he ran. God, does wonders for your self-esteem that, eh? Your son does a runner at the sight of you.'

'He could have forgotten something, gone back for it,' Annie suggested. 'Perhaps he didn't actually see you.'

'He saw me.'

'Don't worry about it – he'll reappear in a minute. Just wait.'

It was a long time since she'd felt sorry for her brother. Not since he'd come to tell them he and Shona were divorcing. Then, Rob had been a tiny blond child, cuddled in his father's lap, sucking the ear of his cloth dog. Alistair himself seemed to feel the worst thing to happen was his redundancy. This was what he'd told her, sitting in her garden in Aberdeen. But Annie had not pitied him then.

'I don't know how I'm going to break it to Mum and Dad,' he'd said.

Annie wanted to exclaim, *It's only a job*, but because he genuinely seemed to want her advice for once, said instead, 'They're getting old, it's—'

'That's what bothers me. Maybe I shouldn't even tell them.'

'No, I mean, they . . . well, it's not that they won't mind. They will – for your sake. But, oh, I suppose, when your friends start dying – Lewis Craig had a heart attack – did you know? – nothing else is all that important any more. It doesn't really seem to touch them.'

'But your own son, redundant in his forties!' Uncomfortably, Alistair became aware that perhaps his family would not see this tragedy as he saw it. 'Annie, that job was my whole life.'

'You were obsessed with it.'

'No, not at all. You don't understand. You've never had a real job. What am I going to do, that's the point?'

'Well, yes it is. Have you any ideas?'

He had, of course, plenty, but didn't feel like airing them.

'Any chance of food?' he asked instead. 'British Rail sandwiches are not all that sustaining. And a drink. I could do with a drink.'

But she didn't jump up, apologising, heading for the cooker, as he expected. Instead, she went on sitting on the kitchen chair she'd brought out for herself while he talked.

'I don't know,' she said. 'When one obsession fails, maybe it's not such a good idea to replace it with another.'

Now, having made it clear the loss of his job was the worst thing, Alistair had no words for the way he felt about Rob's disappearance. He could only make a joke of it. And Annie pitied him. He looked odd, a city man in unaccustomed shorts, his designer T-shirt not quite loose enough to conceal the soft fold of belly over the waistband. When he took off his glasses to rub his eyes, the face beneath looked naked and hurt.

'Come on,' Annie said, 'we'll walk down the path, and have a look for him. I'm sure he just went back for something.'

'Don't be too long,' Tom said. 'I've put supper in the oven.'

'We won't.' Annie's voice drifted back to him as the gate swung shut behind them. He turned into the house.

Annie and Alistair went along the path, and took the left fork that led up to the road to Hamish's house. Alistair began to recover. The steep climb exhilarated him: he'd been working out in the gym twice a week lately, and it was beginning to pay off. He was scarcely out of breath at all.

'So, how are things with you?' he asked, feeling they'd better not talk about Rob just now. 'You've listened to all my troubles.'

Annie half-turned, smiled. 'Aye, all the way up the A96.'

'Sorry if I bored you.'

'Ach, stop it, Ally. What a self-pitying, self-centred man you've turned into.'

'I have not!' He glared at her. They were children again, and he wasn't taking that from his wee sister.

'Poor Ally. Not a good week for you, is it? Sorry.' She looked past him down the path, over the bushes to the shore. But it was the beginning of July, and everything was lush and green and high-growing. She could see only the sea and not the sand. She did not catch a glimpse of Rob, walking as far as the caves. And yet, a shiver caught her, and for a second she was giddy.

6

When Alistair arrived to convey his momentous news, Jamie felt much as Annie had done. Time Alistair realised there were worse things in life than losing your job. But he sympathised, made coffee, and waited to be asked how Ruth was. Or indeed where she was, but Alistair didn't seem to notice Jamie was on his own. In the end, Jamie said, exasperated, 'Sorry Ruth's not here to add her condolences.'

'What? Oh yes, Annie said. But I hadn't realised she was still in hospital.'

'For God's sake, that was the beginning of *May*.'

'Was it? Sorry, my timescale's out of sync with everything outside London. Or it was. She's better then?' Now he was aware of being ignorant. 'Not back at work, though?'

'No, she's away with her mother for a couple of days. That's all.'

It was really Ruth Jamie felt annoyed with, for leaving just as she seemed to be getting strong again. Only for three days, but how could he be sure her mother would look after her properly? The woman never stopped for a minute, and Ruth needed to rest.

'But she's made a good recovery?'

'Yes, she's OK. Fine.' He couldn't be bothered explaining to Alistair, trying to make him understand the difference in Ruth, the way they were now. The guy lived on another planet, always had.

When Alistair had left Aberdeen, Jamie called Annie. He wanted to see her, now he had some free time. He could take her out to lunch or something, cheer her up. What had Tom said? Graham was back in the fold. Obviously hadn't gone off

with this woman after all. But they were still *working things out.*
So lunch somewhere out of town, a bit of spoiling, would be a
good idea.

But Annie wasn't there to be spoiled.

'She's in the Black Isle,' Graham told him when he telephoned.
'Went up with Alistair.'

Jamie looked round his empty flat. He could go too, couldn't
he? If they were all at the High House.

'Thanks,' he said to Graham, 'I'll call her. Might even take
a wee jaunt up there too. You on holiday yet? Don't fancy
a few days by the sea yourself?' This was a tease, given the
way Graham felt about Annie's family. But the pause before
Graham answered went on so long Jamie got worried: *What if
he comes?* Then he would have to sit with Graham all the way
up that awful road to Inverness. What could they talk about –
his bit on the side?

But Graham said only, 'Maybe later. Term's not over yet.'

After he'd put the phone down, Graham stood for a few moments
in the hall, head bent, tracing the edge of the table with his
forefinger. Then he picked up his jacket, called the dog, and
went out. He'd do a couple of miles round Hazlehead woods,
then go over to Jan's.

It was evening, still and warm. This heat couldn't last, it was
unnatural. As he opened the tailgate of the car to let Mac jump
in, he nodded to an elderly neighbour, dead-heading roses in
his front garden.

'Fine night.'

'Aye, a bittie fresher now.' He watched Graham get in the car
and gave him a wave as he drove off.

Does he hear us, Graham wondered, has he heard Annie
crying, me shouting, the rows in the night? Maybe he thinks
I beat her up, give her bruises where they don't show. He was
the one who felt beaten, was aching. End of term, lack of sleep,
the strain of it all. No wonder he felt ill. He had thought, when
Annie left with Alistair and it was much easier to see Jan, that
he'd feel all right about it, freer. But it hadn't worked out like
that. Guilt closed in. But not when he was with her, not in bed,
between sheets, wrapped round each other, deep in the one act

that blots out thought, moves the world away the width of a universe, light years.

She lay in the crook of his arm, one hand idly stroking down his stomach, taking hold of his subsiding penis, teasing it gently, then cradling his balls in her palm.

'Lovely,' he whispered, 'I love that – you're so good at it.'

'I know, I know . . .' She smiled at him, then sat up, pushing her hair back. 'Ah, I'm going to miss all this.'

'Your choice,' he said. He got up on one elbow and looked at her, naked, breasts drooping as she leaned forward. 'You're the one who applied for the job. You're the one who did so well in the interview that she got it.'

'What choice? What else could I do? You're terrified anyone at school finds out. And you're not going to leave your wife, are you?'

'Of course not, you've always known that. And of course I don't want anyone at school to find out. As they will, they're bound to, if this goes on. But you never wanted me to *leave* Annie, did you?' His stomach lurched. They hadn't said any of this openly till now, but maybe he'd been a fool, maybe her agenda wasn't what he thought.

However, all she said was, 'You couldn't anyway.' *It's not your wife*, she wanted to add, *it's the house and the dog and cat and the friends you've both got, and family – a whole life, and you're in it like a net, you've become part of the net, woven in.*

He knew all this, of course.

'What – leave? It's not that easy.'

'I did it.'

'You *want* me to?' Now he had to harden himself. If she cried, if she pleaded – but then, why had she gone ahead with this job, not even telling him till she went down for the interview?

'No, no. All I'm saying is, if you really want to, the other stuff doesn't matter. You don't give a toss about the sofa and chairs, the bricks and mortar, what your mother will say. When nothing's as bad as staying, that's when you leave.'

He recognised this: he had had moments – Annie crying, his own impatience, the terrible itch to be *out of it*, when this was just how he'd felt himself.

She laid a hand on his arm. 'But it's OK. I'm moving to

Glasgow to work, and be near my boys, and see their father often enough to discuss them sensibly, keep tabs, but not so often we start hating each other again.'

A throb of jealousy. 'You want to see your ex?'

She shrugged. 'We used to . . . I still like talking – och, leave it, Graham. The basic thing is, I need to get away from you, from this whole fucking banal situation.'

He shrank from the tone of her voice, didn't like this language from a woman. But it wasn't his business how she spoke, what she did. It was over, and she'd be gone in August, the house up for sale, her job somehow filled. They had two and a half posts to lose next year, because of the cuts in spending, so the head had let her go without the term's notice. Other people would swallow her work, piecemeal. It would be as if she hadn't existed in the school, had left no mark.

'Come here,' he said, 'all this discussion – it's academic, isn't it? Pointless – you're leaving.'

'Och, I know. We shouldn't talk about it. But I'm not sorry Graham, you've given me a lot, you know. Given me back a really good feeling about myself, my body. All that.' That's the truth, she thought, as she drew him in with the easy welcome of open arms, parting lips, clinging thighs. And yet, a tiny sigh escaped as she fitted her body to his.

'If I'd thought to bring the dog over,' Graham said, much later, 'I'd stay the night.'

'Bring him back with you,' she offered, 'if you think he'd settle.' He hesitated. She waited, then shrugged, offended. What did the bloody dog matter? 'Please yourself. But tonight, tomorrow, maybe Friday – it's all we've got, Graham. Colin's camping trip finishes at the weekend, and he's working through the rest of the holidays. I need to be around to get him sorted out for the new term. He's going to stay with me the first year. That's another reason for moving to Glasgow. These kids at university – it works out expensive.'

'I suppose it does.'

'And anyway – look, if it's over, it's over. Right? All we're doing here is prolonging the agony. Eh? Don't you think?'

'Yes,' he said, 'you're right.' He lay back, staring at the ceiling.

Jan moved away and got out of bed. 'Sleep with your wife, why don't you?' She headed for the bathroom, tossing her remarks over her shoulder like a dry bone for a dog. 'She's the one you've got to live with for the rest of your life.'

Graham dressed and went home. There, he sat with a whisky, the dog beside him, head resting on his feet. It was too late to ring Annie, and yet he wanted to, wanted – what? To be comforted for his loss. Who better than Annie, who had washed his back as he soaked his bruises in the bath after a hard rugby game, who had cooked and cleaned and cared for him all this time. He closed his eyes, but saw only Jan, felt only the clutch of her, heard her moan as her spine arched till she was taut as a sprung bow, and came in his arms, beneath his hand, shuddering, pleading. To give so much pleasure, and to get so much – of course it couldn't last.

Jan sat in her kitchen with a mug of tea, wondering if she should just go to bed. He wasn't likely to come back now, not after she'd said that. She'd been teaching *Romeo and Juliet* to her third years, and she'd quoted them Friar Lawrence's line, *These violent delights have violent ends*. 'What do you think that means?' she'd asked. Blank faces.

Then one of her bright girls suggested: 'Juliet says it's rash and unadvisable, and that. They're like, too keen on each other right at the start. They don't, see, get to know each other first.'

In her head she heard Juliet's words again. *It is too rash, too unadvis'd, too sudden*. There now, she told herself, getting up to rinse her mug, Shakespeare always has a quote for it. And laughed, though anyone seeing her might well have thought she was crying.

In the morning, Graham phoned Tom's house, but there was no reply.

7

It was late, and for all it was July, getting dark. Stuart couldn't
see the clock from where he sat without his glasses, but it must
be after eleven. He had dozed off. He closed his eyes again, feeling
sleep lap gently at the edge of the chair. No. Get up, go to bed. He
sighed, and pushed himself to his feet. Nowadays, he seemed less
and less able to fix a time for going to bed. He no longer had to rise
in the morning, since there was no shop to go to. He wondered if
Tom stayed up later too, and lay in bed in the morning. But Tom
had the boy now, probably got up to see him off. However late
he stayed up, Stuart still woke at seven, and rose before eight. It
was during the day he flagged, dozing off after lunch or supper.
An old man's habit, he scolded himself, disliking the sour taste
in his mouth as he woke, the stiffness in his legs and back.

His newspaper had fallen to the floor. He picked it up, folded
it, and took it with his spectacles and half-drunk mug of tea,
through to the kitchen. It struck cold, now the weather had
broken. Rain was spattering on the window, that was what had
wakened him, wind and rain. The end of the hot weather they'd
had for more than a fortnight. He ran the tap, thinking of the
kitchen at the High House, where the Aga's warmth filled every
crack, and flowed out into the hallway. Sometimes, for a moment
or so, he missed the High House, and wished himself back there.
But it was only a twinge of nostalgia, an ache for something that
would never come back. The house could not have provided it
anyway: youth, his dead wife, his lost daughter. Family life.

In the bedroom, before he drew the curtains, he listened to the
growl and wash of the sea as it climbed the shore, then retreated
with a faint splashing. Despite all the bluster of the storm, he
could still hear this known sound. He was closer to the sea here

than at the High House. The cottage was only a strip of tarmac
and a few yards of pebbly sand away. Listening to wind and rain
and sea, the rage of weather, he imagined as he had before on
stormy nights, that the water had risen over the low sea wall,
and crossed the street to his cottage. It had crept between step
and door, curled round the crack between door and lintel, and
flowed along the hall. It had come seeking him. He welcomed its
cold salty smell, yielded to its surge as it swelled on the bottom
stair, and began to fill the downstairs rooms.

He shook his head, and drew the curtains shut with a clatter
of wooden rings. This was all nonsense; the sea did not come so
far, never had. As he turned towards the bed, he became aware
that the telephone was ringing.

'Dad?'

'Yes.'

'Is Rob with you?'

'Rob? No – I haven't seen him today. Not since . . . Sunday,
he was here. We watched the football, an English game, but *he*
likes it, of course, supports Ipswich, did he tell you? Mysterious, that.'

'But Dad, he's not with you now, you haven't seen him
tonight?'

'Not today. I said so. What time is it?' Stuart peered at his
watch in the gloaming, then reached over to switch on the hall
light. 'Oh, it's not as late as I thought. He'll be with one of his
pals, surely. What's that boy called, the one who—'

'No, I don't think so, because he just—' Stuart heard the
hesitation, and knowing it meant *How much should I tell the old
boy?* was offended.

'What? What did you say?' Tom's silence. The first cold lick of
fear, around the centre of the breastbone. 'Is something wrong,
Tom? That you're concerned.'

'He came home, saw Alistair, and turned and fled. We don't
know why. No one's seen him since.'

'Alistair?'

'Yes, he arrived with Annie today. He's been – och, never
mind all that. It's just – you don't know, do you, with boys that
age, when to start worrying. When it's justified.' Tom sighed.
'I'd leave it myself, but Annie's getting agitated.'

'You must tell the police,' his father said. 'You must call them at once. No time to be lost.'

'Oh come on, Dad, it's eleven o'clock at night. No, we'll leave it till morning.' This time Stuart's silence, very cold. 'Dad?'

'Just as you like. I'll ring you in the morning.'

'Yes, you do that. And I'll let you know if he – when he – turns up.'

Stuart stood in the hall, listening to the patter of rain against the glass panel in the front door. Then slowly he went back upstairs to bed. But he would not sleep. How to sleep, when a child is missing?

He saw her so clearly still, his bonny lass, running ahead of the rest, down on to the beach, hair swinging behind like a sheaf of wheat, her voice clear and strong. He had closed his eyes so that he might sleep. But opened them again, to look at darkness, and not at what his mind conjured: that last morning. The garden sloping to the sea was visible from the open kitchen door, and his daughter was eating cornflakes at the sunny kitchen table. The light on her hair, tangled from sleep, her cotton pyjamas with a pattern of forget-me-nots.

'I'm off then.' His hand on the boys' dark heads, then her fair one. 'See you later, alligator.'

She wiggled her fingers at him without looking up, bored with the old joke, but answering to please him, 'In a while, crocodile.'

He could still recall how her hair had felt under his hand, the warmth of her, still see the way the kitchen was, a blue dishtowel on the Aga rail, his wife with a basket of clean washing on her hip, that she was going to hang up outside.

See you later.

In a while.

But had never seen her again. Alive.

During the endless two weeks they searched, in that waste land between terror and loss, and terror and despair, he heard the other children tell each other what had happened, make a story of it, trying to understand what none of them would ever really know.

A bad man magicked her away, Jamie said. *Maybe she's gone into the sea, like a mermaid,* Annie wondered. Liz had been reading them folk tales at bed-time; that was where they'd got these ideas. But how young they'd been, believing such nonsense. A mermaid, her hair floating in the water. He thought of his dream of the encroaching sea. He could have forgiven the sea, for the sea had no feelings, no will. If the sea had taken her, I could have got over it better.

He opened his eyes. Darkness, the wind keening. Closed them, to worse darkness. *My bonny lass.*

There was no point in this. He should give up the pretence of trying to sleep, and sit downstairs with his whisky bottle. Years since he'd done that, surely. There were not many nights now that he would call bad nights. The years diminish, if they do not destroy, pain and loss. And if it came to it, he knew how to sit it out, how to dull memory with the sweet and peaty malt, how to turn the long night into day.

At the High House, Annie, Tom and Alistair sat up late. Tom got out a packet of Gauloises that had been in the kitchen drawer for some time.

'They'll be stale,' he said. 'I don't know why I kept them.'

Alistair had given up smoking ten years ago, even longer than Tom. 'Give me one,' he said. 'I don't care if it's stale. Won't know the difference now.'

'If you two are going to make a fug in here—'

Tom held out the packet. 'Here.'

'Oh well.' Annie took one. 'What does it matter anyway? One cigarette. In the scale of things.'

They all sat smoking.

'God,' Alistair coughed and rose to crush his cigarette end in the sink. 'Tastes like shite.'

'Sorry about that.'

Then they were laughing, all three of them, laughing and coughing.

'What are we laughing for?' Annie gasped. 'Nothing's *funny.*'

'Hang on,' Tom said. 'I've got something that won't be stale.' He came back with an unopened bottle of malt whisky.

'What's that? I've never heard of it.'

'I have.' Alistair took the bottle from Tom and studied the label. 'Something special, eh?'

'The best.' Tom put three glasses down on the table. 'I meant to keep it for a celebration, but somehow we never get round to those in our family.'

'What were you hoping to celebrate?' Annie asked.

'My last Munro is what I had in mind. I suppose.'

'You *suppose*?'

'How many have you done?'

'Two hundred and five. Last three at Easter, before that – oh years ago. I'll never do them all.'

'Why not – people often take years, don't they?'

'Lost the impetus. Seems pointless somehow, like most other things.'

Annie brought a jug of water, but both men waved it away. 'It's raining,' she said. 'I thought I heard thunder.'

'Where the hell is he?'

'Rob?' Tom poured whisky into Alistair's glass. 'Not at Hamish's. He hadn't seen him since he left at five. He said he'd come through in the morning to help us search.' There was a long pause.

'Search?'

'Ach, Annie, he's thinking Rob's a wee boy, like Dad saying get the police. Rob's grown up, he's at some pal's house.'

'You rang them all, you said.'

'The ones I could think of – I'm sure I don't know all the lads he goes around with.'

'No, but—'

'It's not the first time,' Alistair said.

'What isn't?'

'That he's gone off. As a kid he was a bit of a wanderer. Shona's fault, I used to think, not keeping him on a tight enough rein.'

'And the way he came here,' Annie said, 'first to me, then Tom. Maybe he's just decided to move on.'

They went on sitting there, drinking whisky, trying to believe this. In the end, the bottle was almost done, it was three in the morning, and they'd played gin rummy till they couldn't stand it any longer, or even tell one card from another.

In the morning, Annie woke with a headache and went to run a bath. As she swirled water round, mixing hot and cold, the memory of the day before unfolded, so she turned the taps off, and went to look in the turret room. Rob was not there. He had not come home. But everywhere evidence of his existence overlaid, almost obliterated, Jamie's childhood presence. On the floor a T-shirt, several pairs of underpants, a towel, dirty socks; on the chest of drawers and the window-sill a litter of empty crisp packets, mugs with an inch of cold tea, teaspoons, and empty plastic cartons that had once contained chocolate mousse or yoghurt: the detritus of a life still being lived, here, in this place. The bed was unmade, but Annie knew it was always left like that. He had not been in it for more than twenty-four hours. She went to have her bath.

No one else was up. Downstairs, she made tea and forced herself to eat toast, so that the headache would clear. She fed Bracken and let her out. At the open back door, the air was fresh and cool, smelling of dust laid by water, the drenched earth, wet leaves. The rain had stopped and the wind died away, but the sky was heavy with low cloud.

'Where is he?' she asked aloud. Bracken, snuffling round the gate, looked up. 'Rob, Bracken, where's Rob gone?' The dog's ears lifted, and she yelped, once. Annie turned back indoors. As she did so, the telephone rang. Stuart.

'No. No, he hasn't. Tom's not up yet. No. Yes, you do that. Come now, if you like. OK, fine.'

A few minutes later, it rang again.

'Hi, Hamish, how are you? No, no he hasn't. Not yet. Yes, if you like. Stuart's coming in an hour or so. We'll sort out what to do then. 'Bye.'

In the kitchen, the familiar Aga, too warm in summer, not quite hot enough in winter; the fat kettle on the closed hotplate, warming water all day; the table, big enough for eight to sit round, or even ten. And in the air, the smell of the cigarettes they'd smoked the night before. When they were children, all the adults smoked. Liz wouldn't let them do it in the kitchen, though, or only in summer, if the door stood open. Annie closed her eyes, and saw them again, all the grown-ups, with Mrs Macintyre from the post office, and Hamish. *Have you found her yet? Not yet.*

The creak of the door.

'Morning.' Annie opened her eyes: Alistair, looking grey. He picked up the empty whisky bottle. 'My God, we fairly killed this last night.'

'Mostly you and Tom.'

'You had your share.'

'I must have – my head's sore, anyhow.'

'Well, it can't be the malt – you don't get a hangover with that. It's pure, unadulterated.'

'*You've* got a hangover.'

'Aye, well, after you went to bed, Tom found this bottle of red wine.'

'You never drank that as well.'

'Think so. Can't really remember, to tell you the truth. Haven't been so pissed for years.' He glanced round. 'Here it is.' An empty wine bottle, on the floor by the bin. 'Yes, killed that one too.' He went to run the cold tap, filled a mug, and drank. 'That's better. Mouth tastes like horse dung. No sign of him?'

'No.'

'You check his room?'

'Yes.'

'Which one's he in?'

'Jamie's.'

'I thought so. I'll just go up and have a look.'

'He's not been in it, Ally.'

'I know, but there might be something—'

'Like what? A map with "Treasure" marked with a cross?'

'You OK, Annie? Just a bit tense, like me?'

'Just a bit.'

'Well, as I said, he's done it before. Not to worry. He'll turn up. Probably at his mother's.'

Annie did not even bother to answer this.

Tom came down as his father arrived at the front door. He had driven over, and as he parked, Hamish's Land Rover drew in behind him.

'I'll make coffee,' Tom said.

They all sat round the table. Annie, coming in from the pantry with the bowl of sugar and a tin of shortbread, halted.

Have you found her yet?

Not yet.

'Annie?'

'Sorry – here. I brought some shortbread, if anyone wants it.'

'What we've decided,' Alistair said, 'is to go round his pals, see if anyone's got any ideas. But somebody should stay here.'

'Dad – you stay. You're not fit to trail about.'

'The waiting game,' Stuart said. 'The waiting game.'

'I know. Sorry.'

'Look,' Alistair leaned across the table, tapping it for emphasis, 'there's really nothing to worry about. Not at this stage. He's just skipped out for a while. He'll turn up. Bound to.'

'I'll go along the beach,' Annie said. 'In case he's gone as far as the caves. He could have slept out there. Maybe he's, I don't know, turned his ankle or something, can't walk back—'

'Streuth, there are tourists galore,' Alistair broke in. 'One of them—'

'Well, anyway, that's what I'm going to do.'

Stuart put a hand over both of Annie's, where they quivered, locked together in her lap.

'Keep calm, lass. We all need to keep calm.'

'I know.'

When they had left, Stuart sat down again in the kitchen with Annie.

'It's a queer thing.'

'What is?'

'Time.'

'*Time?*'

Annie walked the length of the beach and back. If he's still not appeared, she told herself coming up the path to the house, we must ring the police. I really think we should. She pushed open the gate and stepped into the garden. The door to the house was shut, but between gate and door, standing uncertainly on the path, was a child with long red-gold hair. Annie stood still, not breathing. Could not breathe.

It's a queer thing.

What is?

Time.

Then the girl turned, hearing Annie, and she was not a child at all, but sixteen or seventeen. She wore leggings, and a huge ballooning T-shirt, and she was at least seven months pregnant.

'Sorry,' she said, 'this is the back door, isn't it? I should've gone in the other gate. But I was told this way—'

'It's all right. Everybody comes to the back door – unless they're driving.'

If it hadn't been for the belly, the breasts swelling with milk, she'd have been a skinny wee thing. With fair skin that freckles, and burns in the sun. Nothing like Lindsay, when you looked at her. Nothing at all. Just that hair, and it was much redder than Lindsay's had ever been, it was only the way the sun had caught it, had made it seem gold. Annie glanced up at the house, thought she saw someone moving in the window of the turret room, but not Rob. Then nothing, a blank piece of glass. She thought of how she'd stood there with Jamie ten years ago, watching Ruth walk up to the house. Who had this girl come for? Not Jamie.

'I'm Lucy Philips,' she said.

'Are you sure you've got the right house?' It was a mistake, that was all.

'It's a Mr Mathieson, right, that lives here?'

'Tom, yes.' Tom?

'Well, I'm right then, are you his wife?'

Tom?

'No, no, I'm Annie, his cousin. Tom's out – I think he's still out. Can I help?'

'Actually, it's Rob I was looking for. Rob Fraser? She – his mother – she said this was where he was staying now.'

Then Annie knew.

'You'd better come in,' she said. 'Come in, Lucy.'

8

Annie had no idea what she was going to say to Stuart about Lucy, when they met. But Stuart was not in the kitchen now, and when she put her head round the living-room door, she saw he'd fallen asleep in an armchair, the crossword in Tom's *Scotsman* half-finished. The one day in his life when this wouldn't drive Tom wild.

'Sit down,' she said to the girl, as she came back into the kitchen. 'Everyone else is still out, except Tom's dad, and he's having a nap. Can I get you a drink? Coffee or something?'

'No, thanks. I don't drink coffee.'

'Squash, then – I don't know if there's anything like that here . . . Hang on, I think – yes.' In the pantry she had found cans of soft drink, and two large bottles of lemonade which Tom had bought for Rob. 'Come and look. See if you'd like any of these.' Lucy came and looked, and took her time choosing. The pantry was cool.

'Years ago,' Annie said, 'when we were children, this was stocked to the ceiling. Jam and chutney on the top shelf, bottles of raspberry wine standing on the floor. Everything else in between. No fridge then, so if it was the day the fish van came, or the butcher, there'd be whatever was for supper, sitting on a plate, under a mesh cover . . . I bet that's still here, somewhere.' But she couldn't see it, and they went back into the kitchen.

'Did you live here, then?'

'No, Tom and Jamie lived here. But I came every summer, with my brother. Rob's dad.'

'Right.' The girl unzipped her Diet Pepsi with a hiss of escaping air. Annie had put down a glass, but Lucy drank from the can.

'When is your baby due?'

'Four weeks.' As Annie silently counted back, Lucy sighed, and her silver earrings quivered: a moon was hanging from one ear, a sun from the other, both with smiling faces. 'I'll be glad when it's here. Fed up being as huge as this.'

'Uncomfortable, in the heat.'

'You said it.'

Annie thought, there must be a question I could ask, that would make everything clear, without causing any offence, or risking any assumptions. But what?

'I'm sorry Rob's not here just now. Did you . . . was he expecting you?'

'I doubt it.' The girl shook her hair back, and the earrings danced. Above the sun and moon, two more holes held silver hoops. But she had no other jewellery, no rings. 'My auntie lives in Inverness, and she's been saying for ages I should come and stay with her, and Mum said why didn't I go now, it's the last chance I've got to have a holiday on my own. So I came up on the train. I'd have come on the bus, it's cheaper, but my mum said the train would be better, with me like I am.'

'I'm surprised she's let you go so far from home, so near the birth.'

'My auntie's a midwife, so she wasn't worried, really.'

'So . . . you thought you'd come and see Rob at the same time?'

A deepening pinkness spread up the girl's slender neck, but did not reach her face.

'Well, yes, that was another reason.'

'Does he . . . have you spoken to him since he left home . . . I mean, recently?'

'I sent a letter.'

'So he knows . . . he knows you're going to—'

'He knows I'm pregnant. Anyway, his mum's talked to him. My mother went to see her.'

Well, Annie thought, that's surely clear enough.

'But when he left, I mean at New Year, he didn't know then?'

'Sort of. It was early days, but I kind of suspected.'

'You must have been – weren't you frightened?'

The girl nodded. 'You better believe it. I was mega scared.'

'How did your mother react?'

'She was OK. After a while. I mean, she's been fantastic, really.'

'So, what are you going to do . . . afterwards?'

'Oh, I'm keeping it. Her. It's a girl.'

'You must have had a test . . . a scan?'

'Yeah – that's *incredible*. There's this fuzzy like film and the baby's kind of floatin' about – but that's not how I know, of course. They did this test, because of my funny blood group, and they said they could tell me what it was – but you can just keep it to be a surprise when it's born, some people like that better. But I never thought, I just says, is it a boy or a girl, and the nurse says it's a little girl.' Lucy took another gulp of Pepsi. Her eyes seemed unfocused, dazed with remembering.

'Your blood group,' Annie hesitated. 'Are you all right, then?'

'Oh yeah, it doesn't mean nothin' dangerous. Just they were checkin', right?' Lucy tilted her head back, and drained the can.

'How will you manage, though?' Annie persisted. 'Have you left school? Well, I suppose you had to.'

Lucy set the earrings off again. 'Oh no, you can stay on now, they let you stay if you've got exams. But you don't feel sort of right at school, once you start showing. I left at Easter. My mum, she wants me to go back and take my A levels. But see, I completely *love* babies. I was always the one looked after all the little kids in the street. I've made loads of money, baby-sitting. I want to be a nursery nurse, or a nanny. But Mum keeps on at me to get A levels. She never went to university, and she's got this idea that's the best thing to do.'

'Well, yes, it is usually.' Annie felt she should support this absent, and (it seemed to her) unfortunate mother. But on the other hand, if the girl wanted to work with children, and had gone and got pregnant at sixteen . . . Fifteen? *Rob* had been fifteen. No wonder he'd headed north. His furtive sullenness those first weeks. No wonder.

'But you're not thinking of getting married?'

'What – to Rob?' Lucy grinned. 'Shotgun wedding? Nobody does that, nowadays. People just, like, live together, don't they?

Well, I'm actually gonna live with my mum, she'll be a lot more use, don't you think?'

'But, he'll have to . . . contribute. I mean, it's his baby too.'

'Boys aren't really interested, though, are they? I mean, it'll be nice for him to take her out, and that. When she's a bit older.'

Annie gazed in fascination at Lucy, the blush on her neck, the narrow freckled hand holding the can, a fragile girl submerged in the bulk of pregnancy. She seemed both naive and experienced, a child, and yet ancient with received wisdom. But Annie warmed to her. The very openness of this extraordinary conversation made her feel privileged, flattered.

An hour passed. Annie knew all about Lucy's family, her cat, her father's tropical fish, her married sister, her taste in food.

'I felt sick at first, I kept thinking I was going to throw up. But now I'm starving all the time. I'll eat anything. My mum says that's one good thing, I'm not picky about my food any more.'

'Food,' Annie said, looking up at the clock. 'Tom and Alistair will probably be back soon. Maybe I'd better think about lunch. And wake Stuart, if he's still sleeping. You'll stay, will you?'

'Oh yes. My auntie dropped me off – she's gone home. I said I'd ring her when I wanted to go back.'

Annie went foraging in the pantry and fridge.

'There's not much, actually. Plenty of eggs, and bread. Not much cheese. I don't know – omelettes?'

'What's that called when you fry up the bread with eggs soaked through it? Eggy bread.'

'French toast, we called it,' Annie said. 'Yes, I could do that – with a bit of salad, maybe.' She got out a bowl and a whisk. 'You beat up the eggs, while I get dishes to soak the bread in. We won't start cooking till they get here.'

Together, they began to get the meal ready. And Lucy went on talking. Annie heard about GCSEs, Lucy's best friends, her married sister's flat.

'She's got this cute little bathroom, everything blue and white, even pictures up in it, and white ducks with blue bows on the windowsill. Really neat. I'd love that, a place you could do up yourself.'

'Yes,' Annie said, 'it's lovely. Great fun finding all the right bits and pieces, choosing them. But that can take years.'

'Oh no,' Lucy said. 'Emma, she got everything at the one time. All new.' She licked raw egg from her finger, before Annie could stop her. But she didn't look like a girl to go down with salmonella. She looked, Annie realised, indestructible. Not fragile at all.

'So,' Lucy went on, 'what's your house like then? Is it near?'

'No, no it's in Aberdeen.'

'Oh right. My dad says that's the dearest place to buy a house, next to London. Because of the oil boom, and the Americans moving there.'

'Well, it was at one time,' Annie agreed. 'Not so much now maybe. Still expensive though. But we bought our house years ago – it's in an Edwardian terrace.' Annie was still proud of her house; she liked talking about it.

'Oh, a terrace, don't you fancy getting a detached? That was what my parents did. A terrace first, then when Emma was born, a semi. Now they've got a detached, with a double garage and everything.'

Annie hid a smile. 'Ours is an old house,' she said, 'and in Aberdeen they're granite, solid. You can't hear a thing from next door.'

'I like old houses,' Lucy said. 'They're a lot of upkeep, aren't they? How old are your kids? They're not here, are they?'

'We've no family.'

With a rush of astonishment, Annie realised she had not thought of Graham all morning. Alistair's crisis, Rob disappearing, Lucy's arrival, her non-stop talking, had blotted him out. Tom is right, she thought, I could live without him. I could leave. I love the house, but on my own I could leave it, it belongs to our marriage anyway. She was giddy with freedom, and leaned her hands on the table, as if by letting go, she'd lose her balance altogether.

Stuart appeared in the doorway.

'Nodded off,' he said. He seemed faintly surprised to see Lucy, but no more than that. Just wait, Annie thought, wait till he finds out. But she could not imagine this. Tom, yes, but Stuart, Hamish . . . Alistair? Oh God, what are we going to say to Alistair?

'Stuart, this is Lucy, she's a friend of Rob's. She's staying with relatives in Inverness, so she thought she'd come over for the day.' She turned to Lucy. 'This is my uncle Stuart. Tom's father.'

There, that was enough for now. Let Lucy explain everything else. Wasn't that what she'd come for, really?

'I can hear a car stopping,' Lucy said, her hearing quick and young. 'Maybe we should start cooking some of this if that's your cousin back. It takes ages when there's a lot of people.'

'I'll go and see. See if they've tracked him down yet.' Stuart went back through the house to the front door.

'I should tell you,' Annie touched Lucy's arm. 'No one's seen Rob since last night. That's where Tom and Alistair have been. Out looking for him.'

But Lucy, who'd seemed flustered by the arrival of the car, was unmoved by this. 'I wouldn't bother if I was you. He'll turn up, eventually.'

Annie smiled, comforted against reason by Lucy's easy dismissal of all their anxiety.

'It's Jamie,' Stuart said, coming in followed by his son.

Annie, who was always so pleased to see Jamie, easy with him, very nearly left the room, walked down the path and escaped, as Rob had done. For here were Stuart and Jamie, who had lost their children, and Annie who could not have any. And following them, Alistair. But Alistair had not lost his son, he had not, Rob would come back.

Tom appeared a few minutes after Alistair. 'I've just rung Andrew Jack,' he said, entering a kitchen where the smell of frying eggs mingled with a series of confused introductions and explanations. Annie was doing her best, but made sure she didn't meet her brother's eye, after the first wild surmise she saw in his face when she told him Lucy's name.

'Who? What did you say?' she asked Tom.

'The local chief inspector. I know him quite well, so I thought I'd just talk it over – but he agrees with me. Leave it another day, before we make it official. He might have turned up at Shona's by then.' Then he saw Lucy, took her in, with no more than a faint narrowing of his eyes. Perhaps Annie need not say anything after all – certainly not yet. Lucy herself had gone quiet. She helped Annie cook and serve, was deft and capable, though her size made it difficult for her to move round the table, and between chairs.

Hamish came in as they began to eat. So Annie gave her untouched plate to him, and sat in the Windsor chair instead, eating an apple. She was far too hot with cooking and standing by the Aga, and with anxiety, to eat. Hamish, she saw, was quite unsuspicious of Lucy. Whether he even took in who she was, where she'd come from, was doubtful. He was thinking only about Rob, for of all of them, it was Hamish who was most agitated.

'Lucy thinks he'll just turn up,' Annie said.

'He always does.' Lucy calmly forked food into her mouth and smiled round them all. 'And he's not a kid. I mean, you get really worried if a little kid goes missing, don't you? In case some pervert's got hold of them. But not a lad of sixteen.' She went on eating, oblivious.

'He's been a great help to me, your boy,' Hamish plunged in first, talking fast with his mouth full. 'Plumbing, joinery – get him a trade, I say, forget all this varsity stuff. Never did me any good.'

'Hamish,' Tom leaned forward, 'Hamish, you did look in the cottage, didn't you?'

Silence. And they all knew, as Hamish's face reddened, fell, that he had not.

Then they got to their feet, all four cousins, and Tom said, 'We'll take my car – you haven't blocked me in, have you, Hamish?'

'No, no, left it outside, on the verge.'

They disappeared so quickly, in unison, with one accord, that Lucy found herself left with the two old men. And the dishes.

'I'll wash up,' she offered, getting to her feet. 'One of you can dry, and the other one put away. OK? I don't know where things go, in this house.' She ran hot water, squirting washing-up liquid lavishly into the bowl in the way of someone from a hard-water area, amazed at the resulting froth of bubbles. 'Look at this – I only put in a little bit.' She had to lean forward to reach the sink; her belly got in the way.

Dazed, meek, the old men stacked dishes, and waited for her with tea towels, ready to dry.

*   *   *

'Can we just be clear about this,' Alistair said in a tight voice, turning round from the front seat to look at Annie and Jamie in the back. 'I'm not under some crazy delusion – wish I were – this girl, this Lucy whatever she's called, is having a baby. Right?'

'Well done,' murmured Jamie. 'Your years in the city have certainly sharpened your powers of observation.'

Alistair ignored this. 'And the implication is, Rob's the father. Am I wrong?'

'Oh dear,' Annie sighed. 'No, I don't think so. It looks as if that's what's happened.'

Jamie thought his cousin looked more than ever like a man heading for a heart attack. His face was brick red. But he turned to look at the road ahead again, and said nothing more.

No one spoke till they turned up the track to the cottage.

'This is what I can't understand,' Annie said, as the car bumped over the ruts.

'Why Hamish didn't look here in the first place?' Tom suggested.

'Is this the house they've been doing up?' Alistair indicated the cottage, as it appeared over the hill.

'Yes, Hamish is supposed to be letting it out. Next summer, at this rate.'

'Bloody obvious, you'd think, to look here first. To anyone with a modicum of intelligence.'

Tom laughed. 'Poor old Hamish. He does his best. And actually, he and Rob have got on very well.'

'That's not what I mean at all,' Annie broke in. 'I wasn't talking about Rob. It's just – it struck me today – why did I never think of this before? Maybe I did – only now it seems so clear. Why did none of us know where Lindsay had gone?'

'That's what I used to wonder.' Jamie tuned in to this at once. 'We were together all summer. Everybody knew everybody, much more so then. If it was some holiday-maker, we'd have known.'

'I see what you mean.' Tom slowed the car; the last part of the track was even rougher. 'Those boys from the caravan site Alistair went off with. And there was a wee lass with a snotty nose you took a fancy to, Annie, for a week or so.'

'Did I? I don't remember. There was a girl with curly hair—'

'So what you're getting at Annie,' Jamie interrupted, 'is how could she have a secret like that, and none of us know anything about it?'

'What we seem to be suggesting,' Tom said, 'is that she'd gone up to the guy's hut before.' He turned the car into the space Hamish and Rob had cleared for parking.

'Yeah, that's what I think. She must've.' Jamie opened his door, ready to get out, but no one moved.

'It wasn't a secret.'

'What?' Tom switched off the engine, and in silence Alistair felt them all looking at him.

'It wasn't a secret. I knew about it.' More silence.

Annie glanced at the cottage. It looked empty, but what if Rob was there, had seen them, was slipping out at the back, while they all sat in the car, on the verge, at last, at long last, of talking together, all four, about what had happened to Lindsay. She had waited so long for this conversation.

'For goodness sake,' she said, opening her door and getting out, 'that was all over *long ago*. Let's find Rob first.'

The door was not locked. Their feet thrummed on bare boards in the tiny hallway and living room, and slapped on concrete in the kitchen. Annie ran upstairs first, and found Rob in the front bedroom. On the floor were several empty Coke cans, and half a white sliced loaf.

'You didn't starve then?' she asked.

Rob was sitting on some blankets, leaning against the wall. He grinned at her, a wide nervous grin. 'Hi.'

'What were you up to – we've been frantic.'

'Sorry. Couldn't face Dad.'

'You'll have to now.'

They'd followed her upstairs. The little room was full of people, all looming over the boy on the floor.

'Sorry,' he said again. 'Needed a bit of space.'

'I suggest,' Alistair said, 'you abandon that notion and come back and meet your friend, since she's come all this way to see you.'

'What friend?' He thought of Kevin, then, absurdly, of the dog. She?

'Lucy's here,' Annie said. Rob went very white, and struggled fast to his feet. 'She's at Tom's with Stuart and Hamish. Are you coming back, Rob?'

He shrugged. He was surrounded, and had no choice. Captured, he submitted, and followed them out to the car. Annie put the Coke cans and bread in a supermarket bag lying by the window, and took them with her. Guessing (rightly) that the blankets belonged to Hamish, she left them where they were.

Then they drove back to the High House.

9

'They've been very good about it, considering,' Lucy said. 'Your family. I could see it was a shock to them.'

'It was a shock to me.'

'I wrote to you. Didn't you get my letter?'

'Yes.'

'Well then.'

'Never read it.'

Lucy raised her eyes heavenwards. 'For crying out loud . . .'

'Well, if it said what I thought it was going to say, I didn't *want* to read it.'

'All right for you – I couldn't pretend nothing was happening, could I?'

'No. Right.'

'So?'

'So, what?'

'What you doing, you coming back to your mum's?'

'Maybe.'

Lucy lay back in the sand with a sigh, and closed her eyes. If she lay flat, she could hardly feel the breeze, and the sun was warm on her face.

'It's nice here. I didn't like it at first, but I do now. I don't know I'd want to live here though, not all the time.'

Rob didn't answer this, but sat up on one elbow and traced the horizon of her stomach with a finger.

'Don't. You're tickling me.'

'You look weird, lying like that.'

'Thanks.'

'What's it feel like? Does it feel like you've got something alive inside you?'

'Here.' She took his hand and guided it over her T-shirt, then kept it still in one place. Beneath his palm, the warmth of her flesh, then a sudden bump, there and gone again like a wave, a heartbeat.

'Is that it? Where's it gone?' He moved his hand, seeking. Again, something poked at him, a heel or an elbow. 'God, that's mad, that is. You think it could be an alien? Hello? Hello? Anybody there?' He laughed, but he kept his hand on her, waiting for another signal from the life to come. Lucy lay still, putting up with this.

'One thing,' she said eventually.

'What?'

'Who's Lindsay?'

In the house, Annie answered the telephone. It was Graham.

'We'll wait for you,' Tom said, 'before we open the wine.' He put the bottle back in the fridge. But twenty minutes later she was still talking, so he took it out again, filling her glass and leaving it by the phone. The rest he took outside for Alistair and Jamie and himself.

'With everything that's happened,' Annie was saying, 'I suppose I've got a different perspective. I don't know. Nothing seems to be certain, any more. But come up tomorrow, then, if you want to. I'd like you to. I do want to see you.' She took a deep breath. 'And Graham, if you're sure, if we are going to try . . . oh well, we'll talk about it later. Now's not the time. It's just, children are children, aren't they? Whoever they belong to, they all need looking after. Anyway, I'll see you tomorrow. And I think it's a good idea, we haven't been over to the West for years.'

In the garden, they finished the first bottle, and Tom opened another.

'I have to go home tomorrow,' Jamie said. 'Ruth'll be back in the afternoon.'

'So glad you came,' Tom murmured. 'Wouldn't have wanted you to miss out on all this fun.'

'It's fine for you two,' Alistair complained. 'You just drift along, pleasing yourselves. No proper jobs, God knows what you live on, no responsibilities . . .'

'Sybarites, hedonists, locust eaters . . .' Tom lay back on the rug he'd flung on the grass, and closed his eyes. 'That's us.'

Alistair glowered. 'If you say so. Whatever *they* are. But here I am, my career finished, an estranged wife who keeps expecting money from me, and a son who's been stupid enough to produce a grandson at the worst possible time.'

'Granddaughter,' Jamie said. 'It's a girl.'

'What?'

'We had a long chat this morning, Lucy and me. She tells me the tests showed it's a girl.'

'Bloody hell.' Alistair poured himself another glass of wine.

'All your experience proves,' Tom told him, 'is that things fall apart.'

'Sometimes they can come together again,' Jamie grinned. 'I think both Annie and I have hinted to Lucy that she could have the baby adopted, and it needn't even go out of the family. But she seems determined to hang on to her offspring. Probably best, in the long run. The child will never learn to speak, being unable to get a word in edgeways, but otherwise, she'll be an excellent mother.'

Before Alistair could decide whether he would in any event approve of a grandchild of his being brought up by Jamie (Annie, perhaps – he could go on having some influence there) Annie came out and joined them. Jamie got down on the rug next to Tom, giving her his chair.

'What happened to the other garden chairs?' He kicked his brother.

'Went mouldy in the garage,' Tom answered, without opening his eyes.

'I don't think it's warm enough to sit out here today,' Annie said. 'I'm going in in a minute.' But she let Alistair fill her glass, and watched for the sun to reappear as the high breeze moved clouds across the sky. 'Graham's coming up on the train tomorrow. We're going across to the West coast for a week or so. Skye maybe.' She turned to Alistair. 'You can go back with Jamie, can't you? I'll give you the key, if you want to use the house. Graham's putting Mac and Tibby in the kennels.'

'I might stay on,' Alistair said, 'if that's OK with you, Tom. See if Rob's going to come back south.'

Jamie considered this. 'I think everybody should stay on,' he said. 'Why don't we all move into the High House?'

'God forbid,' Tom muttered, but Jamie went on.

'Lucy seems to like it here. She came back quick enough this morning. She could bring up her brat surrounded by sand and sea and kindly relatives.'

'Oh Jamie, don't be ridiculous.' In a moment he would say it was the perfect place to bring up a child, Annie thought, and of course it was, our parents thought so too: the big house, the beach so near, all the freedom in the world. She put down her empty glass on the grass beside her chair. 'Alistair, you said yesterday you knew where Lindsay had gone.'

'No, I didn't say that. I had an idea, but I didn't *know*. I'd have told the police, told Dad.'

'What then?'

'It was a bargain we made. One of us was supposed to be around with the wee ones, you and Jamie, all the time. Usually, it was her. She said that was OK, as long as I stayed whenever she had to go away for a while. We must have fallen out that day, I don't know. Or she said she was going after I'd made plans. I was going to play football with those kids from the caravan park. I mean, that's what I wanted to do, not hang around with my wee sister all the time. Building sandcastles, exploring . . . I was past that. And so was she, that was the trouble. Auntie Liz always said one of us had to be there. "But not Tom," she said, "he's forever got his head in some book. He wouldn't notice if they drowned, or were carted off screaming by white slavers."' Alistair swallowed wine, no longer cold and sweet, but sour in his mouth. Then he went on. 'So I said *I* was going; she said *she* was. Neither of us would give in.'

'But did you know where she was planning to go?'

'I didn't really care. She always had to have a mystery, a secret. She wanted you to ask her, be curious. Then she could smile, and tell you nothing. But she'd mentioned him, I think, I'm sure, because I did think of him. I suspect she fancied herself, chatting up this old man, being the pretty young thing brightening up his life. It was like a dare she'd set herself. It seemed a bit dangerous.'

'It was dangerous – he wasn't just some harmless old drunk, as everyone thought.'

Tom sat up and pushed his hands through his hair, the way Jamie did. Annie saw how alike they were, how you'd know they were brothers, and Stuart's sons. But Lindsay had been different, sturdy and fair, like her mother.

'Two weeks she was missing,' Alistair said. 'Two weeks, and I didn't say anything, because I wasn't sure, and I thought they were searching everywhere, so if she was in his hut, they'd find her. And I thought if I told them, I'd be in trouble for not staying with the rest of you, not saying right away what had gone on.' He shrugged. 'Stupid.'

'Too right it was stupid!' Jamie exclaimed. Annie put a hand on his shoulder but he shook it off. 'Thinking of your precious bloody self, as usual, Alistair. If you'd said something, if they'd found her sooner—'

'She was missing two weeks, and she'd been dead two weeks,' Tom said quietly. 'Come on, there's no point in this. We all know what happened, as far as it's possible to know. The police must have searched that hut – in fact they had – she wasn't there at the time she died. He took her there later, she died somewhere else – on the beach, in the woods. Who knows? And all the evidence went up in smoke when the hut was set on fire after Duncan was arrested. Feelings ran very high, Dad said. People were scared.'

'The whole thing was a farce,' Jamie said, but he was calmer. 'They storm in there, find her, arrest Duncan, who's wandering about the lanes so far out of his head on whatever it was he got his fix from – surgical spirit, lighter fuel – he'd no idea what they were on about. Then, before they can get him sobered up enough to talk, his heart gives out. Or his liver. Whatever. Dead in his cell in the morning – end of prosecution.'

'Well,' Tom said, 'everyone wanted to believe it was him. And who else could it have been? But I think myself, he didn't kill her on purpose. *Something* happened. But not a mark on her – she was dead, and that was all. Not strangled, or stabbed – maybe suffocated, that's what they decided in the end—'

'Stop it,' Annie pleaded. 'Don't talk about it any more. It was horrible, it's still horrible. There's not one of us can read to the end any newspaper report about a missing child. Even now. But it is over. It *is*.'

Death had sealed up whatever secrets Lindsay had carried: there was nothing to unravel, nothing more they would ever know. They were silent, and Annie shivered.

'It's getting colder. I'm going in.'

The three men sat on for a few minutes longer.

'Sorry,' Jamie said at last. 'You were only a kid.'

'It's all right – I agree with you. I do blame myself. Why d'you think I'm such a prick, eh? Could *you* live with somebody like me? I have to.'

'Too much cheap wine,' Tom said, gathering up the glasses. 'We should stick to whisky, I say. Right, come on then. Somebody's got to clear away the lunch dishes, so that I can make supper. And after that, somebody's got to be sober enough to drive that lassie back to Inverness. I'm scared she might move in. And I've got two book reviews to write by Tuesday.'

Across the empty garden, shadows edged away the last of the sunshine. One of the cats sniffed a forgotten wine glass, drew back, went on as if in slow motion to a gap in the hedge, and disappeared.

'You should have told me before now,' Jan said. 'About Annie being so upset. If I'd known she was in such a state—'

'Exactly. I couldn't – I didn't want this to end. I know, I was wrong, I'm a bastard. But I was crazy – I think I went crazy for a while.'

'We both did. It's just as well I didn't know, really. I'd have felt I should stop seeing you, but . . .'

'But what?'

'Och, I didn't want it to stop either.'

'But you do now?'

'Do you?'

A long silence.

'It's going to, isn't it? You're leaving, I'm taking Annie away on holiday, trying to mend our marriage. Isn't that right?'

'Yes.'

'I'll miss you.'

'You'll miss the sex.'

'No question.' He slid his hand along her thigh, but she put her hand over his, stopped it there.

'It'll be all right,' she said. 'You care an awful lot for Annie, despite everything. I've always known that really. But marriages do break down, it's nobody's fault. Sometimes you just outgrow each other. And you did give me the impression she only wanted you to provide kids, didn't want you for yourself. But that's not true, it seems. Going by the way she's reacted.'

'Well, I did feel like that – for years.'

'Hm.'

'Come on,' he said, his mouth at the opening of her blouse, his fingers unbuttoning. 'One last time.'

And why should she not give way to the luxury of this last time, why not give all they could, take all there was from each other? I don't know how long this has to last me, she thought. But one thing – I won't wait so long again. I'm different now.

Graham, knowing he too was changed, but unable to tell yet how much, had promised Annie a new start. Jan's leaving would make it easier, he could concentrate on his marriage undistracted. Why then did he feel as if he were turning his back on something glorious and happy, in favour of – what? The old struggle, the old misery. However much he still loved Annie, he did not want that. But he lay with Jan in his arms, deeply relaxed and still, and told himself he meant well, he meant to do his best.

Midnight. Annie was reading, without taking in any of the words. I wonder if he's with her tonight, she thought. One last time, before he comes back to me, and she goes away. But a comforting numbness stood between her and all the pain this would once have evoked. Graham had sounded subdued, but was kinder, had listened when she told him about Rob, and Lucy, laughed at Alistair (well, he always did that), and was, perhaps, her friend again. It might be all right, in the end. But I must hold on to this separate feeling, she told herself. And if it's too late to foster, or adopt, or if Graham really doesn't want to (he did once, it was my fault we never went on with it), I'll get a job, retrain, learn to use computers. I'll make my life anew. She leaned back, closing her eyes. *Oh, please God, make it all right.*

Someone tapped on the door.

'Come in.' She looked up to see Rob. 'Hello. You all right?'

'Yuh. OK if I sit on the bed?'

'Yes, of course.' She shut the book.

'I spoke to Mum. I phoned her, like you suggested.'

'Good. What did she say?'

'Oh, nothing much. I just wondered . . . do I have to go back?'

'Well, if you want to stay on in this house, you'd better ask Tom, eh?'

'I don't think he's bothered. Mum said it was up to me. Anyway . . . I might not actually live with Tom. I meant, stay in Scotland, in this area, like.'

'What about Lucy, and the baby?'

He reddened. 'Well, Lucy could bring it here in the holidays. I mean, I know it's my kid and all that, but it doesn't seem . . . real. It's just . . . I was going to do joinery, and Hamish says I can move in with him, and if I help him with his house – he's got this idea we could do up the house for B & B if there's two of us – he won't charge me rent or nothing. And I can go to college. Then when I'm *earning*, I can help Lucy out, can't I? Anyway, Dad says he's goin' to see Lucy, visit the baby an' that.'

'*Alistair?*'

Rob nodded, and his face had a glint of mischief she had not seen in him before.

'Yeah, he says to me he's been a rubbish father, so he's goin' to make up for it bein' a grandad.'

'*Alistair* said that?'

'Well, he never said them exact words,' Rob admitted, grinning, 'but that's what he meant.'

Something had happened between them at last, father and son, Annie realised. Not much, but perhaps enough. So easy, she thought, to imagine the whole of the past can be wiped out by a new baby, another girl with red-gold hair. And she had a pang of jealousy so strong she was blinded by it. But whether for Alistair, or Lucy, or Rob himself, she could not tell. Then she was calm again. That was not how she was going to be any more.

'So what d'you think then?' Rob was asking.

'What about?'

'Me doin' joinery and that.'

'Oh Rob, I think . . . I think I can't think straight any more.' She smiled. 'Too much, all at once.'

'Yeah, I know what you mean. But – I could do that, couldn't I?'

'Yes, if it's what you want.'

'Yeah, probably.'

He smiled at her, and she put a hand on his arm for a few seconds. Somewhere inside her head, his head, Annie felt the pieces slide back together, form a different picture. But still, something coherent again.

'Right then.' He was about to go, when something made him pause, turn back. 'Annie—'

'Yes?'

'What happened to Lindsay?'

The Past

Thirty-four years back – The Beach

Sunlight lies on the kitchen floor like a flat yellow pool, and catches the edge of the table, where crumbs glint. Liz wrings out a dishcloth and wipes away the crumbs. It is the quiet time of day when nothing has just happened, nothing is about to happen. Three o' clock.

Stuart is at work; Christine and Matt have gone into Inverness to shop; the children are on the beach. It is a day like all the other days of the summer, and she should be in the garden by now, tackling the weeds. But a blackbird singing his heart out in the forsythia bush by the back door, the faint cries of holiday-makers on the beach, seem to make her lazy. I'll have an afternoon off, she decides. It's my holiday too, and I won't get another, a real one. Worry nibbles at the edge of her mind: Stuart, the shop not paying enough, whether she should take the chance to teach full-time next year. But Jamie is still so young, and . . . She sighs, and gets down the tea caddy from the shelf by the Aga. I'll make tea, she thinks, lifting the hotplate for the kettle. I'll have a cup of tea and finish reading my chapter.

She stands by the open back door waiting for the kettle to boil, and the blackbird flies off. The kettle is humming already, but she lingers, caught in sleepy July heat. The garden is littered with toys: an overturned bike, a naked doll with a surprised expression, a dozen Matchbox cars and lorries, a skipping rope. Lindsay, with great patience and (she has to admit) bossiness, has been teaching Annie to skip. Annie's not got the hang of it yet.

When she's made her tea, Liz carries it out to the garden with her book and sunglasses, and settles herself on the bench. It creaks as she sits down. The children jump on it, make it by turns a horse, a plane, a spaceship. It has not stood up well to all this attention. The heat soothes her, smoothes away the worries. She feels peaceful. She can't, of course, know there is to be no peace after this day. Very soon, the children who are left, playing peacefully too on the busy beach, will hold unaware, the knowledge of what is to come.

On the shore, Lindsay is turning cartwheels. She does it fault-lessly, legs absolutely straight, arms strong and stiff, wheeling across the sand, a starfish of a girl, rhythmic and graceful. Upright at last, she dusts sand from her hands, rubbing the palms on her shorts.

'Right,' she says to Annie, 'you try.'

But Annie can only do bunny jumps, and even they aren't very good. When she tries to make her legs go higher, and straighten out, she tumbles over.

Alistair laughs. 'Look at you,' he jeers. 'Call that a cart-wheel?'

'No,' Annie says, red-faced, 'of course not. It's a special jump, I meant it to be like that.'

'More fool you!' sings Alistair. This is his phrase for the summer. Whatever Annie says or does, he shouts *More fool you!* She hates him. Look at the way his thick hair sticks straight up off his forehead, not like Tom's, that's always floppy and smooth.

Tom is lying on his stomach, on a towel, reading. He reads more than anyone else in the world. He reads at dinner, though he's always being told off for it; under the covers at night with a torch when it gets too dark to see; on the school bus, he tells Annie, even when it makes him feel sick; he act-ually reads in the bath. Annie has not of course seen him doing this, but once the book fell in the water, and he had to dry it out over a towel on the Aga, so she knows it's true.

Jamie is whining; he kicks sand over Tom's legs.

'Come and *make* one, you said you'd *make* one. Come *on.*'

Lindsay goes down to the damp sand near the water's edge, and begins to draw patterns. Annie follows, and watches. She is perfectly content: while Lindsay is here, she's proof against Alistair's teasing, Tom's all-consuming book, Jamie's nagging. She doesn't need any of them. Her only slight niggle of dissat-isfaction is about the shorts. Lindsay has shorts; she has to tuck her dress into her knickers. It's not the same. But tomorrow, Auntie Liz has promised to go into the loft to look for Lindsay's old clothes, and among them, Annie is sure, are some pairs of shorts.

'Look,' Lindsay says. 'This is Ally – and that's Tom.' She is drawing faces. Alistair's has hair sticking up in spikes, like Oor Wullie. Annie laughs.

'Do me,' she says. 'Do me.'

Lindsay draws a round smiling face with curly hair. She sits back on her heels.

'You do one.'

Annie tries to draw Lindsay, her large eyes, her long hair. But of course, it is nothing like her: just a circle in the sand, and some squiggles.

'Very good,' Lindsay says, so Annie is satisfied. Lindsay does another one.

'Who's that?'

'Just somebody.'

'Who?'

'It's a secret.'

'I won't tell – who is it?'

'A man. A man I know.'

Annie stares at the sand face, but can make nothing of it. 'My daddy?'

'No.'

'Your daddy – Uncle Stuart?'

'No.'

'Hamish?'

'No, even madder than old Hamish.'

Annie laughs, not understanding. She likes Hamish – what's mad about him? Except his swooping voice, his funny trousers that he tucks into socks. Maybe that's what Lindsay means. But Lindsay leaps up and tramps all over the sand faces, scuffing them out in an odd, stomping dance. Annie joins in and they both dance, till the sea comes up and over their feet.

'Poor faces,' Annie says. 'They're all gone.'

'The tide was away to get them, anyhow.' Lindsay stands still, the water creeping between her bare toes, over her feet.

'What'll we do now?' Annie asks.

'I'm going for a walk.'

'Where – can I come?'

'No, it's too far.' Lindsay starts running back up the beach.

Heart sinking, Annie follows, hears the dreaded words.

'Ally – you're in charge. I'll be back soon.' She walks backwards away from him, grinning.

'No, I'm not,' he says. 'I'm away to play football.'

'That's up to you,' Lindsay says, not caring, 'but if anything happens it's your fault. I put you in charge.'

Annie's heart, which is in a low, uncomfortable place, lifts slightly. Alistair plays football with boys from the caravans. He usually finds company at the caravan site; these last two summers he's been sick of his own family, on the lookout for new friends. There will just be Tom and Jamie left, and in the end, Tom, who is good-natured, will put down his book and think of something more interesting for them to do.

Lindsay turns, and her hair, swinging sideways, glints gold in the sun. Alistair goes after her, and she stops for a moment. Annie can't hear what they're saying. Lindsay tosses her hair back, and goes off by herself. Alistair comes back and kicks sand over Tom.

'Hey – you're in charge.'

Tom comes back from the other world that not even Jamie's whine could disturb.

'Why?'

'Lindsay's off again. I'm goin' to play football.'

'Where's she gone?'

'See her boyfriend.'

'She hasn't *got* a boyfriend!' Annie is furious, but Alistair shrugs.

'Much you know.'

Tom gives up the book, knowing he's beaten. 'OK,' he says. 'Stop it, Jamie, we'll dig the trench. Tide's coming in now. I was waiting for that.'

Jamie dives for the buckets and spades. Alistair heads back along the beach towards the caravan park.

For a little while, before she starts digging with Tom and Jamie, Annie watches Lindsay go. In a moment, she'll be beyond the next crop of rocks, and out of sight. Annie aches to be thirteen and independent, but more than that, she longs for Lindsay to change her mind, and come back.